GLUTTONY

A DEADLY SEVEN NOVEL

GLUTTONY

LANA
PECHERCZYK

also by lana pecherczyk

The Deadly Seven

(Paranormal/Sci-Fi Romance)

The Deadly Seven Box Set Books 1-3

Sinner

Envy

Greed

Wrath

Sloth

Gluttony

Lust

Pride

Despair

Fae Guardians

(Fantasy/Paranormal Romance)

Season of the Wolf Trilogy

The Longing of Lone Wolves

The Solace of Sharp Claws

Of Kisses & Wishes Novella (free for subscribers)

The Dreams of Broken Kings

Season of the Vampire Trilogy

The Secrets in Shadow and Blood

CARDINAL CITY MAP

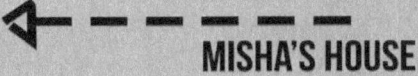

MISHA'S HOUSE

AIRPORT

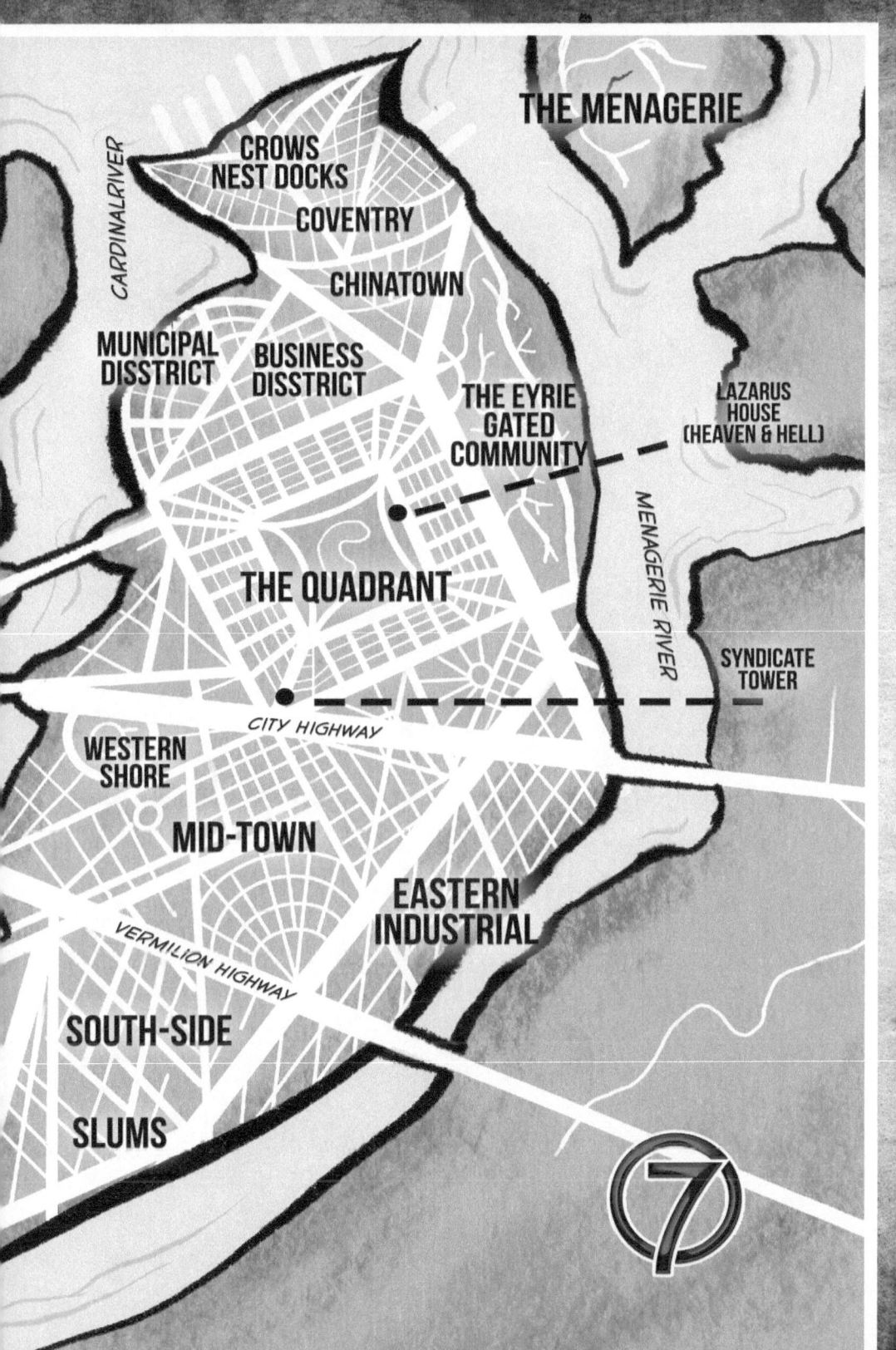

"A glutton is one who digs his grave with his teeth."

PROVERB

prologue

IN THE DANK UNDERGROUND corridors of the Syndicate Black Site, a bone-numbing alarm sounded. It echoed through the empty ex-military base.

A solitary life form slithered and crawled across the sticky red-stained corridor leading toward the elevator. Its barbed vine-like tentacles tumbled and twisted, belying its physical form. The plant moved with purpose, leaving carnage in the shape of its last meal. Bones and blood littered the path behind it. Each meal gave it something different, something beyond leaves and roots. It took four legs from the rat, thought from the humans, and soon it evolved beyond the confines of its original form. But it needed more. It was hungry—thirsty—and it had not been sated.

It needed more.

More.

More.

It snaked its morphing mass into the cracks surrounding the elevator until it found the cable. Reaching toward the light, it slithered up.

IN A DARKENED ALLEY, Clyde McGee faced off with a rabid gorilla, a psycho and his female hostage. Rain pelted him, stinging his skin. Hair stuck to his face and his torn shirt clung to his muscled torso. Blood from wounds blended on the white fabric creating an abstract masterpiece. Clyde aimed his gun at the psycho's head, then his gaze darted to the roaring gorilla as it thumped its chest in warning.

The psycho pressed his knife to a redhead's pale throat. Her torn lab coat fluttered with the breeze. Each man narrowed his gaze at the other, watching for telltale body language signaling action.

A twitch of Clyde's trigger finger.

A whitening of scarred knuckles as the psycho tightened his grip.

The redhead's frightened whimper.

The gorilla's snarl.

The woman implored Clyde with her wide, mascara stained eyes. *Please. Help.*

The psycho, a man with a goatee and a Mohawk, sneered at Clyde.

"Give it up, Magnus," Clyde shouted, his voice booming like thunder through the rain. "You've nowhere to go. You're done. Tell your monkey to stand down."

Magnus looked behind him. The alley was a dead end. With the whites of his eyes showing, he backed up until he hit the wall and pulled the woman in front of him, using her body as a shield.

But Clyde had trained all his life for this moment. He was the best bounty hunter the city had seen. He ate perps like this for breakfast.

"He's not a monkey, he's an ape, and we're connected." Magnus tapped his head. "He does whatever I do, and if I go down fighting, he does too."

Magnus roared, and the ape mimicked him, but Clyde wasn't afraid. He knew something they didn't. Magnus and the gorilla were only connected as long as Magnus lived.

The woman caught Clyde's eyes, her mouth hardened, and she gave an almost imperceptible nod. She was more than the love of his life. She was his partner, and she trusted him. He fired the gun. Red spray burst from her shoulder and she slumped forward, clutching her wound. The man behind her dropped to the ground. The bullet had gone straight through her to pierce the psycho's heart.

The gorilla let out a deep huff. It slumped. The rage left its eyes, and it backed up, confused.

Clyde ran to his love. He gathered her in his arms and held his palm to her sticky shoulder. "I'm sorry, Trix. There was no other way."

She blinked through the rain. Her trembling hand lifted to touch his jaw and curve around his neck. She pulled his lips to hers and kissed him softly, with intent, and then with passion. When they broke, she gave him a weak smile. "You did good, baby. You did good."

He frowned. "Not good enough."

"We're alive. And the gorilla is saved. That's all that matters."

They paused, staring into each other's eyes, waiting.

One. Two. Three.

"CUT!" shouted the director behind Tony Lazarus. "Perfect. And, that's a wrap."

A buzz rent the air. The rain stopped. Floodlights came on. Production crew suddenly emerged from the shadows of the studio set, but Tony was still staring into his co-star's big brown eyes. She winked at him.

"You wanna get a drink after this, Tones?" she asked, her Boston accent thick. "You know, celebrate the end of an era?"

Maggie O's classic good looks, perfect curvy body, and lips that locked you in a trance were the talk of Hollywood. But her dry personality switched from happy to vixen in the shake of a lamb's tail. Stories of her bedroom exploits had traveled through the staff, as Tony's had. She probably thought a hookup between them was inevitable, especially since his no-dating-co-stars rule had expired when the director had shouted "It's a wrap."

"No can do, Maggie. I'm dry, remember?"

Her voice thickened and her eyes smoldered. "You look pretty wet to me."

He smirked but disengaged and helped her upright. "Sorry. Not today."

"I'm up for a drink!" Desmond, a.k.a. The Psycho, jumped up from his death position on the floor behind Maggie.

The gorilla which was actually a man in a CGI costume, also stuck up his hand. "I'm keen."

Maggie pouted at the intrusion before she turned back to Tony. "But the movie's over. Surely you can enjoy a drink now."

Jeez, woman. Have a little respect. His recent exploits weren't exactly a secret. He shouldn't have to remind her. "After holding up production for two months so I could go to rehab, they've written abstinence into my contract. I'm clean until the premiere."

She gaped. "Abstinence from everything?"

He winked. Let her think whatever she wanted from that.

"A coffee then?"

Desmond scooted forward and raised his hand. Again. "Where are we going?"

Maggie folded her arms and blocked him. Poor guy.

Or was Tony the poor guy? This woman wouldn't let up. Probably wanted them to be the town's next power couple and rustle up a bit of publicity for the film release.

The bustle of a closing set swarmed around them and Tony turned to the set assistant arriving with a robe in each hand. She was a tall, willowy woman about thirty. A Bluetooth headset covered her ears and the clipboard under her arm looked like it was about to drop.

"Thanks, Peta," Tony said and received his robe but didn't put it on. He didn't mind the wet clothes and fake blood. Been in worse. "You need help with that clipboard?"

Despite having worked with Tony for the past few months, Peta's smile was still shy. "No problems, I got it. Great scene, by the way."

"Yeah, thanks." Tony wasn't so sure. That last interaction had felt stilted on his side. The chemistry between Maggie and he wasn't so translatable. He'd done better before.

"Also," Peta added, "you might want to know that Donatello is on his way."

"Shit." Tony scrubbed his face. Not good. The demanding producer was the last person he wanted to see. Maybe if he hurried, he'd get to his trailer before Donatello. He could crank some music, lock the door, and feign deafness to any knock.

Peta's smile dropped as she turned to Maggie and thrust out the remaining robe. After Maggie received it, Peta turned without a word and left.

Desmond shouted after Peta. "Where's my robe?"

Tony gave him his.

Maggie's lip curled. "Honestly. What do I have to do around here to get a little appreciation like you? That girl has had it in for me since day one."

Saying *Please* and *Thank you* would be a good start.

He lifted his brows. "The director doesn't appreciate me. I told him that final shot was unbelievable. Civilians don't carry the kind of bullets that pierce through two bodies—it's irresponsible to do so—but do you think he listened to the feedback? Let's not even talk about the unbelievable plot."

Tony knew if the film failed at the box office, they'd blame him for messing up production, but there was nothing he could do about that now. He just hoped his acting had been up to scratch.

Hugging her robe tight, Maggie responded. "I don't know why you care. We're only here to look good and play the part, not to think. Besides"—she slapped him playfully—"what's wrong with that, right? It pays the bills."

"I care because I don't want the movie to be a flop."

She was only half listening. Her eager look told Tony she was about to ask him on a date again. While on a normal day, he might say yes, this wasn't normal. He hadn't felt normal for the past few months, not since before rehab. Since he'd caught the sharp end of a soft tongue belonging to a woman with honeycomb eyes and a body cut from sin.

Bailey Haze was toned, athletic, but full of plenty. Plenty up top, plenty down behind, plenty of personality. His mind had been stuck in the gutter, dreaming of indulging. He'd wanted to every night. But he hadn't seen her since she'd looked at him with scorn.

I don't expect you to know anything.

The memory of her biting words invaded his mind, and he shut it down quickly.

Maggie opened her mouth, but Tony only saw Bailey's lips.

"Later," he said quickly and strode away.

Maggie shouted for all to hear, "See you at the wrap party."

He waved nonchalantly over his shoulder and kept walking, because a wrap party was exactly what he didn't need. To be surrounded by a bunch of actors and assholes gulping down booze, snorting up powder, or vaping the latest craze, meant his internal gluttony radar would go haywire. Being within a foot of anyone ingesting in excess was enough to make him sick. This sense was supposed to be useful in tracking down deadly sinners. The closer he was to someone with deadly levels of gluttony, the more his gut twinged. Unless, of course, he'd dulled that sensation with the very thing he was meant to be fighting. Alcohol and drugs had been his saving grace. How ironic.

But after the night Bailey Haze had come around, wanting information about Max's disappearance, and all Tony could give her was a few drunken words, he'd had enough. He was tired of this monkey dance.

Arriving at his trailer, he wrapped his fingers around the door handle and pulled. The metal door tugged open just as two people arrived on his six. Damn. He turned around.

One was a tall, potbellied, balding man with sweat stains under his pits. His thousand-dollar suit oozed sleaze. The other person was Peta, hugging her clipboard to her chest. She bit her lip and averted her gaze.

"Donatello," Tony greeted.

"You're expected tonight at the wrap party." The man's voice was grime down a wall.

"I thought these things were optional."

"You're the star of the film. It's non-negotiable."

"It's just for the staff and fan club. No biggie."

Donatello ground his teeth. "Do I have to remind you of the setback you caused with your little vacation to Darling Greens?"

Tony wanted to roll his eyes. As if he'd ever live that down. "No. I get it. I'll be there."

"Good. Because it's in your contr—what the fuck is that?"

Tony looked up and caught the disgusted look on Donatello's face. Peta behind him also featured an expression he could only place as intrigued. Twisting his neck, he followed their gazes into his trailer and blinked. His fingers cramped on the door handle. What the hell? A Barbie and Ken doll hung from his ceiling, twine around their necks like a hangman's noose. Each was dressed like the characters from the movie—his with the torn white shirt, Maggie's with red hair and the same dress she wore in the final scene. He leaned forward and spied two more dolls, a gorilla and the psycho, both with red paint splashed on them. The heads were at odd angles. But the doll representing him was pristine... apart from the noose. There was a note pinned to his doll's shirt. He plucked it off and read it.

I know.

He inwardly groaned, thinking immediately of his younger sister Sloan. Jesus Christ. This was exactly the kind of nineties teen horror bullshit she'd come up with to mess with him. She still hadn't paid Tony back for the elevator prank he'd pulled months ago. She had been royally pissed at one point. It was not unlike his sister to pretend she was cool with it, hold a grudge, wait months for the right moment, and then pounce to get the ultimate payback, just to prove she could.

He scowled. His prank had been in good faith. Forcing her and Max into a locked elevator to talk their shit out had been a good call.

They were soulmates—a balancing influence for each other. There was no escaping it, and they were being stubborn at the time. His plan had worked, too. They got together in the end, and now they were very happy. So, fuck the bullshit.

"Godammit, Tony. You have a goddamned stalker," Donatello snapped.

"What? That's nothing. Just a prank." The words came out, but an unsettled feeling niggled in Tony's gut. Sloan had been deliriously happy planning her wedding these past few weeks. If she'd had time to prank, he'd be surprised.

The producer was already turning to Peta. "Get set security up here, also get the head on the phone. We need to hire pretty boy a bodyguard."

Malice simmered in Tony's blood. *Pretty boy?*

Peta also glared at Donatello.

Then something he'd said clicked. "I don't need a bodyguard." That was the last thing he needed. His family was more lethal than the entire security team put together. He could not, would not, allow someone to follow him around all day, every day. Under the cover of darkness, he slipped out in a masked battle uniform to fight crime. Granted, it had been months since he'd joined the rest of the team on a patrol of the city, but he planned to. Soon. Once the film was done.

The only reason he was in the movie industry was to make use of his martial arts skills, do his own stunts, and because no one in their right mind would think a film star was Gluttony, the city's hooded vigilante. He didn't bring dates home. He didn't date, period. He had flings and affairs out and about. Never at his place. He certainly wouldn't allow someone to shadow him.

"Like I said, I don't need a bodyguard, Donatello." Tony folded his arms.

"Are you fucking kidding me right now? You've got dead dolls hanging from your trailer ceiling. After your selfish behavior almost shut down production permanently and lost us millions of dollars, we've finally finished shooting. I'll not let anything get in the way of this film coming out. I want no more bad press. We keep this quiet. We shut it down. We stick a guard on you until opening weekend, capeesh?"

Donatello turned to Peta and opened his mouth to speak, but Tony cut him off.

"My family has a security company on retainer. At least let me hire one of them."

"No. The studio will handle it."

Fuck. "Don, I've cost the studio enough money. Let me do this."

Donatello chewed his cheek and stared at Tony. He checked his Rolex, then huffed. "Fine. Make the call."

two

BAILEY HAZE

BAILEY HAZE WAS A SIMPLE WOMAN, or so she thought. She dressed in the same black pantsuit and tailored white shirt every day for work. She ate the same breakfast of blueberry oats. She drank Green Tea every morning at six over a crossword. And she did what was asked of her in her job, no matter what, because the alternative was going back to the CIA at Langley, to mind-numbing loneliness.

She wanted friends. She wanted a say in how she lived her life. She wanted this. Unfortunately, *this* came with a jumbo side-serving of compromise.

Looking around the sprawling back lawn of a diplomat's house, she wasn't sure she could call it living her life. The daily grind, perhaps. Witness of excess, even more. Babysitter to the disgustingly rich and entitled.

It was four p.m. and the children's birthday party was almost over. Her partner from Nightingale Securities, Damien Holden was manning the opposite end of the lawn, watching the only other exit to the festivities. He got the good side, the side backing onto the rear private parking lot. Bailey got the exit leading up to the mansion, meaning she got to witness excess in its purest form.

This was the one percent. Their trees were green and their sky was blue, but they lived in a different world.

From her vantage point at the middle of the marble steps, Bailey had one eye on the apex of the stairs, and one eye at the base where children shrieked, chasing a dog with a balloon tied to its tail. Little shoes slapped loudly on the pavement. The dog barked several times and managed to escape under a bush, leaving the tear-stained clown an opening to start his balloon show. Between lulls in the party noise, the soft lull of adult conversation and music came from inside the house. Unfortunately, at the top of the majestic steps stood a tall graying man slurping from a grubby glass of bourbon. To the right, on a balcony overlooking the party, was a group of women sipping wine and champagne without even the occasional glance at their darling children interacting with a clown from a horror movie.

The bourbon-drinker's attention was on Bailey. His lazy eyes drifted to her every so often, then back to the glass he twirled in his fingers, clearly contemplating something she'd hear about soon.

He obviously didn't think she noticed him through her Aviator sunglasses, but that was the beauty of mirrored lenses. Those without a sense of self-preservation would only think she watched the direction her head was pointed. She gave him a veiled look of disgust. The top buttons on his collar were popped, giving everyone a flash of hair on his chest. The tie was loosened, and the jacket and pants were crinkled. His gold watch and cufflinks looked tarnished, and he had a chain around his neck. He wore expensive clothes badly.

Tony Lazarus on the other hand. Now there was a man who pulled off luxury without making it look extravagant. There was something about the way Tony presented himself. It was both casual and elegant at the same time. To be honest, he could throw on any old t-shirt and make it look good. With those muscles—

Good Lord. She mentally smacked herself in the head. *Stop thinking about Tony Lazarus.* He was *not* the kind of person she needed to lust after.

Irritated, she tapped her microphone on her wrist sleeve and brought it to her mouth.

"Damien. We almost done here?" she asked abruptly.

From across the lawn, she saw the broad-shouldered man lift his wrist to his lips in response. "Yeah, mate. I reckon we give 'em until the clown goes home, and then we're done."

Damien was one of the two Australians Max had brought with him from their home country to start the security firm in Cardinal City. Damien was tall, thickly muscled, bearded and an ex-soldier for the SAS regiment in the Australian army. Like his friends, he was a lethal addition to the team. Bailey liked the Australian men. They didn't mince words. They said what they meant. They treated her like a friend, an equal, and they didn't push her personal boundaries.

"Party seems to have run over time," she noted.

"Contract's a contract," Damien replied.

As if he overhead the conversation, the man with the bourbon stumbled down the steps to where Bailey stood vigilant, hands clasped behind her back, jaw clenched.

"Party's run over," he slurred. "You need to stay a few more."

Bailey winced at the sour fumes coming from his breath. "Sir, that would change the terms of our contract and would need to be renegotiated by the boss."

"Only you need to stay. Not your friend. I have need of you all by yourself."

What are you doing up here all by yourself? The slurred voice from her memory made her shiver with disgust. She tried to blink it away, but it crowded her mind. She had to remind herself that nothing had happened. She'd escaped the drunken man at her parent's party by locking herself in her room. This wasn't then.

"My partner and I come as a pair, sir," she added.

"I hope you change your mind."

Damien, having heard the exchange, coughed over the comms to hide the insult he shot at the man. Her lip twitched, and she lifted her chin. "Not happening, sir."

"Richard."

Damien laughed through her earpiece, making another less veiled insult about the man's name. Fortunately, none of what he said could be heard by their client. She cleared her throat and slid her gaze back to the children.

When she didn't respond, he kept talking. "Name's Richard. You know that."

The children squealed and jumped, all letting go of their red helium balloons at the same time. One by one, the little balls of landfill floated into the air, lifting into the cloudless blue sky. The kids ran circles around the lawn. So innocent. So ignorant.

For a moment, she didn't see their backyard lawn, but her old childhood home. Her own drunk and disorderly parents. A loud bang *popped*.

Senses on alert, Bailey unclipped her firearm from her underarm holster and pulled out the gun. She released the safety and held her wrist mic to her lips. "You got eyes?"

A crackling came back, then Damien's deep voice: "It was a balloon Bai, just a balloon."

Heat flushed to her cheeks and she sheepishly holstered her weapon.

"False alarm. Got it."

When she lifted her sight back to Richard, he watched her with an amused and yet equally leering expression. Somehow, even though he looked at Bailey's head, she felt his attention on the swell of her breasts pushing against her stiff, white button-down shirt. The damn shirts never fit her properly. Her waist and height were too small for a larger size, yet her breasts were too big. She clenched her jaw.

"A few more hours," he decreed. "I'll pay double."

Awful, awful man.

And Damien was most likely enjoying every moment of her squirming, knowing she had to hold her tongue, or lose their paycheck. He would also be across the grass in a flash if he thought there was any serious danger to Bailey. Thankfully, she spied the clown walking toward the edge of the lawn where his trunk supplies were. The children were dispersing.

"Looks like things are finishing up here, sir."

The man blinked, then turned to the children rushing up the steps to find their parents. A pretty brunette girl in a pink and white fluffy dress came stampeding up. A painted green butterfly covered half her face. She held a balloon animal in her hand.

"Did you see, Daddy? Did you see me make the balloon?"

He swayed. "Yeah, doll. I can see the balloon."

The jerk's eyes were still on Bailey.

"No, daddy, I said did you see me make it. I did it first go. No one else did it first go, but me."

Richard blinked again. "Why don't you show your mother?"

The little girl screwed up her face and aimed her gaze at the glass in her father's hand. Something clicked inside the little girl and her enthusiasm disappeared, replaced by a look of pure indifference. Her arm dropped, the balloon animal lowered and fluttered to the ground. It rolled down the steps on a hesitant breeze and skipped over the limestone toward the pool, on a path to clog the filter.

The girl continued up the steps. She didn't even turn at the balcony platform to find her mother but entered the house through the enormous open glass doors.

Bailey recognized that look of defeat. She'd seen it in the mirror many times herself as a child. Alcohol made memories disappear. It made children disappear. And when you had a lot of money, you tended to spend a lot on booze. Anger burned the back of her neck, prickling her skin.

Richard leaned toward Bailey, brought another waft of his sour stench, and she snapped. "You know, *sir*, if you weren't so concerned with seeing the bottom of your glass, or watching me, you may have enjoyed the brief time you'll never receive again with your daughter."

She checked the lawn. Most of the children had dissipated, along with the clown. "Looks like the event is over. Our contract is done," she said. "I'm not sure what threat to your family we were protecting you from, sir, but I suggest next time you look closer to home before you call us again."

Richard spluttered, but Bailey didn't give him a chance to respond. She walked the last two steps down to the lawn and crossed to meet Damien. Also wearing mirrored Aviators, his head followed her as she came closer.

Dammit.

She said nothing when she arrived. Just stood there, gathering her calm.

After a few moments, he asked, "We working for this wanker again?"

"Nope."

"Good." He nodded, but then added, "Max won't be happy."

"Max can kiss my fat ass."

"Your arse isn't fat."

"You're just saying that because you're scared of me."

He arched a brow, tilted to the side, looked behind her at her rear, then straightened and shrugged. "Maybe p-h-a-t phat. As in, fully sick phat."

She blinked. "What did you just say?"

"You know, *fully sick*. As in—never mind." He shut his mouth and tried to look innocent. "It's all coming out wrong."

"Goddamn Aussie." She cursed, but there was humor in her voice. "All right. Let's go."

"Good. Max needs us back at the office. He's got another job for you tonight."

WHEN BAILEY and Damien arrived at the Nightingale Securities headquarters, their leader waited for them. A few months earlier Max had been taken hostage by a bomb wielding terrorist. No, that wasn't quite right. Max had been strapped with a bomb and left with a dead man's switch attached to a ton of C4 and a cell phone detonator. Prior to that, he'd been missing for weeks. Missing whilst in the employ of the Lazarus family.

Bailey was still dark over that. Still peeved at how no one told her what had really happened during those two weeks, or what Max had really been tasked with for the family. His recent engagement to Sloan Lazarus was the only thing keeping her from commencing an all-out investigation of the suspicious family brood. But she wasn't CIA anymore. It wasn't her job to snoop in other people's lives.

Live your own life, she reminded herself. *Make your own choices. Be free to forge your own path.*

Freedom came in all shapes and sizes. It wasn't just the liberty of one's body from incarceration or capture; it was the power to think and act how she desired, without manipulation, without suggestion, and without oppression. It was the ability to think for herself and make her own decisions.

Max gave that to her. The CIA hadn't. Her family hadn't.

But she wasn't going to cry into her protein shake every morning over the matter. She was going to take that freedom and live her own life. Until Max's disappearance, it had gone well. Now she was questioning things she shouldn't.

Taking a deep breath, she faced Max—a perpetually blond, tanned and hard man. Since his near-death experience, he'd been different. Distant. Curt. Then he announced his engagement to Sloan and he became happy, and dare she say, jovial at times. She almost preferred the hard-as-nails Max.

Almost.

She'd investigated the three-person Nightingale Securities team before applying for the job, and she knew all about Max's tragic history during his service with the Australian army. She believed he was a good man, despite his reason for being dishonorably discharged. Over the past six months, along with the rest of the small security team, he'd become the only family Bailey cared for.

Not that they knew it.

"Max," she stated as she placed her black leather handbag on her desk. It was on the tip of her tongue to apologize for the way she'd left her previous assignment. Word would get back to Max soon, if it hadn't already. But she didn't want to make an excuse. That drunken asshole deserved the tongue lashing he got. Behaving like that at his daughter's party? He should be ashamed of himself. Bailey wouldn't apologize for sticking up for herself.

Dressed in a pair of black jeans and a tight muscle-bound T-shirt, Max was a catch. Just like the other two Bailey worked with, a fact the barista at the restaurant over the road constantly reminded her of.

Bailey didn't see it. She did, but she didn't. Her mind had locked away those feminine emotions and feelings a long time ago.

Only one person had come close to triggering any sort of response, and it didn't make an iota of sense. He was a poster boy for everything she despised but also the very thing every woman in the world would do anything to be with.

Maybe that's why she couldn't stop thinking of him. Must be. He was a conundrum. A mystery she needed to solve. A puzzle. The moment the thought entered her mind, her stomach revolted. Nope. Stay away from him.

Tony Lazarus was trouble in the shape of a gorgeous, smiling cocktail glass she didn't need.

Max collected his keys and strode to the entrance. "I'm on my way out, but I need you to work a double shift. I have another job for you. Tom-Tom is still on assignment."

"I'm listening." She supposed she had nothing else to do tonight.

"Details are on the folder on the desk. They're waiting for you, so you need to hurry." Then he gave a two-finger salute and went out the door, at the last moment saying, "It's the least you can do after losing us a client today."

When Max was well and truly gone, she twisted to eye Damien as he sat heavily at his desk and pulled his Aviators off. He rubbed his eyes and then trailed his big hand over his beard for a scratch. It was a little on the ginger side, despite his short crew cut being dark brown.

"You told him?" she accused.

"Nope."

"Is he pissed?"

Damien shrugged. "Doubt it. That sleazeball you mouthed off at was a worm."

Bailey exhaled relief. "So. Any idea what the job is?"

"Nope. Just that you better hurry. Max said they're waiting."

Right. Bailey quickly made her way to Max's desk and picked up the folder, glancing at a nearby picture frame showing the smiling faces of Max and his girl somewhere in the wilderness near a waterfall. Bailey frowned. That carefree vibe, whilst welcomed for her friend, went against her theory that the Lazaruses were keeping secrets.

She shook it off and opened the Manila folder. Inside were the job details.

Shit.

"Um," she said to Damien. "I forgot I had plans. Can you take it?"

He leaned back in his chair, a roguish glint to his eyes.

He knew. The bastard.

"Can't," he stated. "Got a hot date. Tom-Tom won't be back until late either."

"But... my plans."

"Can't be too important if you forgot them."

She darted a look back to the papers.

No.

"You've already lost one client today," Damien pointed out. "You'd better hurry."

She narrowed her eyes at him. Easy for him to say, he was a man. He didn't get leered at or propositioned by the clientele. But he was right. You don't put your personal feelings into a job. You do the job. You get out. You get paid. She knew that. She *knew* that.

A frustrated growl ripped from her throat and she collected her handbag. "Why am I always the one to do overtime?"

Damien smirked. "Well, if you had a life, you'd have a real excuse not to do it."

Stupidly, she had no reply until she was mid-way to the Cardinal Film Studios, fifteen minutes away.

three

TONY LAZARUS

THE VERY IDEA that Tony needed a bodyguard was laughable, yet he remained in his fake bloodstained T-shirt while he waited for one to arrive. He didn't like waiting and almost wished he had an entourage to help him pass the time. With nothing else to do, he stayed in his trailer and reclined on the brown and cream checked table settee. He launched the scrunched stalker's note across the Winnebago's expanse and watched it hit a hanging doll near the door and bounce down to the small sofa.

Huh.

That was fun.

Again.

Rubbing his palms together, he turned to the table next to him and pulled the top leaf off the unread manuscript and balled it up. It was only a courtroom drama. He threw again. And again. And again. It might be a stretch to say this kept his battle skills sharp, but he was saying it. The alternative was to work out, or have a nap, and he had the inclination for neither.

He'd not been invited on a family mission since his return from rehab, or more accurately, since he'd missed the call to action when Max had been kidnapped. He'd not been asked to spar with any of his family—apart from when Sloan needed impromptu acting classes— and he'd not been included on any strategy talks. Not a single text message, nor a comment at the family dinner. Nada. Bupkis.

Feelings about that tried to surface, but he pushed them down instead, preferring to numb his brain in the monotonous action of paper ball throwing. While he shot at the dolls, aiming for their swinging feet, he kept one eye on the flat screen to the left of him. It broadcast the local news network, but nothing of note excited him. It rarely did.

Sliding his attention back to the dolls, he knew he'd have to get up soon and collect the trash. He was also running out of projectiles, and there was only so much manuscript he could ball up before his agent realized he hadn't read the damned thing.

"All right. Here goes." Tony screwed up his last piece of paper. "Two points if I hit one hard enough to make it swing and hit the ceiling."

He shoots.

He scores!

"And the crowd goes wild. *Hhaar.*"

Tony threw his hands in the air, jumped up and did his best Rocky Balboa impression, but even that got dull after a while. There was no one to watch him.

He went back to his game until a familiar voice spoke on the television, nabbing his attention. He squeezed the crumpled ball in his fist and sat down on the sofa near the door, eyes on the screen. Griffin's wife, Lilo, stood outside the Cardinal Copy network studio about to give a news report. Her lively brown hair caught a breeze and lifted, but her attractive face was focused, gaze turned inward as she listened to the communication microphone in her ear.

Damn, Griff was lucky to have her for his mate. All of his siblings who had paired up had scored well, but the idea of coupling up—falling in love—was a foreign concept he couldn't relate to.

Women helped him sate his appetite temporarily, but that was it. He was too hungry... for sex, for pleasure, for conversation, for... more. It was always more with him, and one woman had never been enough for his insatiable urges. He could never have a relationship because soon enough, he got hungry again, and he hated it. Unchecked gluttonous desire eventually turned every taste to cardboard.

But Lilo, she was the center of Griffin's universe. Lilo had come a long way in the past six months. She used to want to unmask the Deadly Seven, but then she fell in love with one of them. Now Griffin and his wife were inseparable, much like Wyatt and Misha, or Evan and Grace. Max and Sloan were the latest of his family to catch the bug.

On the screen, Lilo was about to cross to another reporter in a neighboring city when a knock came at Tony's trailer door.

Thank Christ.

Without removing his eyes from the news report, Tony leaned over and opened the door for Max. "Guess who's about to report?"

Light flashed in as the door rocked open, but no answer to his question. Tony looked over and tensed.

Not Max.

Bailey.

Now, there was a woman he'd happily sate his urges on.

Still standing at the foot of the steps wearing her hot-as-fuck Aviators and a black pantsuit, there was so much more about her that appealed to him. Killer curves. Smooth brown skin. Big eyes. Full rosy lips. *Plenty.* It was the only word that kept coming to mind. She flicked her jacket open and rested her hands on her hips. Such a casual move, but it drew his attention to the fullness at her chest in a way that made his blood heat.

His mouth watered.

This woman was his bodyguard.

He casually swung his legs around the sofa and stood. He moved toward her, eyes never leaving her face until he ducked to avoid the dolls. At the doorframe, he lifted his arms to grip the top in a pose he knew exhibited the best his rigorous gym schedule had to offer. And then he slid her The Smile. Empire Magazine called it the look of the year. TMZ said it could kill. Cosmo said a bunch of things he probably shouldn't repeat. He just knew it made life easier.

Except Bailey didn't react. Not a twitch. Birds flew past in the sky, crickets chirped, and the world kept turning.

After a beat of silence, his grin dropped. He glanced down at himself and patted his chest and abs. "Is this thing on?"

When he glanced up, he caught her sucking her teeth, unimpressed. Right. Well, Plan B, then. Plan A was a long shot, anyway. He smiled again. "We have to stop meeting like this."

"You hired me."

"I hired Nightingale. You didn't have to come. Admit it, when the job came in, you were the first to stick up your hand."

"Don't flatter yourself. No one else was available."

His swagger faltered. He shrugged. "A man has to try."

She removed her glasses, folded them and used them to point to the dolls behind his head. "Care to explain?"

The torn shirt was beginning to make him feel a little exposed. He hopped down the trailer steps and gestured at the dolls before folding his arms to hide the battered shirt. "Your Honor, may I present Exhibit A; The reason I apparently need a bodyguard."

"I'm asking who you think did it. Why they did it. Whose wife did you screw this time?"

He covered his heart in mock offense. "Objection. Speculation."

It was a jest, but a glimmer of tightness constricted his chest and her words from months ago came back to haunt him: *I don't expect you to know anything.*

No matter how hard he tried, he couldn't stop them from cutting him. The sad thing was, she'd been right. He knew nothing. He was a smile on a face and a dick on legs. A monkey who danced to someone else's beat.

"What's with the lawyer talk?" she asked.

"I might change genres and try a courtroom drama. What do you think?"

"I think you should stick to telling me about the job."

"Oh, but it's much more fun pretending to be someone else."

"What's wrong with being yourself?"

He plucked at the hem of his shirt, saw his skin through a hole and folded his arms across his stomach to cover it. When he didn't answer, Bailey stepped into his trailer, leaving him out in the cold. She went to great pains to avoid touching him as she passed and then inspected the dolls with her sunglasses poking, brows puckering. "Do you have a copy of the police report?"

"No."

"Why not?"

"We didn't make one."

"Are you kidding me?"

"For a few dolls?"

Her eyes narrowed. "You taking me for a ride, Lazarus?"

"Babe..." He paused just in time, a smirk lifting his lips at the insinuation. He would say more, but that kind of line wouldn't work on this ice queen. Nothing in his normal arsenal had worked.

Silence.

Their eyes locked.

She did this little confused flinch, shook her head and cleared her throat.

Tony rejoined her in the trailer, squeezed by and collected his wallet and cell from the tiny dining table. He shoved it in his rear pocket and then retrieved his skateboard from its spot near the sofa. His Ducati was at the lot, and it was a ten-minute walk to get there. He preferred to use the board for the journey; nobody stopped to talk to you when you skated.

He reached for the TV remote. Lilo was saying something about water catchments being inexplicably drained around the tri-state area, but he switched it off. It was an interstate issue. Feds would handle it. One day the Deadly Seven envisioned themselves being split across the world, to help in any way they could, but not today. Not yet. Not until after the Syndicate was eliminated. Since the Syndicate were close by, Tony's family would stay local for now.

Bailey pulled her gaze from the dolls and began a slow scan of his trailer, pausing when her eyes touched the double bed, and then again when she caught the personal gym attached in a conjoined trailer.

"Did the stalker touch anything else?" she asked.

"I'm going to stop you there. Calling it a stalker is overkill. It's probably Sloan's retaliation for the time I locked her and Max in an elevator together."

"Heard about that. Didn't think Max was holding a grudge, though. Didn't think Sloan was either." She glanced at him and quickly looked away.

"What?" he asked.

"Nothing." She straightened her spine and then turned her unwavering gaze back to him. "I thought what you did was nice, actually."

Nice?

The weight of her stare buzzed against his skin. "Stop looking at me like that."

"Like what?"

Heat flooded his cheeks. "I didn't play match-maker, if that's what you're thinking. They were being annoying. I wanted it to stop. That's all."

"Right." She rolled her lips to try to hide an obvious smile. "Well, for what it's worth, I don't think the dolls are Sloan's doing."

Still scowling, Tony averted his gaze. It didn't matter who the prankster was. If anyone seriously thought about taking him on, they were in for a surprise. Just let them come. He may be a little rusty around the edges, but he knew how to protect himself.

Suddenly the trailer air became stifling, and he had to get out of there. He jogged down the steps and plonked his skateboard down, stopping it expertly with a boot. With a furtive look down Trailer Row, he checked for oncoming foot traffic. The majority of production had finished months ago, and today's take was only a make-up session. Most actors had gone home shortly after the final scene take, and the only staff left were preparing for the party. Food carts were gone or shifted. It was a ghost town.

"Where do you think you're going?" Bailey asked, doing that hands-on hips thing, looking down at him from the doorway, all traces of softness gone.

"I'm leaving. I have a party to get ready for."

Her lips pursed. "Get inside. We're not done."

"Babe, we're going," he stated. "I got places to be."

"Don't call me babe. It's Bailey. And I said, get your ass back in here, Lazarus. We need to talk about this. I need to know what I'm up against before we go parading you in the streets. Then I need to update your producer."

"It's Trailer Row. It's hardly a street, and you can call Donatello on the way."

A shout from further down the laneway drew Tony's attention as a male co-star on his way out waved. "See you tonight, Tones."

"You want to air your dirty laundry in public, be my guest," Bailey hissed. "I can talk about it down there."

She had a point. He'd thought everyone was gone, but obviously not.

"Fine." He stomped on the skateboard tail to flick up the top and grab. Then he went back inside.

Bailey slammed the door behind him. "Sit."

"Yes, ma'am."

"Take this seriously. You have dolls hanging from your ceiling. Not just hanging, but with blood painted on them."

"The blood's not on my doll," he joked.

"Why on earth wouldn't the studio call the police?"

Fiery eyes pinned him, giving him a taste of that x-ray attention again. He held back a squirm. This was ridiculous. He was better than squirming under a lady's attention. With a forced exhale, he loosened up.

"Guess they don't want another scandal," he answered.

"We need to find out who did this, or you'll be a sitting duck. You'll permanently need a bodyguard. Is that what you want?" He opened his mouth and she shut him down, continuing to berate him like a child. "Don't answer that. I'll answer for you. No. You don't want a long-term bodyguard, because next time, it won't be me, it will be Tom-Tom or Daymo if you refuse to act like an adult."

He leaned back and rested an arm lengthwise over the top of the sofa. "All right, Scooby-Doo. What do you suggest?"

A muscle in her cheek twitched. "The stalker had access to your trailer. I'll need the studio records of who's been allowed on the lot. We can start there."

"Sloan can get in anywhere without a trace. You know that, right? So if it was her, you wouldn't know, anyway."

"And exactly how does she manage to do that?"

The world thought Sloan was a slacker gamer, not a hacking and tech-wise vigilante. He'd said too much.

"I meant, she's family. I've given her an all-access pass to the set," he fibbed.

"There will still be records. We'll ask her too. Anything else I need to know?" She pulled out her cell phone and began to take notes. "Disgruntled colleagues. Crazed fans?"

He rolled his eyes. "They all love me."

"Right. Because that's so believable."

That was the last straw. He didn't need this crap. He didn't need a fucking bodyguard. He straightened, tensed, and instead of shrinking away, she blocked his exit at the door with a challenge in her eyes.

"You have something to say to me, Lazarus?"

Long seconds passed. "I was just about to ask you the same thing."

"I don't know what you mean."

"You don't like me, Bailey. Be honest."

Her jaw tightened and Tony saw the truth in her eyes. It was more than not liking him. She didn't respect him. Suddenly, the fight went out of him and he sighed. Just get this over with.

"There was a note," he admitted and found the scrunched paper ball to hand to her.

She opened it. "It says 'I know.' That's it?"

"That's it."

She folded it and put it in her pocket. "You have a secret. Someone knows. They don't like it."

"You want your Scooby snack now?"

Attentive eyes laced with suspicion weighed on him.

He was done. "I don't need a nosy babysitter. I can take care of myself."

He moved for the door, but she stopped his exit with her body. The pure retribution in her eyes cut him to the core.

"I am *not* a babysitter. I am a trained security specialist. Eleven years serving my country, which far outranks your drop in the ocean."

His three collective years of training with the SEALs and the SAS (both Australian and UK) was a public fact and she knew it. He'd completed all in record time. It helped build his action-hero credibility. Granted, the public didn't know about the four other years traveling the world, learning the Art of War, or his old nighttime escapades bringing the city's worst to justice. They didn't know about his training by one of the most lethal women in the world—his mother, a deadly assassin.

She continued. "*I'm* the bodyguard. I make the rules. Everywhere you go, I go first. Understood?"

Her scrutiny made him realize he was supposed to be acting like the dumb playboy actor. The one who hated responsibilities. The one incapable of being one of the Deadly Seven. Without another word, he reached around her, got in her personal space like only a narcissistic actor would, then opened the door and used his body to get by.

She let him.

"Bodyguards don't investigate," he pointed out. "You guard."

The fidget of her fingers told him he'd hit her right in the squirming spot, just like she'd done with him earlier. She didn't like being told not to investigate. She thought she was better than a bodyguard.

"You coming?" he asked over his shoulder. He put his skateboard down, planted a foot to stop it rolling and waited for her. He should be used to people ordering him around by now.

She shut the trailer door and, after giving a searching look around, gestured down the alley in the direction of the parking lot. "Let's go."

Watching her stride away, he felt a growing hollow in his stomach... a hunger forming. There was nothing he could do but follow.

MUCH TO TONY'S CHAGRIN, Bailey insisted she drive him back to his place in her SUV, meaning his bike had to stay at the studio lot. The woman was serious about the bodyguard business. When they'd arrived, she made him stay in the car until she exited first and checked their surroundings—even though they were in the private Lazarus House underground garage. They took the civilian elevator up to his level, and then she checked the corridor leading to his apartment before she let him out of the lift.

"Alright," she said, waving him out. "Let's go."

His lips twitched. "Are you sure it's safe?"

She shot him an apathetic stare. A thrill tripped in his stomach.

"Which room is yours?" she asked and then checked her watch as though she had somewhere better to be.

"On the left."

He followed her down the hall. There were only two doors. The one on the right belonged to Griffin and Lilo. Each apartment was penthouse sized and took up one half of the building. Of course, the top floor was the real penthouse. That belonged to his eldest sibling, Parker, and spanned the entire expanse of the building, complete with a pool and jacuzzi on his balcony.

32

Bailey held out her palm. "Keys."

Don't think so. He ignored her and wrapped his hand around the knob.

"Stop," she snapped.

"Christ. I can open my own door."

"It's unlocked?"

"Yeah, of course."

She waved him aside. "Let me go in first."

"This is private property. No one gets in but the family. And maybe the cleaner, but she's had a background check." A very extensive check. Plus she was paid handsomely for her exclusivity and silence.

Her black brow arched indignantly. "I go in first."

He took a step back, palms up.

"Wait here." She unclipped her firearm and released it from the holster. Then she nudged the door open and proceeded with caution.

Tony waited in the hallway, hands in pockets, leaning his head against the wall. This bodyguard schtick was getting old. With nothing to do but wait, he focused on Griffin's door and pushed out his sixth sense to feel for the sin of gluttony. Nothing. Didn't mean there was no one home, but most likely the happily married couple were still at work. They were both workaholics.

His neck itched. Come to think of it, his chest itched too. The fake blood had caked on his skin. Normally he'd be out of makeup by now. He sniffed under his arm and jerked back. Yep. Shower needed pronto.

"Clear," came Bailey's voice from inside his place.

Perfect timing. He dragged his shirt over his head and entered his apartment. The decor was slick designer chic. White tiles contrasted with granite features. Potted plants were placed at random intervals around the space, including a daisy bush near the balcony he used more than the open-plan kitchen. An acoustic guitar leaned against the wall in the living room. But the pièce de résistance was the theater room—two level cinema seating, sunken floor, wall to wall projector screen, and a surround sound system. When they'd built the building years ago, he'd knocked out the spare bedroom to make the theater bigger.

Shower.

Right. He scrunched up his shirt and then popped the top button on his jeans as he toed off his boots. He almost got to his bedroom door before he heard her.

"What are you doing?" she squeaked.

He pivoted, a slow smile forming on his lips. Bailey was near the kitchen, a hip leaning on the bench, head cocked, lips pursed, and eyes wary of his naked chest.

"Taking a shower. Want to join?"

There went those brows again, but she didn't speak.

"Didn't think so," he added and then gestured into his room. "I stink. I itch. And I need to be at this party soon."

She cleared her throat. "Um. What time?"

"About an hour."

She checked her watch and then met his eyes again. "You don't need to go anywhere else before then?"

He shook his head. Unlikely the family needed him, or if they did, they wouldn't ask.

"I'll be back in fifty."

"I'll only be a few minutes. Help yourself to a drink in the fridge and make yourself at home."

She didn't even consider it. She just checked her watch again. "I'll be back for you. Don't go anywhere."

He frowned. "Where exactly do you have to go?"

Instead of answering, she cast her eyes around his place. "Do you ever think about using your celebrity status for something else other than making money?"

"What's that supposed to mean?"

She sighed. "Nothing. I have to go."

"It doesn't mean *nothing*." He strode back toward her, only to have her back up from him. Then she planted her boots squarely on the floor and folded her arms.

"Fine. You want to know what I meant?"

"I'm all ears, babe."

"You're a big-budget movie star, yet you squander your income away on booze and things—"

"Objection, Your Honor!" He held up his finger. "Conjecture."

She frowned. "Don't you ever have a serious conversation?"

"I do when there's something serious to talk about. Besides, I'm practicing. What do you think, does lawyer look good on me?"

"You could be using your celebrity for good, for giving back to the community, but… never mind. It's none of my business. I don't know why I said anything."

It wasn't her business, that was the truth, but she was the first person who had ever asked him to do something better with his money—with his status. Strangely, this meant something to her. She didn't think he noticed the way her cheeks heated and her eyes brightened when she spoke about it. Whether she was just an opportunist who'd seen the chance to get in the ear of a celebrity, or a woman with altruistic tendencies, Bailey Haze had ideas about the world, and Tony didn't fit into them.

Or she was hiding something. Unease squirmed in his stomach, and he had to remind himself the woman was ex CIA. She was adept at keeping secrets. He didn't get a chance to push the subject. She holstered her gun and left, leaving him watching the empty space she'd vacated.

The woman intrigued him. She'd kept checking her watch during the drive. At first, he'd thought she was just eager to get her shift over, but...

He slipped his cell phone out of his back jeans pocket and dialed a number.

Two rings later, Sloan picked up. "Bras," she greeted.

"Sloanie."

"Wassup?" Muffled giggling came through, then it sounded like a hand covered the handset and—

Tony held the cell away from his ear. He did *not* need to hear his sister making out with her man. Jesus. If this is the reason why Max couldn't meet him at the studio.

At least someone was seeing action. Since his rehab stint, he'd been encouraged to step back from all gluttonous activities. No drinking. No drugs. No gambling. No sex. That last one wasn't in his contract, but he'd still followed the rehab rules.

He had to, or risk falling.

His stomach rumbled. Yep... hungry. On all accounts.

Sloan came back. "Sorry, about that. Max is... um"—more giggling—"did you want something?"

"You owe me."

"Max!" More shuffling, then the sound changed. "Okay, okay. I'm in another room. What do you need?"

He paused. "I want information on one of Max's employees."

"Bailey?" she teased. "The same woman you so gallantly offered to go and speak to a few months back?"

"She's the bodyguard Max assigned to help me. I don't trust her. I want every piece of information you have on her."

"Well, it just so happens that I've already presented my background checks on Max's staff, so I'll just shoot that information through."

"Presented? When did you do that?"

Sloan paused. "The other day at a family meeting."

"Without me?"

"Don't act so surprised. You were probably told."

Except, he didn't think he was. They'd just stopped asking. And he'd stopped pretending it didn't hurt.

BAILEY HAZE

IT WAS one thing for a client to act cocky, but it was another for him to strip before you and offer to share a shower. What was with men today? Did Bailey have a sign over her head that said *Hit on me?*

In her small kitchen, Bailey stewed over the fact as she prepared herself a Cosmopolitan. She also tried not to think about his perfect torso and disarming smile.

Honestly, what kind of man said things like that?

Tony Lazarus, that's who.

Bailey measured out the cranberry juice and poured it into the cocktail mixer. She added the ice, vodka, triple sec, and lime, then popped the cap on and shook the damn thing like she was Tom Cruise, or rather Tony Lazarus in his latest college-boy film.

She scoffed and shook her head. The man was blessedly endowed with all the right physical traits, and any woman would have jumped at the prospect of having a shower with him, but she wasn't a one-hit-wonder kind of woman. She liked to take her time.

Her ex-partners had called her intense. She just knew what she wanted, and Tony couldn't give it to her. She liked it long and slow, not hard and fast. She liked it to last all night.

Unless you'd like to join me. As if they could get any satisfaction with a quickie in the shower before heading out to a party. But then Tony had sardonically added, *Didn't think so.*

Which irritated her more, and she didn't know why. It wasn't like she was disappointed... was she?

Absolutely not.

She retrieved a martini glass from her cupboard and placed it onto the speckled kitchen bench. She poured the canister contents into it. Then she washed her cocktail shaker and upended it on the sink. When she returned to the Cosmopolitan, she didn't pick it up. She touched the cool rim. A drip trickled down the stem and a memory rose to the surface.

The condensation on the inside of a car window, trickling. Her heated breath. Wind buffeting outside. Metal creaking. The pain in her chest at the cold, vacant stare of her dead best friend, her body half through the windshield. Bailey dug the heels of her palms into her eye sockets and inhaled deeply. On the exhale, she glared at the Cosmo glass.

I will not let you ruin me.

You destroy lives.

I am better than you.

For another two minutes, she watched her drink and reminded herself of all the pain alcohol caused in her life. The loud angry slurs late at night. Her friend's hair fanned out on the hood of the car. The empty harrowing hallway of the rehab center when she'd visited her mother. The gravestone of her parents at the cemetery.

What a waste.

Heartache wrapped around her chest and she used the feeling to steel her resolve before crippling doubt set in. Two minutes was all she allowed herself before she turned her back on the drink. She leaned her butt against the bench and folded her arms.

Her living room wasn't much to look at, but it was homey. It featured a cozy high-back winged lounge chair she'd found at a thrift store. Cushions and throw rugs galore. Crossword books on the coffee table—the kind you could win a prize with. A modest flat-screen television on the wall, and two paintings of a tropical hideaway graced the other walls. There was a matching set in her bedroom. In all her time working abroad with the agency, she'd never visited a tropical island. It had been the dreary parts of Europe, and not exactly what she'd envisioned when signing up. One day she would visit those places. She'd just rather not do it alone.

She took a deep breath. Time for a shower.

Moving to her room, she pulled out a black suit from her closet and laid it on her bed. Next to that, she placed her underwear—a cute blush-pink satin number with a bow between the balconette bra cups. She thumbed through a collection of hanging white dress shirts in her closet and settled on a black one. A white shirt would show her bra, and she felt like a little private luxury under her shirt. She wouldn't concede to a flesh toned T-shirt bra tonight, especially when her expectations were of a night no doubt dealing with a drunk and intoxicated client. She deserved a little something for her trouble. She didn't have high hopes that he would stick to his abstinence from booze. Addicts never did. And for some reason, bodyguard was a word synonymous with babysitter in this high-profile world.

How did she get herself into these situations?

Heading to her ensuite, she turned the shower faucet on, undressed and went under the spray.

Tony may have pointed out that it wasn't her job to investigate the stalker, but she couldn't let it go. Not only had his comment hit too close to home, but she hated that he was hiding something.

Besides, being told not to do something was the quickest way to ensure she did it.

On her way back from his place, she'd not only grabbed a bite to eat, but put in a request with his studio for the security footage near his trailer. Unfortunately, because it was after hours and the indisputable fact that everyone in that industry worked on their own time, she'd have to wait until someone got back to her.

To get to the bottom of the stalker, she'd have to work on discovering what Tony's secret was. Probably an affair, these things always were. But something else tumbled in her gut... intuition, premonition... an inkling. Call it what you will. She only knew it meant something was not right with that family. She'd known it since Max disappeared on a secret mission for them and ended up with a bomb strapped to his chest.

The part of her brain she'd fostered in the CIA was screaming at her to pay attention, and every cell in her body wanted to investigate further, but she'd promised herself that she'd put all that behind her. No more cloak and dagger business; she was on the straight and narrow. Stick with the stalker. Not everything was some grand conspiracy she had to crack. Being paranoid with life was one of the reasons she got out. She wanted something real. She wanted a nice life, not ruin. After years of loneliness, the Cosmo had started to look too good.

Maybe she was over-thinking things. Maybe Tony wasn't coming onto her. Maybe he was just being himself, and she didn't even know quite who that was. There had been an obvious shift in his body language earlier, after he'd accused her of not liking him. It had been more than conceit. He'd been hurt. He wasn't the person the public saw. He was guarded, obstinate, and perhaps even caring. Despite what he'd said, she knew he'd wanted his sister to work it out with Max. That blush of his had proven it.

Tony was a hopeless romantic.

That last word hadn't meant to slip out. She held her breath and dunked her face under the hot stream of water. But... while she was at it, she may as well explore those thoughts. She couldn't very well do her job tonight if she was focused on his good looks. And boy were they good. Better than good. Damned hot. The kind of sexy that shouldn't exist. The kind that made you lose your words and hold your breath and squeak like a little mouse when he popped the top button on his jeans as you glimpsed a taste of the hard sacrilegious flesh beneath... his lack of perceived underwear.

Good Lord.

Another dunk under the water.

The silver screen didn't do him justice. She'd watched a few of his films after her first encounter with him months ago. For research. But seeing him in person today, in the hot-blooded flesh, was an experience she hadn't been prepared for. It was different this time. Last time, he'd stunk of alcohol and acted like a slobbering loser. This time, he had his shit together. She saw the man who earned the multi-million-dollar paycheck. Charming. Charismatic. Playful. From his picture-perfect face, square jaw, wide lips, to eyes that smoldered and made you feel as though you were his whole world—simply by landing on you—he had presence. His shirt had fit his body like a glove. Every ropy muscle, line and curve demonstrated the gym in his trailer had gone to good use.

She shut her eyes. His intense gaze was right there, stealing her breath. Goosebumps erupted over her flesh. Her nipples hardened. Desire bloomed low, and she pressed her thighs together to dispel the feeling.

Maybe if she just... her hand slid down her wet body, bumping over her sensitized breasts and went lower... and then she remembered her interaction with him two months prior, when she'd accosted him in the Lazarus House lobby. He'd been with a woman at the time, but the moment he'd seen Bailey, he'd discarded the model on his arm like she was an afterthought.

Nope. Hell, no.

You will not ruin me, Tony Lazarus.

She stepped out of the stream and shivered. He may not be a cocktail in a martini glass, but he would be an addiction all the same. He was a client. A playboy film star. There were quite literally millions of other women in the world who wanted to be with him, and there always would be. He would chew her up and spit her out. She was better than this.

He couldn't give her what she wanted.

Packing her lust away—because that's all it was, run-of-the-mill handsome-boy, lonely girl lust—she turned the faucet off, opened the shower stall door, and froze.

The sound of her fridge door closing filtered through. Glass and metal tinkled. Someone was here.

The shock of revelation drilled down to her bones, petrifying her, and then a muffled bang sounded from somewhere outside the ensuite. Maybe from the bedroom. Maybe still in the living area or kitchen because the bedroom door was open.

Every muscle tensed. Every sound amplified as she reached with her ears. Another boot scuffle. Someone was definitely in her apartment.

And she'd left her firearm on her bedside table.

Shit.

As quietly and efficiently as she could, she grabbed her dusky pink silk robe from the hook and then wrapped herself in it, drawing the strings closed across her waist. Water on her body darkened the silk in blooms of deep maroon, reminding her of blood. Holding her breath, she inched the ensuite door open with a toe and assessed through the crack.

Her gun was on her bedside, locked in its holster. Her laid-out clothes were untouched. Nothing had been ruffled. The big duck-blue pillows were immaculately placed, and not a wrinkle existed on her matching coverlet.

On the count of three, she opened the door a tad more. She waited. The intruder was quiet. Too quiet. As though he'd heard her turn off the shower and lay in wait.

Who would be in her condo?

Tony's stalker, that's who. Damn, she hated being right. She'd *known* it was a real threat. She just didn't think the stalker would come after her first. Whoever it was must have seen her take Tony to his place and then followed Bailey home. This could be a misplaced preemptive strike.

She opened the door wider, but as she did, the open doorway on the other side of her room filled with a shadow. On instinct, she moved. Forget the gun. Rush him. Get him down.

She took two light-footed strides across her carpeted floor, but the shadow kept moving. She'd barely caught a glimpse of a purple covered shoulder, and then he was gone. He hadn't seen her. Slowing her trajectory, she eased and flattened herself against the bedroom wall two feet from the door that led to the living room. Her chest lifted and fell with each schooled breath.

Bailey craned her neck to see out and glimpsed a masculine hand rifling through her crossword puzzles. There was a crunching sound. It took her a moment to realize what it was. The damned bastard was eating something he'd taken from her fridge. From the crisp, clear intonation, it was probably the cucumber she'd been saving to use in her salad tomorrow.

Darting a glance back to where her gun was on her bedside table, she considered going for it, but that would mean leaving the safety of her spot. She'd have to cross the open doorway zone, and that meant he'd see her. If he had a gun, he'd get to her first.

From the casual way the hand rifled through her things, and his eating, it didn't seem like he'd noticed her finishing her shower after all. She had the element of surprise.

She used it.

She rushed toward the stranger with his back to her. She slipped one hand under his arm, and the other around his neck to take him in a chokehold. She dragged him back to throw him off balance. It was supposed to give her more time to apply pressure to his throat, but his big hand came up to cover hers, and he rolled to the side.

In a blink, she found herself on the ground beneath him.

The wind knocked out of her lungs. Her eyes watered from the thud. When her vision cleared, she saw Tony Lazarus's perfect face looming over her... still holding her hand. His hair was messy and a touch damp from his shower.

Tony Lazarus.

In her apartment.

And he'd outmaneuvered her.

"What the fuck?" she burst. That move had *always* worked on someone bigger than her.

He frowned, eyes on their joined hands as if she'd burned him. "It's you," he murmured.

"Of course, it's me. This is my condo. What are *you* doing here?"

Her response shocked him out of his daze, and he tugged to pull her up. Screw that. As he lifted, she hooked her heel around his ankle and used the changing momentum to push him backward. This time, it was he who landed with a jarring thud, and she who landed on top of him, trapping his arms to his sides with her thighs.

The cucumber knocked from his hand and rolled across the carpet until it hit the base of her kitchen bench.

Throwing her forearm onto his windpipe, she applied pressure with all her weight. "What the hell are you doing in my home, Lazarus?"

His remarkable blue eyes watered, and he tried to move his arms. They pushed against the inner walls of her thighs and she clenched. Strangely, she had the sense that he could break from her hold but didn't. He relaxed and his cheeks colored.

For the second time since she'd met him, she saw a crack in the veneer of his movie-star composure. Sweat beaded across his brow, but he wasn't afraid of her. It was something else. Was he ill? She eased off his neck, but kept her forearm gently there, ready to push at a moment's notice. Her face was inches from his when she lifted a brow. "I'm waiting."

"I-uh... I..." He swallowed, and then he groaned in an almost sexually, pained way.

His eyes darkened. The scent of hot-blooded male filled her senses, hitting every nerve and instinct, and when his mouth parted on a hissed breath, she was overcome with how divine those lips looked. Soft. Wide. Moist.

"It's you," he murmured again, as if that explained everything.

The baritone of his voice worked with his drugging scent to loosen every muscle in her body and warm her blood. She melted against him until her aching breasts touched his hard chest. The physical connection snapped something inside her—a slap in her mind's eye. She shook her head to dispel the amorous feelings. What was wrong with her?

He was an intruder in her home! Not some sex toy.

She fisted his shirt on either side of his neck, lifted and shoved. "What. Are. You. Doing. Here?"

"I got tired of waiting. So sue me." The words came out of his mouth, but his eyes drank in her features as though he was a thirsty man and she, an oasis.

Tired of waiting? For heaven's sake. "How did you know where I live? Did Max tell you?"

He shrugged. The action moved his arms still pinned beneath her thighs and, damn if it didn't bring an infuriating awareness there again.

"How did you get in?" she pressed, her voice huskier than intended.

Again, another shrug. Another minute flash of attention—*there*.

A moan escaped her lips. Her eyes widened in surprise. He craned his neck, reaching for her with his mouth.

Every logical thought fled her mind. All that was left was his intoxicating scent tickling her senses. Musky, heady and natural. He wanted to kiss her, and—*goddammit*—she wanted to let him. Inch by inch he strained closer. Closer. Electricity and anticipation hummed between them. There was no other reasoning but his lips as they met, and the seismic reaction afterward. The earth moved. The sky tumbled. The air thickened. He was the destruction of her world, of her inhibitions. This was raw, powerful and inescapable. She tunneled her fingers into his damp hair, and he slid his hands out to grip her waist and hold her to him until the pressure between their hips became unbearable and she rocked. Her mind began to shut down to make way for all the sensations of pleasure Tony brought as his tongue dueled with hers.

They kissed, lost in each other until a single word pierced her haze: ruin.

She pulled away and reason flooded in. Connection severed, she blinked, catching her breath as Tony resumed savoring her with his eyes.

This was wrong. She *knew* that, but she hadn't been able to stop. Her lips felt tainted, bruised, wet. She wiped the back of her hand across them and huffed. Then her face twisted into fury and she slammed her palms on his chest.

"Ow," he groused.

"You don't get to come into my home, eat my cucumber, accost me, and then kiss me like..."

"Like I've been waiting for your taste my whole life?"

"I'm not one of your groupies, Tony. Those lines don't work on me."

Amusement flickered in his eyes, and then his attention dropped from her face down to her chest. They were back up in a flash. "Sorry. Shit. I'm not looking, I swear."

He squeezed his eyes shut.

"Not looking at wha—?" She glanced down. Her robe gaped, giving him unfettered access to her precious cargo. Both parts. Upstairs and downstairs. She readjusted to cover up. "Boy, I'm not going to ask again."

His eyes opened and crinkled. "Boy? I like that. Cute."

Goddamn it. It was what her grandmother used to call her father when he was in trouble, and the trouble had lasted well into his adult years. Tony wasn't a child, but she felt like he needed schooling, and the word had just slipped out. She climbed off him. He gave a disappointed sigh. She started stalking to her bathroom, but pivoted at the last moment and came back to him as he lifted himself from the ground.

She pointed at his face. "This isn't going to happen."

"It already has."

"You know what I mean." Smug bastard.

"I know."

"For the record, we're not compatible. Men like you and women like me don't mix."

"Says who?"

"Me. I'm not into"—she waved at his face—"all *that*. And you can't handle all of this."

They were the wrong words to say to Tony Lazarus. He didn't cower, he didn't shy away, he stood tall and let his dark gaze drift down her body. "Maybe that's a good thing."

"What's that supposed to mean?" *Go on. I dare you. Just say something about my body and I'll throttle you to Kingdom Come.*

"I mean, I have a big appetite. I *need*"—he gestured around her body—"all of that."

Bailey opened her mouth for a retort, but Tony suddenly turned his back on her, hunching over his hands. "Fuck, it," he cursed. "I'll wait for you outside."

Then he left her condo.

Just like that.

"Yeah. You go wait outside," she said, as though it was her idea.

Stunned, and a little confused, she strode to her room. What just happened? Did he come onto her and then change his mind? Typical. Exactly what she expected from a mercurial movie star.

But as Bailey dressed into her suit, the back of her mind flashed an image of when Tony turned his back on her; a blue glow had refracted against the wall. Had he pulled out his cell? At the idea of him either filming, recording, or dismissing her so suddenly, irritation battered her nerves. By the time she was done preparing her makeup and hair, she was ready to call Max and have a quiet word with her boss.

This kind of behavior from a client was wrong. She didn't care if he was Max's future brother-in-law. It was goddamned wrong. She would request to be reassigned first thing in the morning.

five

TONY LAZARUS

SENSING SIN WAS no walk in the park. For a skill steeped in righteousness, it wasn't The Rapture, and it wasn't divine. It was grime and damnation wriggling in Tony's gut, and it was only through sheer stubbornness, or complete intoxication, that he survived this semblance of what some people called life. Gluttony was something that occurred every hour, minute, and second. It was the indulgence of the rich and powerful. It was the meal of an infant or the excess of a friend. And now that he was forced to stay away from the toxins that drowned his discomfort, gluttony was Tony's nightmare.

When he crossed the studio threshold, the sense of sin grew heavy in his gut. A crowd of revelers would always do that to him. Sickly and like a beacon, the sense tugged him in one direction and then the next. Whoever imbibed the most would cause the biggest reaction. Not all piggish excess was deadly, not all was sin, but he felt it all the same.

Party already in full swing, production staff and actors milled about on the stage set where he'd filmed his last scene. To the world who'd see it from the other end of a lens, it was a city alley and street complete with upturned cars from the action sequence, and other fallen debris. One of the giant gorilla costumes sat on a chair, pretending to drink at the temporary bar underneath the window of a fake barber shop. Music played from somewhere, but Tony's eyes had halted wandering, and zeroed in on the bar with longing.

His mouth dried, he swayed a little, and he shoved his hands in his jeans pockets to keep them from glowing accidentally. So far he'd managed to suppress the new, strange power, but it crawled beneath his skin, needing to get out and he had no time to investigate it. So he resisted like a junkie yearning to itch his veins. He'd had plenty of practice stifling his urges, and also plenty of practice succumbing. The sooner he was done with this party and his contractual obligation, the better.

"You okay?" Bailey asked as she came up next to him.

"Why wouldn't I be?"

Her clever eyes made a pointed dip at his hidden hands. "You've put your hands in your pockets. You're also sweating and your face has paled."

For a moment, he stared at her, undecided on how to respond. The woman read him like raw post-production footage. He felt naked. Unedited.

"Do you like watching me?" he asked.

She blinked and then turned her gaze back to the crowded room. "Yeah," she answered dryly. "Sure. Let's go with that."

"It's okay. You can admit it. I saw your Netflix watch list."

She gaped. "You turned on my television?"

"Had to do something while waiting for you to get out of the shower."

A muscle in her jaw twitched, and he grinned. "Not one, but *three* Tony Lazarus films."

She rolled her eyes and waved her hand toward the party. "After you."

Crisis averted, the tension in his shoulders eased. He didn't need her looking too closely at him. Turning back to the crowd, he steeled himself. *Showtime.* Plastering the playboy persona on his face, he sauntered further into the joint and raised his hands, shouting, "Let's get this party started!"

Already halfway inebriated, most of the crowd turned and cheered. Before he knew it, he was surrounded by co-workers, strangers, and more—all wanting a piece of him, or rather, the person he wanted them to see. One by one, the carrion picked him apart until only bones remained. Through it all, he grinned and beared it with one eye on them, the other on his mate, standing stoically to the side, watching his back... or more correctly, watching him.

An hour in, his agent sidled up to his side, interrupting Tony's selfie shot with two winners from the studio fan club competition. Chet Truscott was a man Tony had once identified with. He'd spent the first years of their business together asking Tony what he needed. Now, the fifty-something-year-old man wearing Armani only cared to ask what Tony could do for him. He wasn't meant to be at the wrap party, but there he was.

"Tony," the man stated with a dismissive glance at the groupies. "I need a word."

Tony held his finger up at Chet, then beamed at the two enthusiasts. A robust woman in her fifties, and her younger, pink-cheeked daughter. They both wore T-shirts that had a picture of his face. "Thank you, ladies for your time. I hope you enjoy the rest of the party. Those shirts are hashtag-adorbs." He kissed each woman gently on the back of her hand. It was pretentious actor shit, he knew, but he didn't care. They loved the attention, and he loved the response. Giggles and blushes abound. Spending time with his fans was something he'd always loved. There was something in the way they saw him. It wasn't Tony, nor Gluttony, but the character he played. Some actors complained at being confused with their characters, but he loved it. He lived for it. Any chance he got, he encouraged it.

After the women reluctantly turned away, Tony's smile dropped, and he focused on his agent. "Didn't think this sort of party was your thing, Chet."

"Oh, you know me, always at the beck and call of my clients." Chet swirled the amber liquid in his whiskey glass.

Tony scoffed. "You haven't becked my call in years."

Chet's eyebrows lifted at Tony's mocking tone. "Really? That's how you're going to play it?"

"Don't know what you're talking about." Tony averted his gaze toward his bodyguard. Bailey stood in a quiet corner, hands behind her back, stoically watching him.

"Let's get something straight, Tony," Chet said, drawing Tony's attention back. "This industry moves fast. You're already a has-been so don't get cocky. You're not my biggest client, yet you're my biggest time suck."

"I love you too."

"Have you read the scripts I sent over?"

"Maybe."

"For fuck's sake. If you don't pick something soon, you're no good to me." Chet shot back the remaining whiskey from his glass. "Have an answer to me by the end of the week or you're dropped."

The sad truth was Chet was the best agent in town. He had connections. He'd *made* Tony, and he knew it.

Chet pointed his empty glass at Tony with a warning in his narrowed eyes. "End of the week."

Then he was gone, lost in the crowd of noisy revelers.

The scent of Chet's whiskey still burned into Tony's olfactory and before he knew what he was doing, he found himself at the makeshift bar. The tall lanky barman wore coke-bottle spectacles that turned his eye color a cloudy gray.

"What can I get you?" the barman asked.

Tony considered. The night had taken a turn and the rolling in his gut was becoming unbearable. It was either leave or get a drink and become numb. Make that shell fill up with *something*.

Just one.

"Scotch on the rocks," he answered.

The man nodded and left to prepare the drink, pulling out a clean glass from the rack.

Tony exhaled a long, drawn out breath. He placed his palm on the back of his neck and squeezed. Just one drink. No harm, no foul.

A change in the atmosphere to his right signaled her arrival. Talk about a craving. She was the temptation he couldn't have. The haven in his nightmare. Just touching her would block out all sin-sensing, and she knew nothing about it. She thought he was a jerk. Maybe he was. *This is torture.*

"You don't want that drink," Bailey stated, her velvet voice low enough for his ears only.

His gaze slid sideways. Standing half a foot shorter than him, she was an impressive woman. Classically beautiful, tall, and striking. How she managed to slide under the radar was beyond him. Throughout the night, rarely a person looked her way. She tried to play down her beauty with boring pantsuits and little makeup.

No colleague asked why she shadowed him. He'd originally assumed word had gotten around about the stalker gift in his trailer, and the need for a bodyguard. Gossip like that was always front and center, and his co-stars were always the first to enjoy a bit of friendly ribbing. But if word had indeed gotten out, he'd have known it by now.

No, he believed no one noticed Bailey because she was good at being a ghost, at pretending she blended with the furniture. There was something about the decor in her condo. It felt like a display model home. There was no connection there. No life. It seemed furnished by the salesperson. Not a single family photograph, no identifying paraphernalia. Only the pictures of a tropical getaway merited pause. Sloan's quick report over the phone earlier today had been lacking in regard to Bailey's pre-CIA life. Boarding school in her youth. Rich, dead parents she never visited, or took their money. She'd donated it all to charity instead. Before she worked for the agency, she was basically a ghost. Exactly what the agency liked.

Tony tore his gaze from her and brought it back to the barman. He placed the glass on the bench before heading off to the next customer. Tony reached but was stopped by long, elegant brown fingers wrapped around his tanned wrist. The contrast between their two worlds was never so evident as that joining, but when the grimy sense of gluttony in his gut disappeared, he knew he had to have her. He stumbled, adjusting to the new serenity. It was a biological response that had been programmed into his DNA. Each of the Deadly Seven reacted upon contact with their mate with an almost medicinal response. The sick sense in their gut disappeared, and the concentration of sin in their blood reset. They felt human. He could have wept at the sudden absence of queasiness, and he could have gathered her into his arms. Instead, he took her calming scent in and breathed. She smelled like soap with a hint of coconut.

Mistaking the reason for his fumble, Bailey's grip on his wrist tightened, and she steadied him.

"Are you okay?" Her sharp eyes scanned the crowd for danger.

That was the second time she'd asked that tonight. The awareness hit him squarely in the chest. He'd only a moment to comprehend, *maybe she doesn't hate me,* but then he remembered her wiping her mouth with the back of her hand after they'd kissed.

No, she was disgusted with him.

His power—whatever it was—throbbed beneath his skin. It started with a light drum and strengthened to an aching hammer. From his legs up his torso… in his neck.

Aghast, he looked down. A blue glow pulsed in his veins, keeping time with his ever-increasing heart rate. Anyone with their eyes on him would see. Something powerful, untamed, and hot wanted to get out of his body. Here. In front of everyone.

This could be dangerous.

Bailey's grip released, and she took a step back, stunned eyes on his forearms, on the light coalescing in his hands. "What the hell, Lazarus?"

He shook his hands, flexed his fists, and instinctually suppressed the powerful urge. "It's nothing. Special effects I forgot to wash off. The paint glows under these lights."

Pulsing. Throbbing.

He ground his teeth and held his breath.

Need to release.

Come on, come on. Hold it together, Lazarus. Breathe in. Breathe out. *You're an actor, so act normal.*

Tony calmed, the blue glow faded, but it was too late. The look on Bailey's face said she didn't believe him. Casting a glance over his shoulder revealed they were alone in their observation. The party-goers were too busy ingesting whatever substance was their poison. None had seen his slip up.

Scotch forgotten, Tony turned and headed for the exit. Barging through the crowd, he ignored greetings thrown his way. He had to get out. Had to go home.

His Ducati was still in the parking lot.

The instant he slipped out of the studio warehouse, he broke into a jog, knowing full well that Bailey would come after him, and he couldn't explain what happened. Not yet. Not without knowing if he could trust her. Even then, what would he say? Oh, that blue glow? It's nothing. Doesn't do a thing but look pretty. Typical.

TONY'S INSIDES wanted out of his body.

He had barely registered Bailey's shouting as he'd exited the lot and drove from the studio without looking behind. She had come running after him, but he'd not a moment to spare. The napalm in his veins flickered and flashed, casting a blue halo of light on his surroundings. Now speeding through the Cardinal City streets, all Tony could think was to contain the intense pressure under his skin. It was an alien urge in his body, and he didn't like it.

How did his siblings accept their new powers? Because to him, the foreign sensation felt like a demon under his skin, and every time he envisioned letting his control slip, he saw his body splitting monstrously. He didn't want it. He wouldn't have it. He refused to acknowledge whatever was happening to him.

Tony shook his head to dispel the thoughts.

Just get home. Get to Lazarus House.

Everything will make more sense there.

In what seemed a blink, he roared around the street that led to the underground garage. He revved on the throttle while waiting for the garage door to lift, and when it had, wheels spun as he wrested the vehicle into the safety of the darkness. He parked between Parker's Bugatti and Liza's Ford sedan, cut the engine and exhaled slowly, only now registering that he'd not even put a helmet on.

But he made it. And his insides were still inside. No more blue glow.

"What happened to your bike?"

Tony jolted at Liza's voice. Tall, Amazonian, and tough as nails, his sister emerged from near her car. Dressed in her standard detective's outfit, jeans, brown leather jacket and white shirt, Liza gathered her long brown braid over one shoulder and frowned at him.

"Lying in wait for your next kill?" he joked.

"I just got here, numbnuts. You would have noticed if you hadn't driven in like a fucktard on steroids."

"Shut it, Liza. I'm in no mood for your attitude tonight."

"You know I love you." She jerked her chin at his bike. "Is that the reason for the carrot up your ass?"

He climbed off and checked the tank. Keyed scratches covered the previously pristine black paint. The words "I know" were repeated all over, just like the dolls. A trickle of fear, of helplessness, creeped in. He bit his lip and screwed up his face as the ghost of energy pulsed again, like distant war drums beating beneath his skin. With this new emotional turmoil, his power—whatever it was—wanted out. It seized on his weakness and insisted. He squeezed his eyes shut and concentrated on forcing the urges away. Stifle it. Swallow it down.

"No," he growled and clenched his fists.

"I'm sorry?"

Shit. She's coming over. He hid his hands behind his back. "You're home early," he noted casually.

Garage air brushed icily against sweat on his upper lip.

"Crime's down and I'm not stupid, Tony. You can't deflect with me. I have eyes." She gestured to his vandalized bike. "What's going on?"

"Nothing. Probably Sloan," he mumbled half-heartedly.

"That's not Sloan's doing."

Bailey hadn't thought it was Sloan either.

The moment his thoughts went to his mate, his body reacted, doing the thinking for him. Heat zipped up his spine and the drum beat in his blood grew to a percussion, thrumming incessantly. Phosphorescent blue light pulsed in his veins. Heat came in waves until a prickling sensation ran over his feverish skin. Suddenly, Tony didn't feel so good. He swayed.

"What the hell is that?" Liza asked, shrewd gaze on his forearms.

"Special effects." With the blue light from his arms to guide him through the shadowed garage, he strode toward the door leading to the headquarters. He shouldered through the heavy door, hardly hearing the warbled sound of Liza's voice calling behind him.

Everything felt dark, despite the light escaping his body. He pushed the urge to release down and wouldn't let it out. Only one directive rang clear in his mind—get home. Get to his apartment. Shut the door. Lock it.

The faster he walked through the dark underground corridor, the more he suppressed, and the darker his vision became.

He had to get to the elevator leading up to his room. Get there. Get in the lift. Go up to the safety of his apartment. But as he rushed through the Deadly Seven operations room, passed a surprised Parker and Flint working on technical adjustments to a Deadly suit, he couldn't see straight. It was all shadows and delirious blue patterns in front of him.

"Bro!" Liza shouted, jogging after him.

"Leave me alone," he growled.

He kept going. One foot in front of the other until he'd passed the medical room, the gym, and the weapon's room. He hit the "up" button next to the elevator and braced himself against the wall, breathing deep. The power inside wasn't listening to him, it had a mind of its own and it wanted out. *Keep it down. Keep it down.* He exhaled slowly through his mouth and waited for the car.

"Stop," Liza ordered.

Her authoritative tone had Tony lifting his head only to be confused by what he saw. His sister had her state-issued firearm aimed at him. She stood, feet slightly apart, arms braced, and with a determined scowl across her face.

"I won't say it again," she warned.

"Are you shitting me?" he snapped, anger rising.

"You're behaving erratic, Tony."

"Get lost." He hit the "up" button again.

"Goddamn it, Tony, talk to me."

"You won't shoot."

"You've met your mate, haven't you, and you're trying to hide it."

He tensed and his world came crashing down. She knew. They all knew. He shook his head and grit his teeth.

She continued, "Step away from the elevator and let's talk about this."

"Get that gun out of my face."

"No can do, bro. You've got this look in your eye. The last time one of us was separated from our mate and became out of balance, an innocent almost died. I won't let that happen."

She referred to when Sloan accidentally sent a room full of them to sleep with her power, and then tried to kill Barry Pinkerton, the ex-Syndicate geneticist. Sloan had snapped out of her berserker state just in time to avoid strangling the man to death. Everything flashed cold in Tony and he leveled his glare at his sister. "You think I'm out of balance?"

She widened her eyes in accusation. "You're always out of balance."

"Screw you. I've been sober for months."

"Show me."

He shouldn't have to, but he did. He held out his wrist tattoo out. It told her jack about his sobriety, but it was a clear indicator to whether gluttony saturated his system. Shaped in a Yin-Yang symbol, the black bio-indicator ink would darken to cover the entire symbol if he had too much gluttony present in his blood. If he held not enough gluttony, the ink would fade to leave a white, empty symbol. Both unbalanced states were equally dangerous and conducive to a berserker rage. Except, since his time with his mate today, it was still virtually balanced.

The elevator door pinged open to reveal two more of his siblings, Wyatt and Sloan. From the look of their battle-ready faces, they'd been called down the moment he'd entered the basement.

Great. Just fucking great. Everyone was here to watch the show.

He tried to push his way into the elevator car, but Wyatt, the invulnerable mountain, put his palm to Tony's chest and stopped him.

Tony backed up like a cornered animal. From the corner of his eye, he could see Parker and Flint come up from the operations room. So many pairs of eyes were on him, watching, assessing. Judging the monkey in a cage.

"Go away," he said. It was meant to be a shout, but the words came out a snarl. He wiped the back of his hand against his feverish forehead and his vision flickered, but the worst thing was the undeniable urge building under his skin like a pressure cooker about to blow. "Why can't you all just leave me alone?"

"Because you're family," said Parker, and then he instructed Wyatt to secure Tony.

Family.

The word bounced around in his head. And just exactly what was family? Someone you could boss around? Someone you took for granted? Someone you never truly saw.

As Wyatt advanced, the pressure beneath Tony's skin strained to bursting point. He didn't know why he kept holding it back. They already thought he was a screwup. He should know by now that nothing good ever came of bottling things up... so he let it out.

An almighty roaring filled his ears, burned through his veins. Ozone drenched the air. Someone shouted to take cover. A blinding blue light turned white and then Tony's vision closed in. He remembered no more.

six

WAYNE BOSCH

WAYNE BOSCH always thought he was an agreeable man, perhaps too much. He gave his wife whatever she wanted. Diamonds, a yacht, a house on the river. He even took a job with a morally ambiguous company because it paid better, and he could provide more good things. Well, that wasn't completely true. It also let him gray the lines of science in the name of human advancement. One day he hoped to have his name up in lights for making the next big scientific break, and until this day, everything had been going swimmingly... or should he say, *growing* swimmingly.

But over the past few days, his carefully planned life had turned to blood colored mud. He stared at the mess in the conservatory side of the laboratory he shared with another scientist, Barry Pinkerton. Unbelievable. Once it had contained the most forward thinking scientific experiments in his field of botany genetics, and in his lab partner's field of animal genetics. On the far side were empty open cages. Pinkerton had created a new species of animal that sensed deadly sin, hunted it down and extinguished it. On Wayne's side, he'd created a new species of sin-sensing plant that was almost sentient.

Wolves could scent fear. Bugs could hunt using pheromones to lure their prey. Plants could actually seek out areas where the sun shone, and the water ran free. Using all this knowledge, Wayne had taken pieces of each puzzle to fit into his new sin-sensing design. The plan had been to breed and graft hybrid plant species together, introduce a little human, animal, and insect DNA to then create something far more sinister than Barry Pinkerton ever could.

Wayne had tweaked the ability to sniff out sin, to hunt it down like a source of sustenance, and then eat it. His experiment had stalled until a few months ago when he'd discovered his plant not in its cage like he'd left it, but out in the laboratory, tendrils wrapped around a rat, or the mummified husk that was left of the rat. How the plant had moved from its cage to the center of the room was beyond him, but it had moved just enough to reach the rat a few feet from the cage.

Wayne had only designed the plant to unfurl tendrils, to latch itself onto any sinner within arm's reach. He'd never in his life expected a plant to physically shift from one location to another, like it could walk.

It shouldn't have been able to move like that. And in the months since, he'd not seen a repeat incident, leaving Wayne to surmise that the Deadly Seven intruders must have left the cage door open when they'd infiltrated the base to extract Pinkerton.

Stupid man. Pinkerton should have done his job like he'd been told. Now there was a target on his back, and if Pinkerton ever showed his face again, he'd be eliminated. And his family too. How was Wayne going to explain this mess to the boss? He hardly understood what happened himself. A plant moving across the room like an animal? Impossible. A plant wrapping its tendrils around and then absorbing any living thing in its path? Inconceivable.

But it had happened.

And now there was a mess.

Wayne scornfully collected a dustpan and brush before the cleanup crew made their way to his lab. If they arrived before he'd taken care to preserve the evidence for further study, he'd have no chance at understanding how his virtually inert plant had become mobile and carnivorous. He was just about to resume cleaning the fallen leaves scattered around the lab when his cell phone rang. He picked it up with a smile.

"Hello, love."

"Honey," his wife said. "You left so quickly this morning. Is everything okay?"

"Yes, yes. It's fine. I just received an emergency call to come into work."

"Oh. Okay."

"Is everything okay with you?"

"Well, it's just…"

"Sweetie?"

"We received a notice from a debt collector."

Wayne took his spectacles off and rubbed the bridge of his nose. He was hoping to have more time. And with this latest setback, it was unlikely the boss would give him an advance on his next research grant. Wayne had already cut corners with the quality of supplies. There wasn't much wiggle room left.

"Wayne?" His wife's voice came through warbled. "Why are we receiving a notice from a debt collector?"

"Must be a mistake, Gabrielle. I'll sort it out. Don't worry about it."

"Are you sure?"

"Yes, yes. Now you go off to your salon day with your sister and enjoy yourself. I have to get to work. Actually, maybe you should stay with her for a while. I'm going to be tied up here for a bit."

He cut the call just as two men in white overalls and face masks entered the lab. The taller man gestured at his companion, and they made moves to begin cleaning up the biological mess.

"Wait!" Wayne shouted. He scuttled over. "Please don't start. I have to secure the samples."

"That won't be necessary, Mr. Bosch."

Wayne's blood turned to ice at the sound of his boss's cultured and confident voice. Standing in the doorway to the lab was Julius Allcott, the man who ran the Syndicate show, and the man who had Wayne's fate in his hands. Behind him was the infamous Falcon, the Syndicate's enforcer.

"M-Mr. Allcott," Wayne mumbled. "I was just telling the crew I need to collect some samples before they—"

"Like I said. Not necessary. We're shutting this little disaster down."

"B-but…" He couldn't lose it all, not now. Not when he was so close to having everything he wanted.

Julius held up his hand and sneered. "You've accomplished nothing here, except failure."

"My plant has achieved the impossible. The inconceivable! It's not a failure."

"And where is it now, hmm?"

"Um."

"You have achieved nothing if we have nothing to show for it." Julius stepped into the laboratory and sneered. "Nothing except dead bodies and bleeding funds. I cannot afford to keep this division open any longer. Our focus lies elsewhere."

Wayne skirted around the central lab bench to get closer to the man. "Give me another chance. I'll find it. I'm the only one who can."

Julius's fist hit the lab bench, rattling the wayward tools on top. Wayne startled.

"How did this happen?" Julius roared, fury protruding the veins in his neck.

The entire room stilled. No one breathed. This was the first time Wayne had ever heard of the boss losing his temper. Even his always-collected enforcer flinched at Julius's outburst, and if she was rattled...

Wayne gulped. "It was the plant. Its diet was never meant to be carnivorous. It was meant to sense out sinners and poison them surreptitiously. It somehow got out of its cage." He hesitated. "It ate a rat."

"How long ago," Julius demanded.

"Um. Maybe about two months ago."

"After the infiltration to extract the betrayer from us?" Julius turned to his enforcer. "Do you think it was them? Was this the next stage of their attack and we missed it? Have they contaminated everything?"

She ran her tongue over her perfect teeth as she considered, then she looked away from her father. "It wasn't them. It was me."

Wayne blinked. Julius gasped. The two-man clean-up crew slowly edged out of the room.

"What are you talking about?" Julius asked her.

"I only wanted the plant to be free, unbound from its cage. I sensed its despair. I didn't expect this to happen. I apologize. I will fix it."

Despair?

Odd, Wayne thought, that a plant could feel any emotion at all. Odd even more that the woman could sense the sin. Who was she really?

Julius stared at her for long hard seconds, and then he turned back to Wayne. "No," he said. "You will both fix it."

Wayne released the air he'd held in his lungs. Thank God.

"And if you can't fix it, you eliminate it. Quickly. We can't have this thing running around uncontrolled. We don't want to unleash chaos until we're ready, and we're not ready."

Falcon's fists clenched at her side. "You want me to eliminate it?"

"It"—Julius waved at the cage—"him"—he waved at Wayne—"whoever. I don't care. Just fix it."

Her violet eyes flicked toward Wayne, then back to the leaf littered cage. "But the plant had no choice in its existence. It had no choice in what it became. It was hungry. I released it to feed. It shouldn't die for my mistake."

"For Christ's sake, darling. What's gotten into you? The plant is something we created to *use*. If it can't be useful, we get rid of it. Call it a practice run, a failed experiment, a pile of trash, whatever you need to get the job done. Just bring it back and under our control or exterminate it. We do not need this kind of attention. If we can't salvage this massive hemorrhage of Syndicate funds, we cut our losses. Understood?"

She nodded. Julius cast a disparaging glance at his enforcer, who raised a questioning eyebrow in return, then he left.

Falcon, or whoever she was, watched the empty doorway for what seemed like an eternity. She was so still that Wayne began to believe she'd turned into stone, or the plant had left some of its petrifying venom behind. Light from the LEDs brightened her silver hair and accentuated the red stains on her white leather jacket lapels. The blood wasn't from the corpses littering the base. It was the old blood of men who hadn't done their jobs. It was failure. When she finally moved, it was for her shoulders to droop, and a sigh to escape.

"Find the sentient plant," she said in a low monotone voice. "And I might let you live."

She walked out of the room, leaving Wayne to think debt collectors were the least of his worries today. If he failed to find this plant, there would be no tomorrow.

seven

TONY LAZARUS

TONY CAME to with his eyes glued shut. Around him, people spoke in hushed, urgent voices. He could open his eyes, but his training had taught him to always seek the advantage. Whether it was higher ground, information, or to make the enemy come to you, a battle was won if you were smart about it. Keeping his eyes closed— for strategic reconnaissance, he told himself—he focused on gathering what information he could.

He was cold.

The air smelled like disinfectant.

The voices were hollow, echoing as though they were in a room with hard floors and walls.

A bright light shone behind his eyelids, trying to push through.

A rhythmic beep to his right... a heart monitor.

He was probably in the medical room, which made sense if he'd blacked out.

What were they saying?

"...bioluminescence isn't supposed to be hot." Parker's deep grumbling tone was unmistakable. "It's a cold light. I don't under-

stand how he's turned something benign into something so destructive. Frankly, he's a menace in this state."

"Goddammit, Parks. It wasn't his fault," Liza mumbled under her
breath. "See how well you control yourself when you first meet your
mate."

"I control myself fine."

"You haven't met your mate yet, ass-wipe."

A masculine huff. "We're just lucky Flint was in the back, and no
wives or girlfriends were in here. Misha's pregnant, for Christ's sake."

"Wyatt took the brunt of it. Misha was far away. Stop your whin-
ing, *mijo*." Tony's mother, Mary, had joined the group, or perhaps
she'd been there all along. A warm pressure on his hand meant she'd
taken it within her own. It took every ounce of self-control for Tony
to hold back a reaction.

Mary had stood with her children, through thick and thin. She'd
defied orders from the Hildegard Sisterhood to eliminate them as
children, instead choosing to rescue them from the Syndicate. Her
entire life had been on the run, and it was only through her inexplicable psychic abilities that she'd kept the family hidden. She'd taught
them how to fight, how to be deadly, how to love. Now that their
destiny was calling and Mary's abilities were failing, she'd been unable
to hide her increasing feelings of inadequacy from the Seven. But
she'd been there. Always. So had Flint.

Whatever was going on with Tony, he knew Mary and Flint
would never judge, never leave. Could he say the same for the rest of
his family?

A huff and a grumble that could only come from Parker. "I've
only managed to decipher half of Gloria's notes. She mentioned
bioluminescence, but nothing to explain how the photons could be
amplified into some kind of emission of electromagnetic radiation."

"Speak English, bro."

"Tony's body is converting energy into visible gamma rays. He's got the power of a blue sun inside him. If he can't control it, his life will never be the same."

"Dum, dum, *duuum*. Don't be so dramatic." Tony almost laughed at Liza's attempt to lighten the situation with her ominous sound effects.

But Parker was having none of it. "He went supernova in our basement. The elevator is lucky to be functional. Sloan is nursing second-degree burns. What about this is funny to you?"

Second-degree burns. Sloan?

"Sloan will heal fast. The elevator can be fixed..." Then Tony was sure she said underneath her breath, "Pity about your personality."

Tony's mouth felt dry, like he was eating dirt.

"Enough with you two. What are his vitals, doc?" Mary asked. "Any improvement?"

Doc? Must be Grace, Evan's mate. Another light touch at his wrist. "BP is down, as is his temp. Whatever he did back there seemed to ease the toll the ability was taking on his body. I don't have any stats to compare with prior to the release of energy. I'm just going on what I collected immediately after." Grace moved around Tony, shuffling and shifting things he couldn't see. Probably checking other medical instruments attached to him. He slid his focus down his body and noticed an uncomfortable pressure at his inner elbow. Could be an IV. Tightness across his chest and sides of his forehead— some sort of electrodes monitors. Grace continued, "I think you all need to give him some rest. The blue glow has abated. I don't think he's a danger to anyone."

"Do you have any idea why his body reacted the way it did?"

"I'm not a geneticist, and I'm no genius like you."

"But if you had to take a physician's educated guess?"

Silence. Then, "His temperature elevated, and he exhibited the same signs as a patient rejecting a transplant. I don't know, maybe I'm way off."

"But maybe you're right," Parker assured. "He could be rejecting the new power, but why? Would his addictions be a factor?"

"That's a stretch, but not impossible. It could also be psychosomatic. It could also be that your biological mother made a mistake when she created him. I'm not a geneticist, so I don't know for sure, but if this is true, and his body continues to grow to fever and burn through his cells, then I'm afraid the outlook isn't good."

"Are you saying he could die?" Mary gasped.

"I don't know. We need to run further tests."

"I agree. Maybe I'll get Pinkerton on the case. He owes us."

"I'm late for my shift. Are you okay if I head off?"

A low mumble further away. Tony recognized Wyatt's gruff tone. Liza had said he'd taken the brunt of Tony's... what could he call it? An explosion of light? Of energy? Power like a blue sun. Wyatt was invulnerable. He must have jumped on Tony to block his explosion.

"Yes, you can go," Parker responded to Wyatt, then he added, "You too, Grace. We appreciate you running down here."

"Don't mention it. You'll let Evan know when he and Griff are back from the field?"

A grunt of assent. Tony rolled his eyes beneath his closed lids.

"Doc is right," Liza added. "Everyone should get out of here to give Tony some rest. Someone should stay. I'm off duty, so I'll do it."

Chairs shifting and scraping against the tiles. Shuffling and murmurs. A final light press on Tony's wrist. Then retreating footsteps.

"You can open your eyes now."

Tony screwed them tighter. Damn it. Liza had known. One by one, he peeled each eyelid open and flinched at the bright lights. He blinked until his vision came into focus and saw that he was right. He lay on a gurney in the medical room in the basement headquarters of Lazarus House. To the right of him was the operating table and lights, cupboards and instruments. To the left, more cupboards and a mirrored two-way window. Still in the basement. They hadn't had to drag him far, then. He licked his dry lips and rolled his head to the side.

Liza sat in a chair, leaning forward, elbows resting on her knees. Her brown leather jacket had scorch marks on the edges of her arms and he smelled barbecue. A hard expression was on her face. She lifted her brows. "You fucked up, bro."

He rolled his head back the other way.

"You're lucky my hair is still in one piece. And my eyebrows. Jeez. If you'd taken them, I'd be truly pissed."

He shook his head and grit his teeth.

"I'm kidding." She laughed. "Jesus, Tones, take a joke."

"But you're right," he croaked. "I fucked up again."

"Hey." Liza touched his arm, bringing his attention back to her. "You didn't do anything different to what Evan, Griff, Wyatt or Sloan did."

"What do you mean?"

"I mean, they all had a moment when their powers came in. It just so happens that your moment was a little more... extravagant." She smirked at her brother with fond eyes. "I guess we should have expected that from a showman like you, right?"

"True." Tony shrugged. "I always do things in style."

"You realize what this means, don't you?"

"What?"

"You're an actual star."

"You're hilarious. Kill me now." He yanked the IV out of his arm, ripped off the electrodes sticking to his bare chest and temples, and sat up.

"Cool your jets. Lay back down."

"I feel fine."

"But you weren't a few hours ago."

With a sigh of capitulation, he leaned back to rest. "Seriously. I'm fine."

"You thirsty?"

He arched a brow at her. "When am I not?"

"Sorry. Stupid question." Liza sidestepped the operating table and lights in the center of the room to retrieve a glass of water from the sink against the wall. She handed it to him.

He took the glass and gulped water down his parched throat. It was almost as though the burning energy he'd released had scorched the inside.

"Easy there, tiger," Liza said. "You don't want to edge toward being unbalanced."

Tony paused with the glass still to his lips. She was right. Unless he was within a certain radius of his mate, he couldn't indulge in his sin, that meant a simple guzzled drink of water could edge him the wrong way. The fact that he'd gone to rehab was even more prudent now. It had given him the tools to temper his urges. He had to remember them because if he couldn't keep his appetites in check, lives were at stake. Entering an unbalanced berserker rage now would mean certain death for anyone in his radius, not just the target sinner. He wiped his mouth and handed her the glass.

Liza took it and studied it with a furrowed brow. "You want to talk about it, about her?"

Not particularly, no. But he couldn't bottle things up again. For all he knew, that was the cause of the power explosion.

"Her name is Bailey Haze." His voice came out way too gruff, so he cleared his throat.

"I know."

He shot her narrowed eyes. "Did I tell you?"

"Dude, I'm a detective."

"Right. Sloan told you."

"Yep."

He snorted. "Well, did she also tell you that Bailey used to work for the CIA? Maybe still does." *Yeah, right, buddy. Let's go with the CIA schtick.* That's definitely the reason he's in this state. "She knows how to fight. She must have been an operative. I don't trust her."

Liza sat back in her chair, a thoughtful look on her face. "You think she's investigating us?"

"Maybe."

"Nah."

"No?"

"Yeah, you heard me. No."

"Why not?"

"Because if someone was investigating us, it would be the FBI, not the CIA. Maybe Homeland, or even the NSA, depending on whether they classed us as a threat to national security. But it would start with the Bureau, or the local cops and I'm all over the latter. Unlikely the spooks would bother with us if we're just based in this city."

"But the Syndicate isn't. It's worldwide."

Liza clicked her jaw shut. "Goddamn. You're right."

"The initial background check Sloan ran came up with nothing major prior to her being in the agency," Tony added.

"Nothing. Nobody has nothing. Even *we* have something."

"*Our* something was fudged high school records to make it look like we studied abroad when we were really training how to cross a frothed up stream after recent rain with Master Yoshi—I still don't get why we had to do that."

"It was a metaphor." She blinked at him. "We had to wait until the froth settled before making a move."

"Yeah. I knew that. Was just checking if you did."

She snorted. "Point is, maybe she's just squeaky clean. Or maybe all her trouble happened before she was eighteen and on the record."

A few moments of silence passed by as they both ruminated. While Tony's mind wandered to Bailey's past, Liza pulled out her cell phone.

"What are you doing?" he asked. "Calling Max? I don't think that's a good idea."

"Shh." She lifted her finger. "I'm calling Joey Luciano."

His brow furrowed, confused. "From high school?"

Obviously they were thinking very different things in those few moments.

"He's in the FB—Hey bud, guess who?" The tone of her voice changed completely when she switched her attention to the person on the other line. With Tony, she was hard and sarcastic. With the man Tony assumed was Joey, she was all sugar. *Interesting.*

With her cell held to her ear, Liza turned away, half obscuring her face. She toyed with the end of her braid. "Yeah good to hear from you, too. Listen, I have a favor to ask." A pause. A secret smirk. "Yeah, you'd love that, wouldn't you? Seriously, I need you to see if someone is still active in the CIA." A longer pause. "Not even just to see if she's still gainfully employed? Please, Joey?"

He couldn't believe it. Joey from high school. He was on the football team with Tony. He had no idea Liza still kept in contact with him. And he was FBI.

"You are a legend. Thanks, bud." She paused, her eyes flicked to Tony, then she relaxed at something Joey must have said on the other side. "Maybe next time." Then she cut the call. "He said he'll try, but he's not positive he'll get access. We'll have to ask Sloan, which means

Max will know, which means…" Liza rolled her eyes to the ceiling. "We're going to cause shit between them."

"Sloan already did some digging for me. Maybe it was enough. I'll go through what she found tonight."

Liza sat heavily back down on her seat. "You want some help?"

"Nah. You look tired."

"Gee, thanks."

"Serious bags under those eyes. I've got some cream that will do it wonders—ow!" Tony flinched from Liza's right hook to his pec. "That hurt."

"It will hurt more if I have to take you down for real next time." Something dark flickered in her gaze. "I'm serious, Tones. If you get out of balance, I won't hesitate next time."

"I get it," he said quietly. "I need to work out this business with Bailey."

Liza scrutinized him. "It's more than the CIA thing, isn't it?"

"Hell, how do you do that?"

"Detective." Two thumbs pointed at her chest.

"Bullshit."

She smirked. "Your lust spikes every time you speak about her. What happened? You couldn't get it up? She rejected you? Oh, that's it. She doesn't like the hot-stud movie star type." Liza pointed her cell at him. "You know, all I need to do is to be in the same room as you two. I'll find out how she really feels. Easy fix for you."

"No!" Tony snapped a little too quickly that he surprised even himself.

Did he not want to know? Was he afraid? Or maybe it was simply the fact that he was used to everyone liking him. So why not her?

"I'll find out on my own," he growled.

With that last word, he swung his legs over the bed and left, smiling to himself as Liza shouted after him, "You're welcome!"

TONY SPENT the next few days hiding out in his apartment, avoiding phone calls and doing every kind of reconnaissance he could think of on one Miss Bailey Haze. Being a hermit helped keep his power safely below catastrophic levels. But his agent called. His producer called. The studio publicist called. He'd ignored them all until finally, on the fourth morning of hiding, he could hide no longer. He had a press junket booked to promote the new movie later the following evening. It meant he had to go out into the real world, and that meant he'd have to call Bailey.

She'd not called him.

He tried to sort through his thoughts but came up with nothing satisfying. She was being professional. She worked for Nightingale Securities, and Max doled out the jobs. Tony should approach him if he needed her again. But because he'd been avoiding contact with Bailey, he'd had to be rigorously studious about keeping his sin in balance, which meant keeping an eye on his bio-indicated Yin-Yang tattoo, and using Griffin's method of timing any gluttonous act by balancing it out with an equally weighted act of temperance. He caved to a craving once, denied it the next. The last thing he needed was to be out of balance and to accidentally blow a hole through his apartment floor.

Timing everything he did was tedious, and boring, and he'd rather pluck his eyebrows out than have to keep doing it. He didn't know how Griffin had managed it for so long.

But now time was running out. He'd not uncovered any more information about Bailey's CIA history on his own, even with the family's artificial intelligent management interface, AIMI. The in-house computer was a source of much intel for Tony, but there were places she couldn't hack because her program forbade it. But Sloan programed AIMI. She could also hack into the CIA records.

Grabbing his cell phone and wallet, Tony shoved the two items in his distressed jeans pockets and checked his appearance in the mirror.

"Where's Sloan at, AIMI?" he asked the air.

"Good morning, Tony Spazarus," came the female computerized voice over his apartment's internal speakers. "Sloan Lazarus, the Queen of all Things, requests that her whereabouts remain unknown for the next minute and twenty-five seconds."

Tony's fingers paused mid swipe on his hair. Tony Spazarus? *You've got to be kidding me.* He clenched his jaw and waited a few minutes and then asked AIMI again. This time, she replied with, "The Queen of all Things is currently in her apartment. Would you like me to call her?"

"No. That's fine. I'll head over now."

"Would you like me to notify her you're on your way?"

"No. Just lock the apartment after me."

Normally he left his rooms unlocked, but Bailey's paranoia was rubbing off. He took a deep breath and headed down a level to Sloan's apartment door. After a knock, Max opened it. He folded his arms across his black Nightingale Securities shirt and gave Tony a judgmental once over.

Tony was about to ask what gives, when he realized it must be because of Sloan's injury from a few days ago. He probably should have been around earlier to check on her.

"Sloan here?" he asked.

Max sucked his teeth, then stepped aside... only for Tony to cop a load of something hot, wet and hard in the face.

"Jesus!" He flinched back.

"That's for not coming to check on me, dumbass." Sloan stood two feet in front of Tony, blue eyes blazing, black hair flying like some kind of magical sorceress, and... she held a pizza box in her hand, half empty.

Tony looked down at the floor where a black cat lapped up the fallen squashy yellow debris that had slid off Tony's face.

"You threw pineapple chunks at my face?"

Sloan shrugged, eyes still furious.

Tony checked her bare arms. No scars in sight. "You're all healed. *You* should have come to see *me*."

She stared, wide-eyed. "True. But you're all healed, and you should have come to see me!"

"I just said that."

They faced off.

"You two need a minute?" Max asked, clearly unimpressed.

Sloan suddenly smiled and trotted over to him and gave him a kiss on the cheek. "Nah, we're all good now. See you at lunch."

"What for?"

"Wedding cake shopping. Duh."

"Right," Max laughed. He hooked her around the waist and pulled her in for a possessive kiss that made Tony look away. When Max was done, he patted Tony on the shoulder. "See you later."

Then Max left and shut the door behind him, leaving Tony very confused and inside Sloan's territory.

"You want a slice?" she asked, holding the box out to him.

"Um. Is it poisoned?"

"Yes, I mean, no. I mean..." Sloan burst out laughing. "Look at your face. You..." Then her humor dropped. "You don't really think I'd poison you, would you?"

He shrugged and wiped something sticky off his nose. Gross.

She bit her lip and jogged to her kitchen, only a few feet away. She collected a towel from a hook, wet it under the faucet, and came back to him. "Sorry, bras. I thought you liked all this prank business."

He snatched the towel and began to wipe his face. "Yeah maybe I liked it before it became about hanging bloody dolls in my trailer or scratching up the Ducati."

"Say what?"

Tony paused, mid swipe on his face as the cold hard truth solidified. He kind of knew it already, but now he had no way of pretending it was her. The alternative was to believe his life was in more of a shambles than he admitted. Goddamn it. "Fuck," he mumbled into the cloth.

"Someone scratched up your bike?"

"Yeah," he balled up the towel and three-pointered it to the kitchen sink.

"I mean, I knew about the dolls. Max told me." Sloan waved him in further and indicated to take a seat on her couch. She flicked an empty packet of crisps out of the way and then sat herself. "What else went wrong?"

He lowered himself onto the couch. "What's *not* going wrong right now? Between this power that explodes uncontrollably—sorry about that by the way—and my mate potentially investigating me, to the fricking stalker shit, to my goddamned dickwad agent trying to push me into another movie I'm not ready for, to—" he cut himself off. He wasn't ready to voice the rest of his concerns about Bailey.

"You said you didn't trust Bailey, but you didn't say why."

"Just a feeling."

"Well, maybe this will help with your feelings." Sloan reached into the space between her cushion and the couch headboard and pulled out her laptop. Sticking out of the port was a thumb-drive. She pulled it out and handed it to him.

"What's this?" he asked.

"Your wish is my desire. Wait. That's wrong. Is it wrong?" Sloan screwed up her face, thinking. "What is the saying? Doesn't matter.

The point is, I got your back, bras. I owe you big time for how you helped me get a hold of my powers. I'm here for you."

"Thanks." He took the drive from her.

"And if you need help to control yours, just ask. But maybe ask Wyatt. Cos, you know, that burn fucking hurt!"

"Sorry."

She smiled gently, placed her elbow on the couch, and rested her head in her hand. "She's not working for the CIA anymore as far as I can tell, but just because I couldn't find anything, doesn't mean it's true. Those guys are sneaky. And the reason there's not much about her past is that it was a shitty one. You should really ask her about it instead of snooping. She's volunteering this morning down at Hudson House. It's a youth addiction center on Fourth."

Tony lifted his gaze to his sister. "Addiction Center?"

"Like I said, she's had a shitty past."

Tony cast his mind back to when he'd broken into her apartment. She'd had a cocktail glass sitting on the kitchen counter. And when they'd left, he caught sight of it still there, untouched. He'd assumed she just didn't have time to drink it, but maybe there was more to the story.

"How long has she been volunteering for the center?" he asked.

"Since she's been in the city, working for Nightingales."

"Could be part of a cover."

"If it was, she wouldn't actually be working there. She'd be doing CIA shit."

"Only one way to find out, I guess." Tony stood up and pocketed the thumb-drive. "Thanks, Sloan."

"No problemo, Spazarus."

eight

BAILEY HAZE

ON THE MORNING Bailey walked to the sobriety house, the temperature dropped to around fifty. She blew on her hands and wished she'd brought a coat, but all she'd taken from home was a light yoga style jacket. It went with her yoga pants and Sketchers, so she'd thought it was perfect. How wrong she'd been. Summer was well and truly over and Cardinal City was in the grip of a cool fall. The coming winter would be cruel.

She blew on her hands again, and stomped up the steps to Hudson House. It was just another Brownstone type townhouse in a street of identical soldiers, but inside, it was a haven for any youth needing help to unlock the handcuffs of addiction. The place functioned as a half-way house, a sobriety house, and an education and medical clinic. It survived purely on donations, and lately—Bailey spied the holes in the fly-screen on the door—they were running low on funds.

On the stoop, a skinny, brown-skinned boy with a shaved head flicked through his smart phone silently. Beside him, a Latino girl wearing a pink beret over her long hair tapped her own screen. If they heard her coming, they didn't show it. Bailey didn't recognize them, so plastered a pleasant smile on her face in case they looked up. She had to be friendly if she wanted the kids to come to her martial arts self-defense class.

They failed to look up.

Not surprising. Most kids who ended up at Hudson were closed off from the start. Many didn't last longer than a few days before heading back out into the city. Some came from broken homes, others lived on the street, used, and were in gangs; all had suffered addiction of various substances at some point. Bailey's job was to teach them something, anything she could, to give them focus, hope and a reason for staying. It was important they knew that no matter what mistakes they'd made in life, they could make something of themselves. They didn't have to let addiction rule them, whether it was theirs, or their parent's.

Her own pitiful home life had been far from normal. Her mother and father were no role models. They'd believed their money meant they could get away with anything. Bailey had thought so too, at first. She'd thought drinking copious amounts of booze until you vomited or lashed out was okay. And when her girlfriend had pressured her, she'd thought driving inebriated was okay, too.

"You're making the wrong turn," Becca screeched.

"I am not!" Bailey yanked on the steering wheel too hard, and the tires spun on the wet street. The landscape through the car windows twisted, making her dizzy. She almost couldn't see straight through her alcohol-induced mind, but the car stayed on the road. She should have never listened to Becca and driven. "I know exactly where I'm going."

"Oh my God, Bailey. You don't. That was the turn off!" Becca pointed across Bailey's face with a red fingered glove.

Tires screeched.

Glass broke.

Bailey shook her head to shake the memory. She still stood on the stoop, knuckles white as she gripped the old wrought iron handle on the door.

Tires screeched again, and she whipped her head around. At the bottom of the stoop, between the two brick pillars marking the beginning of the Hudson House property, a black Cadillac rolled along the street, blowing smoke from its exhaust. Every nerve in Bailey's body pinged with danger.

The black car slowed. A man with a handlebar mustache and tattoos on his skin watched them with lurking intent as he passed. Bailey caught sight of another two men in the back. Thugs. And they were paying way too much attention to the house.

They stopped and spoke in Spanish to the teens behind Bailey. Obviously, they didn't think Bailey spoke the language, but it was one of the many she understood, and one of the reasons she'd been a prime candidate for the CIA.

"*El canala, we find you,*" the driver said.

The teen boy tensed. His eyes widened. But it was the girl who turned a whiter shade of pale. Bailey's hands balled into fists. If only she had her pistol.

Instead, she recited his license plate out loud. "*And I'll find you, asshole,*" she replied… in Spanish. In English, she added, "Come around here again, and I'll call the police."

The two men in the back of the vehicle shifted just enough to show they held onto cold metal weapons. Bailey wasn't afraid. She stared the men down until one in the back made a gesture for them to move on. She waited until they were long down the road.

"Get inside," she said to the teens. "Come on. Class is about to start."

The boy scowled up at her, but the girl stood. She glanced briefly in the direction of the black car, then walked through the door Bailey held open. Bailey watched as the girl disappeared around the bend, body hunched.

"What's your name?" Bailey asked the boy. "I've not seen you two here before."

"Akeef. That's Elena."

"I'm Bailey Haze. I teach the self-defense martial arts class."

"Yeah. So?"

"So, you know self-defense?"

Akeef glanced down the way the car had gone but said nothing. He plugged his earphones in and then shoved passed her to get inside the house.

She sighed. She could speak multiple languages, kick a rogue foreign agent in the ass, but she had zero experience getting teenagers to trust her.

BAILEY HAD POSTED flyers over the walls of Hudson House for the past month. Each flyer said she'd be there at nine once a week, willing to teach anyone who wanted to learn to defend themselves, and even when she'd popped her head into the media room and spruced the class, not one teenager was interested. There were at least eight in the room, and they all ignored her with dogged determination, Akeef and Elena included.

Agnes, the house custodian gave Bailey an understanding smile as she passed in the hallway. Bailey guessed she couldn't compete with the Tony Lazarus action movie playing on the big screen. She'd seen it, and it was good.

As she watched Tony on screen, blowing up cars and shooting guns, the irony was not lost on her. She couldn't even hold Tony Lazarus in her sights long enough to keep him safe. Something strange had happened to him at the wrap party and he'd fled. She couldn't comprehend those blue lights. Logically, it had to have been special effects like he'd said. But the way he'd fled... She was a terrible bodyguard. The man had hid out in his apartment for the better part of the week, and she'd not a chance to prove she could protect him. She even had some grainy footage of an unidentified woman entering his trailer, but Max had said to leave it with him to pass onto the studio.

Max's reception had been frosty, and Bailey put it down to her recent string of failures holding her snark and forceful personality at bay. The same qualities had benefited her in the agency. It kept her tough and resilient. Getting a foreign agent to cross to your side took a lot of convincing and sometimes a bit of creative manipulation.

But this was real life.

These kids had been manipulated enough.

Bailey tried not to be disappointed as she leaned a shoulder on the scratched up wooden door frame. The room smelled musty. The couches were old and stained. But there was coffee and tea in the corner on a table, and cookies and snacks on a small tray. Agnes always kept it well stocked. Sometimes, they just needed a place to relax, or somewhere the gang leaders couldn't enter without causing trouble.

"You sure none of you want to learn how to pull some of those action moves for real?" she asked. "Learning self-defense can come in real handy when you find yourself in a situation you don't want to be in."

Tyson, a short, pimply faced boy turned her way, his expression taking on attitude and then suddenly deadpanning when he took in something over Bailey's shoulder.

"Holy shit." The pimply kid whacked his hand on the girl sitting next to him.

Then one by one, every teen in the room forgot about the television and paid attention to Bailey.

No. Scratch that. Every eye was focused on an area slightly to the right and behind Bailey. She turned around. Shock skittered up her spine.

Tony Lazarus in roughed up jeans, a designer T-shirt, a blue baseball cap, and his hands in his pockets.

"Tony," she said. "What are you doing here?"

His lips curved hesitantly on one side. "Yeah, about that. Can we talk?"

Bailey cut a glance over her shoulder. Every kid in the room was finally engaged. Maybe this was her chance to teach them something valuable. She glanced back at Tony. *Forceful personality.* Use it.

"I need your help first," she said and hooked her hand around his wrist, dragging him into the room. "Guys, this is—"

"Tony fucking Lazarus," the pimply kid said and nervous laughter broke out around the room.

She grinned. "Language, Tyson. But yes, this is Tony. Now, wouldn't you like to learn a few self-defense moves from a master? He does all his own stunts. Did you know that?"

Tony stiffened beneath Bailey's hand, and she prepared herself for rejection, but it never came. Instead, Tony almost leaned into her touch, as though he wanted more.

"Who's joining us?" she asked the group.

Every female jumped immediately to her feet, including Elena. The boys were slightly less accommodating, but they stood.

Elation prickled Bailey's skin. Great.

"You don't mind, do you?" she asked Tony. "It will only take a few minutes. Thirty tops."

"Um." Doubt flickered in his eyes.

"Please?" She leaned in until her lips hovered near the shell of his ear. "I've not been able to get them engaged all week, and you'd be great at this."

Tony tilted his face until his cheek hit hers. Heat scorched along her face. His lashes fluttered closed, and he gave a soft nod. Then the actor replaced the reserved Tony. Excitement livened his expression, and he addressed the crew.

"You're all in for a treat," he started, eyes brightening. "You think I'm the best in this room, but this little lady here—" He pointed at Elena. "She will be the one to take me down. For reals. You wanna see?"

Cheers. Actual cheers burst out in the room, and Bailey almost cried. When Tony looked to her for guidance, she gestured for him to help shift the furniture around the room.

nine

TONY LAZARUS

THEY HAD MOVED the couches and television to the side for the class. Tony sat on the floor, cross-legged between a girl named Elena and a boy named Michael. For the past hour, he'd been helping Bailey show various scenarios. They'd lost a few of the group when it became clear Bailey would actually teach a class and not turn the session into some sort of exhibition of his celebrity. They were almost done.

"So," Bailey said to the class. "We've learned about an active shooter, and now we will learn how to defend ourselves from an active killer with a knife." She pointed at Tony. "Once again, first, I'll demonstrate with Tony as the attacker, and then I'll need a volunteer to do the same as me and take him down."

Tony nudged the girl and leaned into her. "Your turn, right?"

She gave him a contentious look.

"Come on, Elena." He smiled. "Give it a go."

"Tony?" Bailey gestured at him. God, she was hot when she was all business like this. "You ready?"

He zipped his lips. "Sorry, coach. I'm ready."

"Okay," Bailey continued. She paced along the carpet at the front of the room. "As soon as you register the danger, you need to get up. Sitting makes you vulnerable." She stopped pacing and raised her brows at Tony.

"Oops. That's my cue." He jumped up, and shook his hands out, grinning as he turned to the group. This was so much fun. "Roar. I'm a baddy."

The kids snickered. But Bailey didn't. "You're not a lion. You're a knife wielding fiend. Be serious."

"Okay. One second." He crouched before Elena and nodded at the cell phone in her hand. "Do you think that will make a good knife?"

She gave her cell an incredulous look, but handed it to him. Good. That was better interaction than before. He'd get her to open up and take part before the class was done. She wouldn't be here if she didn't want to be. She just needed a little push.

"Got it, coach." He made a jabbing motion with the cell.

Bailey turned to the students. "When you notice an imminent attack, sometimes you need to shake other bystanders awake. Many people freeze in the face of danger. It's normal. Inform others of the threat and leave if you can. Shout if you have to. If you don't have time to escape, then this is what you do."

She launched into a series of demonstrations involving different maneuvers. From kicks, to using furniture, to twisting the weapon out of his hand. It impressed Tony. And turned him on. It had taken all his focus to remain stoic every time her body brushed up against his. When she'd grasped his arm, twisted so her back was to his front, and he felt the cushion of her ass against his crotch, he had to think of baseball to stay unaroused. She had no idea how she affected him, and when it became time for a volunteer, he pointed at Elena, grateful for a respite from the sensation of Bailey's body.

"Come on, Elena. You know you want to." He took her hand and dragged her to her feet, despite the belligerent look on her face. Tony knew that look. He'd caught himself making something similar many times in his youth. It was self-doubt. She needed her confidence boosted, so Tony asked the rest of them. "What move do you think she should pull on me? The twist and body slam. The kick to the guts. The elbow to the face."

A few shouts of suggestions came back, but it was Elena's voice that had him.

"Kick to the guts," she murmured, then immediately rubbed her arms.

Bailey stood back. "Good girl. Legs are longer than arms. Use your surroundings to give you an anchor. Tony will come at you, and you keep his body away by holding onto something, and then kicking."

Tony lunged toward Elena, pretending the cell was a knife. She squeaked. But then glanced over her shoulder, shuffled back until she hit the couch, and when Tony came at her again, she braced and kicked him—right in the gut. It knocked the wind out of him.

Eyes watering, he grunted and went down, clutching his middle. He was only half-acting. She really did have a strong kick. On someone less trained than him, it would do damage.

"I did it!" she exclaimed, eyes flashing and excited.

"That's good," he bit out. "Good."

"Now what?" Bailey prompted.

"Um." Elena's gaze darted around. Then she bit her lip, unsure. "Run?"

Bailey clapped. "Yes! You run." She turned back to the group. "Don't be heroes. Get out of there."

"Let the Deadly Seven do the rest!" A kid with a nose ring piped up.

More snickers and shouts. Somehow, the conversation shifted to which of the vigilantes was the best. Feeling awkward, Tony rolled to his feet and handed the cell phone back to Elena.

"Which one do you think, Tony?" someone's voice rose above the rest.

"Huh?" he asked, frowning.

"Which is your favorite?"

Tony searched and found the voice belonged to a boy of about fifteen. He had dreadlocks and wore a hoodie.

"What's your name?"

"Simon."

"Gluttony," he answered without thinking, then inwardly groaned. He should have said Pride. What kind of idiot said he liked himself the best?

"Pfft," Simon replied. "He's not been sighted for ages. Neither has Lust. They could be dead. Anyway, I think I'd trust the ones I hear about more. Like Envy electrocuted some dude when…"

A rushing sound stole Simon's voice and Tony's thoughts grew loud. The kid was right. Tony hadn't been out in a while. Months. He rubbed his forehead, mouth going dry. They thought he was dead.

His entire body felt heavy with shame.

Bailey looked at him strange, as though she could read his mind, then clapped her hands loudly. "Right. That's it kids. We're over time."

Any wrongness he'd felt immediately dissipated when the chorus of booing and moans filled the small room. Each student begged Bailey for more. They'd watched avidly throughout the demonstration as though it was a movie. It may as well have been with the acting prowess Tony put into his performance. Every kid loved it, except a quiet one toward the back. Brown-skinned, shaved head, and with headphones in the whole time. A hip-hop beat blared loud enough that Tony could hear. Seeing the class was ending, he surreptitiously unplugged his ears and folded his arms. But he stayed. He watched. And now he was listening.

"Right, everyone on the mat." Bailey clapped her hands again to cut through their raucous babbling. "As soon as you're quiet, it's question time."

That hushed everyone up. Tony went to stand next to Bailey at the front of the class. He dusted off his baseball cap and held it to stop his hands fidgeting. And to stop him reaching out to touch Bailey. A visceral reaction had rocked him every time they'd connected, and the residual echo still rode his system. He wanted more.

But the defensive way she'd reacted to their first kiss played on his mind. *She'd wiped her mouth in disgust.* He'd have to gain her trust before trying again. From the moment he'd stepped across the threshold to Hudson House and seen her leaning against the doorjamb to the media room, he knew she wasn't an active agent. She was there to help the kids. He could trust her. Everything else was his own paranoid delusion.

"Who's got the first question?" Bailey asked the students, a grin brightening her face to something so extraordinary, Tony's heart stopped beating. This was the first time he'd seen her smile. Beautiful.

"Tony?" she asked, interrupting his thoughts.

"Sorry, was there a question?"

"Ooohh," one student teased. "Lazarus has it bad for our lady."

Another wolf-whistle punctuated the air, and Bailey's cheeks reddened. "They wanted to know if you'll come back."

Tony shifted his smile to the group. "Absolutely."

"Can we get a selfie?" Michael asked.

He grinned and waved them up. "Yeah, but we have to be quick about it. Your lady here is my bodyguard, and we have to go to work."

"Bodyguard!" Elena exclaimed. "A woman?"

"That's right, and…" Tony paused and looked at Bailey. "Can I tell them where you used to work?"

A little frown marred her brow, but then she nodded.

Tony's eyes lit up as he faced the group. "She's ex-CIA."

"No way!"

"Get out!"

"As if!"

This time, Tony couldn't help himself. He slid a proprietary arm around Bailey's shoulders and squeezed. "She's pretty special, right?" After a wave of nods and exclamations, he added with a twinkle in his eye, "So you see, everything she taught you about protecting yourself is the honest-to-God truth."

"Damn," Akeef muttered. He studied Bailey with a new interest. "So, you be like, from a good family, yeah?"

Bailey shook her head. "That depends on your perspective. My family had money, but there was addiction in my home like most of yours. That's why I'm here."

"But your college was paid for," Akeef added bitterly.

Bailey tensed. "My parents paid for boarding school, but I worked hard to get a scholarship for college so I didn't need to rely on them. We have many facilities here to help foster opportunities. We're all ready to help. You just bring the will, and we'll try our hardest to help you succeed. And success doesn't have to mean a fancy job. Sometimes success is just making your own choice."

The class started chatting amongst themselves, already lost. Akeef scowled and left the room.

It seemed like the class was finished, so Tony used the opportunity to pull Bailey aside. "We need to talk."

"Just give me a minute to officially wind up, and we'll head out. I have to talk to Agnes about a few things."

While Bailey packed her things, Tony took a few pictures with the teens. He enjoyed spending time at the house and couldn't quite put his finger on why. It was more than the one-on-one with Bailey, or some time with fans. He rubbed his chest. It felt good to help.

ten

BAILEY HAZE

BAILEY FILLED Agnes in on the success of the class and Tony's input. She had to sign him in and keep a record of his attendance. When she was done, she went to find Tony. Half expecting him to have left, or maybe just to be standing around waiting, it surprised her to find him in another room, lying on the floor with Akeef.

She stopped outside the door and kept herself hidden. With a hand on the wall beside the door, she tilted her head. Tony hummed a tune she couldn't place.

"So," Tony said from inside. "Put your hand on your stomach and focus on your breathing."

"Like this?"

"Yeah. And when you sing, doing it from down here can really teach you how to access that deep part of your lungs. You want to give it a go?"

Silence.

"What makes you think I want to sing?"

"Come on, kid. I heard you in here when you thought no one was listening."

"Singing is for pussies."

"I sing. Am I a pussy?"

"Guess not."

Tony sang?

"Come on, try it. At least give the humming a try."

When the kid started, Bailey's hand went to cover her smile. Tony did it. With only an hour or so here, he'd chipped away at the armor of more than one troubled youth. Maybe she was wrong about him. Maybe he had the capacity to think of someone other than himself.

After five minutes, she was about to walk in, but something Akeef said stopped her.

"How did you get away from it all, man? You know, the need."

Tony's deep inhale was audible. "It's there all the time, bro. But you keep yourself busy. You remind yourself of your goals, and you power through. And you get help."

"I don't know."

"Sure you do. You love this shit." A pause. "Tell you what. I'll come back next week and we'll record some stuff. Make a Youtube or something. Keep taking steps forward, and before you know it, you're far away from your doubts."

Bailey placed her palm over her heart. Tony was doing this all on his own. She'd not asked him. He'd offered. There was no one else in there but the two of them. Her mind whirled. He was nothing like she'd expected. The man in there was humble, caring and generous. Why did he hide that part of him?

eleven

TONY LAZARUS

TONY HOOKED up a time with Akeef to come back to the house. The kid didn't ask, and he kind of fobbed off the suggestion to make a music video, but Tony had expected that. Building confidence took time and in the end, Tony casually suggested they hold a video game tournament. He'd slip in a few sneaky karaoke moments while they played. He had a plan. And Sloan's old X-box console would help. The media room had been grossly understocked with things teens actually enjoyed doing. He left Akeef and went to find Bailey.

He didn't have to look far. She was right outside the room. Coming up behind Tony, Akeef cast a sideways glance at Bailey, then plugged his earphones back in. He lifted his hand for Tony to fist bump.

"Later, bro," Akeef mumbled.

"Laters." Tony's heartbeat quickened as he turned to Bailey. "Um. Hi."

"You're fantastic with them," she noted, eyes crinkling at the sides.

He shrugged. "It's part of my job."

"You were acting?"

He thought about it. "No, I wasn't."

"So it wasn't part of your job."

Huh. "Guess not."

When she spoke next, it was with a shy lowering of the lashes. "You know, this is the kind of thing I was talking about using your celebrity for. It's not always about money or donations, but about hope."

He couldn't help it. He hooked his finger under her chin, lifting her gaze to meet his. What stared back at him was something raw, earnest, and for once unguarded.

"Go on a date with me," he said.

She blinked. "Date?"

"You heard me." His fingers trailed up her jawline to tuck a stray hair behind her ear, and then, as if it fit, he curled his hand around her warm neck. A breathy grunt of approval rumbled through his chest.

Hot breath fanned between them. Electricity sizzled in the air. And when she spoke next, it was as if she had trouble breathing.

"And what does a date with Tony Lazarus look like?"

"I wouldn't know. I've never been on one."

"None?"

"You'll be my first."

She lifted two incredulous eyebrows.

They both burst into laughter.

"Not that kind of first," he added. "There have been many... others." Heat rose up his neck. Aw, hell, this was coming out wrong. "Just no one I wanted to date."

The roar of an engine blared from the street. It was so loud, it filtered through the house. Bailey tensed under his touch.

"Wait here," she said. "I'll check it out."

Fear skipped up his spine. Alarm shot through his veins. He

should be the one checking it out. Not her. But it had been months since he'd relied on his deadly skills. Did this situation even need those skills?

Realizing she'd already left, he jogged after her through the house and out the front door. Some kids were sitting on the porch, chatting away. Akeef had music playing on his cell phone speaker, and they all bopped and danced.

When Bailey caught sight of the vehicle making the noise, her eyes widened.

Turning toward the kids, she snapped, "Get inside now!"

Bailey ushered them through the doors. Taking her lead, he blocked any of them trying to get down the steps for a look, but before they had a chance to safely ensconce themselves inside, a prickle of intuition ran along the back of Tony's neck. He turned back to the street.

A black Cadillac filled with rough-looking men had settled curbside. Each car window began rolling down, giving him a good look inside. A flash of metal, of promised violence, and Tony's years of training had him moving before his mind registered what was coming for them—guns. Lots of them.

Enough to spray through the doors if the kids still stood on the other side. The blood drained from his face. He had to do something.

"Keep them inside," he ordered Bailey.

She opened her mouth to protest, but he launched from the porch up onto the concrete balustrade and surfed on his shoes down, assessing the situation as he went.

All windows were open.

Two in the back, one in the front.

The occupants looked this way.

The narrow sidewalk made a six-foot gap to the car.

A plan formed in his head as he got to the end of the balustrade, jumped onto the top of the gate's pillar, bounced across to the other, and then dove. He sailed over the sidewalk and landed on the Cadillac's roof, stomach first. Skidding across, he braced, reached down and inside the opposite window. His fist closed around the scruff of a big thug and heaved. The man came shoulders-out before Tony jammed an elbow into his temple. Tony dropped to the ground. As he wrenched the door open, he let his power advance, feeling the rush inside his blood. A blue glow rose within him so swiftly that he'd wondered how he'd ever had trouble controlling it before. But this felt right. Protecting those kids was right. With the open door, the body in the window tumbled down, giving Tony ample opportunity to get in the car before its two surprised occupants realized what was happening. They adjusted their aim, but Tony's hands snapped out and took hold of each muzzle. Then he let his fire out and couldn't help feeling amazed as his power rushed to do his bidding. Maybe he was good at this too.

A bright blue flash blinded the interior.

The men shouted, screamed.

Heat scorched Tony's palms and he winced. Parts of the car smoldered. Okay, maybe he wasn't so good. But better. When the light faded, he knocked any weapon out of range. It didn't matter. They wouldn't have been able to discharge the guns. His power had melted them into macabre twisted sculptures.

Tony leaned back and kicked the man in the back seat, knocking him out. Then he looped the seatbelt around the driver's neck and choked. Tony eased off the pressure as the tension left the driver's body. Once he'd completely passed out, it was only a matter of readjusting the belt to secure his wrists. Tony did the same for the second man in the rear. The residual blue sparks from his hands almost set fire to the cab and he had to swat them out.

Bailey's shouts warned of her approach. Tony's heart leapt into his throat and he clamped down hard on his power. Painful heat blocked up, and he pushed it down some more. Couldn't let her see this side of him. The complete turnabout of power direction was like shutting a valve suddenly. Everything inside him screamed in denial. The energy wanted out. It kept building inside, but he wanted to confess his truth to Bailey on *his* terms. He wanted to be the one to decide. So he pushed, he stifled, and he acted calm.

He *was* calm.

My terms.

And he'd just taken down three assailants on his own. The kids were safe. Bailey was safe. He guessed he wasn't so rusty after all.

Scooting out of the car and into the street, he quickly grabbed hold of the fallen thug under the arms and dragged him into the open passenger side.

"Tony." Bailey breathed hard as she came around the car. She collected the dropped rifle, and then aimed it like a pro at the thugs. He put his hand on the muzzle and lowered it.

"Situation is contained."

It took her a moment to adjust to what he was saying, but she lowered the rifle and switched her attention to Tony. "Are you okay?"

Out of the corner of Tony's eye, he could see a twisted gun at the bottom of the car, right under the thug's feet. Trying not to look conspicuous, he picked up the thug's legs and folded them into the cabin, then secured the man's hands with the seatbelt. He shut the door, straightened, and acted like nothing was wrong.

"You called the cops?" he asked.

But Bailey had a horrified expression on her face. She must have seen the melted weapons. Her eyes smartened. "What the hell is going on, Lazarus?"

Damn. This wasn't going to plan. He'd wanted to tell her in his own way. He glanced over the Cadillac to see the teens filter out of the house again, crowding onto the stoop to watch. A few had their cell phones out, recording on their cameras. Shit. Hopefully most of his damning action had been hidden in the car.

He swallowed. "I-uh... I told you we need to talk."

"Hell yeah, we need to talk." She eyed his hands, and for a moment he thought they were going blue again, but nothing. Didn't matter. She grit her teeth, jaw flexing. "But first, we have to sort this out. How the hell am I going to explain that the city's favorite film star single-handedly took down a gang of armed and dangerous men during a drive by? I'm supposed to be your bodyguard. Some of that stuff you did was insane." She gaped and waved at the roof of the car. "You flew across the—Godammit, Tony!"

"Hey, hey. It's all good." He tried a comforting grin. "They'll just think I'm a method actor or some shit."

"That was reckless and stupid. This isn't a movie set. For Christ's sake, these are real people. Those are real kids."

Seeing the group gather on the porch stoop, Tony flinched. They must have all come out of the house. Hopefully none had seen him in action. But Bailey had. And she was furious.

"Don't forget I served," he offered.

She cocked her hip. "Real life action hero, huh?"

"Something like that."

For a moment, she just stared at him, jaw clenched. "That was pretty impressive. And I mean, *impressive*." She didn't look impressed. She looked pissed. "You just took down three armed men, inside a vehicle, with nothing but your bare hands."

Shit. He'd have a hell of a time explaining this.

Then she said something he never expected. "Is this some kind of joke? Are you making fun of me?"

"Wh-what?"

"You have all these... skills, and yet you hired me to be your bodyguard. And then you let me school you in self-defense moves!" Her face went beet red. "Well, screw you, Lazarus. I know when I'm being made a fool of."

"That's not it. I swear." He reached for her, but she shirked away.

"Do me a favor, Rambo." She jerked the rifle toward the street, in the direction of the distant sirens. "When the cops get here, maybe try telling the truth for once."

He opened his mouth but shut it. Maybe now wasn't a good time to tell her everything.

Police sirens got louder. Bailey pinned him with her big brown eyes. "Don't you dare run off. We are definitely having that chat."

He wasn't so sure. She already thought he was a philandering addict. Back at his trailer, she'd accused him of having an affair, and that was why someone stalked him. What would she say when she discovered he was prone to random explosions of blue light that burned like fire? And she was his mate. And he'd been lying to her.

The whoop of a siren, and the flash of red and blue against the house's gate made many of the kids disappear inside. Bailey jogged over to meet the cop car as it arrived. Tony used the commotion to slip away.

twelve

WAYNE BOSCH

BEFORE SETTING out on a hunt beneath the sewers of Cardinal City, Wayne Bosch and the enforcer had gathered their intel and pooled their resources. Or, perhaps he should call her Despair. It had only taken him a moment or two to connect the dots. She could sense the sin. She was the same age as the Deadly Seven. They were original Syndicate experiments. For all Wayne knew, there were plenty of others like her out there.

Between the two of them, they'd collected evidence of random suspicious activity matching their parameters across state lines, moving west from the black site, and toward the coast where Cardinal City lay.

From random bodies of water being drained to farm animals going missing, only to turn up with their corpses as dried out desiccated husks. When Wayne and Despair had gone to investigate, they'd recognized the same striations on the husks that had been clear on the corpses in the lab. It looked liked indents from vines. From the lack of actual plant-monster sightings, they also believed their prey to be traveling by night, or perfectly camouflaging itself amongst other foliage. The creature was smart.

But one thing was certain, it was getting a taste for living meat, and it wasn't sated. It was hungry.

Despair crouched at the opening of a manhole and heaved the sewer grate open. "After you."

Wayne peered down into the dark unknown, flinched at the smell, and then glanced around their surrounds. They were in the middle of a street on the outskirts of the city, nestled between an old abandoned warehouse and an industrial factory. Since it was the weekend, traffic was quiet. The only moving person he'd spotted was a homeless lady pushing a shopping trolley filled with a hodgepodge of belongings. He shifted his gaze up and noted the fading light. The temperature was dropping, which meant it would be cold under-ground, and his flimsy houndstooth-patterned suit would do little to protect him from the elements. They had maybe an hour or two of light left until nightfall. But none of that mattered down there where it was dark twenty-four-seven.

Despite knowing this, he couldn't help asking her, "Are you sure this is a safe time to go down? Shouldn't we wait until morning?"

Couldn't she go without him?

Dressed in her white leather battle outfit, she'd neglected to place the half-face bird mask on. Instead, he was treated to the full exposure of her stunningly pale and expressionless face. Unblinking violet eyes studied him.

"The trail will go cold," she stated simply.

The trail... meaning the educated guess they took based on the pattern of incidents moving across the state. Considering its nature and its hunger, it made sense that the plant would head to a more populated area, and if it was here in the city, it made sense it went underground. More water to drink. More rats to eat. It had sucked most farm animal corpses dry of fluid to leave desiccated husks. The animals were alive before the farmers went to bed, and dead in the morning. Same went for the bodies of water that had been drained, confirming the attacks occurred during the night hours.

Wayne pushed his glasses up the bridge of his nose. He didn't really have a choice, did he? He needed his funding to remain. He needed a job. Thoughts flickered to his wife, the debt she knew nothing about, and the hopes and dreams he wasn't ready to give up on. Not yet.

He had his trusty torch and a can of spray accelerant he would use together with a lab-sized blowtorch to make his own flame thrower. Despair had a net slung over her shoulder, a bullwhip attached to her hip, and some kind of feudal Japanese sword strapped to her back.

"This is insane," he mumbled. "How do we hunt a sentient plant?"

"Any way we can," Despair answered, and then booted him down the manhole.

DESPAIR

DESPAIR LANDED GRACEFULLY in the ankle-deep sewer water of the culvert leading through the underground tunnels. She watched the bumbling scientist flounder on his knees, hands blindly splashing about him.

"My glasses. I can't find them," he shouted. Contaminated water splashed into his open mouth and he gagged.

She crinkled her nose. It smelled rather bad there—a mix of

mildew, sour trash and human waste. The sooner she was out, the better.

The only light came from the open manhole directly above, but it was enough for her to see the water at her feet and the double-barreled brick walls around them.

More splashing. More shouting.

She clicked on her torch. White light illuminated the tunnel, casting the damp domed walls into sharp relief. Sounds of the scientist echoed down into the black caverns beyond their sight.

Every nerve in her body woke, including the one in her gut. Somewhere in the tunnels, she sensed fading despair like a scrape of nails down the lining of her stomach, getting lighter with each stroke. It must be the creature. She shouldn't be able to sense a plant, but it had mutated into something else. Back in the lab, it had wanted freedom from the shackles of its life. She'd known, because she'd sensed its sorrow. When she'd released it from its cage, its despair stopped. She'd never thought it would leave a senseless trail of bodies behind. She'd thought the creature would only attack sinners, but even the poor farm animals weren't discriminated against.

"I need my glasses," the scientist wailed. "I can't do this without them. Please."

Keeping her eyes glued to the direction she sensed the plant, she bent, dipped her hand below the waterline and retrieved the man's spectacles. She pushed them into his palm and ignored his stumbling apologies and gratitude.

"Shh." She moved her torchlight around the tunnel. The sense of despair flickered and waned. The plant was there, yet it became less sorrowful. Perhaps more purposeful, more clouded with hunger. Its desire was changing.

Pausing, she listened. Water dripped from curved walls. Cockroaches scuttled. She angled the torch low at the water. Reflections refracted onto the walls, shimmering eerily.

The hairs on her arms lifted in warning. She stepped forward, then thought better of it. She turned, took hold of the scientist's collar. "Walk."

She pushed between his shoulder blades and he lurched, slushing forward.

"B-but, my torch," he protested.

"It's in the water. It won't work. Move."

He shuffled along. Trembling hands moved to unclip his weapons from his belt. With each sloshing step, rats scuttled and squeaked, water splashed, and something... something moved in the shadows.

Slowly, slowly they approached a junction where four sewer tunnels met in the middle. Water sporadically dripped from above, giving a hollow acoustic sound that revealed the sewerage system went on for miles.

Her torch flickered. Darkness threatened to swallow them whole.

She sensed it again and swung the torch in the right direction, just glimpsing movement in the dark. The light flickered again, then went dark.

"What happened?" The scientist hissed into the vast dark.

She hit the torch to correct the light. The beam came back on. When she looked up, the steady stream of light illuminated the space behind the scientist, and incomprehensible black slithering lines moved against the concrete tunnel walls. Adrenaline shot into her system.

What the hell?

The torch failed and darkness engulfed them, but the squiggling lines had burned into her retina. She couldn't unsee them. Squeezing her eyes shut, she shook her head, as though to smack sense back into her mind, for what she'd glimpsed had not been logical. Black slithering vines massed over the entire tunnel. Above their heads, on the sides... perhaps below. Gathering her wits, she smacked the torch until it worked. The scientist's hand shadowed his squinting eyes under the glare of her spotlight.

"We should go back," he said, unaware of what was amassing behind him. "I lost my torch, and yours is fault—"

The scientist froze, body going board stiff. Behind his misted spectacles, his eyes widened in panic.

"What is it?" she hissed, but he didn't answer. He was petrified, arms pinned to his side, fingers balled into fists from fear, or something else.

Why wasn't he moving?

"Bosch," she hissed. "What..." Terror stole her words. Thin tendrils appeared from beneath the collar of his shirt, as though they'd been inside his clothing the entire time, climbing, slithering up his torso.

Bosch had mentioned earlier that the plant had a natural poison. It was supposed to wrap a tendril around any sinner who got too close and numb them. She hadn't thought the toxin was selective, she'd thought it was always there, but Wayne Bosch wasn't stunned or petrified as each little squirming spike slid up his neck, over his jaw and onto his face. He struggled against the vines, even when the tendrils entered his mouth... his nostrils... his ears.

Could the plant enjoy watching its prey squirm? Could it use its toxin selectively?

The scientist's spectacles fell with a splash.

A scream froze in Despair's throat. She backed up.

Bosch gurgled, mumbled, choked, but the vines soon filled his mouth.

She didn't know what to do. She should help him, shouldn't she?

But the plant... the one she'd helped escape was wrapping itself around him, slowly making him disappear as though it were bandages and he the mummy.

One foot back, then another, she backed up. She should run. Forget about the scientist. But Julius insisted she had to end this.

Choking wet sounds filled her ears, and she lifted her hands to cover them, but she still held onto her torch. She couldn't keep out the disgusting wet sucking sounds. All she could do was watch in horror as the man disappeared while the plant fed. Its writhing vines and tentacles and leaves growing plumper by the second, filling with the lifeblood of a man as it became one with it.

There was no telling how many creatures this thing had absorbed while hunting between the black site and here. It had started out as a simple plant in the lab. Security footage showed it eating rats, physically morphing in shape, and then crawling out of the black site. The creature had taken on characteristics and mannerisms of its prey, mimicking them, becoming something else, something unbiased towards sinners, and just hungry.

Wayne Bosch was no longer. There was no husk this time. All that remained was a coiling collection of vines shaped like a man, and when the thing approached Despair, she flattened herself against the brick wall. She reached for her sword, but something stopped her. The moment she'd moved, the sense of despair flared in her gut. Slowly, she lowered her hand from the hilt of her sword and returned her fist to her side. Hoping against all hope that she would survive, she held her breath and tried not to whimper as a tendril unfurled itself from the being and came toward her face. A scream gurgled in her throat as it brushed against her cheek. She squeezed her eyes shut, trying to hold her breath steady, but all she wanted to do was lose the contents of her stomach. When she next opened her eyes, the creature was gone, as was its despair because it was free.

thirteen

TONY LAZARUS

TONY WALKED HOME from Hudson House, sucking on a raspberry slushie and kicking an empty can at parked cars lining the well-to-do city street. With his baseball cap down low to obscure his face, he'd meandered the time away with no wayward fans or paparazzi mobbing him. He drained the slushie with big slurps.

He would rather drink something else, taste *someone* else. Bailey's hot, curvy body entered his mind. Again. For the zillionth time that walk. The entire morning with her had been filled with arms brushing against each other, body heat jumping from skin to skin, a casual smile thrown his way. He'd craved no one so much. But the woman who gave him a great morning had also made him feel two inches tall. She thought he was making fun of her, when in fact, it had been the opposite.

When his feet brought him back in line with his can, he booted it with renewed vigor. The tiny metal projectile went airborne, spun, and hit the side of a slick black Maserati.

The alarm went off.

"You've got to be fucking kidding me." Could his day get any worse?

"Hey, dickhead," someone shouted from behind him, but he had no fucks to give. He ignored studiously and kept walking until a police siren *whoop-whooped*. Fuck! He threw his head back and roared his frustration, staring at the darkening sky, only then realizing he'd been walking aimlessly for most of the day. He gripped the slushie, ready to launch it.

"Get off the road, you big lug!" came a feminine voice from the cop car behind him, and for the first time all afternoon, he relaxed.

Finally. Something going his way. Pivoting, he came face to face with Liza as she climbed out of her unmarked detective's car.

"What the hell are you doing?" She glanced around the tree-lined street, probably looking for his imaginary friends. "Having a pity party for one?"

An affluent couple walking their Japanese Spitz down the sidewalk stopped to watch the excitement. Out of habit, Tony ducked his head to avoid being recognized. He growled at his sister, "How did you know where I was?"

"All of us have microdot trackers on our cells."

Of course they did. "Here to check up on me?"

He'd meant it as a joke, but she hesitated. "It's time to go home, Tony."

"Why? So you or Parker can lecture me about what happened?" Because he knew, without a doubt, that word had already reached them. If it wasn't Bailey who'd told Max, it would have been Liza who'd heard about the incident at the sobriety house through law enforcement channels. It could even be all over social media. Didn't really matter. It wouldn't change the fact he'd stuffed up. "Or because you don't think I can handle my power and I'm going to blow up in front of these poor people."

"Come on, get in," Liza growled. "I'll take you home."

There was no point in arguing, so Tony threw his almost empty slushie cup into a trash can and let himself into the front passenger side of Liza's car. He adjusted the seat back to accommodate his long legs and then helped himself to a stick of gum from the console. He started poking the buttons on her cop computer dashboard while she entered her side.

"Touch another button and you die," she warned as she removed her magnetic siren light from the car roof and put it on the dash.

"Jeez. Touchy. Someone needs to get laid."

Brown eyes hot as the sun burned into him. "Are you fucking kidding me right now?"

"What?"

"You left the scene of a crime. I had to cover for you, *again*." And there it was. She'd been called out to Hudson House and disapproved of the way he'd handled things. She continued, "I had to talk your woman down from the ledge."

His ears perked up. "What do you mean?"

"I mean"—Liza planted her foot on the accelerator and launched them forward—"that your mate was in all sorts of twists worried about you."

"Worried?" That wasn't right. The woman had snapped his head off.

"God, you're such an idiot. All men are."

"What did she say?"

"She left immediately after giving her statement." Liza's jaw ticked, but she wouldn't take her eyes off the road. "You need to go to her and explain the truth. She's already been hounding Max and Sloan. That woman does not give up."

A small smile tilted Tony's lips. She was a strong woman. A

sneaky sense of pride puffed in his chest, and he looked away in case Liza noticed.

She was worried about him.

Bailey.

He conjured his memory of the morning, about to indulge in nostalgia, but the moment he thought of his mate, his body reacted viscerally. His hormones skyrocketed. His hands heated with the promise of power, a constant reminder that he had no choice in this life. Damn it. Every time his hormones went into turmoil, he couldn't control himself. Heat prickled his skin, and then he felt a little off. No doubt, his body didn't like him stifling his powers, but he didn't enjoy being forced into a situation.

"Tony. I said you need to go after her, did you hear me?"

"I'm not the guy who goes after the woman," he stated. The very thought of putting himself out there, open to rejection, made his stomach twist into knots.

The car screeched to a stop.

He barely avoided hitting his head on the dash. "What the—"

"Are you kidding me?" Liza screeched, furious. Livid. It was so out of character that Tony could do nothing but stare. Cars beeped behind them, but she only rolled down her window, snapped her siren back on top, and then gave their tooters the finger. Back at Tony, she lowered her brows. "You *have* a woman, Tony. Whether you or she admits it, you already belong together. Your biology has done half the job. The only way you can fuck this up is if you keep saying shit like that... *OOoh. I'm not the guy who goes after women,*" she mocked. "Get your head out of your ass."

Tony squirmed. "Chill out."

Hell broke loose on Liza's features and she punched Tony in the arm.

Both of them went still, shocked.

She blinked.

He blinked. She'd really punched him. It hurt.

Then her face screwed up and she repeatedly jabbed him until he cried out for her to stop, half laughing at the absurdity of it. He tried pushing her back, but it was like trying to stop a hurricane. He was five again, and his six-year-old sister was punishing him for stealing her favorite rope of raspberry licorice she had been saving for a rainy day. But this was different, or maybe it was the same all along and he was only just getting it. This wasn't Tony stealing her licorice. This was Tony having what she couldn't. Because lust made her sick.

He stopped fighting her, braced, and took it. He let his sister punch him until he was sure bruises formed. She needed this.

A man in his forties came up to her open window and peeked inside. "You need a hand in there, miss?"

Her firearm was out of its holster and pointed at the surprised man's face before he could blink. "I'm a city detective, asswipe. *I'm* punching *him*." Then she rolled the window up and resumed driving, mumbling more curses at the stupidity of men in the city.

For minutes they drove in silence. Tony was almost too afraid to speak. He cleared his throat. "You'll find someone, you know."

Her fingers gripped the steering wheel so tight her knuckles went white, and he knew he'd hit the mark. When she spoke, her voice was strained. "It's just, you have your person right there. Some of us—me, Daisy, maybe even the arrogant King of Pride—we'll never have what is staring you in the face. She's waiting for you to go to her and explain everything, and you're not going to do it. Why?"

That she might say no, that she would see the real Tony was all an act... it terrified him. So he changed the subject. "I have a theory about our mates. I think they only need to embody the exact opposite of our sin right at the start, right when our powers are triggered.

Think about it, Max has embodied his share of sloth lounging in bed with Sloan. Misha has exhibited a touch of wrath and blasted Wyatt on more than one occasion. She's definitely not always the opposite of wrath, yet he still can't sense the sin in her. She's still his haven when they touch."

A pause. "What are you saying?"

"I know you're afraid you won't find someone you can have a relationship without feeling sick every time you—"

"Stop right there. I'm not talking about sex with my brother."

He shrugged. She was Lust. She got the picture. There was hope. Maybe even for Daisy to overcome her despair. God knew Parker had no chance with his pride. Getting through his thick head would be a chore.

The car pulled up next to Lazarus House. Liza looked at Tony with serious eyes. "Here's your chance, brother. She's in the lobby waiting for you. Has been for the past hour. You either head in there, explain everything, or just go straight to Hell and drink your sorrows. Either way, you need to make a choice and stick with it."

His heart stopped beating.

She was in the lobby.

Bailey was in the lobby.

Here.

It was just a small foyer with a desk to one side where the doorman sat, and an elevator that went up to their apartments, or down to the secret underground base. But it was so much more than that with her in it.

Lazarus House was an impressive multi-story apartment building with the restaurant Heaven on one side of the lobby, and the night-club Hell on the other. Both places were frequent haunts of his. Good food, good drinks, and good women. Plenty of women, but never enough. Not until Bailey.

He shifted his gaze to the line of patrons outside Hell. Celebrities visited the popular nightspot. It was notorious for its privacy and no media rule. Everyone wanted to see inside and get a taste for themselves. Most of them would be turned away because Parker held a very exclusive list for hand-picked clientele.

"What are you afraid of, Tony?"

As if in answer, the blue in his veins lit up the interior of the car. "Shit. I can't go out like this."

"Yes, you can."

He growled when she reached over him to open his door. He whacked her out of the way.

"Oh, don't be such a baby," she said and did it anyway, then gave him a testing look.

The door swung open, giving everyone on the street the perfect view into the car, and to him. He clamped down on his power, suppressed the shit out of it, and ended up sweating from exertion. It felt like his veins had twisted beneath his skin. His body didn't like being told to wait. It had to. What if he couldn't control it?

But there he was.

Unlocking his seatbelt, he shot his sister a glare, and then unfolded himself from the car. He made it two steps across the sidewalk when someone called his name and he froze. It wasn't Bailey. She was still standing inside the lobby, talking to the doorman and unaware of his approach.

He turned and relaxed. It was Peta from the studio.

The tall assistant was almost unrecognizable. She detached herself from the line for Hell and came trotting over, heels clicking on the concrete. A tight navy dress hugged her form from hips to breasts where the straps held the top together in a halter. Out of its usual bun, her hair tumbled down her shoulders.

"Tony!" A grin stretched her red lips. "I'm so glad you're here."

"Peta." He leaned in and gave her a peck on the cheek. She blushed and sort of twisted toward the line. Tony guessed it was to see if any of her three giggling friends noticed. "Good to see you."

Peta's expression drew all businesslike. "I've been trying to call you all day."

"Oh? You want to get on the list?" He whistled to the bouncer, pointed at Peta and then to the door of Hell.

The bouncer nodded and waved Peta's friends out of the regular line.

"No, um, actually... although thanks... it's the questions for the press junket tomorrow. I emailed them to you. Donatello wanted you to look them over."

"Shit. Yeah, sorry. Thanks. I don't know what I'd do without you."

"If you need a hand going over them, just let me know."

"I think I'll be fine, thanks. See you tomorrow."

She bit her lip. "We also need to know if you'll have a plus one for the premiere next week."

Premiere.

Fuck.

While his life went to shit, the world kept turning without him.

"Yes, I'll have a plus one."

For a moment, Peta's eyes flashed with some unnamed emotion that made him feel a little awkward. She seemed to want to add something, but thought the better of it, and relaxed.

"You're not coming in?" she asked, pointing back to Hell.

This was his chance. If he was going to forget about his responsibilities, avoid Bailey and everything else, this was his opening. Easier to fuck up now and never face the failure he knew was inevitable. The drink was calling. Peta's perfume smelled heady. He could so easily...

He shook his head and stepped away, out of Peta's scented cloud.

His body already sensed Bailey in there. Another scent tugged at his memory. Bailey's coconut shampoo.

"Not tonight," he said to Peta.

"Oh. Okay. Tomorrow, then."

He waved and headed into the lobby.

BAILEY HAZE

BAILEY WATCHED Tony talk to the leggy brunette and couldn't help the irritation swimming in her chest. Having no idea where he'd gone after she'd snapped at him, it had tied her in knots all afternoon. The man had just disappeared. He'd saved lives, and then he'd disappeared before she had the chance to thank him.

And to ask what the hell he was hiding. She kind of knew, but needed to hear it from him. She wouldn't let him leave her sight tonight until she found out.

"I'm clocking off for the day. You okay to keep waiting, Miss Haze?" Gus the doorman asked. The older man had kept her company while she waited for Tony to arrive home.

Bailey had become friendly with Gus over the past few months. The first time she had been in the lobby was when Max was kidnapped, and the Lazarus family had tried to hide it from her and the rest of the Nightingale crew. She'd all but burst down the door demanding information. While Damien and Tomas had believed Parker's lame excuse about Max being on a sudden secret assignment, she wasn't nearly as trusting.

That same niggling suspicion picked at her nerves. Tony was hiding something. She knew it. No one had the combat skills he had unless they kept up to date with training, and a movie star simply did not train the same way. They trained in slow motion. It was all fake.

"Miss?" Gus asked again.

"Sorry, Gus. I was lost in thought. Tony's here. I'm sure I'll be fine letting myself out after I have a word with him."

Gus saluted her with his aviator cap and then headed out. He passed Tony coming in at the same time. They said a few cordial words, Tony clapped the man on the shoulder, and then it was just Tony and Bailey alone in the small, cold lobby.

He wore the same jeans and T-shirt he'd worn earlier that day, and with his baseball hat now off, his brown hair still looked like he'd just gotten out of bed. He'd not returned home since he'd left Hudson House. Bailey folded her arms.

This was it. The moment of truth.

She'd been gathering clues regarding the Lazarus family sketchiness since Max went missing. At first, she'd kept telling herself, it was her CIA paranoia kicking in, but as the evidence mounted, she'd had no other option but to arrive at the indisputable truth. The Lazarus family were the Deadly Seven. They had to be. It was the only answer that made sense.

"I've been trying to contact you," she stated.

He put his hands in his pockets and hunched. After a breath, he lifted his long-lashed gaze to meet hers. They were ten feet apart, yet she could feel his body heat across the expanse of the tiled floor. Her body hummed with awareness of him. It threw every demand out of her head.

"I wanted to thank you," she added and took a step in his direction. "And I'm sorry I lost my cool, but it's my job to keep you safe, and at the time, it hadn't hit me yet that you obviously don't need my help..." Her voice became breathy and trailed off when she caught the intense longing on the man's face. His eyes were glued to her lips, lids lowered, mesmerized as she spoke. He wasn't even listening to her words. It was distracting.

"Tony."

His gaze snapped up to hers.

"What's going on?" she asked. "This time, tell me the truth. No running away."

All sultriness evaporated from his expression. He scratched his head. "I-ah-I." Then he looked at his exposed hand, eyes wide.

Thin lines of blue glowed along the back of Tony's hands, tracing the network of his veins like lace needlework. He appeared confused. Disorientated. *Definitely not special effects.*

At Hudson House, she'd accused him of making fun of her and had immediately regretted it. She'd overreacted. She'd never been in a life or death situation with someone she had feelings for, not for a long time. And she couldn't deny it now. She had feelings for him. Big ones. The size that couldn't be ignored. She'd been surprised at the genuine way he'd interacted with the kids at the sobriety house, even when he didn't know she was watching. Tony Lazarus was just as charming off screen as he was on it. That morning had crossed a boundary for her, and she couldn't go back. She saw a side of him he rarely showed anyone else. And if her suspicions were true about him, she'd only just scratched the surface of knowing him.

Bailey stepped forward.

"Tony," she started, but he backed up.

"You shouldn't come near me. Not like this." He frowned and hunched over, shaking his head. "I don't want you to see me like this."

She took another step. "Like what? The glow? It's okay, I've already seen it."

He shook his head. The blue glow grew brighter, and a sheen of sweat broke out across his brow.

"You're one of them, aren't you?" She held her hand out, eyes already enthralled by the glittering blue threads now delineating his forearms, casting them into the perfect shape of masculine strength. "You're one of the Seven. If I had to take a stab, with your excessive lifestyle, I'd guess Gluttony. Am I right?"

She thought it would calm him, or he'd feel like a weight had been lifted from his shoulders, but he looked pained. Hurt. Like his world was tumbling into chaos, and she couldn't help but feel a sense of kinship with him. She knew what it was like for events to spiral out of control. She still remembered how it felt to sit in the hospital, a police officer telling her that her best friend had died in the accident she'd caused as a teen. As a *drunk* teen.

She wanted to help him.

Most law enforcement officers thought vigilantes were a thorn in their sides, but Bailey had left the CIA for the same reasons people became vigilantes. Red tape stopped a lot of good being done and let many criminals go free. She'd been living a one-woman hopeless mission to reduce the hard drugs getting into the country. The CIA may color outside the lines of law, but with every bad guy they'd nabbed, it was always just a stepping stone to a larger criminal. Often those smaller criminals were let go because *there are always bigger fish to fry.*

"You can trust me, Tony. I'll keep your secret."

If he heard her words, she couldn't tell, because the man's eyes promptly rolled back in his head and he collapsed onto the tiled floor. For a few seconds, she stood there, unblinking.

Seeing a large, healthy man collapse was simply something she'd never seen. And when Tony began to shake and convulse, her heart leaped into her throat.

"Tony?" Her voice came out shaky and she inched closer. She kneeled and placed two fingers to his carotid. He sighed and his lashes fluttered at her contact. His trembling subsided, but he didn't wake. His pulse was weak and erratic. A fever burned so hot she almost had to take her hand back.

Tony was in trouble. He wouldn't want her to call an ambulance, but did she have the luxury not to do it?

Bailey searched the lobby for help, but it was empty. She looked through the glass doors to the street where people walked on the sidewalk. There were windows on either side of the lobby that peeked into the two establishments, Hell and Heaven. But from the way no one noticed them, the windows were one-way. She had to get him out of sight from the street until help arrived.

But first, she took her cell phone out and called Max. Then she placed the phone on the ground while she hooked her hands under Tony's arms and dragged him toward the elevator. Good God, the big guy was heavy. Those muscles weren't for show.

He groaned.

"Don't worry Tony, I'm calling for help." She ran the back of her fingers down his cheeks. His big hand came up and engulfed hers.

"No," he mumbled. "I'm fine."

"You're not fine, Tony. You have a fever. You're sick."

Bailey's call connected.

"Haze," came Max's gruff voice. "I told you to wait until you speak with Tony. I'm really sorry, but it's not my place to—"

"That's just it," she blurted. "I'm with Tony now and something's wrong. He passed out."

A pause. "From booze?"

"No! His veins glowed, and then he just passed out."

"Shit. Stay there. Wait. Where are you?"

"I'm in the Lazarus House lobby."

"Don't wait there. Get inside an elevator, ask AIMI to take you down to the basement. I'll get everyone to meet you down there."

Then the line went dead.

Goddammit!

"Who the hell is Amy?"

"I'm AIMI. Your artificial intelligence management interface." A computerized feminine voice came over a lobby speaker.

Bailey jolted. "Um. I need to get Tony to the basement. Can you help me?"

"Please lift your face to the camera so I can confirm your identity and security access."

Camera. Camera. Bailey searched the ceiling. She couldn't see the camera and was about to explain when AIMI spoke.

"Identity confirmed. Bailey Haze, Tony Lazarus's mate and security specialist for Nightingale Securities. You may enter the elevator."

What the fuck? It knew her. The doors to the elevator opened, and she heaved Tony inside. Getting his legs inside was a feat, and she had to rest him against the mirrored walls, but she did it. She retrieved her phone, and then the moment they were both securely inside, the elevator door closed, and the car descended.

"It will be okay, Tony," she said and touched him again. He seemed to like it. The truth was, she had no idea if it was going to be okay, but she had to trust Max knew what to do.

She'd yet to meet the entire Lazarus brood, and had mainly been assigned to watch the wives and girlfriends when she hadn't been on external security assignments, so when the elevator pinged and two tall, built men were waiting, she took a moment to recognize their faces from the pictures in their files. One was covered in tattoos and wore a dark shirt and gray sweatpants. That would be Evan Lazarus, the artist. The other was unmistakably Wyatt. Tall, dark and brooding, he often accompanied them on outings with his girlfriend, Misha.

"What happened?" Wyatt growled. He indicated for Evan to help him pick up Tony and carry him between them.

"He just started glowing blue. All over his hands and arms." God, that sounded insane. She rushed after them down a long, concrete hallway. It was scorched near the elevator, but cleared the further they went. "He said he didn't want me to see him like that and then passed out."

Tony started to convulse again, moan and fight against his brother's hold. They passed a few shut doors. As they came to a wide opening of the hall, Bailey glimpsed a big operations room beyond. Televisions on a wall, glass cabinets with Deadly Seven suits on mannequins. Tools. Benches. Two faces peeked out from the room, watching as Bailey rushed by with the men. One was Misha, another was a solemn woman in her fifties with her long dark hair in a braid.

"Is he okay?" Misha asked.

"Stay there, Misha," Wyatt ordered. "Don't you dare come out. In fact, Mama, take her upstairs. Neither of you can be here if he goes off."

Goes off?

Wyatt and Evan barged into a room filled with dim lights and medical equipment. They placed Tony down on a gurney in the center of the room, beneath operating theater lights. Evan switched on a lamp that illuminated Tony. He fought against the two men restraining him, but he was no match for their combined strength. While Evan held him down, Wyatt tore Tony's shirt down the middle as though it were made of paper.

Bailey gasped at what was beneath. Sparkling light pulsed as though on an electrical circuit, and the wires were his veins. Wyatt wheeled over a heart monitor and switched the machine on. He attached two electrodes to Tony's sweaty chest.

"Can you get Grace on the phone?" Wyatt asked.

"She's in surgery," Evan replied.

"Parker?"

"Work. Not answering."

"Shit. Fucking shit fuck." Wyatt cursed some more.

"What can I do?" Bailey stepped forward. "I've had triage field training with the CIA."

"So have we, the triage training, I mean." Evan looked at her, his dark brows joining in the middle. "I know you."

"Not the time, brother," Wyatt ground out.

But Evan wasn't to be deterred. He pointed at Bailey. "I've seen you before."

"I work at Nightingale."

"That's not it." Evan fumbled in his back pocket and pulled out his cell phone. He thumbed through pictures.

"What the fuck are you doing?" growled Wyatt.

"Trust me," Evan mumbled. "There."

He showed Wyatt a picture on his cell. Both men looked hard at it, and then at Bailey.

"What?" The walls began to close in around her. "Why are you looking at me like that?"

"But will it work?" Wyatt asked Evan. "How long ago was the dream? What else do you remember?"

"Um." Evan's eyes glazed as he appeared to remember. "She was sitting with him. Alone. I don't remember."

"For fuck'sake, Evan. I'm not leaving her with him on an *I don't remember*."

"She's his mate!" Evan pointed at Bailey. "Stranger things have happened."

There was that word again. *Mate*. She had the sense it meant much more than Max's Aussie comradely word for companion.

Tony thrashed about, sweating, in a feverish daze. A permanent frown flawed his handsome face. "No. Can't see me like this." He kept repeating the words, holding his breath, legs thrashing. The tendons in his neck and every sinew of ropy muscle bulged in sharp relief.

And then it all stopped. The sparking lights faded to a blue ghost beneath his skin.

Wyatt pushed Evan toward Bailey. "Take her out to a safe spot. I'll cover him in case it happens again. We don't have much time."

"No." Bailey dodged Evan's reach and went for Tony's hand. She picked it up in her own and squeezed. He was searing hot, but she refused to let go. "Tony. It's Bailey."

He moaned and shook his head, but his grip tightened. She wouldn't leave.

"I'm here," came a deep grumbling voice from behind her.

It was Parker, the eldest. Tall enough he had to crane his neck to fit through the door, and broad shouldered enough he had to angle sideways. The man was a mountain made of flesh. Straight nose, square jaw, long hair tied at his nape. If they lived a few centuries ago, he would have fit in well with the Vikings. He wiped his hands with anti-bac and calmly came to stand over Tony.

"Temperature?"

Wyatt and Evan shrugged.

A muscle in Parker's jaw twitched, and then he picked up an electric thermometer from an instrument tray on a side table. He held it to Tony's forehead until it beeped. "He's off the charts. This isn't good."

"Should we run an IV?" Evan asked.

"Grace didn't do that until after he released."

"Released what?" Bailey asked. One of these days, someone would start talking, come hell or high water.

Parker blinked at her, only just registering she was there. "What's she doing here?"

Both Evan and Wyatt answered in unison. "She's his mate."

Evan showed Parker the elusive picture on his cell phone. Parker gave her a grim look and then turned to his brothers. "Get us two chairs."

Within moments, both Parker and Bailey were seated beside Tony. Bailey still grasped his hot, sweaty hand, and he still gripped back. Parker leaned pensively toward Bailey, fingers laced, wrists on his knees.

"What has Tony told you?"

"Nothing!" she gasped. "But I guessed a damn lot. I figured out the rest once I got down here. You're all the Deadly Seven."

"And what has he told you about his power?"

Parker hadn't blinked at Bailey's revelation. He didn't seem to care that she knew their secret. "Nothing. He only said he didn't want me to see him like that. I know it's something to do with a glowing light, but he keeps hiding it from me."

Parker rubbed his stubble. "Grace said he's acting like a transplant patient rejecting the organ. He must suppress what comes naturally." He met Bailey's gaze. "He needs to accept what's happening to him. He needs for you to accept it."

"What do I have to do with this? I've barely learned of his power's existence!" She rubbed her temple with her free hand. This was all too much.

"Bailey," Parker said. "You're Tony's mate. Do you know what that means?"

She shook her head.

Parker signaled for Evan's cell. When he got it, he showed Bailey the picture. It was a drawing of Bailey sitting bedside with Tony. This very bed!

He saw her surprise and said, "You're his mate. It means that out of everyone in the world, you're the one his body recognized as the perfect antithesis of the sin he battles daily. You're his balance. The sin we sense is a constant feeling of wrongness in our stomach, but when any of us touch our mate, it goes away. The wrongness in us is reset."

Parker paused, letting Bailey soak that in for a while. She'd heard the rumor about their sin-sensing. Stories told of them hunting down the worst criminals, eerily knowing of their whereabouts in a way that was too accurate to be anything but supernatural. At first, she'd believed it to be an urban legend they let circulate to put the fear of God into criminals. *You can't hide, we'll find you.* Her mind latched onto the second thing he'd said. Mate. As in soulmate?

Her mind whirled. What was she supposed to do with that?

"You will help him," Parker decreed when Tony thrashed again.

"When you say jump, does everyone say how high?" She raised a brow.

Outrage flared in Parker's golden eyes. "If you don't accept being his mate, he could not only go nuclear right now, but it could happen anytime he's out of balance. On the street, on set, teaching a bunch of teens at a sobriety house. Only through regular contact with you, can he live a life without wondering if that next bite of food will send him over the edge, or if he drinks too much water and wakes up one morning in a pool of other people's blood, knowing he's the one who made the mess, all because someone didn't want to make the jump."

Bastard.

She bit her lip and looked at Tony lying helpless and in pain. "I didn't ask for this."

"None of us did, yet here we are. You joined the CIA because you wanted to be proactive, not reactive. I'm not saying you have to get married. I'm just saying, here's your chance to help, so you must."

"How?"

"He's trying to stifle his powers." Parker stood and folded his arms, looking down at his brother's prone form. "He's stubborn. Probably the best fighter out of all of us, but he doesn't believe in himself. He thinks he's better off pretending to be someone else. You need to convince him differently."

Parker dimmed the lamplight, and then gestured for his brothers to exit the room. They left her with a ticking time bomb. Who was her soulmate, or rather, she was his.

She swallowed the lump in her throat and stood to see his face better. "Tony? Can you hear me?"

He frowned and turned away.

"Don't you turn away from me, boy." She heard her grandmother's clipped tone coming out of her mouth and cringed, but she couldn't work with his stubbornness. "I'm here, so you can damn well get used to it."

When he didn't respond, she placed her palm on his slick, warm stomach and felt him breathe. In. Out. She did that for some time while her mind ran a million miles per hour. She wanted to help. It's all she'd ever wanted to do. It's what sent her into the agency. It's what kept her there for years on end, even when she felt herself slowly distancing herself from life.

With each passing minute, Tony grew more twitchy, more agitated, and she couldn't help hearing his last words to her. *I don't want you to see me like this.*

He was ashamed of who he was. Tears burned her eyelids. She sniffed. Everyone wanted a piece of Tony Lazarus, but he'd not even been on a real date. He'd never shared his true self with anyone, until her, until this morning. And she'd only just learned his truth. Maybe he didn't know who he wanted to be either. Wiping her eyes, she pushed his heavy body to one side of the gurney, and then climbed on next to him. The moment she laid down and entwined her body with his, he tensed, but she didn't stop. She slid her arm over his front, hooked her leg over his, pressed her lips onto his hot neck, right beneath his ear, and whispered, "I see you Tony Lazarus. I see the real you, and I'm not going anywhere."

He shuddered. His lashes fluttered, but didn't open.

"You make people laugh. You entertain them. You take time with your fans, and even with those who aren't. You make troubled teens feel better about themselves. You put yourself in danger to save—"

Tony's hand wrapped around her palm and gripped tight. He was still tense all over, muscles hard as a rock, but he turned to face her and opened his glazed, fevered eyes.

"You can't be here," he said, voice scratchy. "I can't control this thing inside of me."

"Yes, you can."

He shook his head.

"Parker was right. You're so damn stubborn." She leaned up to get a better view of his face. "You went to rehab, right?"

He nodded, confused.

"What's the first step of AA?"

She saw in his eyes when it dawned on him. "Acknowledge and accept," he answered.

"That's right. This is happening. This is *you*. And that's okay."

He squeezed his eyes shut. His lips flattened.

"Shh," she crooned and nuzzled into his neck. He was so hot, like lava, but she kept herself there. "It's okay. This is you, and this new power isn't going anywhere. Neither am I."

They held each other until bit by bit, his breathing grew steady, but the heat was still there. He still hadn't let go.

"You're going to have to release that blue fire, Tony," she whispered. "You have to accept it as part of you."

"I'll ruin you."

Her breath hitched at his words, and goosebumps erupted over her flesh. Those were the exact same words she'd used to stop drinking herself into oblivion, from falling off the cliff. Every time she'd had a rough day, she'd make her Cosmo and stare at it, telling the drink, *You won't ruin me.*

That's how he saw himself, as the thing that people were addicted to, the poison, the destruction. It was fucked up. And it was cruel. She exhaled slowly. This had been a long time coming, but she had some things of her own to accept too.

"I was ruined a long time ago, Tony, and I pulled myself back together. I made a life for myself, and now I'm here." She rolled on top of him, not caring if anyone watched through the viewing window. She only had eyes for the blue, sparkling seas of vulnerability staring back at her. There was only one way she knew to get him out of his own head. The last time she'd kissed, she'd been disgusted with her feelings for him and he'd seen it. She'd wiped her mouth. But he wasn't the man she'd thought. She'd been wrong to do that. Sliding her fingers into his damp hair, she tugged until the message was clear. This was important. Listen now.

"I've seen ruin, Tony, and you're not it."

She lowered her lips to his in a slow, passionate kiss. At first, he stilled, but when she refused to give up, he acquiesced. His tongue darted out, tasted her lower lip and then bit into the plump flesh. An anguished groan released from his throat, as though he held back the floodgates.

She whispered, "Let it go, Tony. Accept."

Kiss by kiss, his body softened beneath hers. His hands moved to her hips, bottom, thighs, and roamed. Light leaked from his veins, but she wasn't afraid. He was distracted, licking and tasting her mouth, pushing his tongue in with new demands. From the corner of her eyes, blue glittered over the dim room—beneath her, around her, above her—as though he was a living firework, or they were underwater. She couldn't decide. She was either about to combust in his heat, or drown in his sweet, salty scent that made her heady with desire. Tiny sparks of his power shot into her body, but it was more like the burn of embers than a maelstrom of flames. It pinched, tickled and sizzled with sensation.

"You're beautiful," she breathed, taking in his wonder. Horrifically beautiful were the actual words bouncing around in her head and she couldn't look away.

Drugged eyes latched onto hers and then shifted to take in the celestial room. Everywhere they turned, luminescent blue reflected and danced off the metallic medical instruments, the monitor, the glass widow. The sterilizing canisters. The shiny tiled floor. Chrome trims on faucets. He slid his gaze back to her. Whatever he saw in her eyes, it must have been enough. A slow, smug smile curved his sensuous lips, and then he flipped their bodies, as though she weighed a breath. He growled when he took in her yoga top, now riddled with holes. Poking a finger through one, he lifted her shirt and smoothed her hot skin. The bioluminescent lines of his body faded, but she didn't think he was repressing his power. It seemed spent.

"Hey." She pulled his head back to hers. "I think you did it. You let it go bit by bit. I'm fine."

His eyes glazed again, and he swayed.

"But you're not," she added.

A masculine clearing of a throat near the door.

Parker tried not to look at them but gestured at the IV stand. "Doc said he'll need his fluids replenished."

Bailey slid out from beneath Tony and helped him settle back down. When she pulled her hand from his front, he grabbed it and frowned. "Don't go."

She gave him a small smile. "Wasn't dreaming of it."

But while Parker busied himself around the room, preparing the IV drip, she couldn't help the niggling thoughts entering her mind. She'd somehow talked Tony off the ledge, basically kissed his pain away, but despite what she said about knowing him, she didn't. Only moments earlier he'd been flirting with another woman in front of the lobby. If they were meant to have some kind of soulmate connection, maybe it wasn't as solid as they'd led her to believe. Perhaps she wasn't as strong as she thought. Perhaps she could be ruined again, because Tony was fast becoming the addiction she worked so hard to control. What had she gotten herself into?

JULIUS ALLCOTT

"SO YOU SEE," said the Dutch geneticist Levi Van Jansen to Julius Allcott. "The new replicates are proceeding as planned."

Van Jansen was a man in his late fifties. He had experience in the industry and was without scruples. After the betrayal of Pinkerton, and the disaster with his lab partner, Julius had head-hunted Van Jansen. He'd scoured the world's top journals, awards and research projects, and then found the man who'd been too forward thinking for society to appreciate. He'd found the man who'd had his funding stripped and been vilified in the media. He'd found Van Jansen. The stodgy man with white hair had fluff growing out of his ears. He had dirt under his nails and saggy eyelids, but he was a creative genius. Julius should have hired him long ago. He'd done in months what Pinkerton had failed to do in years.

Finally, there was hope.

Van Jansen tapped on the tank of a young man floating within the viscous amniotic fluid and squinted at the replicate body. It had taken eighteen months to grow this sixteen-year-old body. His shoulders were broadening, his body developing into pure muscle and strength. At his current growth rate, he'd be fully grown in less than six months.

Julius strode along the vast collection of seventy-five glass tanks. Half contained the pubescent bodies of replicates, waiting to be born; the other half contained varying prepubescent and youthful bodies, still in early stages of growth. They would belong to the second wave of attack on the sinners of the world.

It had been almost eighteen months since Envy had destroyed the initial replicate lab and eliminated all functioning clones. At first, Julius had been furious, outraged, but eventually saw that they had done him a favor. The first round of clones were imperfect, only living a few months before expiring. None were powered with special abilities, not like these. Not since they'd gathered the unlocked DNA samples from half the Lazarus family. But Julius aimed for more. He wanted eternal. He wanted life everlasting with his family.

"It is imperative these new replicates are born without flaw," he stated.

"I am confident that with the new DNA samples we've gathered from the original test subjects, we can reach perfection. We are almost there."

"How many more unlocked samples do you need?"

"We've already isolated the genome sequence that unlocked their powers. Any more samples will just give us new paths to new abilities. What we need is to solve the expiration problem."

"And how do you propose to do that?"

"I have been looking over the notes of my predecessors and believe there has been something they've been keeping from you."

"This is?"

"Stem cells."

Julius glanced over at the door to the warehouse where two soldiers guarded the entrance. He wanted no one else within earshot.

If Van Jansen was correct, this would be valuable information to his enemies, and to the rest of the Syndicate. When he was satisfied no one listened, he turned back to Van Jansen.

"Please explain."

"Your first creator, the woman who made the Deadly Seven."

"Gloria."

"Yes, Gloria. She was the surrogate for each child born, was she not?"

"Correct."

"So she had full control over the biological samples of all projects?"

"Yes."

"Were there any failed experiments prior to Despair?"

"There were a few. Maybe two."

"And these were born of her own body as well, ja?"

Julius nodded. "What are you getting at?"

Van Jansen clicked his tongue. "This is the key. The stem cells she collected from the waste of her own failed experiments."

"But the children she bore weren't clones."

"Yes, I know this. But the problem we're having with the replicates after birth is that their cells continue to produce. This is a similar process to how this Deadly Seven family can heal and regenerate their damaged skin and yet stop once the job is done. You understand where I am leading, ja?"

Julius pulled out the locket contained on a chain around his neck. Inside held biological matter from his departed wife and daughter. Both had perished decades ago in an accident caused by corporate negligence... *sloth*. This was all for them. The ending of sinners in the world, the razing of the old civilization to start anew, the creation of perfect life. All so he could see their faces, hear their voices, touch their skin, and give them a world where it wouldn't happen again.

Unable to help himself, he opened the locket, just to check. There, inside, were two strands of hair. One thick wiry afro that belonged to his wife, and the softer, smaller black silken length. There was only one strand for each one chance. This had to be perfect.

Boots squelched behind him. He snapped the locket shut.

Turning, he found Despair striding toward him, her white leather uniform splatted in mud and reeking of sewage. The guards by the door barely contained their grimaces, despite her now being only feet beyond their entrance. Her silver-white hair hung around her shoulders, leaves and bits of bio-matter lodged in its dirty, stringy lengths.

Julius waved Van Jansen away. When the scientist had left, Julius turned to the woman.

"Is it done?" he asked.

Thunder clouds flittered over her expression. "No. It is not done."

His lip twitched. "My darling, do I sense a note of sarcasm?"

She took a breath, folded her arms with the creak of wet leather, and stared at the tanks. This was the most emotion he'd seen in his progeny for some time. The sarcasm, the pink stain to her pale cheeks, the brightness in her eyes. Perhaps her sin wasn't taking hold of her as he'd come to accept. He rubbed his throat. Although, her recent attacks on him begged to differ. She'd been blacking out too much lately because of her sin. She was of no use to him like this and it was too early in his plan to set her loose on the city's despondent. Perhaps she'd last until they gathered biological samples from the rest of the originals, but this change in dependability was not placating. She'd become erratic in behavior since exposure to her siblings. This was yet another of her tasks she'd failed to complete.

"I can't capture the creature alone," she revealed. "It has evolved beyond anything we'd imagined. Bosch's body was completely absorbed. He is gone, somehow part of the creature now walking around on two legs and hissing like a living thing."

"Curious."

"I hold no burning desire to pull it out and study it. It seems to be content in the sewer. Perhaps we should leave it be."

Julius took one look at the defeat in his bird of prey's eyes and knew she was becoming soft, ineffective. He needed her cold, without scruples, holding no mercy, not—his mouth twisted in distaste—full of empathy for a plant. Cold spread throughout him. First, she released the plant. Now she wanted to leave it be?

"We can't have that, as you well know. It is one thing to have the Lazarus family onto us, but they have limited resources and we have their identities. This Cold War of ours is serving us well. If this creature is left to its own devices, you invite the attention of the local law enforcement, and worse, the FBI, CIA or Homeland." *Not when we're so close.*

"But you have investors all the way to the White House. In the military, and beyond. Why do we have to keep hiding so much?"

"My darling," he said, voice placating. "Our benefactors are not omniscient. We have come too far and gone on for too long to have our plans derailed by law enforcement, or the public. There is much to be said for mob mentality. I shouldn't have to remind you of that. Take some Faithful with you next time. Get help."

Her jaw clenched. "The Faithful are pitiless vile sheep who know nothing about battle."

"At the very least, they would make a good shield. We have plenty of tanks free for their rebirths. Fresh blood for our cause is always needed."

Cold violet eyes locked onto his. "And what of me? What will you do if I am the shield and I do not come back?" She flicked her gaze to the locket around his neck, seeming to see it right through to the strands of hair within. "Will you bring me back as *fresh blood* for your cause?"

Unbidden, his hand went to the locket and squeezed. It was a tiny cold thing in his palm. In it, there was no room for the battered hope he saw in her eyes. Anguish wrapped around his heart because he knew if this didn't work, if he failed at bringing his family back, then what was the point to creating the world without sin? What was the point in making utopia if he couldn't share it with them? He'd rather raze it all to the ground than fill it with anything else. Everything he'd ever done was for the two strands of hair he'd kept safe and close to his heart.

There was no room for more.

Despair's eyes watered as she took Julius in. "You keep saying you're my father, but you're not, are you? You're not even family. You are a sperm donor, and that's it."

Anger rose swiftly in him to color his vision red. "I saved you from that burning building. I—"

"Came back for me when they didn't. Yes, I know. The story is getting old."

Flummoxed, he shook with fury. How dare she? "I gave you everything you needed."

"To be a monster. To kill indiscriminately for you." She sneered at him. "You keep me separate from the rest of your family. You don't want me." She choked up, waiting for him to prove her wrong, but he couldn't. It was true.

She was a dark thing he'd created to help him achieve his goals. She was the evil he wanted rid of in the world. She was the last thing he would consider family.

He gave her a dismissive wave. "Do as you're told. Then you can get back to the business of collecting unlocked blood samples from your brothers and sister."

The light faded from her eyes, her expression went lax, and then a perfect calm stole over her storm. The hairs on Julius's neck stood on end, and he'd barely a chance to shout at the guards before she was upon him, choking the life out of him, with only one directive firing in her eyes—*kill*. End the sin.

He should have known better than to allow himself to despair around her, but with the end so close, with fruition in sight, he was blind to how close she'd been to the edge of oblivion. His rapidly increasing emotion must have set her off.

Two thwacks ripped through the air in rapid succession. Tranquilizer darts pierced the leather between her shoulder blades, and within moments her eyes rolled to the back of her head and she collapsed, releasing his throat.

"Get Van Jansen back in here," he rasped at one guard. To the other, "Once the scientist has looked at her, put her to bed. She won't remember the attack."

Van Jansen came bustling through in the wake of the first guard. He came, pursed his lips and widened his eyes at the fallen angel at their feet.

"How many times has her switch flipped?" he asked Julius.

Julius rubbed his tender throat, only just healed from her previous attack five days prior. "Too many to count. We are losing her to despair. Her usefulness is fast reaching its expiration date. Since her siblings are all coming into their powers, I was hoping she would soon be too. But she is the eldest."

"Mm," Van Jansen replied. "Thirty-five, ja?"

"Something like that."

"If she hasn't triggered by now, it is unlikely she will."

"Soon she will be of no use to us. Our only choices will be to let her loose on the population, or extermination."

"Untrue. She is still of childbearing age. There are always her stem cells."

"Yes. There is always that."

sixteen

TONY LAZARUS

TONY WAS STUFFING his face with his third jam-smeared croissant when Bailey woke and joined him in the kitchen of his apartment. It was six a.m. and his rumbling stomach had woken him with a ravenous appetite. The intravenous fluids he'd had the previous night had done nothing to sate his hunger.

Still, once on the lips, forever on the hips. He grimaced at his last bite and put it back down. If his trainer knew he'd indulged with buttered pastries, he'd make him do a million burpees.

Bailey padded up to the bench with dark hair tousled, puffy lips and bedroom eyes. It was a shame she still wore her hole-riddled yoga attire and they'd done nothing but sleep by each other's side. God, she looked incredible in the morning. The more he learned about her, the more he wanted her. It took all his restraint to keep his hands calmly resting on his porcelain plate, and his heart steady in his chest.

She still had a long way to go before she accepted and trusted him. Perhaps further until she was ready to be with him wholly. There was always a sense of restraint with her. Even when she'd slept next to him, she'd used a pillow to separate them. But he wouldn't be deterred. Not for long.

He aimed his remote at the flat screen on the wall beyond the kitchen counter and turned it off. Nothing much interesting except the city's plumbing problems near the Quadrant Central Park.

"Morning, babe."

"Hungry?" she joked, eyeing off the empty packets of croissants.

"Always," he replied without taking his eyes from her.

He hadn't thought his response offended. Maybe there was a slight lewd overtone, but she would have heard worse. Whatever the case, she'd taken it strangely. A nervous flitter ghosted across her expression, and when she spoke, her reaction became clear.

"And this is the sort of thing having a mate can help with? I mean, you're free to—" she cut off as her shrewd gaze took in the empty plate.

He waved at his crumbs of devastation. "Gluttonize is the word I use. I'm free to gluttonize. Say it with me, Glutt-on-ize."

"Very funny."

"Not funny, fun. But yes. I can eat without reprimand, of course, apart from watching my weight. I'm all about these abs." He patted his naked torso and enjoyed the simmering flash of lust in her gaze. Yep. Not broken, and definitely still *on*. "Basically, touching you makes the sick feeling I get from being near other people imbibing go away. You reset my internal levels so I can eat my fill. As long as you're around, I don't need to freak every time I guzzle a drink or have a feast."

At the word *feast*, his gaze ran down her body. He'd only had a small taste last night, and he had been delirious with fever. He'd savored nothing. When he'd woken this morning, she slept so soundly he didn't have the heart to disturb her. But now, it was all he could think about.

He slid a plate with the last remaining croissant her way.

She shook her head.

"Coffee?" He pointed at the percolator.

Say no. Tell me to take you to bed.

"I have my protein shakes at home. I should be going. I have work today and shouldn't you be preparing for this press thing you have?"

He couldn't help the sag of his shoulders. "It's fine. I'll just turn up and smile and all will be forgiven."

He winced. That was a stupid thing to say. Now she was going to think he was entitled.

"I wish we all had that luxury," she said.

"What do you mean? Something wrong at Nightingale?"

"Forget it." Her eyebrows flicked up, and she shuffled awkwardly. "So, I guess I'll see you."

"Wait." He hopped up from the stool. "You're leaving?"

She ruffled her hair in an attempt to style it. "Yes."

"But... don't you want to talk about it—us?"

For a long hard minute, she looked at him carefully. He thought she would turn tail and run, but she folded her arms, cocked her hip and gave him pursed lips. Immediately, Tony went hot and flush all over.

Being one of the "beautiful people," he got used to things. He would smile, people would stutter and stumble over themselves to get to him or acquiesce. He would walk in a room, and people stopped breathing. But this proud, independent woman gave him an unprecedented thrill every time she looked at him with those spirited eyes, those I'll-talk-about-it-when-I'm-good-and-ready eyes. This was his woman. She would keep him satisfied, thrilled, for days, weeks, months. An eternity. He just had to convince her to stay.

"I need you," he said, eyes lazily drifting down to her lips. The unmistakable lift of her brows brought a deeper smile to his face. "I need you to be my bodyguard at the junket," he continued, enjoying the way he made her squirm.

"Gluttony doesn't need a bodyguard."

"But Tony Lazarus does."

"I guess that's Max's prerogative. I've not heard from him yet, and since I'm hole-ridden, I need to get home, showered and dressed. There may be other jobs for me."

Right on cue, her cell phone rang, and she fixed him with a curious look before answering, knowing full well who would be on the other end of the line. "Yes?" she said into her handset, still glaring at Tony. "Yes, boss. I understand. I'll take him to the press junket. Bye."

When she cut the call, a grin split Tony's face. "There's no way you're the embodiment of temperance. I don't know what my biology was thinking, picking you."

"What's that supposed to mean?"

His voice lowered seductively, and he closed the gap between them. "It means that I love your fire. I love your attitude. It makes me hard when I think of you." He lifted his fingers to trail down her chin, watching as she responded to his touch. "I can't stop thinking about the way you tasted last night. I need more."

"Careful," she warned breathily. "Too much of a good thing can be bad."

"I don't have to worry about that now. Not with you." He leaned in and rubbed his nose along her cheek. Feminine musk hit his system and his lashes fluttered. A low rumble cleared his throat as desire began to build.

"I still need to go home," she whispered.

"I can go with you. Or you can shower here."

"No!" she responded, a little too fast and too loud. She pressed her palms to his chest. She looked down at his half naked body and immediately lifted her gaze back to his. "I mean, I need a moment to myself, Tony. This is all a bit much. You understand, right?"

He blinked. Shut down like that.

A bit much.

"Sure. Whatever." He collected the empty croissant packet and put it in the trash. If she needed space, then, whatever. Who was he to press? She had her own mind, and he wasn't the type to wait around and mope.

"Tony, don't be like that."

"Like what?" Like the asshole she always thought he was?

He stopped at the trash can, closed his eyes and counted to three. He wasn't an asshole. He hated them.

"Right, well, just stay here until I come to get you. We're still not much closer to identifying your stalker. And come to think of it, now that I know your secret, maybe the stalker does too. Why else would the words 'I know' be written over your things?"

"Because they're imbeciles." He came back to the bench and continued to clear.

"She. Because *she* is an imbecile. The CCTV footage from the studio showed a blurry female. You didn't read your emails, did you?"

He waved her off, pretending not to care and to be enthralled with doing his dishes. Those croissants weren't sitting well in his gut. If she didn't want company, then he'd go down and use the gym. Perhaps finally try on the new Deadly Suit and make Parker happy. The two of them used to be close, but then he'd turned into a prideful prick, and Tony had become busy with his work. He missed the days they used to base jump from the tallest city skyscrapers.

"You know," she started, voice tight and getting louder. "You can't keep pretending to be this person you're not. I want to get to know the real Tony I met yesterday. If he decides to show up again, let him know I called."

Bailey left in silence.

Damn it.

His energy waned, so he took a seat on his balcony, dropped his head into his hands and listened to the sounds of the city. Traffic, horns blaring, a dog barking, a siren in the distance. Sour trash and something acrid like new bitumen floated up in a breeze. He looked down at his palms and called on his power, testing it. Hot blue light rose in his veins, lacing over his hand in a network of strength, or of potential devastation. This fire inside him was unavoidable. Pushing it down had done no one good, but despite knowing this, he still didn't feel any closer to being at peace with himself.

I want to get to know the real Tony I met yesterday.

At the sobriety house? When he exploded like a blue sun? The pretty playboy actor?

He only had one chance to make her like him, and so far, she'd not fallen for his old act. He had to admit; the act was getting tiresome. At the sobriety house, he'd felt no pressure. Hanging out with Akeef, talking music, helping the kid realize his potential. It was... fulfilling. And then Elena. The look of accomplishment on her face when she'd learned to defend herself. Those moments felt real.

He scrubbed his face, confused, conflicted, and a little afraid. The only surety in his life right then was the constant need to be with the woman who'd calmed his soul, even if she didn't feel the same way. And if she never did, that was going to hurt. Wanting something he knew would make him hurt, but wanting it anyway was just another addiction, wasn't it?

There was only one thing to do. Make it feel good. Make it easy. Make Bailey want him, and hope that she liked the real Tony. The man beneath the act.

seventeen

BAILEY HAZE

FRUSTRATED, Bailey vigorously scrubbed shampoo through her hair. Goddamn, that man. Since she'd come home to get some space, her mind had been crowded with thoughts of Tony Lazarus. Tony without a shirt on. Tony with his wicked smile. Tony offering to make her coffee. Tony with a sad face when she told him she needed some space. *Sure. Whatever.*

She grimaced at the tiled wall of her shower. He had no right to make her feel bad about needing a moment to herself. After everything they went through the previous day, after all the secrets revealed, she needed to gather her thoughts. And he still held her at arm's length. He needed to work out whether he could be authentic with her. What was the point in holding back anymore?

"Don't whatever me," she mumbled, irritated. But when she dunked her head beneath the stream and closed her eyes, she saw Tony's sexy face as he came in to rub his nose along her cheek. She felt the tingle spear down to her stomach.

I love your fire. I love your attitude. It makes me hard when I think of you.

Why were his words so wickedly charming?

I need more.

Maybe she did too. She shut off the faucet and paused, listening. Had she heard a sound? Tony?

Her heartbeat quickened. Getting out of the shower, she nabbed a towel and wrapped her body, and then used another to cover her hair. Holding her breath, she opened the bathroom door and rushed out into the kitchen. Was he here?

There was no one there but an empty home, and no other sound but the beating of her thundering heart. Her recently poured Cosmo sat untouched on the counter, and the television was off. There was no one in the fridge, rummaging through her salad ingredients, no one eating croissants. A sharp twang of disappointment sliced through her and she shook her head. It was stupid. She was being stupid. With a deep breath, she forced herself to slow down and finish getting ready for the day. She needed this time alone. Right?

BAILEY WATCHED the sea of press part to make way for Tony Lazarus as he walked through the simple banquet room in the Ritz Hotel. His waiting cast members occupied a long bench at the top of a makeshift stage. He was a gravitational force that dragged every bit of attention his way.

And he seemed to love it. A grin here, a wink there. He even mentioned one of the paparazzi by name. If you didn't know him better, you'd have missed the twitch of tension in his casual posture. Despite his easy smile for the crowd, Bailey sensed the man would pounce like a wild cat, attack his prey and grin salaciously as he devoured his meal. She was coming to see that he wasn't a man, but a wild, beautiful thing contained in skin. Some kind of inferno made flesh.

Then again, maybe she imagined all these things because she now knew what he was capable of. He could level the entire room if he lost control of his power. *Go nuclear* was Parker's exact term.

Everything had happened so quickly yesterday. She'd gone from wanting to date Tony, to being slapped in the face by his devastating secret, to learning how integral she was to his wellbeing. Not just integral, but intrinsic, biological... inescapable.

And Bailey Haze decided long ago never to be pushed into a decision she wasn't ready to make. Peer pressure had a lot to answer for, and it had taken a beat-up car, and a dead drunk friend to realize that. It took her years of scraping her life back together to become one of the top students in her school to know that she made her own choices.

The problem was, the moment she'd finished getting dressed that morning, she'd found herself rushing to pick up Tony. Not because of her job, but because the emptiness of her home had been too loud, and the memory of his presence had been magnetic, drawing her back to him with inescapable power.

Looking at the rest of the room, she wasn't the only one who felt this way around him. The charismatic lady's man and everyone's friend was dressed in a sports coat rolled up at the forearms. The baseball cap he'd worn in the car to hide his identity must have been stowed in his back pocket. When he climbed the stage, the bulge at his left ass confirmed her suspicion. And it was a fine ass indeed. One she felt perfectly wicked perving from behind the safety of her mirrored Aviators. Oh wait. She was indoors and wasn't wearing any.

She snapped her gaze to the tall brunette assistant who called for attention at the stage and proceeded to filter questions to the cast. Bailey recognized her as the woman Tony spoke with outside Hell last night. Being here, she must be more than a mere set assistant. She might have more access to places around set than Bailey thought.

She could be a potential suspect.

Except, the suspect on the CCTV footage could be anyone. She'd had dark hair, but that didn't mean it was the set assistant. The studio had wigs by the truckload in the wardrobe department. Anyone could have pilfered one and used it as they broke into Tony's trailer to set up the dolls. All this left Bailey no closer than she was the first day she'd started. If it were up to her, she'd have interviewed the entire cast and staff.

But it wasn't up to her, and Max had already reminded her this morning to stick to her job. No investigating. No drawing attention. Leave it to the normal police. And since the studio didn't want them involved, frustratingly, she was left guarding Tony's body, which was ridiculous in itself. He didn't need guarding, and she was a trained CIA operative. She could do more.

Her mind wandered back to which of Tony's peers or acquaintances could be stalking him. There was only one other female she'd noticed; the buxom redheaded costar sitting next to him, Maggie O. More than once she leaned in close to Tony, brushed her bulging chest on his arm, and then whispered into his ear. Every time, Tony tried to avoid her touch by moving to pick up his water bottle, but then she did the same.

Then Bailey looked harder and noticed more. Tony's flinching was in direct correlation to when someone took a guzzle of water, or when the snack cart came out and people dove in. A surge of empathy shot through her. That man would never be able to feel normal around people doing anything in excess.

Unless you help him.

He glanced over at her, and their eyes met. She smiled tentatively. He didn't smile back, but she saw the relief in his posture. His shoulders lowered. His eyes turned soft. Then he went back to answering questions.

After a while, all the questions blended into white noise until Bailey's ears pricked up when someone said, "Tony, is there someone special in your life?"

Her armpits prickled and her heartbeat accelerated. They'd not had a chance to discuss where they stood. She wasn't ready for this.

Tony's lips hovered near his microphone. "Yes."

"Is she here?" A woman with a bow in her hair asked.

He paused, looked a little uncomfortable, then his lips stretched into a winning smile. His spine straightened. "How about I tell you about this great group of kids I've been helping at a sobriety house?"

"Tell us more about your lady!"

"What do you mean by special?"

"Why has it taken you so long to date?"

A barrage of responding quick-fire questions came at him from multiple sources, but he refused to comment further, or give Bailey away by looking in her direction. His jaw clenched and she could tell he was pissed off at the direction of topic. Her heart went out to him. The people only wanted one side of Tony Lazarus, and it wasn't the philanthropic man.

Something eased in Bailey's chest. He could have singled her out, pointed the cameras in her face, but he'd not hesitated to hold that secret close to his heart. It would get out eventually, but for now, Tony had demonstrated he wasn't just thinking of himself. The man respected her privacy. And he'd tried to use his celebrity to promote the Hudson House. She watched him with a new light feeling floating through her body, and this time, she didn't try to block the emotion rising, she accepted it. She enjoyed it.

IT WAS close to five p.m. when Bailey was finally able to get Tony to herself. After the group Q and A, he'd spent another few hours being interviewed one-on-one by a succession of entertainment journalists. Like a piece of meat, he'd been paraded before them, asked stupid questions repeatedly, and then stood up and did it again with the next journalist.

The man never sighed or rolled his eyes. He smiled, nodded and politely answered questions.

When it was all done, and Tony was eying the food cart with longing, she went up to him and touched his wrist gently. He'd mentioned that morning that the action would reset some sort of internal sin gauge in his body. She could help his discomfort. It was hard enough to sit through this thing for hours without sustenance, but wondering how many bites it would take to affect his sin was a burden he didn't need.

"You done?" she asked.

"I am. Shall we go?"

"You don't want to nab a bite first?" She'd had a few herself.

"I'd rather take you out to dinner," he said, voice low and conspiratorial. "Or we can eat at my place. I can call Heaven and have something sent up."

"I'd like that. Dinner, I mean."

He mustn't have expected her to agree, because his head snapped up, his eyes locked onto hers and he blinked. "Okay, then. Let's go."

"Car's out the front." She ushered him out of the room and took him down to the lobby. A tingle of anticipation traveled up her spine.

I'm going to have dinner with him.

Hiding her smile, she slipped her sunglasses on to help her eyes adjust to the glare of the sunset shining through the foyer windows. When they stepped outside and onto the driveway, Bailey's instincts went on high alert. There were too many people. The paparazzi hadn't left and there seemed to be more than the usual hotel patrons and staff milling about. General public. She couldn't get eyes on her car.

Anything could happen in a crowd like this.

She nabbed a valet walking past. "I called for my car, but I can't see it. It's a Ford Explorer."

"Sorry ma'am. There's been a hold up. If you wait over there, I'm sure it won't take long."

Over there was a growing line of put out looking businessmen and posh women in pantsuits.

Bailey took Tony's elbow. "I don't like this crowd. Let's find another way out."

But it was too late. A shout from the paparazzi alerted everyone to Tony's arrival, and every camera, flash and person was turned their way.

Lights popped in their face, and voices bombarded them with questions.

"Tony, care to comment on the rumor that your agent is going to dump you?"

Tony stiffened beneath Bailey's touch. The journalist must have hit a nerve.

She whispered in his ear, "I can shoot them if you like. Got my Taser and my firearm."

He smirked then shook his head, dipping close to say, "Thanks for the offer, but it's cool. Best to not engage with the animals."

"Tony, is that your bodyguard?" a short man wearing a brown suit asked.

"Why do you need a bodyguard?" someone else chimed in.

Bailey frowned, at first rejecting the notion they'd somehow learned of her role, but then realizing it was obvious. She wore black slacks, a Nightingale Securities bomber jacket, and had her long dark hair tied back at her nape in a ponytail slicked down to stop the stray curls. With her Aviators and don't-fuck-with-me face, it was pretty clear she was his bodyguard.

True to his advice, Tony didn't answer the journalists. He ignored them until a man shouted, "Or is she your date?"

Bailey winced as more bulbs flashed and more voices shouted at Tony. The mob of attention closed in, literally getting so close they were inches from Tony. They had to get out of there.

"Is she the special one in your life?"

"Have you finally taken the leap?"

"Who is she?"

"Tony!"

"Tony!"

A flash of red pushed into the group, and Maggie O came between Bailey and Tony. She broke the hold Bailey had on his elbow and latched onto his arm, pouting at the cameras with pillowy lips. Shoved behind, Bailey was left out of the circle wondering what the hell had happened.

"It's me, isn't it darling?" Maggie cuddled into his side. "I'm the special someone."

Tony's brows winged up and he looked over his shoulder to Bailey, stunned.

"We didn't want to say anything in there to overshadow the film, did we, honey?" Maggie addressed the paparazzi. "But since you're all here, you may as well know. We're together, and I for one think it's nobody's business what his agent is or isn't doing."

"No." Tony shook his head, aghast.

"No what?" The man in the brown suit asked. "No to the question about the agent?"

"No to Maggie."

But Maggie didn't hear him, nor seem to care. "Yes we are. After working so closely for months, I *know you* Tony."

Oh no, she didn't. *Nasty bitch.*

Heat flared up Bailey's neck to cloud her mind. She ground her teeth. Maggie wasn't the one. Bailey was. She pushed between them, took hold of Tony's jaw between her finger and thumb, and smashed her lips onto his in a swoon-worthy close-mouthed kiss. The shock move sent Maggie careening to the side, and a chorus of gasps and flashes exploding into the atmosphere. But it wasn't until Tony placed one palm behind her head, one on her lower back and tipped her, that the energy became effervescent. It bubbled up and spilled over. Chaos erupted around them, but it all seemed to fade away under the scent of Tony's soft lips, his musk and familiarity.

She heard nothing but her heartbeat pounding in her ears, could see nothing but the way he adored her. And then her Aviators fell off and reality hit.

They had to get out of there.

She took his hand, and yanked him away, rushing down the driveway and out of the hotel complex. Pursued, but together and in agreement, they jogged along the sidewalk. The paparazzi were hard to shake, and damn, they could run fast with those big cameras.

"Where are we going?" Tony flashed his teeth, clearly having the time of his life.

"We're giving them the slip. There. The night markets have opened." She pointed down the sidewalk to the end of the street. Beyond the city buildings was the entrance to the Quadrant Central Park where people filed through an enormous wrought iron arched gate covered in ivy. Cyprus trees loomed on either side, gilt leaves coming alive in the dying sun. The dense park and market stalls beyond were the perfect place to get lost.

Darting in and out of the crowd, they continued into the markets. The smell of cooked pretzels and garlic filled the air. Immediately inside the park, lined on either side of the double width walkway were food trucks, street vendors, and amusement games. Parents with children and prams, businesspeople finished work for the day and the public idled along, enjoying the last street festival of the season before the weather cooled down too much.

It didn't take much to duck and weave into the crowd, losing themselves in the activity.

Bailey checked over her shoulder and saw a group of unapologetic photographers chasing them, heads swiveling to see where they'd gone. She pulled Tony close to her, behind a stand of sunglasses, then handed him a random pair before putting on her own and hiding behind the turnstile. The makeshift stall was a repurposed open caravan with an annex for wares. The next stall was another caravan selling Jamaican jerk chicken, its mouthwatering aroma of spices invading the space.

Laughter and chatter filled the air. While she kept her attention on the crowd, Tony perused the sunglass selection with avid fascination.

"You know," he joked, pointing a pair of Rayban knockoffs at her. "If this were a movie, we'd be in the montage."

"How can you joke at a time like this?"

"What, this? This is nothing. *This* is a collection of misguided photographers trying to make a living." He pulled out a pair of gold John Lennon glasses. "Now these are more your style."

She put them back on the rack and then added the ones from their faces. "We're not really here to buy sunglasses. We just need to look different."

She removed her bomber jacket and tucked it behind the caravan. She'd pick that up later if they had a chance. She then made the gimme sign to Tony.

He watched her, eyes sparkling with some kind of mischievous thought. Slowly, he peeled his jacket from his sculptured shoulders, and slung it around hers, enveloping her in the warmth he'd left behind. He retrieved his baseball cap from his back pocket and slung it on his head, turning the peak to the back. It made his face even more devastatingly handsome. With a growing grin, he dug his fingers into her hair and gently tugged on the tie that secured her ponytail. Never breaking his intense eye contact, he slid the tie down the silken length until her hair cascaded around her shoulders. She watched the amused light in his eyes heat as he took in a breath of her scented shampoo. And when he touched his nose to her head and inhaled again, he hummed deliciously. The velvet smooth timber of his voice penetrated deep within her body, hitting hotly between her thighs.

God, he was...

He made her speechless.

And when he looked at her like that, her heart pounded.

Satisfied with his handiwork, he cast an appreciative eye over her transformation and gave her hair a final fluff.

"That's better." Then he crowded her with his big body and pushed her toward the shadowed gap between the two caravan stalls. Against the side, he pinned her with his hips, driving her into the corrugated metal wall. She gripped his broad shoulders for balance. His hands slid up her waist, grazed over her breasts and continued up to her collarbone where he pressed her in place while he said, "We'll just have to stay here until they're gone. I'm sure we can think of something to do."

Dipping, he placed his lips on her neck. Nerves combusted. Shivers ran down her body. Sparks of pleasure zipped up her spine, and all from the simple press of his mouth against her skin. She was usually more reserved than this, but her body arched into him, her breath hitched. The swell of her breasts pushed into his chest, and a long strangled growl came from his throat.

"When I get you alone," he promised against her skin.

A lick up the tendon in her neck, a nip on her jaw, a nibble on her earlobe. He would feast on her, and she would like it.

Later.

Right now, they were in public, and over his shoulder she could see the disapproving stares of a woman with her teenage daughter.

"Tony—"

He swallowed her protest with a hot demanding kiss that left her breathless.

"We can't," she tried again, but he lifted her by the waist and directed her thighs until her legs gripped his hips. Then he shifted them around to the back of the caravan where the shadows of the trees provided cover. Rocking his pelvis into her, she lost all sense. She drove her tongue into his mouth and succumbed. He shifted her weight and twisted, stumbling the two of them away from the van, and into the shrubbery behind. Bailey caught a glimpse of rows of bushes, maybe hedges. Tony found a gap and, still kissing, they stumbled through.

Somewhere.

She had no idea where, except the sounds of the market dimmed and the chirp of crickets grew louder. Then Tony tripped. They fell to the grass and rolled, laughing. Ending up with Tony's hard body on top, he braced himself on elbows beside her head. His hat had fallen, and his hair draped over his eyes. Looking down at her with bright eyes, he gave her a quick kiss and then lifted his head, searching around.

"I have no idea where we are," he whispered with exaggerated drama.

It was some sort of grassed clearing, or rather a lack of trees and shrub. The park was huge. If Bailey remembered correctly, the lake wasn't too far off.

"Nowhere," she said. "We're nowhere important."

Blue light sparked in his eyes, giving her a glimpse of his power. He dove to her neck and grumbled against her skin, "Perfect."

She shivered and delighted in the feel of his five o'clock stubble rubbing against her skin. *I can't believe I'm giving in to this feeling.*

It felt good.

Leaves rustled to their right.

Abruptly, they stopped. Both froze, high on alert.

"Did you hear that?" Bailey hissed, alarm needling her skin.

"Shh." He cocked his head, listening to the park, or... perhaps his sixth sense.

She only heard the crickets, a rustling of leaves, and a masculine repetitive grunt.

For a moment, they looked at each other, wide-eyed and about to laugh. Was it another pair of lovers hiding away? But then there was a strangled cry and a feminine shout of frustration. A thud as though something was hit. A hiss. A slither. There were more than two people, and... a *thwack* and *crack*.

Tony leaped off Bailey's body. "I sense gluttony."

She darted a glance toward the market. "Back there?"

He shot her a grim look and pointed further into the bushland. "It's deadly. You should go."

Gritting her teeth, she shook her head, and when a white-robed person in a white Halloween mask burst through the bushes, she unclipped her firearm. What the hell?

Tony cursed. "Faithful."

TONY LAZARUS

TONY PULLED the Faithful by the scruff of his robe. "What are you doing here?"

But the masked man only shook his head. Panicked black eyes flashed at Tony through the simple mask slits. "It's-oh-my-god-it's..."

The man kept pointing behind him, to the crashing sounds behind the shrubs. Suddenly he looked down at himself. Thin dark ropes came from nowhere to slip around the white robe, gathering its folds and tightening.

Jesus. What was that?

"No!" shouted the Faithful. "Get it off me."

"The rope? It's moving. Is this some kind of trick?"

"It's not rope, it's—" The man was sucked back into the bush, leaving Tony with his hands splayed in front of him, grasping air.

"What the fuck was that?" he burst out.

Heaving breaths made him turn around. Bailey's big eyes were like orbs, her face had a greenish hue. She gripped her gun with pale knuckles. She still stared at the spot the Faithful had vacated.

"It wasn't rope," she said, voice trembling. "It was a vine. A living, moving vine. I'm sure of it."

"No. That's not possible." But as the words slipped out, he knew he was wrong. With the presence of the Faithful, the Syndicate weren't far behind. Only a few short months ago Tony had come across some wild, deformed and rabid beasts in the wilderness— results of an experiment to hunt down sinners. A moving plant? He wouldn't put it past them.

"Shit." He pulled out his cell. Who would he call? Parker with his judgement? Griffin or Evan... Wyatt. It would have to be someone powered. Sloan... but who would be best to handle a plant?

All of them?

Damn it. He should have worn the communicator watch Sloan had created a few months ago. It was for moments like this when under civilian cover, he could just hit the alarm and send it back to base. Tony hadn't even worn his Deadly suit recently. He was way out of the game. He just never thought this mess would come to his doorstep. *Shit.*

Somewhere behind the bushes, a gurgled scream punctuated the surge of grimy gluttony rolling in his gut. With a jolt, he realized the sin came from the same direction as the screams. Whatever it was, it was feeding, and from the screams, it was the Faithful who was the meal.

He'd tried to avoid the fact that he was made for this, but there was no escaping it now. He looked at the blue liquid glitter running in his veins, ready to release on his bidding. This was his purpose.

"Call for backup. Parker is on speed dial." He lobbed his cell to Bailey, and then ducked through the bush, aiming for the direction the sick feeling in his gut churned the most. When he burst out of the shrubbery and into another clearing, he couldn't believe his eyes. The member of the Faithful was wrapped up like a Christmas ham, vines tangled around him, slowly choking to death. But the worst thing, the most mind-boggling thing that almost made him believe he'd stepped onto a movie set, was the humanoid plant behind it all.

Standing well over seven feet tall, the two-legged monster was a mass of writhing tentacle vines. Each vine striated along the body like muscle fiber, a botanical cadaver with the skin pulled back. There were slits for eyes and a gaping maw filled with sharp thorns for teeth. Twigs and leaves sprung from the head, as though it were trying to grow hair. Roots from its legs buried into the ground for grip. It had one viney arm splayed to the right, holding another Faithful at bay, and one to the left, wrapped around the throat of a woman dressed in black yoga pants, her long silver hair escaping the raised hood. He wasn't used to seeing her out of her white leather, but the woman being strangled was unmistakably his sister.

"Daisy?"

The hooded figure looked his way, revealing wide violet eyes and a pale face turned red from exertion. Her fingers scrabbled at the vine wrapping her throat. She was choking.

Power rippled up his spine and surged at his fingertips. Blue light illuminated the clearing. He launched at the plant-man with only one thought. He mustn't let Daisy die.

His fingers wrapped around a low tendril, and blue fire shot out of his hands, smoking and sizzling the creature's green flesh. A searing sound ripped through the air. The monster screeched but didn't let go of Daisy. It kicked Tony away and sent accusatory eyes—slits— at Daisy, as if this was all her fault. But it didn't let go. It choked and shook Daisy until her hood fell back. Her long pale hair trailed about as her head moved like a rag doll.

Weapon, Tony needed a weapon.

"Sword," Daisy hissed. It was all she could say. She couldn't point because her fingers were the only thing keeping her neck free enough to breathe. She glanced down to her right.

A long thin metal object, only a few feet away.

Sword.

Tony reached for it, lunged, but something caught at his feet and he fell. It was another vine, or root curling around his ankle. *Godammit.* Stupid move! Quickly recovering, his hand hit the hilt of the sword, and he twisted, arcing the blade overhead. It sliced through the viney arm, severing Daisy from the main body. The monster screeched inhumanly. The length around Daisy's neck hit the floor. Some parts shriveled and stilled, others writhed and slivered back until it rejoined the larger beast.

"What the flying fuck was that?" he gasped, sword rotating in his wrist until it was at the ready. How the hell was he supposed to stop that thing? It regrew body parts.

The two Faithful it ate were already dead. Their masks had long since fallen. A dried mummified husk was all that remained of them. The root around his ankle tightened, cutting off his circulation. He placed his palm over the ropy cord and called on his power. Blue fire spit out, catching the plant and his jeans on fire. The vine shriveled away from the heat. Tony patted his jeans to stop the flames spreading.

Again. That was stupid.

"Tony?" Bailey's voice cut through his heart.

She stood inches from the plant thing, firearm aimed and locked, eyes wide as a tendril crept toward her face in a way that almost seemed inquisitive.

"Don't shoot!" Tony said, holding his palm out. "People will come."

But Bailey was beyond comprehension. She pointed the gun between the plant thing's eyes and fired. A loud crack echoed through the trees, and birds took to the twilight sky. But the creature didn't stop. Its vine kept coming for Bailey. It *wanted* her.

"Don't let it touch her," Daisy rasped. "Neurotoxin."

Shit. Taking a giant leap, Tony shoved Bailey out of the way, and then went for the humanoid mass. He powered up until heat emanated in the air, casting a shimmering mirage of blue around him, and then he dove at its midsection. The moment he connected, the thing screeched in agony. Tony tried to grab hold of it, but anytime his hand connected, it slipped beneath him like a thousand worms wriggling and sliding. The creature recalibrated itself to adjust for the pieces Tony had burned or pulled off. It reformed and reshaped, but most importantly, it fled.

Tony's fire must have kept him safe from the toxin, because he felt no ill effects on his hands as he fired. Faster than Tony could grasp, every last bit of vine and root slithered away, camouflaging itself in the local greenery. When the last leaf and root had gone, Tony rolled and crawled across the grass to Bailey. Sitting on her ass, with her hands loosely hanging at the side, she looked stunned, and he couldn't tell if it was just emotionally, or literally. Had she been poisoned by the neurotoxin? Her gun had left her hands and lay a few feet from her.

"Babe, are you okay?" he asked, searching for signs. He clutched her face between his hands and turned her to look at him.

Blinking, her pupils contracted. "It was alive. The plant was alive."

"I know. It's gone."

"I mean, I've seen some shit, but that was next level cray. You're not doing your prank thing, are you? Like, are you sure we didn't stumble onto a movie set?"

"That's what I had thought," he mumbled. "It's not a prank."

He glanced around the clearing. Two dead bodies—mummified corpses were all that remained. It was gone.

"I can't sense it anymore. It's not feeding."

After a quick squeeze to Bailey's shoulder, Tony pushed up to a knee, and then stood. He turned around and found Daisy standing over the two Faithful. She held her sword in one hand, and Bailey's firearm in the other.

There was something about the scene that gave Tony pause. He studied his eldest sibling without her mask. Her long silver hair was tied messily at her nape, bits escaped and flowing. She had a delicate face accentuated by strong bone structure. Fine white scars laced over one side of her face. She had the same wide lips as the rest of them, a trait he'd learned had come from their biological mother. Those lips had probably never smiled, not since she was seven and he was three and she used to tickle him in the stomach to make him forget about the fact they were locked in a room. Daisy didn't like sorrow, and back then, her way to get rid of it was to make the person happy. Now, she killed them.

Out of her white death-dealer's uniform, she appeared almost normal.

A pang hit him squarely in the chest. Maybe she'd never had the chance to learn to smile. For all Tony knew, the woman had been raised as a robot, conditioned to do the Syndicate's bidding and little else. Sinners from the Hildegard Sisterhood came to mind. Like his mother Mary, they were stolen as little girls from their childhood homes or orphanages, and taught to be ruthless seductress assassins, so when they grew to adulthood they knew nothing of love and affection. It was use your body to infiltrate. Kill or be killed. It was fortunate Mary had met Flint and turned their life around.

But Mary had been at least ten years younger than Daisy was now. Could Daisy still turn her life around?

He wasn't sure. Sloan had tried to give her a chance, and the woman had kidnapped and tortured Max. Max had insisted Daisy held back her full wrath, and in the end there was a note pinned to Max's chest, outlining how to save him from the poison he'd been injected with.

The only thing Tony knew was that his sister was confused.

"Daisy," he ventured.

She looked over, eyes blank. Unlike last time they'd crossed paths, she didn't correct him and tell her to call her Despair. That was progress, he guessed.

"Come home. Let's talk about this."

"I have to find it," she rasped, voice flat. "This is my fault."

He paused, unsure what to say. When no one spoke, he added, "What the hell was that thing?"

She shook her head. "It only wants to be free, but I have angered it now. I have betrayed it by coming here to destroy it. It was so sad in the cage. It was like us."

"It's taking lives."

"It is what we made it." A tiny frown pushed Daisy's straight brows together. Her voice lowered. "It is my fate."

Tony eyed the fallen piece of withered plant arm, severed by the sword. "You said neurotoxin. What did you mean?"

"It can excrete a toxin that paralyzes prey before it eats." She rubbed her raw and puckered neck. "My body is fighting it as we speak."

That's why her tone was still husky. A normal person without regeneration and advanced healing would have choked on the poison.

Concern for Bailey's safety wrapped around his heart. She should have gone when he'd told her too. If that vine had hit her skin, she could be dead. A full body panic, like he'd never known before, engulfed him. Already he couldn't comprehend a life without Bailey.

He could completely understand why Wyatt was so overprotective of Misha.

"You sensed it," Daisy accused. "You must help me find it."

He raised a brow. *Must?*

"You want it dead. I want it dead. We will work together."

Tony turned to Bailey. "Did you call for backup?"

She nodded.

"No," Daisy snapped and pointed the gun at Tony. "Just you." But then she shifted her aim to Bailey. "And you."

"I don't think so. Bailey's not involved in this. Let her go."

"She's the only guarantee I have that you will help me. Give me your cell phones."

They had no choice but to comply. Daisy fired a shot at each phone, not caring about the explosive sound cracking through the park.

He shook his head. "That wasn't necessary."

Pain and hurt and a thousand unnamed emotions warred across Daisy's face before she stamped them down under a blank expression. She stepped toward Bailey and then, with the flick of her wrist, her sword tip was under Bailey's chin. "Don't make me ask again."

Cold fury dropped in the pit of Tony's stomach. Blue light pulsed through the veins on his forearms and sparked at his fingertips.

He snarled, "Sloan forgave you for what happened to Max, but I'm warning you now, you touch a hair on Bailey's head, and I'll come for you. I'll rip you in two."

Bailey gasped and shot Daisy accusatory eyes. "You're the one who kidnapped Max."

Daisy's violet gaze darted between Bailey and Tony. She lowered her sword but used the gun to point in the direction the plant monster went. "Track it."

"Let Bailey free and I will."

"No."

"It's okay, Tony," Bailey stood up. "I'll come. You need someone to have your back."

He gripped the back of her neck and met her determined brown eyes, glistening under the starlight. "Baby, this is dangerous. I can heal. You can't. Leave this to me."

"There's no chance in hell I'll leave you with the bitch who almost killed Max."

"She's my sister. She won't hurt me." He hoped.

"She's your sister?" Bailey hissed. "That nasty bag of crazy is related to you?"

"It's a long story."

She shook her head. "I don't care. I'm not leaving you with her. Parker said you're the best fighter out of all of them. I know if it comes to it, you can keep me safe and you need me. I keep you balanced. If anything else, having someone to watch your back and support you will help."

Parker had said he was the best?

He was going to regret this, but what was the alternative? Fight his sister, perhaps to the death? He nodded, gesturing for Daisy to lead the way.

Daisy shook her head. "You first."

nineteen

TONY LAZARUS

TONY GRIPPED Bailey's waist and lowered her from the manhole ladder to the sewer below. They were underground in tunnels made from old brick and concrete. A pungent stream trickled around their feet in the culvert. Bailey gagged, and Tony took a moment to acclimatize to the smell with his nose buried in his elbow. His new edition Nikes were well and truly stuffed. Mud, silt, gross things and worse had leeched into them.

He shook them out, but it did no good except to disturb the rats and cockroaches as they scuttled past.

Unperturbed, Daisy was already a few feet into the tunnel and stood with her sword and torch at the ready. Her light illuminated the dark passage ahead, in the direction the creature was last seen. Tony sparked the power in his hands, adding a blue glow to the ambiance.

"Not bad," he murmured to Bailey, showing off his hands. "Comes in handy, right?"

She shot him an amused look before hardening her features and glaring at Daisy.

"Thank you," Tony whispered into her ear. "I know working with her is hard for you."

"We're being forced at gunpoint. Not exactly what I call working with her," she replied sardonically.

He cast a glance over his shoulder to where Daisy stood a few feet away. "My instincts aren't so great when it comes to her. She's the one we left behind."

Studying him closely, Bailey nodded. She was law enforcement. She would know what it was like to leave a soldier behind. It simply wasn't a thing you did.

They'd been children at the time, but they now had a chance to mend bridges, to bring Daisy back to them.

"Walk next to me," Tony said to Bailey, voice low.

She came up to his side. "You good?"

He nodded. "You?"

"I'll never get this smell out, but yep. Let's do this."

They joined Daisy. She pointed with her sword, irritated at their delay. "The last time I came with Bosch, we surmised the creature nested in here somewhere. It gets deeper later. It likes water, so if it's drinking, you'll sense it. Alert me, and we'll follow that direction. If I feel its sorrow, I'll do the same. Between the two of us, we have a good chance at locating it."

"And then what?" Tony's gruff voice sounded loud in the small space.

"Then we exterminate it."

Tony nodded and followed her. "Who's Bosch?"

A pause. "Wayne Bosch was the botanical geneticist who created the creature."

"Was?" Bailey asked.

"He's dead." Daisy's raspy voice echoed. "He was absorbed by the plant."

They walked on. The water got deeper and flowed faster. Any time they came to a new open tunnel, they stopped and put their sin-sensing feelers out. Tony sensed no gluttony; Daisy sensed no despair.

They must have covered miles, because Tony's stomach began to growl, and Bailey asked more than once to rest. Daisy tried to hide it, but on occasion, her hand went to her throat and she wheezed when the air became particularly polluted and stifling.

"Does it hurt?" Tony asked, alluding to the wound on her neck. "Do you need to stop?"

Daisy coughed. She hooked stray white hairs behind her ear. It was clear to Tony that she was trying very hard to remain composed, to not let him see her weaknesses. Even in the low light, Tony could see the scars on her skin. Catching his attention, Daisy turned to the shadows. "I've had worse."

Awkward silence dropped like a stone.

He didn't know how to respond, so continued walking. After a few moments of silently trudging through the wet sewage, he was over it, impatient. He had to do something to break the tension. He hummed a snappy repetitive song. It was the first tune that came to mind, and he had no idea what it was, except he'd always sung it to fill the silence. Waiting for another scene check, spending grueling hours in the makeup chair. It made him feel calmer.

Next to him, Bailey's voice lowered. "What is that? I heard you humming that at the sobriety house."

"Don't know. I hum it sometimes when it's too quiet. Catchy. Gets stuck in your head."

"It's the song I used to sing when you were a baby," Daisy answered, surprising them. "At the lab, we used to have our blood drawn at the same time every day. When that time came close, you would get nervous. You were three years old and terrified of needles.

Sometimes they were bigger than my finger. I sang to stop you crying."

Daisy's profound words cut off abruptly. She continued walking, sloshing onward doggedly, completely unaware of Tony's and Bailey's stunned silence.

She'd shared something. Hope flared in Tony's chest. Maybe he could keep the conversation going, keep cutting through that icy exterior.

Hurrying to catch up, Tony asked, "Do you hate us for not coming back?"

Dickhead. Go straight to the most uncomfortable question, why don't you? He mentally slapped himself.

"No," she answered, once again surprising him. "Once I hated you for leaving. Then I hated you for not coming back. Then I hated you for forgetting. Now, I feel nothing."

"I'm sorry. We all are. Especially Mary. You have to know that. We all thought you were dead."

"If you are asking for forgiveness, it won't come. I am beyond the hopes and dreams of a child."

She wouldn't forgive *them*?

Fuck that.

She'd tried to murder them on more than one occasion! She'd hanged Mary from the rafters of a nightclub. She'd set rabid beasts after them. She'd purposefully kidnapped and tortured Max to prove that the mating bond could be manipulated to bring about the deadly berserker state. He clenched his fists, and his blue light flickered.

Tony stopped and gathered his patience. They were at a split in the tunnel and the culvert was deeper. The water came up to his knees. Scanning Daisy, he considered his words but *screw it*. Honesty was the best policy.

"Just because we want you back, doesn't mean we've forgiven you, either. You still have a long way to go before you can redeem yourself, but you're family, Daisy. You get a chance, and so do we. We've only just learned you are alive. We want you back. We want to make it right, and we hope you do too."

"There is no coming back from what I am, from what I have done."

"Yes, there is. You have to see that life with the Syndicate is no life at all."

Daisy stopped and stared at him. "I told you, I feel nothing."

"That's not true," Bailey interrupted. "You warned us about the plant's neurotoxin."

Tony's eyes turned sharp as understanding flowed through him. "She's right. You didn't want Bailey hurt. And for whatever reason, you gave us the clue on how to heal Max. You do feel."

Daisy shook her head and turned away. She stared long and hard at the glistening domed brick walls covered with mildew. "All I have left are empty memories and false promises. Don't think there is something here when there isn't."

"Does Julius know you're with us?"

"Enough conversation." She peeked into another tunnel and shone her torch down its length. "I sense nothing. Do you?"

He shook his head. "I haven't sensed the creature's sin since we were face to face with it, and it was feeding on your Faithful."

"Then this is pointless." She threw Bailey's gun into the contaminated water. The gun landed with a splash and promptly disappeared into the murk. "You can go."

Daisy took off down one of the tunnels, leaving Bailey and Tony stunned and on their own. Daisy's torchlight dimmed the further she went, so Tony flared his power and held it steady, giving them blue illumination to guide their way back. Fatigue ached in his arms. He didn't know how long he could hold his power. The long overuse of it to light his way was taxing. He gave his retreating sister one last look and shook his head.

"I saw a ladder to a manhole not far back." He gestured for Bailey to go in front of him. "Go first and I'll hold up the rear."

Regrettably, he didn't trust Daisy to keep going and not return to stab them in the back.

"I want to say let's collect my gun, but I don't want to stick my hands in that murk." Lines formed in Bailey's forehead and she eyed the water like it was poison.

"Just leave it," he replied. "I don't like the vibe down here. Let's get out."

"No complaints here."

Bailey continued to trudge. She took two steps ahead of him, and then it came out the water. In an explosion of watery action, tentacles shot out, wrapped around Bailey. She aquaplaned and fell face first, splashing loudly.

It's here.

Adrenaline surged through him. He dove for Bailey, aiming for where her body submerged. He gripped her as she thrashed. Blue light glowed in the murky water, casting a cloudy bloom. He heaved, but the creature was everywhere, latching onto her and pulling her down. How had he not sensed it? Because it hadn't been feeding. It was smart. It knew how to hide from him. His fingers lost the battle with the vines and slipped.

"No!" he roared. This can't be happening.

Thousands of tendrils, roots and vines slid and slithered, gathering purchase on her body and trying to grip him. He felt it on his side, around his ankles, *everywhere*.

A burning sensation sliced his arm. The toxin. If any of that got onto Bailey. Maybe it already had.

"Bailey!"

Thrashing vines whipped around, coming up from the water, lashing out at him. Careful not to get his face whacked, he changed tactics and dug his fingers into the thickest appendages, hoping they were integral. Every panic, every fear, powered his fire, and he roared his agony, wrenching it free from his body. Blinding light burst under the water and the thing jolted away, but it wasn't enough. The water dulled his power's effect, but the fire kept the toxin from getting into his hands.

Freeing himself, he went back to Bailey and focused on the thickest roots. Clamping down on his panic, he went at it with robotic precision, trying not to let that niggling doubt push in.

That was not her thrashing getting weaker.

That was not the life draining out of her.

Hurry.

Explosion after explosion, he let loose on the creature. Out of time. Bailey slackened, sinking. Flattening his lips and bracing himself, he lifted her—heaved. Smaller roots snapped away, and he elevated enough to get her out, to give her one spluttering breath, but then she went down under new vines and water.

It was never ending.

"Daisy!" He roared, panicked. "Help!"

Please let her hear him. Please let her come back.

"Daisy! I NEED YOU."

And when the sense of gluttony trickled into his gut, he knew the creature was feeding. Whether it was from Bailey or the water, he couldn't tell. Didn't care. Ripping with all his might, he yanked and shot power into the thing—*Pop! Pop! Pop!*—until his lungs burned, until his arms felt like they would rip from his body, until Bailey started to lose her fight again. The feeling of despair, so hard and so deep, sliced through his heart.

"Don't give up, baby!"

He fired, and yanked, every time ripping a new piece of the creature away, throwing its bio-matter over his head.

And then Daisy was there.

Swinging her sword, slicing into the depths. She chopped and attacked like a machine. "Now!" she shouted. "Lift her now!"

Half submerged and on his knees, Tony slid his hands beneath Bailey's body once more. He dragged her up, breaking the last binding vestiges. Water sluiced off her face as she broke the surface, but she didn't splutter. She didn't breathe.

No no no.

He patted her face. "Bailey!"

This was his fault. He should have refused to let her come. Should have forced her away at the park. But he'd been selfish. Some part had liked that she'd wanted to stay to watch his back.

Daisy continued to hack the creature while Tony shifted Bailey to get her in a better position, reclined against his knee. He rested her neck over one forearm arm so her head tilted up. There was no dry, flat area to do CPR.

Come on. He patted her face. Nothing. *Baby.* He pressed his ear to her mouth and listened for life. Nothing. He shifted to her heart.

Thump, thump.

Yes. Yes.

"That's it, baby. Stay alive." He titled her head to the side and cleared her airway. Wet gunk came out. He pinched her nose and angled her, opening her mouth. Then he breathed into her and continued to do so until she spluttered. Her chest heaved, and she vomited more water.

Sucking in air, her eyes opened with a naked plea. "Tony. Oh my God, Tony."

"I've got you."

"I can't feel my legs."

He scooped her up, one arm under her arms, the other under her thighs. He cast his sister an agonizing glance. "I'm going. I have to get her out of here."

Daisy clenched her jaw, screamed a war cry and stabbed her sword into the water. Vines thrashed as she hit the creature. "Go!"

And then he did the most painful thing he'd ever done. He chose between his mate and his sister. He left a soldier behind.

twenty

BAILEY HAZE

BAILEY COULDN'T FEEL her feet. From her ankles down there was a numbness. She lay in the medical room in the Lazarus House basement, still wearing her stinking sewage outfit and waiting for the antitoxin she'd been administered to take effect. The pain and swelling had gone down, but the numbness around her feet remained. The creature had slid beneath the hem of her pants and wrapped itself around her bare ankles. She could still feel the vines sliding around her torso, her arms... clamping, tightening, holding her down. Her struggle had been impossible. The disgusting water invaded her mouth, her lungs.

She shivered.

Stop. You're fine.

Max paced along her side, silently fuming. She could feel the tension in the air. Now and then, he'd pick up a figurine of Sailor Moon, and then put it back down on the bench. Most likely Sloan had put it there to brighten the sterile place. Sloan had a borderline unhealthy obsession with the manga character, and Max brooded when he stared at it. Most of the Deadly Seven, bar Parker, had returned topside to scout the area where they'd left Daisy fighting the creature.

Raised and flippant male voices filtered back into the room through the open door. Tony and Parker argued somewhere beyond and had been doing so since Parker had seen to Bailey's paralysis with an antitoxin injection. They'd not known what the plant toxin was, but because Tony had been exposed to the venom, they filtered his blood to produce a serum with antitoxin antibodies. Fortunately for Bailey, when administered, it worked.

But she knew how close she'd come. If Tony hadn't been exposed to the toxin, she might not be alive.

The moment she was stable, Parker immediately took the opportunity to blast his brother about failing to wear the Deadly Seven communicator watch. When the backup had arrived where the cell phones had been dumped, they couldn't be found, and the hidden tracker in the watch would have provided them with a beacon to trace their location. Neither of them would have been harmed.

"How long do I have to be here?" Bailey whined to Max. She plucked a twig from her hair and cringed, imagining it still wiggled. She dropped it on a metal operating instrument tray next to the bed, adding it to the ever-growing collection of potential plant matter for further scientific study. "I'm starving and I need to bathe."

"Grace is almost here. Just a few more minutes."

Max stopped pacing. He flexed his fists at his side. The ex-army intelligence-gathering specialist had served with a few of the Lazarus family. He'd also dated Sloan for many years and had known about their secret long before anyone else. He'd been on missions with them, yet he had the nerve to round on her, fuming.

"You should have *never* been down in that sewer with him," Max insisted with a growl.

"Excuse me?" She held out her hand and counted on her fingers.

"One, I was forced at gunpoint. Two, he had zero backup. Three, he was hunting a plant-monster. You heard me. A. Plant. Monster. Four, he is my partner, my mate. You would have done the same for Sloan." Her eyes narrowed at the guilt flashing across his face. "Or maybe you already have, and that's how you ended up with a bomb strapped to your chest."

"We're not talking about me." Max's usual sunny face darkened further. He folded his arms, bulging out his musculature with a display of male stubbornness. "You almost died."

"So did you, but you didn't. I didn't."

"Bailey—" he scrubbed his face, shaking his head in disbelief.

"Have the rest come back?" she asked, changing the subject.

Bailey knew she shouldn't, but there was a sense of culpability where Daisy was concerned. Yes, Daisy had kidnapped and tortured Max, and Bailey would never forgive her for that but, despite working for the enemy, the woman had returned and kept the creature distracted while Tony escaped with Bailey. She'd saved Bailey's life.

She'd also been the reason Bailey was in danger in the first place.

Tony had been beside himself when he'd carried her through the streets, trying to find a pay phone. Shutting her eyes, all Bailey could see was Tony's chest and feel his warmth as he'd held onto her while shouting down the payphone's handset, saying he'd left their sister behind. The tremble in his voice still hit her squarely in the chest.

"No," Max answered Bailey's earlier question. "They haven't come back."

He strode out of the room.

Sighing, Bailey rested her head on the hard plastic pillow and stared at the ceiling. She was itchy, she smelled, and she was over it, but Sloan was still out there, hunting the creature and looking for their sister. Max's irritation and moodiness was warranted.

Was this her future? Pacing back and forth, stressing and snapping, with nothing to do while the heroes did their jobs?

It was clear now why having their identities kept secret was so important. No normal person could fight that creature, and if the Syndicate made more, then... Bailey's throat closed up with dread. Those heroes were vital.

"Here." Max returned to the room with a plate of sandwiches.

"Yes, Lord. Gimme." Bailey didn't care what was in them, or that she still had a layer of filth on her. She took each little triangle of heaven and shoved it in her mouth, hardly chewing before swallowing. Cucumber and cream cheese. Heaven.

"Easy tiger," Max murmured. He filled a glass of water at the sink and handed it to her.

She made appreciative hums as she swallowed, trying not to spill as it hit her mouth. Already, she felt better. A burning prickling began to build in her feet. She flexed her toes, wincing.

"How's the patient feeling?" Doctor Grace Go rushed in, still wearing her green surgical scrubs. She had a stethoscope around her neck, and her hospital name tag pinned to her hip.

With dark hair and a kind smile, she had a way about her that put Bailey at ease, simply by setting her eyes on Bailey.

Tony and Parker came in behind her. Parker keenly watched from the side to hear what Grace had to say. That man had a mind like a sponge, always soaking up the information around him. Tony nudged Max out of the way to take the spot by her bedside. He gripped her hand and looked at her with eyes still flashing with worry. She squeezed back.

"I'm feeling quite good actually," she replied to Grace. Now that she'd eaten. "What Parker gave to counteract the toxin seems to be working." She wiggled her toes. "I can move them, but can't feel much beyond my ankles. It kinda burns and prickles."

Grace went down to the end of the bed and pulled out a pen from her pocket. She took Bailey's heel and poked the nib around the pad of her foot.

Little burning sparks of fire shot through her.

"Ow," Bailey said, jolting. "That hurts."

Grace smiled. "Good. The feeling is coming back. Won't be long now and you should make a full recovery."

The doctor shooed Tony to the side and continued with a basic examination of Bailey. If she wasn't so ready to get out of her disgusting attire, she'd find it humorous to see the three brooding men watching as though it were a life or death situation. Lined up in a row, all had their arms folded, eying her intently, jaws twitching.

Grace lowered Bailey's wrist. "Heart rate is returning to normal. Blood pressure is fine." She shone a torch into Bailey's eyes. "Pupils responsive."

Then she touched Bailey gently on the shoulder and looked deep into her eyes. "How are you feeling?"

Grace looked at Bailey. Really *looked* at her. Something in her tone sent a rush of hormones swimming around Bailey's body. Her eyes teared up, but she pushed them down. She wasn't one to cry in front of other people.

"I'm fine. Looking forward to a hot shower."

"Well, you'll need help with that. At least for tonight." She glanced over at Tony. "You can take her upstairs now, if you like."

Bailey stiffened. "I can't go home?"

"You're coming to mine," Tony insisted.

Grace agreed. "I think it's best that Tony stays with you, at least until you're capable of walking on your own. And he will need to monitor you to ensure there are no adverse effects of the antitoxin."

"How long will that be for?"

"The treatment seems to be working fine, so overnight." She glanced at Parker. "Filtering Tony's blood worked."

His response was an arrogant cock of the eyebrow, as if to say, *Of course. Did you expect any less?*

Grace smirked. "As long as you're feeling fine, there's nothing to worry about. You had a big scare, so get some rest." She scrunched up her nose and laughed. "Maybe two showers."

Tony didn't wait any longer, he scooped Bailey into his arms. She supposed there was no arguing with him, so laced her fingers around his neck. Having a big, strong, actual real life hero carry her wasn't something she could complain about. She didn't want to.

"We'll finish our conversation later," Parker insisted.

Tony ignored his brother's statement and carried Bailey out of the room. Two steps out, they almost collided with Misha and Lilo in the hallway. Misha had a stack of folded clothes resting on her pregnant belly, while Lilo held another plate of sandwiches.

"Whoops!" Misha exclaimed, her blond curly hair bouncing as she stepped back.

"Hi." Lilo gave Bailey a small grin. "You look better."

Tony growled impatiently and tried to side-step the women, but they both united and blocked him.

"Here," Misha handed the clothes to Bailey. "You'll need some clean clothes. I have girly bubble soap in there too. God knows the man stuff is yuk."

"I have more sandwiches if you're still hungry." Lilo put that plate on top of the clothes.

Bailey balanced it all between herself and Tony.

"Okay, grumble bum." Lilo flared her eyes at Tony. "You can go now. But please come down and tell us everything when you get a chance." To Bailey, she added, "We'll come visit you tomorrow, honey, and let you know the goss. I'm sure everyone will come back fine."

Bailey barely had time to give her thanks before Tony grunted and kept walking. Over his shoulder, Bailey saw the women join with Grace and share a familiar rapport. The wives and girlfriends of the Lazarus crew had always been nice to Bailey, even when she'd only been their bodyguard, but once they'd learned Bailey was Tony's mate, they treated her like family. A feeling of rightness bloomed in her chest as they got further from the women and she knew that one day, she'd be right there with them.

"SHH. I'VE GOT YOU."

Bailey jerked awake with a gurgled scream echoing in her mind. *Her* scream.

"You're safe."

She blinked, realizing they'd somehow made it to Tony's apartment. She must have dozed off against his chest while he carried her. The memory of the drowning was still fresh and left its imprint on her nervous system. She'd relived it the moment she'd closed her eyes. Adrenaline pumped through her body, making everything skip—her heart, her breath. *Calm down.*

"I'm just putting you down here while I turn the shower on." The volume of Tony's voice dropped to a calm baritone rumble. It felt so good next to her ear, coming from deep within his chest, that she instinctively gripped onto him when he tried to disengage from her body.

"Babe," he said softly. "I'll be right over there."

He pointed to the open bedroom door.

She was on the sectional sofa in the living room, legs up. The place was cozy. Potted plants on her left and right. An acoustic guitar rested against the wall next to a modern fire place. Designer cushions took the weight off her feet. The sofa was cream. It would need cleaning after this, but Tony didn't seem to care. He left the plate of sandwiches with her and took the clothes package from Lilo and Misha with him into the bedroom.

She wasn't hungry anymore, so put the plate to the side.

Resting her head on the back of the sofa, she watched, bleary eyed as the light brightened in his bedroom. The sound of a faucet being turned on filtered through. Shortly after, he returned. The confident, charismatic lady's man who'd dominated at the press junket was gone. Tony's haggard face and filthy clothes looked like they belonged on a man who'd just completed a marathon through the winter wilderness and lost. His posture did too.

She wanted to apologize for not doing as he'd asked and going for backup, but she wasn't sorry. It had scared her to leave him behind—and not because she had been afraid for herself, but for him. She hadn't wanted him to go hunt that *thing* with someone they couldn't trust. Intense feelings built inside her, and when he crouched down to scoop her up, she kissed him on the cheek.

Confused, he blinked at her. "What was that for?"

A warm rush spread through her as she searched his handsome face. "For being my knight in shining armor."

Storm clouds brewed in his expression. Clearly he wasn't pleased with her words. Silently, he lifted her and took her into his ensuite. Traveling through his bedroom, she glimpsed his comfortable king-sized bed covered in a dark, smooth coverlet. The last time she was there, she'd barely used the toilet before rushing out to go home. Now she took it all in. An enormous black and white painting of Frank Sinatra hung on the wall behind the bed. The curtains were drawn, and the lights were dim.

The ensuite had no door. It was a continuation of the bedroom and looked like something straight out of Vogue Living. Dark granite floor tiles led to a rock feature wall with a rain shower. A steady stream of hot water fell, back-lit by blue LEDs in the ceiling. The other walls were another shade of warm granite, and to the right of the shower, beside the vanity, was a free-standing tub, also slowly filling with steaming hot water. Two potted ficus were the only splash of color. The entire place had a luxurious man-cave vibe.

Tony carried her to a wooden bench near the tub and placed her down gently. "Okay, then, let's get you showered."

For a moment, the two of them stared at each other while the mood thickened with the steaming air. He was going to have to assist her at some point. Bailey became supremely self-conscious.

She glanced at the water running in the shower. The sound of wet sliced through her psyche and compounded. It wasn't the water here, it was the suffocating blanket that had stolen her breath. Her pulse pounded in her ears, and she couldn't work her lungs. Finally sucking in a breath, she looked at Tony. "I can't."

"Babe," he cooed and crouched before her. "You have to wash this crap off."

Closing her eyes, she let the darkness be her friend. She concentrated on Tony's calloused hands running idly against her skin. She concentrated on the movement of her lungs. In. Out. *I'm breathing. I'm breathing.* Pain in her teeth made her aware she clenched too tight. She swallowed and forced herself to relax. Opening her eyes, she was shocked to see pain in Tony's expression.

"This is my fault," he whispered.

No it wasn't.

"If I had truly thought you to be in danger, I would never have let you come down. I should have fought Daisy up the top. Obviously, my sense of reality is warped."

Bailey cupped his face. "We all think differently in hindsight. You weren't to know your power wouldn't work that well under water, or that the creature could stay submerged like that."

"Doesn't matter. Parker was right."

"Right about what?"

But Tony shook his head and changed the subject. "Do you want help getting out of your clothes? I can walk you to the shower, or I can put this bench in there and give you privacy. Whatever you need."

"Stay," she demanded a little too vehemently. She wasn't ready to be under water on her own. She needed his arms around her, the same ones that had pulled her out of danger and saved her from drowning.

He nodded and kneeled down before her to unbutton her pants. Peeling the dried and crusty black fabric down her legs, he was careful to not disturb the welts on her ankles from the poison. When his attention passed the area, he frowned and stared at it angrily.

"Lift your arms," he rumbled.

She did, and he popped her dress shirt down the front, not even patient enough to undo the buttons. When she lifted her brows at him, he shrugged. "It was ruined anyway."

That word sat heavy in the air. Ruin. It punctuated every brisk and stilted move he made. First, taking off her buttonless shirt—*ruin* —then when he rolled the shirt into a ball and threw it in the vanity sink—*ruin*. She was left in her bra and panties, and when Tony's gaze slid back to her, he cocked his head. The clouds in his eyes dissipated, replaced with surprise.

"You're wearing sexy lingerie."

"I know."

"Has that been under there the whole time?" He gave a self-deprecating shake of the head. "Of course it has."

He moved to lift her again, but she stopped him. "Aren't you undressing too?"

He glanced down at his similarly dirty clothes. The Nikes were still on his feet. He had to be just as uncomfortable as she was, yet he never showed it.

"Right." He tugged his shoes off, then stood.

"Uh-uh. There has to be something for me to look forward to." Bailey waggled a finger around his torso. "That comes off."

She held her breath, waiting.

A salacious grin curved up one side of his face, but then he dipped his gaze with a frown. "I can't be held accountable for the actions of Tiny Tony if that happens."

"Tiny Tony?" She giggled.

"Well," he blushed. "He's not tiny, tiny. But compared to me, he's —shit, never mind. Forget I said anything."

Bailey unhooked her bra, letting it fall to the floor. His beautiful eyes lowered to take in her breasts. The liquid heat in his intense gaze made her pulse quicken. Maybe this shower would be okay after all.

Tony slowly disrobed, and she couldn't stop staring. With each inch of flesh he revealed, her pulse sped up. And when he threw in a cocky striptease, all the tension released with a laugh.

"You like this swamp stain?" he joked, pointing to a brown splat on his perfectly defined abs. "Does it do anything for you?"

The grin wouldn't leave her face, no matter how hard she tried to school her features. Dammit. That boy knew how to make her smile.

"How about this one?" He turned and showed her the perfect globes of his ass, still covered by briefs. He hooked his thumbs in the waistband and began to lower it, then grimaced. Checking his rear, he said, "Actually, let's leave that striptease location for another day. Who knows what the waste water collected?"

He turned to face her and lowered his briefs with efficient economy. Bailey blinked, trying not to look at *it*, but like a schoolgirl catching a glimpse of her first naked boy in the pool locker room, she blushed ten times until Sunday. He was well endowed. Definitely *not* tiny. He turned the bath faucet off and then returned to her with a wink.

"Yeah," he said smugly. "Tiny Tony kinda has that effect on women. Just ignore him."

After tersely helping her out of her panties, he slid an arm around her waist.

"Can you stand, or should we do this with me carrying you?"

"Um." She tested her weight. Nettles bit along her feet and prickled around her ankles. She winced. "I don't think I can."

"Okay," he replied thoughtfully. "Carry you it is."

He squeezed her waist and scooped another hand under her legs, so she was back in his arms. She gripped him around the neck as he lifted and brought them under the hot rain falling from the ceiling. Water flooded her face, getting in her eyes and mouth in an entirely uncomfortable way. It wasn't like a jet shower stream, the water simply fell onto her softly, a small suffocation.

She didn't like it.

Shutting her eyes, she frowned, adjusting to the sensation.

"You good?" Tony's voice was low and rough next to her ear. She shivered at the intimacy.

Squeezing her eyes tight, she whispered, "Don't let go."

twenty-one

TONY LAZARUS

IT ALMOST KILLED Tony to see Bailey's vulnerability. He lost control of his voice. No words would come. He'd gently lowered her legs but supported her weight with one arm around her waist. She could stand, but it still pained her a little. There was a hose shower head attached to the rock wall. He used it to wash most of the mess off her body, trying to make the process as quick as possible.

She endured the entire thing with her eyes squeezed shut in concentration, breathing through the water raining on her face. He gave his head and body a quick squirt and then turned off the faucet.

"Time for a bath," he murmured. "It will be easier to soap up in there and I'll hold you the entire time."

Still with her eyes closed, and a frown marring her beautiful face, she nodded. Transferring her to the tub, he positioned himself behind her and lowered them at the same time. They gave a collective sigh as the heat enveloped their aching bodies. He reclined and pulled her back against his chest. The two of them comfortably took up the space with little leg bend. He wrapped his arms around her front and held her until she was ready to open her eyes.

"This smells much better than the sewers," she said, slowly relaxing beneath his touch.

He picked up the soap the girls had given her from the caddy, but Bailey stopped him.

"I want to use what you use."

"This is prettier."

"I don't want pretty. I want you."

Bailey's words hammered on his heart. His body reacted viscerally. Nestled between the pillows of her bottom, his cock grew thick and hard. It demanded attention. So many thoughts swirled in his head. Emotions clogged up. *I don't want pretty. I want you.*

He wanted her too. So bad he ached. With his throat closing up, he lathered his shampoo into her hair, taking special care to massage her kinks. Sandalwood, spices and musk bloomed in the air. When she groaned huskily, and dipped her head back to his chest, his cock tingled and jerked. Shit, this was difficult. He'd tried to hold back his desire but her body was incredible. Slippery. Wet. Soft. Looking down her front while he massaged her hair, he was entranced, tortured. His eyes were windows to the most seductive, erotic scene. He struggled to maintain decorum. Bubbles ran down her slick brown skin, curving and swirling around her breasts, and every time she inhaled, two erect dark nipples pointed out, catching air, teasing him briefly before submerging again.

Jesus.

"I have to rinse your hair," he mumbled, at least he thought he said that. His mouth felt like cotton.

She tensed, coming awake. Wide, panicked eyes swiveled to him. Her bottom lip trembled, betraying her lack of resilience.

"Don't worry, I've got you."

She glanced down at the water around her and inhaled deeply. "I know it's stupid, and completely out there, but I keep thinking vines will come out of the water. They'll sneak up on me when I'm most relaxed. It's all I see when I close my eyes."

"We can get out."

"No. If I don't face this, then this fear will turn into something worse. I won't be beholden to another."

Another fear? He tightened his grip across her ribs and shifted her weight so she was a little higher. He put his lips to her temple. "Do you want me to sing a song?"

A melancholy smile hit her face, giving him the courage to press on.

"I take requests," he murmured. "But no Country."

She scoffed. "I'm not a Country fan, anyway. Hmm. Let's see." She trailed a finger through the water, tracing patterns in the bubbles. "How about... Pavarotti?"

He snorted. "Um... I'm not that skilled."

She laughed. "Taylor Swift?"

"No Country."

"She's not—never mind. What about ABBA? John Lennon? Ooh. Beyoncé?"

She mocked, but Queen B was one of his favorites. A real entertainer to the end. Lightened with amusement, he started to tap a gentle acoustic beat on the tub. She stopped smiling, and when he started to croon the lyrics to *Halo*, she twisted to watch him with avid attention. He caught the way her chest lifted and held, holding her breath captive. Seeing her rapt attention gave him the courage to continue. It was a song about walls coming down, a new addiction, and a saving grace. He'd never been that guy who asked for anything. Words of his own never came easy. And he'd never worn his heart on his sleeve, but with Bailey, he was becoming that guy.

When that creature had her in its vice, and she'd stopped breathing, when every vine and root he'd burned and ripped away from her body grew back, he'd been cold with terror. He couldn't lose her, and he almost did.

While he continued to sing softly, his voice rasping and trembling, he gently lowered their bodies to submerge partly in the water. He scooped water to wash away the shampoo, tilting her head back and rinsing against his chest while she listened. As the song finished, he lifted them back up. The dying note echoed in the air.

She wiped her eyes and then faced him again, eyes glistening.

"You bastard," she sobbed and laughed at the same time.

"What?"

"You made me cry! You sang Beyoncé perfectly in tune, for heaven's sake. Who does that?" She buried her face into his chest and shook her head. Her voice muffled against his skin. "All day I'd not cried, and the moment I hear your voice, I'm done." When she looked up again, her humor fled. "You thought you'd ruin me, Tony, and you have. With a song." She sniffed. "And before you get all worked up, it's a sweet ruin. It's a walls-coming-down-ruin. It's—" she choked up, unable to say more.

"Hey." He hooked a finger under her chin so he could look into her eyes. "But at least I rinsed your hair."

She burst out laughing and then covered her mouth.

He took her hand away. "Don't hide your smile, angel."

When her lashes lifted, and their gazes clashed, desire ignited. The raw sexual intent in her eyes sent every male hormone skyrocketing. His body became hot, prickly and hard. His scent bloomed with musk—pheromones—and then the mood in the tub turned dark and needy. Everything changed.

She pulled him down to meet her lips. The kiss she gave him started chaste and sweet, but soon became demanding.

Tasting her was everything.

She whimpered and arched toward him, twisting to get closer, but he forced her back. He wasn't going to rush this.

"Let me make you feel good," he murmured against her ear.

She shivered, lashes fluttering. After a moment, she gave a small, shy nod. Liquid warmth spread through his chest. He placed her back to his chest again, and slid his hand down her stomach, leaving the other cupped on her breast. Under the water, he twirled a finger around her belly button, circling bigger with each pass until she made an impatient noise. Smiling against her ear, he licked the lobe, enjoying her breath turning ragged.

"Does this feel good?" Pulling her lobe between his teeth, he nipped.

She nodded.

He exhaled, watched his hot breath create goosebumps on her wet flesh, and then rubbed his nose along the skin. "This?"

"Uh-huh." She squirmed.

He bit her shoulder and tested the weight of her breasts in his hands. Gorgeous, full, and peaked with desire.

"And this?" Going deep, he dipped between her legs, sliding through her private flesh with an escaped, hoarse groan of his own. "Here?" He plunged his finger in.

She tensed, gasping, then exhaled with a whimpered nod. "Yes. More."

So tight. He pumped once, twice. He mimicked his finger's rhythm with his tongue on the flesh behind her ear. And when his tongue traced around, exploring her neck, the tip of his finger began a slow, torturous circle of her sensitive nub. She gripped the tub, fingers flexing with restlessness and urgency. He liked it when her knuckles paled.

"Yes, Tony," she gasped. "Make me feel good."

Watching her final defenses crack, seeing how she completely put her pleasure in his hands, it drove his rhythm to match his fierce mood. He was hard, relentless, and driven. He gave her what she wanted. With a final pinch on her nipple, she responded with a cry and a sharp intake of breath. Her eyes rolled back, her body bowed, and she released a long drawn-out, satisfied moan that he felt down to his bones until she finally came down with languid limbs.

She was safe.

She was his.

Smiling to himself, pleased, he unplugged the bath and lifted her, enjoying the way her head lolled against his chest. The sassy bodyguard who always held her own against him had finally succumbed to his appeal.

Getting out was harder than getting in, but he didn't let her know that. He gathered a big towel, draped it over her body, and then carried her back to his room. Placing her gently at the edge of his bed, he stood before her and used the towel to dab her body dry, taking special and attentive care over all the places he'd lovingly touched, learning the areas anew.

She stared, unfocused, in lazy silence, but when he lifted his arms to scrub the towel over her hair, his erection lifted too. Her gaze dropped, and then she took hold of it, fisting it within her grip. She stroked, pumped. His vision went white. Unable to do anything else, he stopped toweling her hair and gave in to the sensation. Tingles zapped up his spine. His legs weakened.

"Babe," he mumbled. "That feels—" *Shit*. So good.

She wrapped her lips around the head and drew his length into her mouth, sucking and stroking, getting faster and more insistent. Her magic tongue took him captive. He was lost in her hands. Frowning at how fast it was going—he wouldn't last, it would be over —he couldn't stop himself from thrusting into her, and when her hands moved to his behind and pulled him deeper, she took all of him. Ecstatic waves of bliss rolled over him, and he almost came undone. But then she pulled off.

Lungs heaving, he looked down into her mischievous gaze. Plump, juicy lips and rosy cheeks. He wasn't finished.

Naughty.

A thrill tripped in his chest. He reached for her, but she scooted back.

"I'm not done feeling good," she said with smoldering eyes. She kept shuffling backward using her feet. He caught her thinly veiled wince.

Was she better, or was she pretending?

Concerned, he studied her face to see if she was in pain, but she waggled her finger at him. "Uh-uh. Eyes down."

Spreading her knees, she showed him everything. A feast. A banquet. He traced his thumb across his lower lip, already imagining her flavor, savoring the memory he'd yet to make. Fuck, he was horny. Ready to go. And she was telling him he could have more.

She'd once teased him, saying that he couldn't handle all of what she had to give. He hoped she was right because he never wanted it to end.

With a low growl of intent, he crawled onto the bed and buried his face between her legs. More. More. *Yes.* He licked and tasted and sucked until he'd had his fill, and then he kept going. He brought her to climax again, with his mouth, with his fingers, and only when she shivered, sated with aftershocks did he guide his cock to her entrance. Teasing her with his length, he whispered near her ear, "Are you ready for this, baby? Are you ready for me?"

"Tony," she warned, bucking her hips. "Give it to me."

He grunted, entering with one stroke, falling down the rabbit hole, knowing that his ruin was inevitable. She was one hundred percent his new addiction, and he would never let her go.

twenty-two

BAILEY HAZE

BAILEY WOKE with full feeling restored to her ankles, but half a brain of common sense. She'd spent most of the night making love to Tony, drifting asleep, then waking up to do it all again. He was insatiable, and she'd encouraged him. Being intimate with him had been the best cure for her fears.

She'd almost died.

But last night she'd lived.

And now that it was morning, and the light streamed into his bedroom, she wondered if she'd done the right thing. Looking at the gorgeous man sleeping peacefully next to her, she felt like she'd stepped into the centerfold for Playgirl Magazine. The man laid on his stomach, his sheet artfully twisted around his hips, a tantalizing glimpse of his taut, tanned ass showing. Even at rest, the musculature of his back was defined. She gently shifted hair that had fallen over his forehead.

His eyes popped open, focused right on her. "Stop the press," he murmured. "I found the stalker."

"Who?" She frowned. "Is it your co-star, because I'm starting to wonder about her 'I know' comment to the paps."

He sat up, rubbing his eyes. "I was going to say you but, okay. I'm not prepared for this level of serious in the morning."

"Oh. Sorry." She leaned back on her pillow and stared at her nails. The French acrylics needed refills, and after last night, they were chipped.

He gave a breathy grunt and climbed on top of her, arms braced either side so he looked down with his gorgeous eyes still puffy from sleep. How could she look anywhere else?

"Babe," he said, voice low and intimate. "What's wrong?"

"I just wish I was allowed to investigate this stalker."

"That's not it." He brushed his nose against hers. "Are you rethinking last night? How are your ankles?"

"It was fine. They're fine."

For a moment, he looked offended, then his brows winged up.

"*Fine*?" He put special emphasis on the word. "Tony Lazarus is not fine. He is *fine*."

She laughed. His cheeks went pink, and he looked away.

"So..." He rolled off her to rest on his elbow and stare openly. "It's about us."

How could she tell him that where he was concerned, she'd always have doubts? He was an actor, and supremely good looking. He'd done nothing to demonstrate his philandering would continue. He'd done quite the opposite, but the truth was she'd known him longer as a playboy than as a faithful partner. Maybe this was about her. The moment she'd woken in his room, and realized her usual carefully structured rules of engagement had gone out the window, she'd become anxious.

She was changing too.

"Babe?" He trailed his fingers along her arm. "Are you okay?"

She hugged her sheet. "I don't know. A lot is happening and I'm still trying to process."

His eyes narrowed. "About us... not last night."

"You know, for someone who receives a lot of attention, you're very perceptive of others."

"I'm an actor. It's my job to read people and then become them."

Taking a deep breath, Bailey held it, then let it out. "I'm afraid, I guess."

"Of me? I'll never hurt you."

"I know you'll never do it intentionally, but you don't have a great track record of staying with one person."

He sighed and rolled onto his back, joining her in studying the ceiling. "I know," he admitted.

Honesty. Bailey hadn't expected that. Maybe a joke, or two, but not an admission.

"I like you, Tony," she said, trying for her own truth. "I like you a lot. You're not what I expected. Tell me I'm wrong, that the partying and the women were a front, and I'll feel better. Was it all a front, another cover to protect your secret?"

"No."

Disappointment lodged in her throat. Okay.

"But." He paused for such a long time, that Bailey thought he'd gone back to sleep, but then he started speaking with his brows drawing together. "It's a front for something."

She sat up to try to gauge his expression. He looked nervous.

"Tony?"

"I—uh..." He licked his lips and his cheeks darkened.

"Hey," she said softly and trailed her finger down his arms. "You can tell me anything."

"I always think I'm going to fuck things up," he said and gripped the sheet in his fist. "So I partied and screwed around so I'd never had to worry about disappointing anyone."

Her heart ached for him.

"Parker used to be so perfect. He was a hard act to follow. But I had my looks, and people outside the family seemed to just do what I asked if I smiled a certain way. It sounds stupid, but it was a relief to not have that pressure. And then, with my sin, it just kind of all snowballed."

"I'm sorry you feel that way," she whispered. "For the record, I think you sell yourself short."

He scrubbed his face, as if he could scrub away his deep thoughts, and then lifted his gaze to meet hers. "Bailey, I didn't know everything tasted like cardboard until I met you. Nothing I did back then makes sense now." His eyes turned dark as they caressed her form. "You make me both hungry and sated at the same time. I can't explain it."

"Oh, I don't know. I think you're doing a good job. Continue."

With a smug curve of his sensuous lips, and a glint in his eye, he shuffled closer and lowered his tone. "You make me want, Bailey Haze. You make me want to be the guy who chases the girl. I'm not going to leave you alone."

Strong hands tugged her closer. He dropped his lips to the side of her neck, bringing delicious tickles all down her body.

She giggled and rolled into him. "Oh, damn. You made me the girl who giggles when her boyfriend kisses her."

He lifted his head, grinning. "You said boyfriend."

"I did." She bit her lip, still smiling.

Her reaction prompted another series of butterfly kisses all over her body. He started with her chin, then her neck, collarbone, between her breasts and lower. His hair tickled and his lashes fluttered against her skin causing the most delicious build up of warmth low in her stomach. Goosebumps erupted over her flesh and he smiled against her skin.

"I love it when I make that happen."

She scoffed. "Cocky much?"

"Come with me to my movie premiere. Be my date." More kisses getting lower.

"You want to go official?" Her breathing got heavy, and she threaded her fingers through his hair.

"I think you already did that when you kissed me in front of those cameras and stole me away like some heathenous woman."

"Heathenous is not a word." Oh, God. Why were they still talking?

"It is now."

SOMETIME LATER, only interrupted by their growling stomachs, Tony went to shower, and although it was a tough decision, Bailey declined to follow him in favor of cooking breakfast. She only needed to mention the magic waffle word, and he acquiesced, leaving her to do her thing on her own.

Bailey swiped a T-shirt from Tony's drawer, put it over her naked body, and went to investigate the contents of his fridge. She found it stocked with groceries and decided to squeeze some fresh juice while she cooked.

She'd fried up an entire batch of waffles but was still trying to figure out his million-dollar price tag juicer when he came out, wet-haired and dressed in only a pair of low-slung jeans. He came up behind her, slid his hands around her stomach and rested his chin on her shoulder. The warmth he gave along her spine spread to her entire body. She smiled inwardly. She could get used to this.

"You need some help?" he asked.

"I can't work out how to turn this damn thing on." She touched a button, and it beeped back at her angrily. She hit it again, and it did the same thing.

"Baby, you have to give it a little loving attention and she'll be putty in your hands." He caressed the juicer as though it had feelings. "Plus, I just ask AIMI to do it. She's got my back." He lifted his chin at a speaker sitting over his fridge. "AIMI, can you please make me some juice?"

"Sure thing, Tony," came the feminine intonation.

The juicer whizzed on, filling the air with its horrendous noise. Tony grinned and shouted over the din. "She likes me."

"Of course she does." Even a computer liked Tony.

"What?" He frowned and pointed at his ear.

"Never mind." With a huff of frustration, she turned and focused on finding some glasses. There were so many cupboards. She began with the doors beside the cooker. The loud whiz cut off suddenly.

"Top left," Tony's gruff voice came from behind. He reached by her to open the cupboard.

Wringing her hands, she stared. Lined in neat rows was a plethora of glassware suited to all sorts of alcoholic drinks. Champagne, highball, wine, cocktail, martini. She scowled at the martini glasses. She'd not mixed her usual amount of Cosmos lately, which meant she'd not reminded herself to stay away from the urges she used to have. It hadn't even occurred to her until now. Testing herself, she removed a martini glass and twirled it in her fingers. It was made from crystal and probably cost a week's worth of her salary, but it was still an empty glass.

"You're staring awfully hard at that glass," Tony noted.

"It reminds me of something," she replied.

His silence had her turning around. The expectant look on his face told her he knew. He saw into her heart and knew the truth, or if he didn't, he wanted to. If this was to work between them, and she wanted it to, she had to be just as honest as he. Trust was a two-way street, and if built properly, it forged a path toward an unbreakable bond. She wanted that. It was her reason for leaving the CIA. She wanted a life, a family, someone to wake up next to.

She took a deep breath and decided to share.

"I got into trouble as a teen," she started. "I got in with a bad crowd. Alcohol was this big cool thing back then, and I knew my parents loved it. I wanted their approval. Their attention. So when my friend pressured me into stealing something from their liquor cabinet, and asked me to drive, I caved. I wanted to do something reckless. I ended up taking their car for a joyride and... there was an accident. My friend died."

"I'm sorry." A line between his eyebrows formed. "I didn't know."

She looked through the empty martini glass. The counter behind was all warped. "Every evening since that accident, I make a Cosmo and then set it on the bench. I walk past it and give it daggers. In my head, I argue with it. I tell the drink it won't beat me. I leave it there, proving that I can resist, then I tip it out in the morning."

"But you've never drunk it?"

"No, I haven't." She put the glass back where it belonged. "This is why I was so rude to you when we met. This mate thing... it feels like a choice that's been forced on me. And"—she took a deep breath, then let it out slowly—"You reminded me of everything I was resisting."

He folded his arms and looked down at his feet.

"But not anymore, Tony," she assured him. "You don't represent that anymore."

Closing the gap, she went to him and touched his unshaven jaw.

Raw vulnerability flashed in his eyes and he touched his lips to hers. "I don't want to be that for you," he murmured against them. "I don't want to be that person, period."

"I believe you." She deepened their kiss. He tasted suspiciously sweet. "Have you sampled the syrup already?"

A guilty look flashed across his expression. "I couldn't wait."

Amused, she tasted him again. "You love eating, don't you?"

"I love this—" he glanced around the kitchen at the mess she'd made. "I love sharing my life with you." Then he shot her a brazen smirk. "Plus I like eating. Do you know I have to dehydrate myself before a naked torso shoot so my skin thins and shows the shape of my muscle beneath?"

"Good Lord, that's rough, and coupled with your sin's restrictions, I understand how consuming unfettered would seem like a dream."

"Pity I have to work it all off later."

"I think maybe I could help with that." She gave him a wink.

Two eyes of molten lust flared with interest, but she held up a finger. "First, food and juice, and then we should probably speak with your family about last night. Do you know if they found your sister? And didn't your brother want to speak with you some more?"

"Party pooper."

Together they set up breakfast on the balcony cane settee. Tony flinched when Bailey took her first bite of waffle, and it hit her... maybe this was why he didn't date. Every meal was torture with someone. He'd feel sick being around gluttony. So she reached for him with her bare foot under the table. When she connected with his ankle, his surprised gaze warmed her. She became bolder and slid her foot up, then hooked around and entwined their legs. For a moment, time stood still as they stared into each other's eyes.

He knew she didn't like being pressured into doing anything.

She knew he didn't like feeling vulnerable.

But they accepted this.

Without a word, he relaxed and made short work of wolfing down his waffles while she ate. When the last morsel was gone, he immediately jumped up and invited her back to the bedroom.

"Tony," she said, leaning back on her cane chair. "Sit down."

"Uh-oh. Am I in trouble?" He winked. "Are you the headmistress and I'm the naughty schoolboy?"

She laughed. "Maybe some other time. I think you're avoiding speaking about your family. Come on." She patted the spot next to her on the cane sofa. "I shared with you, now it's your turn."

Resigned, he sat down and stared broodily at two birds flying in the blue sky. Eventually, he said, "Parker thinks I can't live in two worlds."

"You mean the acting and the... um... crime-fighting?"

"He's right."

She didn't know if she should have an opinion on that, so stayed silent.

"My agent is putting pressure on me to accept more roles where I need to leave the city, and I can't. Not while the Syndicate is still causing havoc. I've already held up production too much with my irregular hours. I'm not building a good rep. The rehab didn't help."

"And if the Syndicate were gone, what would you do?"

He met her eyes. "About two years ago, we had no idea the Syndicate existed, and I was concentrating on the acting and the, um, other stuff. I didn't want to fuck things up when I was so clearly wasted half the time, so hardly went out in battle gear to patrol the city. I still don't go out much. They don't really need me, I suppose."

"Of course they need you. I have a hard time believing that you aren't missed."

He lifted a shoulder, but said nothing.

"Okay, so what *do* you like?"

He tensed. "Don't know."

"So, start with what you do know. Do you like acting?"

"Are you always so pragmatic?"

"Yes. Now answer the question."

"I love acting," he said simply. "It used to be all I ever wanted." He glanced down at his virtually flawless torso. "If you look at my brothers, they're full of scars, but I worked so hard during training to not be marked. I knew then I wanted to be on screen, and it's easier to get a role if you're perfect. Acting meant I could pretend to be someone normal. It was fun."

Parker had mentioned he believed Tony was the best fighter out of all of them. Bailey couldn't believe it all stemmed from his silver screen dreams.

"Do you love it for the fame? Would you still be an actor if you weren't famous?"

He thought about it. "I can't say fame doesn't have its perks, but I'd act anyway. I've always wondered what it would be like to choose my role because I wanted to, not because that's where the money was."

"Well, there's your answer. Why not try theater?"

"I can't." He threw up his hands. "I can't just not turn up because an emergency called me away. If there was a live show, there's no backup."

"That's what understudies are for, right?"

He shrugged. "I guess. Absences are frowned on though."

"My point is, there's always another option. Even if you took some time off to figure that out, you know if you lost all your fans tomorrow, you'll still enjoy acting. And if it gives you more time to help get rid of this nasty organization, then that's okay, right?"

He grimaced. "I hate it when Parker is always right."

"Correction," she laughed. "*I'm* always right. Now, I should probably shower and head to work."

"So... quickie?" He winked.

"Good Lord, boy. I'm still sore in places I never even knew I had."

"That's right, you're sore. Max won't expect you at work today."

She rolled her eyes, but he was right. She did feel an underlying tiredness coating her delicious aches. A day off would be good. "Fine. Let's stay in."

He took her hand. "I'm already planning the perfect Netflix and chill marathon."

Of course he would be, and it sounded ideal. She opened her mouth to respond, but was cut off by AIMI's voice filtering through from the apartment.

"*I hate to interrupt your moment,*" she intoned with a hint of sarcasm.

Bailey lifted her brows at Tony, and his jaw dropped. Was that a jealous tone? Could AIMI truly like Tony? Was that even possible?

Tony's eyes sparkled with humor. He pointed at the ceiling and mouthed, "She's the stalker."

"*But a family meeting has been called in the communal apartment. Shall I tell them you will be there soon?*"

"Thank you, AIMI. You're a doll." Tony lifted his gaze to the ceiling. He waited a beat then made an awkward face when she didn't respond.

"She can't see us, can she?" For a moment, Bailey had a very real concern about privacy.

"Nah. There are no cameras in here."

"Great. That makes me feel so much better." Not. "I guess I'll wait here?"

He frowned, as if she'd grown multiple heads. "You're family. You come."

twenty-three

TONY LAZARUS

WITH HIS PALM resting on the small of Bailey's back, Tony guided her out of the communal apartment elevator. The suite had been stripped of bedrooms and only consisted of living, dining and entertaining rooms. Although, he still preferred his own theater where the sound and picture quality was better.

They were the last to arrive, and Bailey was notably nervous. Black hair cascaded in a beautiful mess around her shoulders, and she wore the outfit Lilo and Misha had brought last night—soft jersey yoga pants and a flowing top. She gathered her hair over her shoulder on one side and repetitively twisted the length.

He didn't blame her for her nerves. His siblings and parents were intimidating. Their powerful, lethal bodies seemed to suck the air from the room. Max stood by the sectional, arms folded, and talking with Griffin. He noticed Bailey and came over.

The rest of the family were spread across the enormous sectional sofa and the dining table behind where Sloan had her laptop out. Parker, Evan and Grace were with her, scrutinizing the screen.

"How are you feeling?" Max asked Bailey.

"A little tired, but feet are doing better."

"Good."

Tony lifted his chin. "S'up, Maxi-Pad."

Max scowled. "Only Sloan's allowed to call me that."

"You let her call you that?" He smirked, then coughed the next word into his hand. "Whipped."

"No," Max growled. "You know what I mean."

"Relax." Tony clapped in on the shoulder. "I'm having a laugh."

"Yeah, you should be a comedian, mate."

It was Tony's turn to laugh, an action which brought the attention of the rest of the family.

Parker came over. "You're here. Take a seat." He cast a glance at Bailey. "You good?"

She nodded and then went with Tony when he sat next to Wyatt on the sectional. Misha leaned forward so she could see past Wyatt's looming body and grinned. She rubbed her protruding belly.

"How's the bub?" he asked.

"Oh you know, kicking me in the middle of the night instead of sleeping." She tried to laugh, but it came out like a wince.

Yeow. Tony'd bet the little squirt had kicks of steel, and with about two months until she was full term, she wasn't out of the woods yet. Those kicks would get more active.

Standing at the front of the room before the flat screen, Parker cleared his throat, eyeing Tony's chatter with distaste. Parker flicked a piece of lint from his shoulder. The charcoal tailored suit was the standard he wore to the office. Judging by the neat man bun and designer trimmed stubble, he must have been there already. God, the man looked like he rolled in a million dollars every morning before going to work. There was such a thing as looking effortlessly awesome. Parker should try it some time.

Tony leaned back on the couch and spread his legs. His knees knocked into Wyatt's spread legs which earned Tony a scowl.

"Those of you who went on the search and rescue last night already know this, but for the rest, we couldn't find Daisy," Parker announced.

Tony straightened. "Did you look where I told you to go?"

Parker lifted an imperious eyebrow.

"Well, did you check under the water? It was pretty dark in there."

"We *all* looked. She wasn't there." Parker folded his arms and ran his eyes around the room, stopping briefly on every person: Griffin at the back with his wife Lilo, Sloan and Max at the table, Evan and Grace next to them... and Mary and Flint, on the other end of the sectional. Mary's face was drawn and dark circles darkened her eyes. She was once a fit, vibrant, fifty-something-year-old, and now looked her age. Flint also appeared older. His beard went unshaven, and his clothes were rumpled.

Their appearance plunged a guilty knife through Tony's heart. While he'd been with Bailey, satisfying his urges, they'd been earning a few more gray hairs.

Snapping a worried glance back to Parker, Tony asked through a lump in his throat, "Do you think she's dead?"

Parker solemnly shook his head and then gestured for Evan to bring him something.

Evan gathered some sheets of paper from the table and walked over. In his hands were scribbled works of art, portraits and scenes most likely taken from his prophetic dreams. Most nights, Evan would see snapshots of the future, or the present, and when he woke, he drew them. Lately, his dreams had been full of whatever subject was most on his mind—Grace. But occasionally, something else would slip through. As the mood turned somber, Tony took Bailey's hand.

There was something on those papers, something no one liked. He could see it in their eyes. Parker shuffled through the papers and picked out one to display. Leaning forward, Tony squinted to make out the picture. Angry black charcoal strokes came together to make a shadowed picture of a crying woman wearing a gag, lying on a bed. She had straps on her wrists and ankles. Evan had overlaid versions of her face, as though she were shaking her head, screaming. The tendons in her neck protruded. But the worst was the sheer terror in her eyes, coming through all layers to hit home. It looked like the drawing of a traumatized, disturbed patient, and Evan had been dreaming it.

Tony looked closer and recognized familiar features. A line formed between his brows. He glanced over at Liza sitting between Misha and their parents. "That looks like you."

She returned his look with trepidation.

"There's more." Parker replaced the sheet with another.

Same scene, different woman. This time, her hair was white. Her features were remarkably similar, but she had fine scarring over half her face. "Is that Daisy?"

So she was alive. His momentary elation deflated when he realized Daisy, too, was being tortured, in pain, or… something not right.

Parker put the third and final sheet on the front of the display. "And we don't know who this is."

A faceless, interchangeable woman. It could be anyone, or lots of them.

"But what does it mean?" he asked, looking to Evan now back at his space with Grace. Evan folded his tattooed arms defensively. Tony got the impression the man was sleep deprived. "Why did you have three dreams of the same thing, but with different women?"

A helpless look flashed in Evan's eyes. "I don't know."

Parker cleared his throat. He paced the floor, as though he were in a board meeting. "Why don't you tell everyone about the dreams."

Evan looked to his mate for reassurance. She gave him a kind smile and a gentle nod of encouragement.

"Okay," Evan started. "I'll try." He took a deep breath and then exhaled. "For the past few nights, I've been dreaming about women being taken and subjected to physical examinations... No, it's worse than that because they're screaming. They're always screaming so hard that someone puts a gag on their mouth, and then they start crying. I can't make out much, but each time I dream, the face of the woman turns into another, and another. Sometimes it's Liza, sometimes Daisy... some of the time, it's a faceless woman I don't recognize. Every time, there are more replicate tanks in the background."

Those goddamned tanks again? Tony shook his head. "Replicate tanks. I thought you destroyed all of those."

"Apparently not," Parker added.

"It's been over a year," Flint pointed out. "The clones only took around two years to grow. These could be a new batch."

"So it's the Syndicate," Tony stated. He rubbed his thumb over Bailey's hand. The repetitive motion soothed him while he mused. "They've rebuilt their army of psycho soldiers, they have at least"—he counted quietly on his fingers—"at least four samples of our DNA. Unless Daisy somehow managed to collect a sample of my blood last night. Then it's five. I don't think she had time, though."

Parker steepled his fingers and tapped them to his lips. "Four out of eight unblocked genome sequences might be all they need to replicate our abilities in new clones."

"But do they know how to stop them from expiring? Wasn't that the issue with Sara?" Grace asked. She reached across the table and clasped hands with Evan.

Sara was Wyatt's ex, a Syndicate spy, a suicide bomber, and after that, a failed clone. She only lived for a few months after being born as a replicate of her original self—with advanced soldier muscle memory—and then her body failed her. As far as the Seven knew, the clones were still failing.

"What did Barry Pinkerton say?" Flint asked Parker.

"He said he'd always known how to fix the expiration problem, but never told them."

"And you believe him?"

"So cynical. But yes, I believe him. Doesn't mean the problem won't be fixed. Barry went out of his way to hide the solution because he didn't want the project to succeed, but now that he's gone, it won't take long for someone to find a work around. They've probably already hired a new geneticist. One without scruples."

Parker's words sparked something in Tony's memory. A name. He picked at the hem of his shirt for a moment, trying to pull it from his mind. When he remembered, his eyes lit up, and he hit his thigh. "Daisy said there was a geneticist whose name was Wayne Bosch."

"He was Pinkerton's lab partner," Sloan added, eyes lighting up with recognition. "He specialized in botany. The entire other side of Pinkerton's lab was covered with cages of different types of plant species."

"Well, one of them somehow ended up alive and eating humans." Tony grimaced, remembering the dried husks. "Did you find the bodies of the Faithful?"

Liza, who'd remained stoically quiet, spoke. "They were gone."

"As though it had never happened." Tony blinked and squeezed Bailey's hand. "It obviously happened. We have the evidence to prove it. Is it too early to get any info about the plant parts we sampled?"

"At this stage, all we can tell is that the bio-matter is constructed of some sort of flexible DNA binding agent. It has a molecular structure we've never before seen." Parker went over to Sloan. He tapped her screen. "See what you can find out about this man, Bosch. Even if he's dead, looking into him might help us understand the creature."

"Um," Evan cleared his throat, looking awkward. "There's something else about the dreams I failed to mention." He shot an unguarded glance at Misha. "Some of the women being tortured were pregnant."

Wyatt shot to his feet. He chopped his hand through the air. "No."

"I'm sorry, bro." Evan shook his head. "I know what I saw. Misha wasn't involved as far as I can see... but... maybe the faceless woman looks indescribable because her identity is fluid, and with the special DNA growing inside her, she's still a target."

"Way to set everyone's mind at ease," Liza snapped, twisting to scowl at Evan.

Tension sizzled in the air. Tony could practically taste Wyatt's wrath as it simmered uncontrolled. Wyatt took his woman by the hand and helped her from the chair. "We're going."

"But..." Misha started, then fizzled off. She rubbed Wyatt's arm and said softly to him, "It will be okay. Don't worry, love."

Still, Wyatt's eyes darkened, and he moved toward the exit.

"Wyatt," Parker warned. "You can't run from this."

Near the door, Wyatt tugged Misha under his arm, and pivoted with a dark glare.

"Honey," Misha said, looking up at Wyatt with big, glistening eyes. "I'm going to be okay. I'm more worried about the actual birth than anything else. You guys have me protected. Don't worry. Stay a bit longer and hear them out."

His eyes softened on her, but when he took in the family, there was panic in them. "This is out of control. We don't have the resources to deal with all this."

Liza hugged herself. "I agree with Wyatt. There's no way we can mount an assault on them, not with our limited intel and manpower. Yes, half of you with your powers count as ten men, but they're building an army of *us*. They're close to completing it. Even if they let the incomplete clones loose until they expire, that's still a minimum two-month shit storm we have to deal with." Her worried glance went to the sketches Parker had rested on the coffee table. "And not all of us will get out of it unscathed."

Her heavy words settled with a storm of tension crackling through the room. Everyone began to argue. Wyatt, barely retaining his stance in the room, placated Misha with hushed tones. Others were barking suggestions on how to get more resources. None of them were practical, and for once, Tony was at a loss for words.

When Bailey shifted awkwardly next to Tony, he realized she would be feeling very out of the loop. Most of what they spoke about had happened before she was in on their secret. He moved their entwined hands to his lap and covered it with his other hand. When she looked up, and he gave her a reassuring smile, she froze.

"I just thought of something," she mumbled.

"What?"

"Back in the agency, if we needed more intel, we would turn someone to our side—create a double agent."

Coming to stand near them, Parker interrupted, somehow having heard Bailey over the din of the family arguing. "We've already got Pinkerton, and the information he gave us hasn't led to much that we didn't already know. It seems like the Syndicate keep most of their information contained in pockets, or silos. None of it runs on a central server. There are probably precious few who know enough to do harm to their organization."

Bailey straightened her spine. "I'm talking about Daisy."

Parker shut her down. "We've tried to turn Daisy. I think it's time to accept the fact she's a lost cause."

On his words, the arguments stopped.

Mary gasped. "Don't you say that, *mijo*. Don't you ever say that." She wiped her glistening eyes. "That's what the Sisterhood said about you all when you were just babies. Thank God I didn't listen to them, or none of you would be here. Frankly, I'm ashamed at your callous outlook. I taught you better than that."

Parker's jaw twitched. "What will you have us do, Ma? Beat her around the head and drag her home?"

"Now that you mention it…" Griffin murmured.

Lilo slapped him on the chest in outrage. "She's your sister. Your lost sister. Your mother is right. You need to stop thinking of her as a lost cause."

Griffin tugged on his collar and nodded at his wife. "Family forgives."

"And we stick together." Lilo took Griffin's hand and kissed his knuckles.

"I have something," Sloan added. "We've tracked her to that building on the far side of the Quadrant. All we need to do is up our surveillance, put a plan in place, and roll it out. There are five of us now with powers. Surely we can infiltrate the place and take her out of there."

"But are there five?" Parker gave Tony a condescending look.

He stiffened. "What's that supposed to mean?"

"It means that you're never here. We plan—"

Tony held up his hand, interrupting. "I'm taking a break from acting."

That shut the smug bastard up. Parker's jaw closed with an audible click. "You are?"

"Yes." Tony glanced at his mate who smiled gently back. "I can't be in two places at once. You were right. I'm telling you all here and now that I'm committing to the team full time. At least until we've dealt with the Syndicate."

"Won't that affect your cover?" Lilo asked from across the room. She had a wily mind, that woman.

Griffin nodded in agreement. "Lilo is right. As much as it pains me to admit, having an airtight alibi is good for all of us. If you suddenly quit and disappear, it could raise questions."

Tony shrugged. "I guess I could do some volunteer work in the meantime. Considering my stint in rehab, I don't think it will come as a surprise."

"I'm proud of your choice, *mijo*."

"You're always welcome at the sobriety house," Bailey suggested.

"Thanks, babe. That's a really good suggestion. In fact, I'm going back this week."

"Okay," Parker said, taking control of the meeting. "So, Tony's on-board. Sloan's looking into Bosch. We're all agreed we need more resources, and we're going to kidnap Daisy, turn her and then use her to take the Syndicate down. Just exactly how are we going to extort the sister we left behind to burn?"

Mary winced, and Flint glared daggers at his eldest son.

Evan threw a scrunched-up piece of paper at Parker with a scowl. "Do you have to be such a dick about it? We're trying."

Liza rubbed her nose. "I can call my friend at the FBI. Maybe it's time to get them involved."

"Assuming they don't know about it already," Bailey piped in. "Hell, even the CIA and Homeland probably know. Unfortunately, there's nothing I can do to check that won't raise red flags. I don't trust any of my old colleagues."

"She's right," Parker added. "This operation is world-wide and the Syndicate has friends in high places. We all saw the breadth of the black site operation. They're preparing for war on a global scale. For all we know, this comes from the government."

"For fuck's sake." Wyatt snapped. "Can't we just bomb them?"

Parker tapped his lip, actually considering it.

Mary stood up. "I think it's time I call the Hildegard Sisterhood."

"No," Flint growled. "They want you dead."

Mary shrugged. "Let's be honest. It's been years since I defected. At first, we assumed we hadn't heard from them because we were in hiding, and we were good at it. But we've been in this city for years and the children haven't exactly been quiet. The world knows about the Deadly Seven and their abilities. It's almost a given that they've already found us." She stood, flicked out her hands and began pacing alongside the couch. Her husband rolled to his side, tugged a dagger from his belt and handed it to his wife. She shot him an appreciative glance full of love and then flipped the dagger with perfect precision. She did this while pacing, thinking aloud. "All the Sisterhood wanted was a world without the destructive influence of men. They trained assassins as sanctioned *Sinners*." She glanced at the newcomers to the family. "I was one of them. It was my job to infiltrate organizations, take down any male-dominated tyrannical organizations from the inside. Toward the end, their objectives moved more toward ending the general world domination type terrorism, regardless of whether women or men were involved." Pausing for a breath, she twirled the dagger attentively, and then continued. "They tried to do good, albeit sometimes misguided. Since the start, they were against the Syndicate. The very fact that they knew about the organization means they have good intel. I wasn't the only psychic on their team." She took a deep breath and then stopped, mumbling in Latin, *"Amicus meus, inimicus inimici mei."*

"My friend, the enemy of my enemy..." Parker's brow crinkled in concentration. "Okay. Let's say we agree. We reach out to the Sisterhood to make them our allies. How would we contact them?"

Wyatt growled and scrubbed his face. "This is insane. I'm bringing a child into the world, and it's gone insane." This time, when he took Misha, they left.

Parker turned to Tony. "Are you serious about your commitment?"

Tony replied with a nod.

"Good. Meet me in Ops at five tonight and we'll gear up and patrol. Sensing gluttony might be the key to finding this plant thing."

It was on the tip of Tony's tongue to say that he had prior commitments, including but not limited to his Netflix and Chill sesh with his lady, but he clamped it down.

Patrolling. He could do that. No problems. He bit his nails.

"Tony?" Parker prompted.

"I'll be there."

twenty-four

BAILEY HAZE

BAILEY SPENT most of the afternoon with Tony at his place. Both had been shaken by the news revealed at the meeting. Bailey, in particular, had not before fully grasped the enormity of the situation. These people who created the plant monster had their operation reaching around the world. They experimented on anything and everything they could get their hands on, including pregnant women and children... and they were preparing for war. Not just any war, an all out apocalypse, and the Deadly Seven were the only ones standing in their way.

Settling into the theater room with a bowl of popcorn and soda, Bailey sat on one of the leather recliners. Tony stood before the screen, using a remote to flick through the available streaming selection of movies. The man had been adamant they spend the afternoon together before reality hit. Tonight he'd be out patrolling the city disguised in his battle suit, making his first appearance as Gluttony in months.

"What do you think their end game is?" she asked.

From the way Tony's shoulders tensed, he didn't want to talk about it, but she insisted. She asked again.

Coming back to the leather recliners, he sat next to her and slid her a resigned glance. "They created us to sense sin. The initial plan was to train us as soldiers and then send us out into the world to execute the ones who sinned the most. Our birth mother thought we were to use our powers to target the worst sinners and convince them to be better, only using our abilities as a last resort. When she learned the Syndicate wanted us be judge, jury and executioner, she made it so our powers would only manifest when we had a mate to balance us, and help keep us sane. So... long story short, they want to raze the world of sinners and build a utopia of saints."

"Surely you're not serious."

He gave a grim nod of the head and then stole a piece of popcorn. "Deadly."

"Wow."

Tony lobbed the popcorn into his mouth. "Mary used to have visions of the future when she worked with the Sisterhood. She saw two variations, one where we were used to create this destructive future, and one where we prevented it. The Sisterhood didn't want to take a chance and wanted us dead. Mary believed we could be saved."

"Oh my God." Bailey slunk low in her chair. "And the people who created you are still trying to replicate what they did with you, but with clones they can grow every two years in a tank?"

Tony nodded, then grinned and pointed his remote at the big cinema screen. "Harry Potter?"

The man could snap off his worries in an instant, but Bailey wasn't so adept. This news shocked her to her core. Forget about the years of work she'd sacrificed to fighting human terrorists, the Syndicate had created inhuman threats, and they weren't even on the CIA radar... not that she'd ever known. If Liza considered turning to her

FBI friend, then perhaps Bailey should reach out to her old agency. Except, she trusted them less than a glass of Cosmo. And Homeland? They feed those guys raw meat for meals. They were ruthless. Going to them with this news might not end well for anyone.

"Bailey, don't worry," Tony said, capturing her hand. "It will be fine."

"How?"

"We fight." He thought about it. "And we do what you said. Turn Daisy to our side and then use her intel to take them down from the inside."

"Assuming she's in a position of trust, and the intel is good."

"She's Julius's only daughter with him. Surely she's his most trusted."

Bailey wasn't so sure it was as clear cut as that.

"Come here," Tony said. He shifted the bowl of popcorn to his other side and then lifted her with strong hands over the armrest until she straddled him. Positioning her hips against his, he lowered his voice seductively. His rumbling purr penetrated her system. "Let's not talk about it now. We have each other. Let's focus on that."

And then he used his lips to brush hers with a tantalizing sweep before nibbling her jaw and kissing her neck. Finding her erogenous zone beneath her ear, he went to work undoing her tension. A moan escaped, and she arched into him, enjoying his grunt of approval when her breasts pressed against his chest.

"That's it, baby," he murmured. "Let's forget our problems, just for the next few hours."

It was unavoidable. The tension left, just leaked out through her skin with every kiss and touch of his mouth. Being with Tony was like something she'd never experienced before. He was attentive, wanting, and loving. He was home.

☯

AFTER TONY HAD LEFT to meet with Parker, Bailey gathered what belongings she could find in his apartment, and got ready to leave. They'd spent most of the afternoon watching precious little TV, but plenty of each other. Tony had been true to his words and made her forget about the outside world and its heavy problems.

She had to admit she liked spending time with him. She liked that he needed her. She liked that he made her laugh. And she especially liked that he came from a family that not only fought to keep the peace, but were dedicated to saving those less fortunate than them. Less fortunate and sometimes misguided. He represented everything she fought for while in the agency.

He was so much more than the movie star poster boy.

And he was hers.

Butterflies fluttered in her stomach and she smiled to herself.

She'd told him she'd be there when he got back from patrolling, but she hadn't, however, mentioned that she would stay in the interim. Her to-do list was growing. She needed her own clothes, and her car was still at the hotel. The valet cost would be astronomical. Not to mention she wanted to speak with Max and the rest of the Nightingale Team. And her firearm was missing somewhere in the Cardinal City sewers. That last one was just going to have to stay there for the mean time. She wouldn't be caught dead fishing around in those muddy waters on her own, maybe never.

Just thinking about everything she had to do made her head giddy.

Since she couldn't find a phone at Tony's place, she needed help to call a cab. Stopping near the front door, she lifted her face to the kitchen speaker like she'd seen Tony do, and awkwardly said, "Hi AIMI, it's Bailey Haze."

Nothing.

She tried again. "AIMI? Just wondering if you could call me a cab so I can leave?"

Immediately, AIMI answered. Funny that.

"*Greetings Bailey Haze. I will arrange for a Cardinal City taxi to meet you downstairs. Where would you like to go?*" AIMI's voice was saccharine sweet with a touch of computerized inflection.

"Home. Please. The address is—"

"*I know where you live. One moment please.*"

She knew where Bailey lived? Freaky.

"Wait," she said. "I think it's best I head to the hotel to collect my car, first. Then I can drive it home. That makes more sense."

"*One moment please.*"

A pause that lasted a few seconds, and then AIMI responded. "*Your cab will be waiting for you outside the lobby in T-Minus five minutes and counting.*"

"Thank you."

No response. Right. Well, guess it was time to go then.

Bailey let herself out and took the elevator down to the lobby entrance where Gus manned his desk. That was a slight overstatement. He sat behind, engrossed in a book with the words *Treasure Hunter Security* on the cover. He had no idea Bailey had arrived.

"Evening, Gus," she greeted.

He jolted, as though he'd been caught stealing. He hid the book beneath the bench and smiled. "Miss Haze, I didn't realize you were still in the building."

Heat flushed her cheeks at the implications, but it was another thing she'd have to get used to. "I'll be back later."

"You need help with any bags?"

"I'm good thanks, Gus. Didn't bring much with me. I'll see you tonight."

He touched the tip of his Aviator style hat in a salute. "Until then."

From the corner of her eye, she saw him retrieving his book and getting right back to the story. Must be a good one.

The cab ride to the hotel was a short one. Bailey had no time to prepare herself for the very real possibility that she'd be accosted by paparazzi camped out since the previous day, and when she caught sight of the cluster of photographers parked where the public sidewalk met the valet driveway, she cringed.

"Great," she mumbled. She tugged her baggy shirt to cover the yoga pants. She wore no makeup and no sunglasses. She didn't even have a bra on. She felt naked. If they recognized her—she shook the thoughts away. *Just get it done with.*

After paying the cabbie, she got out and went straight to the valet.

The man was different to the one who'd parked her car yesterday. This guy was white, looked about the age of the kids at Hudson House, and had blemishes on his new growth stubble chin. His crooked name tag said Angus.

She smiled at him as she approached the desk. "Hi Angus, I have a car parked here since yesterday."

"Do you have a ticket?"

"No." She hid her apprehension and folded her arms when his gaze dropped to her chest. There was no way for her to even pay the man, but perhaps she could bill it. She added, "It's listed under Nightingale Securities. I lost the ticket yesterday."

"ID?"

Now *that* she could do. She pulled out her security license from her pocket. Being on a clip, it was the one thing on her body yesterday that hadn't disappeared into the sewer. She handed it to the man. While he searched on the computer system, she asked, "Could you bill it to Nightingale?"

He nodded. "It's all paid."

"Nightingale paid it?" Wow. Max was onto it.

"Um…" he frowned, scanning the screen. "Cardinal Studios paid."

"Oh." She'd not even considered the studio had validated her ticket. Who would have arranged that?

"I'll be right back," Angus said as he retrieved her keys from the rack.

Casting a nervous glance down the driveway, she checked on the paparazzi. The group had failed to notice her. Thank God for small mercies.

When Angus drove her car up the driveway, a cold feeling settled in her bones. He got out, slammed his door and sauntered over to her with the keys held out, completely oblivious to the state of her car.

"Um," she said through gritted teeth, barely containing her anger. "What the fuck happened?"

He gaped at her, and then back to the car.

The word "Slut" had been keyed repetitively into the side panel.

"Wasn't that there before?"

"Are you insane?" she snapped, voice raising. "Do you think I'd willingly drive around in that thing? No, it wasn't there before."

"I… um," he spluttered.

"How in hell did a car in five-star valet protection get keyed?" She tapped her foot. "I'm waiting."

He went pale. "I can get my manager."

"I don't want you to get your manager. I want you to explain!"

The poor kid took the brunt of her temper. She'd been calmed all day by Tony's soft words and seductive tongue, but now everything wanted to come out, and he was the focus. She opened her mouth to say more, but noticed the paparazzi coming to attention. One of them squinted at her and slowly raised his camera with the large tele-scopic lens.

"Never mind," she growled. "I'll call the manager later."

As quickly as her feet could carry her without raising more suspi-cion, she collected the keys from him and got into the car. She planted her foot on the gas and drove away, hiding her face as she passed the cluster of attentive photographers.

She fumed the entire drive to her apartment, cursing Tony's stalker—it had to be her—before she finally cooled her jets enough to realize that she'd received a vital clue as to the perpetrator's identity. The stalker was someone with access to the studio expense account. Must be. If they'd been able to pay her bill and get close to her car, then surely, they were part of the staff. Nobody else would have been allowed to get down to the garage, unless someone asked to check on it.

Once Bailey had returned to her condo, she quickly showered and dressed in a Nightingale Securities uniform. It reassured her to wear the dark, familiar attire. She wasn't due back at work, but she felt as though, if Tony was going to be out protecting the city, it was the least she could do to find his stalker. She packed an overnight bag with essential items, and maybe a set of lingerie or two, and then headed to her small kitchenette.

Looking around, she took stock. The wooden cupboards and stainless steel appliances were modest, but new. She opened a cupboard. One lone martini glass sat next to a stainless steel cocktail shaker.

The accident that cost her friend's life happened years ago. So long ago that she'd lived the same amount of years since the accident than before. She was sixteen then, now she was thirty-two. How long was she going to keep this ruse up for? It was time to either accept the fact she'd made her own decisions that fated day and not blame the alcohol, or keep using it as an excuse.

She slumped. Deep down inside, she'd always known the alcohol wasn't to blame; she was. All these years she had pretended it was the other way around so she could live with herself, but the truth was, *she* had made the choice to get drunk. *She* had ignored her intuition to not get into the car whilst intoxicated. *She* had chosen to do as her friend asked, even when she knew it was wrong.

Come on, Bailey, just one drink. Your parents won't even know we're missing. Don't be a stuffy old matron.

Memories assaulted her mind.

To capture the attention of her parents, she had made a mistake, a deadly one, and she'd been making up for it ever since.

But was she confident with her choices now?

Was she still that blundering girl?

Was it okay to forgive herself?

Tony may have been the one who rescued her from the sewer, but their time together had shown a vulnerability in him she'd never seen before. He needed her to be strong. She had to stop worrying about destroying lives and start building them.

Bailey took the martini glass and then walked over to her trash can. She lifted the lid and dropped it in.

twenty-five

TONY LAZARUS

TONY CAME to the door of the operations room with a sinking feeling. All the old expectations were exactly where he'd left them. But this time it was different. He had Bailey. He had his new power. So he straightened his spine and continued further into the room. The open space took up a few hundred square feet. Television screens on a wall flickered with the latest from the news networks. Paper, office documents and various computer devices covered the central strategy table. Two of the seven battle suits housed in the glass cabinets on the far wall were missing. At first, Tony assumed two of his family were already out in the city, causing havoc for criminal kind, but then he noticed Parker in the adjoined workshop area, already wearing his suit, hood down. The second suit was laying flat on the bench, interior exposed, and with some wires out.

Flint watched avidly, his spectacles down to the tip of his nose. Sloan was also there, sitting on a stool. Dressed in some grease-stained casual clothes, it appeared as though she'd been working with Flint on some sort of tech repairs.

Damn. Tony had thought he was on time. He should have known

Parker would be early. The three of them appeared to have been at it for a while. A minor splash of guilt hit him when he thought of how he'd spent the afternoon, but then he shoved it aside. He'd needed the time to prepare himself mentally for what was to come.

He'd not been patrolling in months.

Sauntering up to them, he leaned on the bench. "Wha'cha doin'?"

Parker flicked his judgmental gaze at Tony. "Good, you're here."

"I said I would come, so here I am."

The two men shared a tension-loaded look. Parker, no doubt, thought of some condescending response, but kept it leashed beneath a clenched jaw and blazing golden eyes.

Tony's fists flexed at his side. Tonight was not going to go well if the dude glared at him the entire time. Tony's patience was already worn thin, and he had the inexplicable urge to chase down Parker's disappointment with a stiff drink.

The moment Tony thought it, he became acutely aware of how much of his drinking had been bolstered by the weight of expectations pushed onto him. Parker's comment to Bailey about Tony being the best fighter wasn't a slip. It was meant to get back to Tony. It had been a round about way to let him know that he had a responsibility, and he hadn't been filling it.

Maybe it was just a compliment.

Problem was, Tony failed to recognize a genuine compliment these days. Most people he came into contact with always wanted something out of him. A selfie, a kiss, The Smile.

Except Bailey.

Sure, she liked his company, but this past afternoon, she'd let him make the demands.

At the thought of his mate, a warm feeling washed through him, releasing the tension knotted in his shoulders. He relaxed with a slow exhale through the teeth.

There were many issues floating between Parker and Tony. They used to be good friends. Parker's public identity was just as much as a playboy as Tony's. Parker left others running the day-to-day business of his billion-dollar tech empire, while he partied hard and pursued wayward entrepreneurial interests like opening clubs and restaurants, or adrenaline junky seeking activities.

Lately though, Parker had been less of a party boy and more of a workaholic. During his days, he went to his office, then came home and worked, either in the workshop or out on the street.

Tony shoved his thoughts down and shifted his glare to the suit.

Sloan smirked, eyes dancing between her brothers. "You both forget to wear your tampons today, or something?"

Parker bared his teeth at her.

Tony kissed the air in her direction, and she replied by putting her finger down her throat and pretending to gag. Good to see some of them hadn't lost their humor.

Flint watched over the actions of his children with wary tolerance. He cleared his throat. "Right, well, I'm about to head off for something to eat. Your mother has cooked Jamaican jerk chicken and I can already taste the flavor. Do you need me anymore, Parker?"

Parker shook his head.

Sloan's gaze locked onto Flint, slowly widening as though his words had just passed her brain barrier. "Did you say jerk chicken?" She licked her lips, eyes turning desperate. "How much did she cook?"

"Why don't you and Max come over and find out?"

She hopped off her stool and jogged to the doorway. Leaning on the jamb, she shouted down the hall, "You hear that, Max?"

"What?" came a distant voice.

"I said, *jerk chicken!*"

Moments later, Max appeared in the doorway, red-faced and

breathing hard in sweaty gym clothes. Wiping his face with a towel, he glanced over at Parker and gave a curt nod. He did the same to Flint and Tony. Then his eyes turned soft as they took in his woman, now rubbing her hands up and down his slick arms with amorous intent.

"What did you say?" he asked.

"Huh?" Her eyes glazed as she took in his curved biceps. "Did I say something?"

Max laughed and shook his head, an action which prompted a scowl on Sloan's face.

"Don't make fun of me for liking this," she said. "I can't think straight. First, it was the jerk chicken, and then you come in looking all... *that.*"

Max whispered something in Sloan's ear that had her cheeks turning beet red. Tony wanted to laugh.

"We'll be there, Flint," Max said with amused eyes.

"Someone needs to be on comms," Parker pointed out gruffly. "And I thought you could let your crew know about what we spoke about earlier, Max."

Max's face hardened, and he nodded. "Yes, I'll let them know tonight."

"Know what?" Tony asked.

Although Max met Tony's gaze, it was Parker who responded. "Since we all agreed we need more resources, I've asked Max to bring the rest of his team into the fold. Half of them already know our secret."

"Oh." Would have been nice if he'd been consulted.

Sloan pushed Max out the door, shouting parting words to Flint over her shoulder, "See you in thirty, dad. And you two, stop being such tight asses. Go out and have some fun."

Tony slid a tentative look to Parker.

Maybe that was where his problem lied. They used to hang. Chat over a drink. Base jump off a cliff. And then Parker grew the carrot in his ass.

Parker pointed at the suit. "I made some modifications since your powers came in."

"Oh?" Tony's brows lifted, and he shifted for a closer look. The suit seemed the same to him, but he'd never really taken a close look.

With a mini screwdriver in hand, Parker indicated a line from the shoulder to the cuff. "Since power directs from your torso and arms to your hands using a focused photon blast, I've replaced the inner lining with kinetic absorbing fabric engineered to redistribute the flow so the buildup of power is enhanced at the end of the sleeve."

Tony blinked, comprehension dawning. "You made it so any power that leaks through my body and arms is captured and sent to my hands."

"And of course, I've tested the flame resistance to your standard. You won't be catching fire, and neither will the tech built into the suit."

Tony peered at his brother. He didn't have to do all this extra stuff, but he did. For all his pride and ego, Parker was the steady rock who pushed their little group forward. Or his pride was making him do it. Either way, Tony's ire at the man had been misplaced. He owed Parker an apology.

He coughed. "Thanks, bro."

Parker lifted a shoulder in acknowledgement.

Good. Glad that was out of the way.

"Put it on," Parker ordered.

Tony undressed right there. None of them were ashamed of their bodies, or prudes in the least. They'd been stuck with needles, poked and prodded as kids, and they'd spent the rest of their youth conditioning their bodies to be lethal weapons.

Removing his clothes, he stepped into the enormous, seamless outfit. It looked ridiculous unfitted, almost like a baggy garbage bag. Once he got his arms and neck in the right hole, he hit the form fitting button. Air whooshed out as the fabric retracted to hug his frame. He tested the fit by doing a few squats, feeling Parker's assessing eyes on him the entire time.

"Feels good." Felt familiar.

He retrieved his orange face-scarf from the mannequin and tugged it over his head. The elastic fabric could be pulled to cover his nose and mouth, or pool at his neck if he needed to breathe easier. Parker watched Tony reacquaint himself with the suit, and Tony could almost feel Parker's need to add his two cents. When Tony lifted the hood, Parker said, "AIMI's patched in now. And have you tested the syncing ability?"

Tony nodded. "I remember the demonstration."

"Right. You just haven't taken it for a spin."

"I was with you at the black site, remember?"

Tony took Parker's underlying snark on the chin. It was Tony's fault after all. He'd taken a job with little flexibility and slowly forsook his duties as one of the Seven. Maybe his fear of failure had something to do with it. Either way, it was time he started making up for lost time. He fixed his posture.

"Let's get kitted out." Parker waved him into the weapon's room, down the hall.

Inside was a veritable treasure trove for the battle inclined. Floor to ceiling racks of weapon's grade steel, in all shapes and sizes. Swords, guns, rifles, grenades, accessories. Tony spied his old katana on the rack and lifted its weight to balance in his hand. Testing it, he rotated his wrist. Yep. Just like old times.

He sheathed it, then slung it over his back and synced the sword to stick to his suit. While he did that, Parker eyed some magnetic grappling hook guns.

Tony raised an eyebrow. There was only one thing they needed those for. Climbing tall buildings and roof hopping. Thinking the same thing, Parker's lips curved on one side. He tossed Tony a mischievous look.

"Did I mention the new wing-suit capabilities?"

"Fuck off, you didn't."

Parker glued his legs together, and pinned his arms to his side, and then asked AIMI to activate the wing suit. He threw his arms and legs wide in a star-jump. A fine webbing appeared between his legs, and between his body and arms.

"You did!" Amazed, Tony crouched low and inspected the tensile fabric, poking it with a finger. "Where does it go when deactivated?"

Parker pointed at the inner seams, almost invisible. "Similar mechanism to the flexible computer screen on the wrist. Slides in and out when needed. There's a parachute between the shoulders. Automatically retracts after use."

"Shit, Parker." Tony gawped. "If you weren't using your big brain to help us come up with tech like this, you'd be making billions."

His brother deactivated the wing-suit and shrugged. "How do you think I finance our operation?"

"True. Shall we go?"

Excitement zipped up Tony's spine. It had been a while since they'd had some fun... maybe they would catch a plant-monster while they were at it.

twenty-six

BAILEY HAZE

IT WAS six p.m. by the time Bailey walked through the front door to Nightingale. Damien and Tomas were lounging at their desks, throwing paperclips at each other. They were most likely just finishing up from a day assignment or waiting to head off for a night gig. Or there was nothing on the roster. Max had been a little preoccupied lately.

Bailey put her overnight bag on her desk. "What are you two doing here?"

Tomas scratched his shaved head. "Max called a meeting. Didn't you get the memo?"

Max called a meeting without her?

"No."

"Then why are you here?" Tomas's gaze turned sharp. "I would have thought you'd still be at Mr. Perfect's place getting jiggy with it."

Her two co-workers shared a knowing smirk.

"Oh, shut it," she snapped. "Yes, I'm dating Tony Lazarus. You probably saw it splashed all over the tabloids."

Tomas laughed. "Is there something in the water here? How many Lazaruses are left single?"

"Dibs on Liza," Damien laughed, scratching his beard in contemplation.

"Who does that leave me with? Parker?" Tomas snorted. "I think I'm a bit little for him."

It was true, Tomas was under six foot. But what he lacked for in height, he made up for in speed and intimidation. Tattoos covered most of his body, and he had a way of looking at you that made you balk. He was an asset to the team.

Bailey's brows raised as high as they could go. "He'd crush you between his thighs like a walnut."

"Yeah. Hate to burst your bubble, mate, but as far as I know, he's not gay." Damien added, continuing with his tease.

"That hair, man," Tomas added. "I'm jealous."

Damien twisted on his chair to focus on Bailey. "If you're not here for the meeting, then why are you here?"

"I—" Damn. She didn't know how much she could tell them about yesterday. She hated lying. "I lost my firearm. I need a new one."

Fortunately, Max entered from the street, saving her need to defend her rookie mistake. Losing your firearm was a big no-no.

Max's perceptive brown eyes landed on her, skipped over her uniform, and narrowed. "I thought you wouldn't be in for a few days."

"I need something to do."

"And what does Tony think about that?"

"He doesn't control me."

"You know what I mean." Max slid his jacket off. "After our conversation with the family last night, I don't think it's safe for you to be out on jobs. You're a target now."

Aw, hell no. She was not going to lock herself away like a princess in a tower.

"You're a target too," she pointed out. "Does that mean you're going to take a back seat on jobs?"

A loud masculine clearing of the throat brought both their attentions to where Damien and Tomas glared with shrewd eyes that missed nothing.

Tomas's features slackened. "What aren't you two telling us?"

Damien added to the tension with his own flat lips and clenched jaw. He folded his immense arms and lifted his brows. "What's going on?"

Max sighed and walked over to their desks. His was at a quarter angle to theirs. He placed his jacket on the back of the wheelie chair and then braced himself on the desk, two hands flexing on the laminate. After a deep exhale, he shot Bailey a glance. "I just came from speaking with Parker. Since they're low on resources, and two of us know already and are trusted, they want the rest of the team to come on board."

"Do you think that's wise? I mean, they're not protected by another identity." She tapped her finger on her lip. "I suppose you and I aren't either."

"Exactly why Parker's considering expanding."

"Ah-hum." Tomas once again cleared his throat.

"Yeah, dudes. We're *still* here," Damien added.

"Sorry." Max gestured for Bailey to stand next to him, then he turned to his crew and said, "The Lazarus family are the Deadly Seven."

Tomas and Damien stared blankly, blinking. After a full thirty seconds, they shared a confused glance, and then Damien said, "We know."

"You know?" Max frowned.

"Yeah, well, it was a bit obvious." Tomas pushed back on his chair to wheel across the floor. He stopped at the bar fridge near the games area, retrieved a can of beer, and rolled back. "About time you admitted it."

"How long have you known?" Bailey asked.

Damien glared at Tomas for not bringing him a beer, then waved offhandedly at Max. "Since you were kidnapped."

Tomas snorted incredulously. "I mean, come on, mate. You were rescued by a bunch of bloody hooded ninjas. The one who carried you, and who had the genius tech-mind needed to hack the bomb, was a woman. It didn't take us long to work out which woman you know, who's good with computers, and has a bunch of built siblings, who needed bodyguards for their partners, was."

Max ran a hand down his face in a trying way.

"Hold up." Bailey placed her hands on her hips. "Do you mean to tell me that everyone in this team knew for the past two months and no one had the decency to tell me? Even when I was so worked up with the Lazarus family for keeping secrets?"

Damien unfolded his big body out of his office chair, collected his own beer from the bar fridge, and returned with a lift of his shoulder. "We assumed you already knew because of your Spook-shit, and you were using your powers of misdirection to throw us off the scent. Don't you guys know everything?"

"How many times do I have to tell you all, I don't work there anymore? I don't speak with anyone from there."

"Actually, you've never told us that. You're very secretive." Tomas raised his can, pointing at her.

That was hard to argue with.

"There's more you should know." Max headed toward the bar fridge. "May as well get comfortable and grab a brewski. You want one Bailey?"

She shook her head. Still not quite confident to go there.

"Let's sit in the games room," Max added. "This is going to take a while."

Next to a pool table, there were two leather couches. They angled toward a big flat screen hooked up to a gaming console. Two of them sat on each couch.

Max cracked his beer. "It's time to tell you everything."

By the time Max had finished explaining the Syndicate, the experiments that created the Seven, their reasons for needing a balanced mate, and the new replicate clones the Syndicate made today, it had been two hours. Tomas and Damien took it all in stride and were grateful to finally understand the context: they were needed to provide security to the wives and girlfriends of the family. They knew now where the danger lie, and that a war was on the horizon. Nobody wanted that.

Max left them with a decision to make. Things had changed since he'd ask them to travel across oceans to start a private security firm. It was up to them if they wanted to stay and join the new fight or leave and find something else to do. Both had agreed almost immediately that they weren't going anywhere. They were with Max all the way.

Bailey left them not long after ten. It took them a while to decide that even though she was a Lazarus WAG, she'd be okay protecting herself because she had plenty of experience. Tony may beg to differ later, but Bailey would deal with that then. She said goodbye to her crew and stepped outside. Lazarus House was just across the street.

She'd promised to be back when Tony finished patrolling and didn't expect that to be for some time, but weariness dragged her down. Tony's big bed called to her, and she wouldn't mind taking a nice long hot bath. On second thought, maybe a shower. Bathing on her own in a tub was still giving her the heebie-jeebies. She'd tackle that fear again when Tony was there. He made everything seem less daunting.

Hoisting her overnight bag over her shoulder, she smiled to herself. Returning to Tony, to the comfort of his arms was something to look forward to. Ready to cross the street, she stopped when a familiar voice called her name.

"Bailey Haze, is that you?"

Bailey turned and lowered her bag with a sense of dread. The man standing five feet away was someone she'd hoped to never see again.

Tall, dark-skinned and sophisticated, Iman Campbell was a CIA operative perfect for undercover work in the Middle East. He knew three Saudi dialects, not only to understand, but to speak them fluently. She almost didn't recognize him without his long beard, but the distinguishable scar over his eyebrow was hard to miss. And those dark eyes and long lashes… she'd once drowned in them.

"It's been too long." He leaned in to brush his lips over hers, as though they'd never ended their relationship.

She stiffened but tried not to make a scene. Iman was always quick to rile. It was better to ignore it, give him what he wanted, and move on.

She smiled. "I didn't know you were in town." Translation: *What the hell are you doing in my city?*

He switched to French. *"J'ai besoin de te parler."*

Crap. He wanted to talk with her. The language shift obviously meant he was on agency time, and he didn't want anyone to overhear them. She glanced through the glass doors of Nightingale to where Damien and Tom-Tom continued to talk with each other. Now? *"Maintenant?"*

"Oui."

She gave a curt nod. She supposed even if she was done with the agency, this could be a blessing in disguise. Perhaps she could use her personal history with the man to garner some inside information about whether the Deadly Seven or the Syndicate were on their radar.

The moment she thought it, she realized they already knew. That's why Iman was here.

He gave her a disarming smile, picked up her bag with one hand, and placed his other at the small of her back. Body language was clear: She didn't have a choice, anyway.

twenty-seven

TONY LAZARUS

TONY INHALED THE NIGHT AIR, closed his eyes and crouched low on the top of the Lazarus House roof. Above him the starry sky provided both the cover and the light for their shadow activities. Below, the always noisy city street gave him a soundtrack. The rev of cars, the angry shout of a pedestrian clashing with a cyclist, the distant siren of an ambulance.

"Music to my ears," Parker mumbled beside him, scarf and hood down like Tony.

Tony grunted in amusement.

In the dark, the gray of their suits made them virtually invisible to the naked eye. Lazarus House with only a dozen floors wasn't the tallest building in the neighborhood, but it was their building and made for an excellent starting point. From their radius, the architecture grew from brick historical to slick and tall. Tony edged closer to the rim of the building and looked down. A whoosh of air rushed to greet his face, and he inhaled again, savoring the feeling of coming home. Or it could be the garlic from the restaurant that watered his tongue. Hungry already.

Heaven's patrons left the establishment with full bellies, while Hell's anorexic and jewel encrusted desperados lined the sidewalk, milling like bugs. Across the street, the Nightingale Securities building squatted between two taller buildings. The city council trees looked like cheerleader pom-poms. The people walking under the street lights had no clue they were being watched.

Tony could crouch there for hours just watching the world go by, studying the unguarded actions of people. His gaze shifted to movement in front of Nightingale, and he tensed, eyes narrowing.

"Is that Bailey?" Parker mumbled, catching the same thing.

"She's meant to be home," Tony grumbled. He went to lift his hood to bring the internal speaker close to his ear, intending to ask AIMI to give her a message but then stilled. "Who the hell is that?"

A handsome stranger dressed in a slick designer suit kissed her on the mouth. A low growl rumbled from the base of Tony's throat. He could do nothing but watch as the bastard put a proprietary hand on Bailey's lower back. Tony stared as the stranger picked up her bag as though he had the right to care for her, and then he took her away. And Bailey let him. What was she thinking? She didn't appear coerced or uncomfortable. She looked social, chummy, intimate. Anger bubbled in his blood. *What the fuck?*

He stood swiftly, tugged his scarf up and lifted his hood, then he light-footed across the roof, trailing her. His eyes never left the couple still so connected, their bodies touching as they walked.

"Tony," Parker warned. "Leave her."

Prickles attacked his neck. He shook his head. No fucking way.

Tony leaped silently from his roof to the next building, firing the grappling hook mid flight. It connected with the brickwork, a dozen levels up and then retracted, pulling Tony's weight high on the lead. He zipped passed residential windows, catching glimpses of families at their couches, faces flickering with light reflected from television screens. Like a ghost, he kept going. Cresting the top, he detached the grappling hook and scooted to the ledge of the flat roof, one eye on the street below, tracking Bailey.

Two more building hops, and fifty floors up, he almost lost sight of her with the distance making her small, but he couldn't risk sticking to the side of the building. That's when people saw you. With his lungs halting, he watched as his mate stopped at a black shiny sedan. She spoke with the man briefly and then she got into the car.

Friend, lover, colleague... all?

The implications whirled in his mind. Tony's breath heated against his face-scarf and dragged into his lungs. His heart pounded in his chest. City sounds morphed into a roaring crescendo as cold as the air buffeting his face. He froze, limbs locked, as the car drove away, taking with it his rock-solid faith in his woman.

Parker, having come up next to him, stood stoically now that it was clear Tony didn't intend to continue following her. He couldn't track her without her cell phone, and he'd seen enough.

"I'm sure she has a good reason. He's probably just a friend," Parker suggested.

Bailey had no friends except for the Nightingale team. That man had kissed her like an old lover.

Parker must have caught the twitch in Tony's eye because when their gazes clashed over their scarfs, his brother's eyes crinkled around the edges, and he said, "You need to bring the pain?"

Tony gave a sharp nod. Hell yeah.

Parker responded with a sweep of the city horizon. "Which way?"

Focusing inward on his sixth sense, he zoned in on the direction with the strongest concentration of sin—the south. Whether that was the creature, or some poor bastard who'd beat on his wife because she'd told him he'd had enough for one night. There were a few things people got wrong about lust and gluttony. Lust was when you wanted the person, before you had them. Gluttony was when you couldn't stop. For too long the citizens of Cardinal City had been serving up deadly amounts of gluttony, with no recompense for their actions. He flexed his fists, feeling the heat respond to his mood.

"AIMI," he said. "Activate wing suit."

And then he jumped.

Wind rushed his face, his stomach dropped as the ground rose up to meet him, and then he spread his wings and flew.

twenty-eight

BAILEY HAZE

BAILEY WOKE in Tony's bed to complete darkness. But something was off. There was a feeling, an intuition riding her system. It was more than the echo of a disturbing dream, or the sense of being out of her comfort zone. Movement at the window drew her attention, and she went on high alert.

Curtains billowed when the window should have been shut. She was yet to replace her firearm, and she had no weapon, so picked up the closed hardcover copy of her crossword omnibus and gripped it at the ready. Her vision strained in the dark.

"Tony?" she hissed. "Is that you?"

No answer. The air rippled to her right, lifting the hairs on her arms. She spun around.

The looming shadow of a broad-shouldered man was five feet from her bed, resting against the wall, watching her. For a moment, she tensed, ready to hurl the book, but then a bright luminescent blue glittered in his eyes, and she exhaled.

"Christ, boy. You scared me. What are you doing creeping around in here?" She put the book down, but Tony didn't move.

And then she noticed the other things. Blood spatter on his gray uniform, on his clenched fists. The fabric of his face mask sucking in and out at his mouth, his chest heaving and his muscles trembling as though he'd run a marathon—or been in a fight. He blinked, and the blue light winked out, but she felt him, still watching her.

Awareness hummed across her skin, making everything tight.

"Baby?" She crawled out of bed and flicked on the side lamp. "Are you okay?"

He gave a breathy grunt, eyes going down to her bare thighs. She tugged the borrowed Cardinal Studios T-shirt down. It barely covered her bottom, but she'd wanted the lingerie beneath to be a surprise when he came home. With everything that happened with Iman, she needed to feel safe. She needed to be with Tony.

"Tony," she tried again. "What happened? You look..." High. Adrenaline soaked. Not himself.

With her fingers shaking, she went to him and peeled back his face mask to reveal his handsome face, lips hard, nostrils flared. His haggard breath bloomed against her face. She threaded her fingers through his sweaty hair and pushed his hood back. Through it all, he watched, studying, arms never leaving his side.

"Was it... the creature?" she asked, and he shook his head. "Then..."

"I didn't think you'd be here," he whispered, brows joining in the middle. "When I got home."

Now, that hurt.

"Why the hell not?" The irritation in her tone was inescapable, especially after the evening she'd had. Iman's demands from the CIA were ridiculous, but she believed she turned the situation around. Iman wanted intel on the Lazarus family, and she was supposed to deliver. She'd put him off for the time being, so she could discuss it with them, but seeing Tony's post battle condition, she kept that to herself for the moment. He needed her now.

Trembles shook his body. Blue light flickered up his neck, and in his eyes. She'd seen this sort of reaction on other operatives after high stress, high adrenaline situations. The hormone was still coursing through his body, itching under his skin. He needed a safe release, to come down to earth, and she could help him. The last thing she wanted was a fire in the bedroom.

"Come here, baby," she whispered, and brought his mouth to hers.

She licked along his bottom lip and then sucked the flesh between her teeth. A low groan slipped from him, so she delved deeper with her tongue. Tony's eyes lidded, he resisted, and then he kissed her back, all in. Two big hands gripped her rear and squeezed. Desire speared through her, hardening the points of her breasts. Taking a step back, she lifted her T-shirt and dropped it to the side.

Blue heat flared in his hard gaze. He trailed a lazy path down her body. She felt his attention like a caress, going hot everywhere his eyes landed. The mauve lace bra, the matching panties. She palmed his chest, feeling the heat of him through his uniform.

"Let's take this off," she breathed. She looked down at his suit but couldn't find a zip. "Dammit."

He hit the Deadly Seven emblem on his pec. Air whooshed from somewhere, buffeting her face and lifting her hair. When it slowed, she saw the outfit had lost all elasticity and loosened like a melted plastic bag. He stepped out and kicked it aside, attached steel weapons clinking to the floor. Naked beneath, blue light pulsed in veins delineating his body, making his sweat glisten like diamonds. God, he was beautiful. Rock hard abdominals and an even harder erection drew her eyes down.

She licked her lips. *That's mine.*

Her husky moan of appreciation snapped his restraint, and he rushed her, picking her up by the thighs and throwing her onto the bed. With eyes blazing full of need, he flipped her so she was face down, then dragged her back to him as though she weighed nothing. He gripped her hips and lifted her to her knees, then slid a possessive hand between her thighs and found her damp through the lace. He muttered a curse.

Grinding back into him, she let out a whimper of encouragement. He plucked her panties to the side and ran his touch along her seam. "Yes, Tony," she moaned into the sheets.

And then she felt him there, his blunt edge crowning her, centimeter slow. The anticipation was agonizing. She wanted him to fill her now, but he stopped. He pawed at her buttocks, plumping the flesh. He crowded her body and gripped her hair, twirling it around his palm. Craning her neck, she looked back at him and caught his frown of concentration. He was thinking too hard. His mind was somewhere else.

"Baby," she said. "Whatever is going on in your mind, forget it. I'm here. Think about me."

His grip on her hair slackened. Strands of hair fell to her shoulders, tickling, adding to the sensations sparking in her body. Then he tugged on her hair, dragging her head back so their eyes could meet. So much raw emotion, and for a split second, she feared he was retreating back into that other person. She didn't get a chance to ask because when he pushed in a little more, thoughts vacated and she squirmed. Hot breath fanned her neck. But, still, he wouldn't go all the way in.

Screw him, then.

She shoved back, and seated herself with a long, shuddering groan.

"Fuck," he bit out.

"Goddamn it," she cried. "We're in this together, Tony. Don't ever forget that." Whatever was going on in his mind, he had to share. If he didn't, then this wouldn't work. And she wouldn't let them break. She gave them both a moment to adjust.

His stuttering breath pulsed along her spine, as though he battled with himself, with whatever he was refusing to share. Her heart clenched. What if something had gone wrong while he was patrolling? What if he couldn't save someone and they had died, and she'd jumped his bones the moment he'd come home? Maybe he just needed someone to hold him. Or maybe he needed someone to work out his energy on.

She decided he'd had enough time and started moving herself along his length. Out and in. Out and in. An audible hitch of his breath told her she'd surprised him, or turned him on. The hand on her hip flexed. The one in her hair tightened. What was he thinking? Hard? Slow? Needles pricked her scalp where he pulled, and then using her body and hair as an anchor, he began moving with slow, restrained strokes. *That's right, baby. Let go.* His rhythm quickly turned punishing. Harder. Deeper. Faster. Until warmth unfurled in her groin.

"Yes," she gasped. "More."

More of this every night. More of her giving this hero someone to come home to. More of having someone come home to her. As if hearing her silent proclamation, he drove harder.

"You're mine, Bailey," he grunted near her ear.

"Yes."

His body met hers with unfaltering, jarring force, igniting fire in her veins.

"*Mine*," he growled again.

"Oh, God," she whimpered, and bit the sheet.

Her orgasm hit with the force of a hurricane, drowning her senses with ecstasy and skirting the borders of pain. Tony's thrusts took on a desperate edge. He let go of her hair and gripped her waist, taking her with unforgiving passion until he stiffened and collapsed on her back, rolling their sweaty bodies together into the sheets until they were on their sides. Burying his face into her neck, he kissed her, and then held her cocooned in his iron embrace.

He stayed like that until his breathing evened out, until she knew she was alone in her wakefulness, knowing that for all his talk about walls crumbling, his were still up, as strong as ever.

She had to do something to show him how she felt, that it was real, and she couldn't think of a better way than protecting his family from the CIA.

twenty-nine

TONY LAZARUS

TONY AVOIDED Bailey as much as he could over the next few days, but at night he'd come home from patrol, and she would give him everything he'd wanted. At first, because he'd worked himself into a frenzy thinking she wasn't going to be there, he took it without question, relieved she was there. But the longer she'd gone without telling him who the man in the car had been, the more his distrust simmered.

She'd *lied* to him, or at the very least omitted the truth. No mention of the man, only that her car was scratched up. It was probably his stalker taking it out on her. He needed to sort that shit out. All of it. For now, he had a lunch to get to.

Walking out of the Lazarus House lobby and into the street, he cracked his neck to release tension. He was starving, and the family had asked him to lunch at Heaven. They had news about Bosch and his wife.

He was in the mood for neither a family meeting, or life in general.

A week of patrolling had left a brutal handprint on his emotions.

What started out like a fun session with Parker, had ended a twisted heap of despair riddled regrets. While Tony had failed to sense deadly gluttony from the plant creature, he'd caught plenty coming from the vilest of humans.

The first had been a disgustingly fat man sitting before a flickering television, eating a stack of TV dinners, while his anorexic and starving child was locked in a closet, screaming to be let out. Tony had been so furious that he'd pinned the man's hands to the dinner tray with his fork and knife, and then proceeded to beat him within an inch of his life. Without Parker there to level his head, who knew how far he'd have taken it. In the end, the kid would end up in the foster system, and maybe no better a place.

The following night, Tony had found a drunk man using a smashed wine bottle to slice up the bartender who'd cut him off. The scene had been like something out of a slasher movie. The worst part —none of the patrons, or even security guards, had stepped in to help before Tony had arrived.

Each night got progressively worse until Tony stumbled home with sore fists and a raw heart, remembering what had given him the need to numb his mind with drugs in the first place. He'd come home dirty with the feeling of gluttony, and ready to wash it all away with a heavy dose of... something, but when he'd seen Bailey in his bed that first night, his heart had shattered along with his mind. *That lingerie. That body.* All that was left was for him to do was get lost in her untainted touch. He'd taken her every night, and she'd let him. Until the morning when reality hit and he would slip out before she woke.

She was keeping secrets.

Brooding, Tony stepped across the threshold of Heaven, gave a valiant wave to the maître d, and then made a beeline for the private dining room toward the back. With the restaurant at capacity, the sense of gluttony pierced his skin and clawed him down. His footsteps dragged the closer he got to the private room. In a moment of weakness, he wished for Bailey to be at the family gathering so he could touch her smooth skin and siphon his pain away, but like a coward, he'd not invited her. He hadn't even spoken to her during daylight hours, and there was nothing beyond the general lovemaking directives during the night.

He was a coward, but drunks always were. Why did he think he'd be different after meeting her?

Conversation hushed as he passed booths and tables of people. The sudden silence made the kitchen sounds seem to grow in decibel. Shoving his hands in his pockets, he tried not to appear approachable. He was in no mood for a selfie today. Getting to the back of the restaurant, he spotted the private dining-room door open with Sloan glaring at him.

He stopped.

Uh-oh.

Word must have gotten around to Max, and then to Sloan. He straightened his spine and continued.

"So," Sloan said. "Funny story."

"Not in the mood."

She placed her palm on his chest, stopping him from entering. "Oh, I think you'll want to hear this."

He ground his teeth. "Fine. What?"

"Don't *what* me." She looked like she would hit him, but that wasn't really Sloan's style. It was Liza's. He glanced through the door to see if his other sister was there and breathed a sigh of relief when she wasn't. The girls were bossy.

"What the hell, dumbass?" she snapped. "Please tell me you're not being a jerk to Bailey already."

Oh ye of little faith. He could get much worse. "Why, what has she said?"

"She came around looking for you, three times this week." She held up her fingers. "And you've been conveniently out of touch." When he didn't respond, she pulled a burner phone from her pocket and shoved it into his palm. "Because you seem to have forgotten how to buy yourself a new phone, you can have this one. Bailey's new number is programmed into it."

"Stop trying to solve my problems. I'm a big boy." He scowled at the cell phone. It was a leash on his monkey-chain and one he'd blessedly done without. The moment the studio, and everyone else got their hands on his number, demands would come rolling in.

"God, you're a dipshit. Did you know that her car got scratched up by your crazy stalker? The one you keep fobbing off as being no big deal?"

Yeah, he knew. So what?

His sister's eyes narrowed. "So you knew the word 'slut' was the word scratched into her car. You knew that, right? I mean, your girlfriend becomes the center of focus in your public life, and you look after her, right?"

Sloan's words dulled as blood rushed in his ears. *Slut?*

Why hadn't Bailey told him?

Because you haven't been available.

He shut his eyes to take a moment. When he opened them, Sloan's gaze had softened. "If you want to talk about anything, I'm here, bras. You know that, right?"

She watched him perceptively until, startled, he realized she was reading his emotions.

"Stop doing that," he growled. "My feelings are private."

She threw up her hands. "Can't help it if you're broadcasting your mope about the place."

"Tony?"

A female voice had them both turning around. Tony frowned.

"Peta?"

The assistant from the studio.

She smiled warily at Sloan and then met Tony's eyes. "I've been trying to contact you."

"He lost his phone," Sloan explained.

Tony gave her a look and then hooked an arm around Peta. "Let's go outside and talk, where my nosy sister can't hear." And where she can't put the guilt trip on him. He was doing a good enough job of that himself.

He could have sworn he heard Sloan's raspberry behind his back as he guided Peta to the exit. They stopped in the area just outside the Lazarus House lobby. Folding his arms, he looked down at her. The doors to Hell on the opposite side were closed, and a bum reclined before it. His dirty face was shadowed by a hat, and a garbage bag covered his body. Tony shifted his eyes back to Peta.

"What's up?"

"Um." A blush colored her cheeks.

He waited. She turned shy. Sometimes he had this effect on women. It wasn't a brag, just a truth. They got shy, they stuttered, and they swooned. *Bailey never swoons.* He smiled inwardly. She'd never balked like Peta.

Forcing his tension to ease so he appeared less pissed off, he unfolded his arms and took a deep breath, letting it out slow.

"Is it the studio?" he asked.

This time, a nervous expression flickered across her face and Tony thought, maybe there's something else going on here.

"I just—" she started, hesitated. "I'm not supposed to know this, and I wasn't eavesdropping, but I overheard Donatello speaking with Chet."

"Oh?" His eyebrows winged up.

"You're being dropped after this movie. I heard Donatello ask to not let you know until after the premiere. He said you're too much drama, you've cost him too much, and he wants you done in this industry."

"The premiere is tomorrow night," was his first dumb response.

She nodded.

"Wow." He laughed incredulously. He knew it was coming, but to have his producer *and* his agent collude. *Fuck.*

"Tony, they don't know what you're worth. I do. I know," Peta said earnestly. She touched his cheek gently. *What the...?* "Forget about them. They don't deserve you. Some scenes they made you do were humiliating. Casting you in a roll where monkeys and animals ran all over you. Partnering you with *her*. You're worth more. *I know*."

Holy mother of crap. An unsettled feeling shimmied over him. Peta still had a propriety hand on his cheek, and she looked at him as though he was her sunshine... *shit*. She was the stalker. She was the one who scratched up Bailey's car.

Anger rose in him so swiftly, he had to clench his fists to avoid doing something he'd regret. Peta took his silence to mean something else. She cupped his face and pulled his lips down to hers, planting a hard and heavy kiss on his lips.

His stomach rolled.

A bright light flashed and flickered, and the unmistakable sound of an automatic camera shutter filled the air.

What—?

Prying her hands off his face, Tony stepped back, aghast.

Peta still watched him, eyes full of adoration. Behind her, the homeless man took pictures with his enormous camera. And coming out of the Lazarus House lobby, with a stunned look on her face, was Bailey Haze.

Tony's gaze darted to Peta, the woman who'd threatened Bailey and vandalized her property. Panic engulfed him. What should he do?

Pushing the woman away now would only serve to ratchet her twisted mind and paint Bailey as her enemy, and the photographer would see him. He couldn't get rough. He couldn't lay a hand on her. One snap and it would be taken the wrong way. It was one thing for him to fight with his fists against a sworn enemy, but a flesh and blood woman with a twisted mind. He didn't know how to proceed, except to get her as far away from Bailey as he could. Taking Peta's hand, and tossing eyes full of regret Bailey's way, he went in the opposite direction hoping to dear God that Bailey knew by now when he was acting, and when he wasn't.

Peta rushed to keep up with him, almost breaking into a jog.

"Tony, slow down," she gasped.

But his feet chewed the concrete with fast, furious strides. He kept going until he hit the alley behind the restaurant, and then he pulled her after him. Finally alone, he let go of her hand and showed her the full force of his anger. "What the hell has gotten into you?"

Her eyes widened. She paled. "What?"

"You kissed me in front of the paparazzi."

She laughed nervously. "Oh that? That was nothing."

"In front of my girlfriend," he added.

And that was when Peta's real colors leaked through. Darkness shrouded her eyes, and she glared at Tony. "Her? Why her? She's nothing but a—"

"A slut?"

"Exactly, she's…" She shut up, knowing exactly what she'd done.

"That's right, Peta. I know it's you doing all these sick things. The dolls in my trailer, the scratches on my bike, on Bailey's car. You need help."

Peta stepped toward him, held her hand out. "But we're meant to be together."

"It will never happen between us, Peta."

"Why? Because I'm a lowly assistant?"

"Because I'm with someone."

"Since when? Last week? I've known you all year. I know how you like your coffee, I know that you hate anchovies in your Caesar salad. I know—"

He held his palm up, stopping her. "That's enough. Bailey is the love of my life." That's why it hurt so much to be lied to.

Peta's jaw clicked shut.

"If you come near me, or her again, I'm reporting you to the police, and the studio."

And then he left.

TONY SEARCHED for Bailey on the street, but she was gone. He arrived back at the restaurant the same time as Liza.

Dressed in her brown detective jacket, and with her badge on her hip, she'd come straight from work.

His sister took one look at his face and stopped, just before they opened the door to Heaven.

"You got that cat-got-your-dick face," she said. "Girl troubles?"

He rubbed his brow. He should be used to no privacy by now. With a glance across the road at Nightingale Securities, Tony clenched his jaw and went inside Heaven.

"Stalker issues," he said, because Liza wouldn't stop staring.

"You want me to make some calls?" she said.

"Not yet."

Coming back to the private dining room, Tony held the door open and let Liza in first. The boardroom sized table inside had been expanded as their family had. Once, it only had a place for the nine of them, now it fit up to twenty. His parents were there, at the head.

Parker and Griffin were there, as was Evan. Sloan chatted with Wyatt about something to do with her folded origami napkin in her hands. A single empty setting sat at the other head of the table. Daisy's place.

"Good," Parker said, standing up. "You're here. Close the door."

Tony secured the door and then sat down. The quicker he got this over with, the better.

Parker pointed a remote at the wall. A projected image came up.

"This is Wayne Bosch's wife. Notice anything?"

She was pretty. Tall. Dark eyes, wavy hair and brown skin. Plum pouty lips. Good makeup. What else was Tony meant to be looking for here? Apparently he was the only one in the room missing the point.

He lifted his shoulders.

Parker clicked the remote, and another image popped up next to the woman. Bailey.

"They could be sisters," he said. "I don't understand. Why show me this?"

Parker folded his arms. "Did you say the creature went for Bailey first, both times? Up the top and below in the sewer?"

Warmth drained from his body. "You think it was a case of mistaken identity?"

"Daisy said this creature absorbed the man, right?"

"I guess."

"You guess, or she actually said that?" Parker demanded. "Be certain."

"Yeah. She did." Jeez. "You think it means this creature is influenced by Bosch's memories?"

Tony flicked his gaze back to the pictures. The two women had the same chins. Nah, they weren't that similar.

Sloan asked for the remote and changed the screen to stream something on her laptop. A map came up first.

"This is Bosch's house. I sent a drone. It's empty. His wife is not there, and he's not been there for months. We don't know where she is." She pulled up screen shots of someone's Netflix browsing history. "But she's a fan."

Tony cocked his eyebrow at her. "Your point is?"

Parker leaned on the table and peered across at him. "We have the woman's email. Get her tickets to your premiere and we can flush her out. Then we can have a little chat about the activities her husband got up to. We may even be able to get some inside information about the entire operation."

"What if she doesn't know anything?"

"Well then she leaves with an experience she'll never forget."

He exhaled. "Fine."

Parker pulled out his cell phone and handed it to Tony. "Make the call."

Moving out in the hall near the bathrooms, Tony did. Two minutes later, he had the name of Wayne Bosch's wife on the door list to the city's premiere event of the year and a message sent to the woman as an invitation. While he was at it, he put the names of the rest of his family on but didn't tell them. They'd either turn up, or they wouldn't. He wasn't going to beg for their attention. Returning to the dining room, he handed Parker his phone back.

"Anything else?"

"Not now," Parker replied.

"Good."

Tony was thirsty. Without a backward glance, he left. The sounds of the restaurant battered his senses. Their gluttony strangled him. He wasn't sure where he was going, only that he needed to get away. When he found his feet taking him across the way to Hell, he stopped. The photographer disguised as a bum was gone. And why

not? He'd got what he came for. A shot that will sell a million maga-
zines tomorrow.

Tony's gaze lifted to the big red wooden door of the club.

Locked.

But there was a back door.

And walls of booze inside.

"Stop," Liza said behind him.

For fuck's sake.

"Can't you women leave me alone?"

Wrong thing to say. Liza grabbed him by the collar and shoved
him inside the Lazarus lobby. She hit the button on the elevator and
dragged him inside. When the doors shut, she let him go.

"Touch me again, and you'll regret it," he warned.

"Get over yourself, Tony." She glared at the door. "Your girl has it
bad for you, and you kiss another woman in front of her, and then
take the other woman away."

How did she know already?

Liza raised a brow at him, as if hearing his silent question. "It's
already hit the news network. Lilo called and paid the guy off before
it got published."

He swallowed, heat rising up his neck. He'd fucked up.

Liza hit the stop button on the elevator and mumbled, "I don't
know why I'm taking you up, when you should be going down."

"Why?"

"This is the moment you chase after the girl. Don't let her get
away because of your idiocy."

"She's been lying to me, Liza."

"So what? We lied to her for months. Give her a chance to
explain."

Goddammit. She was right. "Fuck."

"Exactly."

thirty

IT TOOK days to recover from what its liberator had done to it.

It had thought she was its savior. It was wrong.

So it stayed hidden, out of sight. It fed when it could and drank the drips of water leaking from the last downpour. It stayed down in the darkness for days, feeding sporadically on the rats and insects that crossed its path. It remembered there was another savior once. She was its world. Its wife. It wanted her. All it could think of was her. It missed her. It needed her.

All of her.

thirty-one
BAILEY HAZE

BAILEY HADN'T STAYED LONG at Nightingale. The moment she'd walked in and seen the faces of her crew, she'd collected a jacket from her locker, and then turned around, taking the file of information with her.

Ignoring the questions from Max, she pushed out the glass door and walked into the cool fall air. She didn't know where she was going. She didn't know which way was up, and which way was down. All she knew was that Tony had looked her right in the eye after kissing another woman—not just any woman, the stalker—and then turned the other way. Like she didn't exist.

It was almost the same thing she'd seen months ago, when she'd first met him. Then, he'd been on the arm of a stunning supermodel. He'd been blind drunk and hopeless. This time, it was a different woman, same scene. This time, instead of coming her way, he went the other. Bailey had overheard some of the conversation. It was clear to her that the woman was the one responsible for all the petty nonsense with the keyed cars and dolls, and she was certain Tony was smart enough to have figured it out. Except, she'd hardly had a moment of normalcy to actually have a conversation with him. She couldn't remember if she'd told him what the woman had done to her car.

God, she was messed up for him. Just like one of his groupies. Just like she'd promised she'd never be.

This was it.

Proof that she couldn't make sane decisions about her life. It wasn't the booze. It was her. Sanity said don't get involved with celebrity. Sure, maybe it seemed like his heart was in the right place, but clearly she'd had it all backwards. He didn't have a heart. It was either that, or her parents were right. They'd never seen her either, no matter what she did or how she'd tried to please them. *She* was the problem. There was something wrong with her.

Barging into the first drinking establishment she could find—a run down hole-in-the-wall bar. It was two in the afternoon, but fuck it. She was a big girl. And she was spiraling.

The place was narrow and long, with only the bar on one side, and small booths on the other. A series of industrial lamps swung overhead, and napkins were pinned to the wall with various signatures scribbled on from famous visiting patrons. Her thighs stuck to the sticky stool. Five people were there, including the barman with the handlebar mustache.

"Cosmopolitan," she said to him.

He gave a short laugh and indicated to the sign behind him. It had a silhouette of a Martini glass with a red line through it.

She picked the only place in the city that didn't sell cocktails?

He took one look at her face and then poured her a glass of straight bourbon. "You need something harder than a cocktail, lady."

Nodding her gratitude, she took the glass in her hand and stared at the liquid. It smelled sweet, sour, heady.

She glanced to her right where she'd put the dossier file on the bar. It was filled with dummy information about the Lazarus family. Just noise. She'd made it up herself and knew it wouldn't keep the CIA off her tail for long, but it would give them a clear understanding that she wasn't giving up any information. She wouldn't be turned.

Iman had said they suspected the family of having ties with international terrorists, but he never said who. He'd also never accused them of being the Deadly Seven, so they'd either not known, or were keeping it to themselves.

Bailey stayed at the bar for hours, staring into her untouched drink, wondering what to do. Go home, give up, or go back to Tony's... again, and be the unseen person he came home to at night time to get his fix. She'd had it all wrong. She wasn't the one in danger of the drink. She was the drink. And she was being used.

Another glance at the folder and doubts crept in. In the reflection of the mirror between the wall of stacked bottles, she saw her face and grimaced. What was she doing here? This wasn't her. She was better than this.

She was trained to think through any situation with a level head.

So start with what you know, Bailey.

She knew she was Tony's mate. She knew this meant he was connected to her like no other. She knew Tony had a pained look in his eyes that had haunted him since that first night he'd come home from patrol and was surprised that she stayed. It was the night she'd met Iman. The night her car had been keyed. *Let's say, for shits and giggles, that Tony knew about all the above, what would that mean?*

It would mean that maybe he'd thought Bailey had cheated on him, or lied about seeing her ex-colleague. Maybe he'd been hurt enough to retaliate and make her jealous?

Her brows pinched in the middle.

"I see people like you all the time," the bartender said, wiping a glass with a towel.

"Oh yeah? Like what?"

He nodded at her drink. "You got a problem. You come in here to test your resolve. You look down at the glass and see your life flash before your eyes, and you wonder if it's all worth it."

"And what do you say to them?"

The grooves beside his mouth deepened. "I say you didn't come this far, only to come this far."

Of course he was right. She'd used her fancy education to put herself into the CIA, and travel around the world, far from home. She'd taken the hardest route to prove to herself that she could save lives instead of take them. That she made good decisions.

This wasn't her.

She paid for the drink, scooped up the file and went home.

IT HAD TAKEN Bailey only a moment to decide home was her condo—at least for tonight. Parking her newly buffed and shined car in her garage spot, she collected the dossier file and got out. Her place was the bottom unit in the three-level building. There was a tiny fenced in courtyard at front, and now that she looked at it, she could see how Tony had broken in so easily. She should have bought a top floor unit.

Letting herself in, she immediately dumped the file in the trash then went to make something to eat. A box on her kitchen bench stopped her. It was big and white with a ribbon around it. There was a note attached to it. On one side, there was a crossword clue. On the other, two simple lines of crossword boxes. Finding a pen, she read the clue.

What your stupid boyfriend says when he realizes he fucked up.

She smirked and wrote, I'm sorry. It fit perfectly.

Opening the box, she found another note stuck on top of the white tissue paper. The note said:

Forgive me, Angel, I've been stupid.
Be my date to the premiere tomorrow night and I'll explain. Tony, xx

SHE PEELED the white tissue paper aside. Turquoise stretch fabric with a tropical leaf pattern taunted her. Holding her breath, she picked it up. The fabric unfolded to a long, sleek one-shouldered dress that would hug her form. Stunning. Something else caught her eye in the box, and when she shifted more tissue paper, her heart leaped into her throat.

La Perla lingerie. Smooth, pale and sexy.

In her size.

He'd gone shopping for her.

She sighed and put it down, running her finger over the items. She was still staring, lost in thought when her cell phone rang. Half expecting it to be Tony, and she wasn't ready to speak to him yet, she almost didn't pick it up. But when she checked the caller ID, she noticed it was from Hudson House.

She hoped everything was okay.

"Hello?" she said into the receiver.

"Oh, good," Agnes replied. "I hope I haven't called at a bad time."

Bailey put the cover on the box. "No. This is a good time. Is everything okay?"

Agnes paused. "Look. I just wanted to get your opinion on something, and I couldn't wait until next week until I saw you."

"What is it?" Tension twisted Bailey's stomach into knots.

"It's... um. Okay, there's no easy way to say this, but I'm not sure if Mr. Lazarus's donation is a bit too much."

Bailey blinked. "Do you mean from Tony?"

"Yes, well, I know he's been coming in and playing games with the kids, which is great. You know, they can always do with a new gaming console, there's so many of them. But the music studio?"

Bailey didn't know what to say. "Tony's been in this week?"

"Oh, I thought you knew. He's been dropping in to spend time with a few of the children. But he promised them a music studio, and I almost didn't believe it, but the contractor has already been in touch with us."

She forgot to breathe. "When was that?"

"Yesterday. Do you think it's too much? I mean, we need some other essential items more than a music studio, if you know what I mean?"

Bailey hummed in agreement, but her mind was still stuck on Tony's generosity. He hadn't told her he'd been going, and he'd given no sign that he wanted to donate a music studio. This was obviously something he wanted to do on his own. She smiled when she remembered Tony trying to direct the press conference toward the sobriety house.

This was becoming as important to him, as it was to her.

"I think a music studio is perfect for them. They all love music. It will give them an opportunity to come to the house, and it will keep them occupied. We can just make sure to let him know not to go overboard with it."

"I don't want the place to be a target for criminals. With expensive equipment, it could be, you know?"

"Absolutely. I'll make sure to tell him to go for the cheaper equipment when I see him next."

"Great. I didn't want to seem ungrateful. Thank you for talking to me."

"No problem."

After she cut the call, Bailey opened the box again. A warm feeling spread throughout her body. She touched the lingerie and imagined a future with him. It involved a happier time, traveling the world together, maybe coming home to have a family. Tomorrow, she thought. Tonight she would sleep on it, and tomorrow she would make her decision.

thirty-two

TONY LAZARUS

CHRIST, Tony was nervous.

Dressed in a tuxedo and standing at the start of the red carpet, he tried not to flinch every time a paparazzo shot went off, capturing his awkwardness. A tug on his bow tie, and a check of his communicator watch every few minutes didn't help.

The red carpet extended from the sidewalk, deep into the entrance of the zoo. Over the din of the crowd—made up of media, fans and giveaway winners—watching from behind red ropes, he heard the occasional monkey whoop and elephant trumpet. It would be interesting to see how much of the noise would be covered when the movie started.

He wasn't supposed to be standing there. His turn to walk had been scheduled toward the end, but he'd wanted to make sure he was there first. He wanted to see Bailey alight the vehicle and take her arm. He wanted her to know that he'd be there waiting.

If she turned up.

He checked his watch for the fifth time. It looked like a Rolex, but the face was digital. No one knew it was a direct line to the rest of his family, and to AIMI. He tapped it to activate the smart screen and flicked through the apps until he found the message confirming the car he'd sent to Bailey's had arrived. If she'd accepted it, she should be here by now. Glancing down the red carpet, he didn't fancy a trip there on his own. The entertainment media were brutal sharks taking a bite out of every star and starlet. Already, he'd seen some B-grade actors get shunned and dropped mid-question when another bigger celebrity arrived. There were sports stars, reality TV stars, and more.

Tony had plenty of opportunity to leave the secure roped off holding bay he was in, but he'd wanted his last red-walk to be with someone he loved.

A smile danced on his face as he thought about Bailey. Yes, he loved her. He should have admitted it from the start, and then maybe he'd not have been so blinded by his jealousy and paranoia. If—when —she turned up, he'd know she felt the same way too. Everything else was just noise. They'd work things out.

Shifting from foot to foot, he straightened when a stretch limo pulled up at the curb. The driver got out and opened the back door. Holding his breath, he watched, waiting for that first long leg to poke out of the car.

It was a male brown boot, followed by navy trousers covering thick thighs... definitely not female. Not Bailey. He almost looked away, but when the rest of the body came out, his lips curved. Parker. The man had his locks tied back in a shiny man bun. His brown facial hair was trimmed to perfection. He looked a million dollars.

Tony walked over and shook his hand. "Wasn't sure if you'd come."

Parker shot him an amused look. "You're the valet now?"

"Wow," Evan said, coming up behind him and dressed in some kind of artfully ripped denim jeans and slick jacket. "I mean, we knew you were quitting, but didn't think work prospects were so bad."

"Asshole." Tony grinned and clapped the man on his back.

Evan sheltered his eyes and peered down the red carpet. "This is going to be epic. I can feel it."

And when Evan had *feelings*, they usually came true.

Then Griffin was there, looking dapper in a tux, his hair parted and slicked back, his spectacles high on his distinguished nose. His eyes danced with humor and he nodded at Tony.

"How many of you are here?" Tony frowned, craning to get a look in the limo.

"All of us." Parker squeezed Tony's shoulder.

Evan assisted Grace out of the car, and then Griffin leaned down and helped Lilo out. The two women looked marvelous in black formal gowns.

Tony inflated with warmth as the rest of his family got out of the limo and congregated on the sidewalk. He moved to Lilo and Grace and kissed each on the cheek.

"Thank you for coming, ladies."

"Wouldn't miss it for the world." Grace gave him a gentle smile and pat on the arm.

"Oh my God. This is incredible." Lilo's eyes flared wide, and she pulled her cell phone out. "Is it poor taste if I ask for a selfie now? The Cardinal Copy want some inside shots for the entertainment pages, and it's just that you'll be so busy soon, I want to get in first. And Oh-Em-Gee, I'm babbling. Cindy is so jealous. We'll see her on the carpet."

"Breathe, Lilo." Tony grinned.

She inhaled as though it scared her, then exhaled slowly, nodding. "I'm good. I'm good."

He laughed and took a few gratuitous red carpet selfie shots with her.

When she was done, Lilo hugged him, and squealed. "I'm so excited."

Griffin's lip twitched with humor, and then he took his wife's hand to lead her to the start of the carpet.

"Congratulations," Wyatt said gruffly as he came up with Misha. He had a black suit on with a black dress shirt, no tie. The pretty blond was stunning in a classy red dress that showed off her pregnant belly. Tony was surprised Wyatt hadn't wrapped her in cotton wool.

Misha shot her man a look and said, "Now, that wasn't so bad, was it?" To Tony, she winked. "You look mighty handsome Mr. Man of the Hour."

"And you're simply ravishing." Tony took her hand and kissed the back of it, enjoying the daggers his brother sent his way.

And then they were gone, Wyatt with a possessive arm around Misha's shoulders, tucking her body into his side. Sloan, Max and Liza walked up and Tony almost didn't recognize them. Liza wore a flesh toned gown covered in beadwork. He blinked. She wore makeup.

"Mention my dress and you're dead." Liza hugged herself and looked over her shoulder nervously. "Mention my face and you're deader."

Tony took her hands and unfolded them so he could see her better. He whistled. "Wow, sis. You got game. Who knew all of this was under that shoddy detective's outfit. Am I right, Max?"

Max went red. "No comment."

"Good answer," Sloan said with a smirk. Her pink satin gown matched the bow on Max's tuxedo perfectly. She lifted her chin at Tony. "Good work, bras. Looking forward to the movie."

The last to greet him was his parents. Mary had on a classic deep red gown with lace flowers over her arms. Flint had scrubbed up well in his black suit.

"Mi amor," she said and cupped his face. She kissed him on either side and then pulled back, eyes watering. "It makes me so happy to see this part of your life doing so well, and it pains me that it can't always be this way."

"It's okay, mama." He smiled solemnly. "It won't be like this forever. I'll get back to it soon."

Mary studied his face. "Are you okay?"

He winced. Was he? "I'm fine. I'll get over it."

"I'm not talking about the acting."

Oh. Tony's mother could see right through his act. She always could. "I don't know. Sometimes I just don't know. What if she doesn't..." He inhaled deeply. His eyes turned downcast. "I mean, I couldn't even keep my job. I left Daisy in the sewer." How could he expect Bailey to...

"Stop it." Mary took his hand and squeezed. "No one is perfect. Believe me, I know. Daisy will be fine. All we can do is our best, and when we mess up, we pick ourselves up, dust ourselves off, and try again. Family forgives. Family gives second chances. Family shows up. This is the kind of person you are. Bailey knows that."

He nodded.

She gave him a teary smile, and then Flint took her hand. He gave Tony a quick clap on the back and took her away.

And then Tony was on his own again. He checked his watch. Nerves flooded back, giving his limbs jitters. He tugged at his bow tie. *Jesus.*

Had he done enough to convince Bailey to come? Should he have picked her up, or called her? Maybe a dozen red roses... but that's not what she liked. Maybe... *Christ.* He should have just gone to talk to her. This was so stupid. She wasn't coming.

Seeing Tony's nerves, Parker hung back briefly.

"Wayne Bosch's wife hasn't turned up," he said quietly.

"Is that good or bad?"

Parker shrugged. "It was a long shot seeing if she had any info, anyway."

Tony nodded, only half listening because another limo pulled up, and when his watch pinged with a message from AIMI, alerting him that this was his car, his heart stopped. A text message popped up on the screen.

"Go get 'em, tiger."

AIMI's message amused him. Sloan must have programmed some more humor into the AI, or maybe she was learning from them all.

"Excuse me," Tony murmured to Parker, and then went to the limo. He waved the driver away and opened the back door himself.

Ignoring the millions of flashes behind him, Tony only had eyes for the beautiful woman peeking up at him through extraordinary long lashes. His heart stopped, his mouth went dry. Slicked back and to the side in a low bun, a turquoise flower secured Bailey's hair. She had some sort of shimmer over the naked skin her dress didn't cover. Instead of holding his hand out, he told the driver to give him a few minutes, and got into the limo, shutting the door behind him.

Scooting to kneel before her, he put his hands on her knees. The dress felt amazing under his palms. Her legs were... that slit showing smooth skin up to her thigh. *Focus, Tony,*

"You look so beautiful," he said. "Bailey, I've been an asshole. That woman kissed me. She was the stalker, but I had to take her away from you when I let her down. I didn't want her taking it out on you. And... I'm a jealous dickhead. I saw you get in a car with this man, and when he kissed you, I—"

"He's CIA," she blurted. "We used to date, but we haven't for a long time."

He stilled. Wow. He'd thought, maybe, but did he really think she was still working for them? No.

She covered his hands with hers. A worry line pinched her brows. "He wanted me to spy on your family. He tried to use his familiar connection to sway me, but I told him I'm with you. I wanted to tell you that night, but you were in a strange mood, and then one night became two and I just thought, I didn't need to burden you with it. I can see how it must have seemed to you, and I'm sorry."

For a few breaths, his mind went blank. "What did you tell him?"

"I said I would see what I could do and made a dummy dossier with nothing special in it. But I haven't given it to him."

"Why not?"

She shrugged. "Even though there was nothing in there, it didn't seem right. My loyalty is to you."

"Why are they interested in us? Do they know we're the Deadly Seven?"

She shook her head. "They think you've got ties with an international terrorist."

"The Syndicate?"

"That's what I thought at the start, but then if they knew about that, they'd know you were the Seven. No, it has to be something else. Maybe I can turn the tables and milk them for information."

A slow, wicked grin formed on Tony's lips. His woman. Turning the tables. For him and his family.

He nudged her knees apart and slotted himself between.

"Tony?" She whispered, licking her lips.

Their gazes clashed, and he blurted. "I love you, Bailey Haze."

Joy splashed across her face. He went in for a kiss, but she stopped him with a finger to the lips. "You'll ruin my lipstick."

"Well, then," he growled, eyes scanning her luscious body. "I'll just have to kiss you somewhere else. But first—" He shook his head to clear his derailing thoughts and reached into his pocket, pulling out a little velvet box. "I have to do this right."

He cleared his throat. With two trembling hands, he held the box between them and opened it. A single diamond ring sat in the middle, glistening as bright as her eyes.

"I know I may not deserve this, and I should have tried harder, but I promise to do better. You're everything that makes me whole. Bailey Haze, will you marry me?"

She choked up. Her palm fluttered to her throat and her eyes glimmered, threatening to spill tears. Then she shut down. Her expression completely closed.

A coldness seeped through him. "Bailey?"

She inhaled and exhaled. "First, you need to promise me something."

"Anything."

"Never again will you keep your worries to yourself. If you have doubts, I want in. I want all of you, Tony Lazarus. Even the parts you're not proud of. Do you understand?"

He blinked. He wasn't crying. Nope. That was something in his eye. He nodded. "I get it."

She grinned and moved to take the ring box, but he snapped it shut and pulled it away, much to her surprise.

"And I want you to promise me something too."

She bit her lip, eyeing him suspiciously. "Okay. What is it?"

"The same thing. Don't think you're on your own. You're part of this family. Whether we get married or not. I want no secrets between us. We talk about everything."

A slow smile lifted her lips, and she slid her hands up his shoulders to cup his face. Her lids lowered, and she cocked her head to the side. "I know what you did for the sobriety house. Those kids are lucky to have you there."

He stiffened. "You weren't meant to find out. Not yet, anyway."

"I know. That's what I love about you, Tony. You didn't do it because you expected something in return. You didn't do it for the attention. And for the record, that is why I came tonight. Not because you bought me a pretty dress, but because I want to be with the man who put those kids first, even when we weren't getting along. Even when—" she choked up. Pain flashed across her face. Her brows slid together and her eyes glistened. "You bastard. You did it again. You're making me cry."

He grinned, giving her the full force of his smile. "I want to kiss you."

"You have to wait, dammit." She tugged the napkin from around the champagne bucket and dabbed her eyes. "Let me finish." She took another deep breath. "I was wrong. You're not the man I thought you were when I first met you. You're so different. And I love you."

He leaned in, touched his lips to hers, and hovered. "So... is that a yes?"

She laughed and nodded, then took his face between her hands. This time, she made no hesitations and pressed her lips to his. "You're the best decision I've made."

"What?"

"Nothing."

She quickly glanced down at the ring box. He opened it again and gingerly took out the ring.

"It's perfect," she whispered.

He slipped it on her ring-finger, trying to ignore the way his lungs seized up as it went on. When he looked up, she wasn't looking at the ring, but at him. If he had any doubts, they were gone in that moment. *Not the pretty. Him.*

"You ready for this?" he asked.

Still with her eyes on him, she nodded. "As I'll ever be."

Swallowing the lump in his throat, he opened the door, and climbed out first. His family had all loitered at the start of the red carpet, causing a bottleneck congestion with the new stars arriving. Maggie O pouted and stroked the fluffy fur around her neck. She glared at Tony, but he didn't care.

He threw up his hands and shouted. "She said yes!"

Cheers went up from his family and the fans. Every camera in the place swiveled his way, and when he turned to help Bailey out of the car, he planted a big soppy kiss on her cheek, murmuring. "May as well go out with a bang."

She rolled her eyes. "I didn't expect any less."

Linking arms, they walked up to the carpet, smiling into each other's eyes. Evan was right, this night was going to be epic.

thirty-three

BAILEY HAZE

BAILEY FLOATED on air the entire red carpet walk into the zoo. Tony lapped up the attention and took every opportunity to show her off. His hand never left her waist. And every time someone made any prying questions about their relationship, he calmly announced their engagement, and then changed the conversation topic to his impending retirement, news which had everyone gasping and rapid-firing questions.

By the time they'd made it through the gauntlet, the zoo was behind them, not in the front with the animals, and Tony was positively beaming with mischief.

"Let my agent deal with that," he smirked as they came up to the brick wall of the ticket office.

"What do you mean?" she asked, frowning.

"It means, my love, that I dumped him. Not the other way around. Tony Lazarus always gets the last word."

"And exactly how did you find out he was going to drop you?"

"The stalker told me." He raised his brows at her. "Can you believe it?"

Oh. Her. Bailey's insides clenched. "What happened to her?"

"I told her not to bother us again, or I'd give her details to the police and her career would be over. I don't think we'll have any more trouble."

"Good. I hope she has a long hard think about what she's been doing."

"All right. Enough of her interrupting our lives." Tony gestured toward the crowd standing before enormous trees lit by atmospheric spotlights. Waiters with trays wandered about, handing out jungle themed cocktails. Pathways to the right and left were shrouded in darkness and had signs to stop any wayward people heading into the unsafe areas of the zoo. A stern-faced security guard stood at each entrance making sure the blockade was respected. That left only one path heading into the trees. A queue was forming, and security ushered people through.

"I think the screen is set up in there," Tony said.

The spotlights flickered on and off, signaling time for everyone to take their seats. A female publicist walked around, calmly but sternly ordering people into the makeshift cinema.

Unable to hide the smile on her face, Bailey followed her fiancé between the arched trees and into the jungle, their hands never breaking hold. Inside was a grassed clearing, surrounded on all sides by thick jungle growth and taller trees. Above them, the night sky twinkled. Lines of white chairs filled the area, and an enormous white screen loomed at the front. The only light came from the two enormous industrial spotlights shining down on the gathering beside the screen.

Wonder filled Bailey as she gazed around. The sounds of the zoo almost made her feel like she was actually in the middle of a jungle. The studio's event team really outdid themselves. Absolutely amazing set up.

"You're at the front, Tony," said the publicist with a brief smile. She gestured and walked, ushering them down quickly. "The rest of the cast and staff are there too. Family and friends to the back."

Bailey glanced down at their joined hands, her ring glittering in the low light. It might take a while for her to get used to this partnership, but she was all in now. No turning back.

Tony stopped at the aisle and waited for Bailey to go in first. Each seat had a swag package resting on top. Bailey picked up her stuffed gorilla and laughed. It was the same shirt Tony had worn on her first day as his bodyguard. She grinned and waggled it at him. "I always knew you were an ape."

"Har. Har," he joked and sat down next to her, moving his gorilla to his lap along with her hand.

They settled in and waited until a few minutes later, the cast were invited up to the front to introduce the film. Tony beamed from ear to ear. This was his last film for a long time. Maybe ever. He may not even survive the Syndicate.

The scary thought popped into Bailey's mind with the force of a freight train. As Tony got up, she tugged his hand and brought him back to her.

"Break a leg," she said, nerves skating up her arms.

"Always." His eyes crinkled at the edges, but when he disengaged, he frowned. His hand went to his belly.

"Are you okay?" she asked quietly.

He nodded and murmured, "Just first hit of the G-word since arriving. Wasn't prepared."

Gluttony. Of course. It would always be rife at a gathering. A deep breath later and he recovered, plastering a mask of entertainment on his face. He bounded over to the stage, taking every eye in the place with him. He made a show of catching up with his peers as though long-lost friends. When it was time for him to speak, there wasn't a peep in the place. Not even the monkeys whooped. It seemed as if the entire zoo had gone still. And by the time the cast returned to their seats, and the lights dimmed, anticipation infused the air. She could feel it on her skin, lifting the hairs on her arms.

Tony settled back next to her, stiff as a board.

"Tony?" she asked, but someone shushed behind her, causing her to frown and face the front.

The title credits played, reflecting eerie flickering glows across the faces of the front row viewers, and a slow violin score filtered through the speakers. Bailey tried to get comfortable, but she couldn't shake a feeling. She reached out for Tony, but he shifted his hand away.

Something was definitely wrong. Risking a glance, she found him not looking at the screen like the rest of the crowd, but inspecting the trees surrounding them. His fists clenched on his knees, and a muscle ticked in his jaw. He noticed her watching and dropped his frown.

"Don't worry," he said. "Just nervous."

Exhaling, she brought her attention back to the screen and immersed herself in the very surreal experience of watching her boyfriend—*fiancé*—on screen pretending to be someone else. And he was so good at it.

He played a bounty hunter down on his luck who'd recently been dumped by his cheating wife and was about to be evicted. No one wanted to work with him because of his grumpy attitude. And then the job of a lifetime came in—help a pretty zoologist track down a wayward gorilla in the city and earn some cash while he was at it. They were just about to learn about the zoologist's morally ambiguous psychic gorilla project... but something was off with her animals. It might have something to do with the nasty assistant with a Mohawk who lurked around.

Tony nudges her with a smirk. "This bit might be scary."

She snorted. Right. After she'd almost been drowned by a living plant, it took a lot to scare her. She returned her attention to the screen just in time to catch a close up of Tony leaning toward an empty cage. High pitched suspense music pierced the air and made the audience hold their breath. Then everything was silent. The suspense was suddenly ruined by a burst of noise from the real zoo animals. Screeches, roars, squawks burst out all around them in the night air.

At the sideline, Bailey could see the publicist's mouth press into a hard line. She probably didn't think the animals would get so loud as to cover the sound of the film.

Next to her, Tony grunted and doubled over.

"Are you okay?" she whispered.

The audience screamed. Bailey jolted and looked up at the screen, narrowly missing the CGI gorilla snapping its jaws from the darkness of the cage. She pressed her hand to her heart in an attempt to stop it rabbiting. It was just the movie. Just the—

But the screen warped and bubbled, as though wind rippled through it. The zoo animals kept screeching, bleeding into the film's audio track. The picture distorted, making the snarling gorilla's face alien-like. Shadows rippled behind the screen. People started murmuring, the publicist and event's people began scurrying. What was happening?

A man with a headset went to the screen to inspect it. Bailey squinted, trying to pull the pattern of shadows into focus, trying to understand what imprint was showing behind the gorilla's face when she put it all together.

Her hand covered her mouth. She looked at Tony. Sweat beaded across his lip when he met her eyes. "I think it's here," he said, casually depressing the panic button on his watch.

The world suddenly became smaller. Sounds muffled while she struggled to process his words. Her heartbeat and intake of breath drowned out all sound—snapshots of the sewer filled her mind, of water invading her lungs—and then life came crashing back in full surround sound.

Tony stood up and shouted at the technician. "Get away from the screen!"

Something burst through the gorilla's mouth on screen, tearing it apart. Tentacles came first, wrapping around the technician's body, lifting him up and sucking him back into the dark abyss.

He was gone.

A shocked hush startled the crowd. Had they all really seen what they'd thought they'd seen?

Jolting, Bailey gasped as long ropes lashed the screen and the creature pulled its monstrous humanoid body through. Screams rent the air, penetrating Bailey to the core. With the film still flickering over it, the creature stopped and scanned the swarming crowd. Bailey's heart leaped into her throat. It somehow appeared more human than before, yet more alien. Its face had expressions constructed from masses of roots twisted into the shape of a human's muscular formation. It searched while its writhing muscled chest puffed out in fury. Tony put himself before Bailey and held her back with a hand.

"We need to get you out of here."

Two dark slashes of eyes roamed the crowd until they settled on Tony—no, not Tony—*her*. Bailey. It hissed through striated teeth. *"Gabrielle..."*

Tony cursed.

"What?" Why did she have the feeling there was more to this?

"It thinks you're Bosch's wife."

When Bailey gasped, Tony mumbled, "You kinda look like her."

And then it came right at them.

thirty-four

TONY LAZARUS

IT ALL SEEMED to happen in slow motion.

Tony watched the creature flash forward on twisted and tumbling feet and knew he was vastly out gunned. Not a single weapon on his body, except the blue fire coursing through his veins, now pushing against his skin, dying to get out. Tentacles grew out of the creature's back and thrashed about like a wild octopus—knocking into chairs, kicking up dirt and grass, bashing into the spotlights. The only light left was from the projector, still showing the movie.

There were too many vines... arms... whatever you wanted to call it.

If he ordered Bailey to run, she wouldn't. He had to give her a job. He pushed Bailey back. "Get that projector turned off. I need darkness." And then he launched at one of the thick vines whipping toward them. He latched on with two hands. It lifted him clear off the ground.

Holy shit.

He hovered momentarily in the air, and then he let his power release. A bolt of blue light flashed, arcing into the limb he held, casting light up to the being's agonized face. It screeched and threw its head back. Its arm split into two between Tony's grip.

He fell and landed on his feet.

That's when the projector died and the lights went out. Tony smiled. Bailey had done what he'd asked, and now she should be heading out of there toward safety like the rest of them. He picked up the dead tentacle and used it like a club.

"Come and get some, Plantie."

BAILEY HAZE

EVERYTHING WAS pandemonium the moment Bailey tipped over the projector, casting the outdoor cinema into complete darkness. The city's elite morphed from cultured and sophisticated to selfish assholes. Screams and shouts became the soundtrack. A woman grabbed Bailey's hair and yanked her out of the way. Bailey fell onto a row of chairs, their high backs cutting into her ribs. A man pushed her, shouting for her to get out of his way. She tumbled over more chairs, her body sliding into the gap in front. Landing on her shoulder, she cried out in pain. She might have jarred something. It was all too much. Her overloaded senses couldn't focus on one avenue of escape. Get up or—

Something hit her on the head and she dove face first into the lawn, taking a mouthful of grass in. Goddamn... Water filled her eyes. She rolled to her side, catching her breath, and ended up looking into the sky bursting with blue patterns of light. At least she thought it was the sky. Stars and blue fireworks danced and swirled until darkness edged in completely. Just before she blacked out, she heard hissing. *"Gabrielle."*

TONY LAZARUS

TONY SMASHED the creature's face with his club but caught a vine to his midsection at the same time. He went flying backward into a fallen spotlight. The metal pole hit him across the spine. White hot needles of agony burst at the site and he cursed loudly.

And then Liza was there, dragging him up, her face fierce under the starlight, her body hard and ready. She'd ripped the bottom off her dress and had used the torn straps to wrap around her fists.

"Where is everyone?" he grunted and yanked his jacket off.

"They're getting the ladies to safety," she stated, and then softer, "And the suits are in the car."

Meaning, they'd be back in minutes disguised as the Deadly Seven and able to use the full force of their supernatural abilities. They just had to keep the creature occupied until then.

"It's too dark. I can't see jack!" Liza snapped and then her feet fell from under her. She landed on her back with a thud. The tendril wrapped around her ankle pulled, dragging her away with her fingers clawing at the dirt.

Tony roared and gave chase, using his power to light his path. Leaping at the tentacle that had Liza, he took the cord between his hands and pulled, straining his muscles, releasing his fire at the same time. But while his gaze was focused on freeing her, another of the creature's appendages knocked him on the side of the head, bowling him into his sister. They went down together in a tangle of limbs. Groaning, they twisted and pulled themselves to their feet.

But the creature was gone.

Panting, Liza said, "You're going to have to get to its head."

"How?" he gasped. "Every time I get near, one of its spindly fucking arms comes at me. Cut one off and another grows back."

"Then you need to go nuclear again. Just explode in its face."

"I can only do that if no one is around." And he wasn't sure he could repeat the experience.

"Gabrielle..."

The hiss came from the dark. Tony went stone cold. His heart pounded in his ears and with painstaking slowness, he whispered to his sister, "Bailey was with the ladies, right?"

No answer.

"Liza?" He let a sliver of blue light release, just enough that he could see the fear in her eyes.

"I didn't see her."

FUCK.

He shot up and charged toward the sense of gluttony, pushing anything in his way aside. Chairs went flying. Stuffed gorillas got kicked. It was after her. His angel. Except... the gluttony faded. It wasn't feeding. Where was it?

He spun in the dark. Where was she? There. She'd been near the fallen projector.

"I'm coming, baby," he murmured. He ran toward the end of the grassy cinema and stopped. Most civilians were gone, so when he made it to where the projector had been, he freely used his power through his hands like torches. He scanned the area wildly, and then he saw it.

A single turquoise flower lying on the ground, half hidden beneath a fallen chair.

A roar of pain shot out of him.

"Bailey!" he roared.

Panicked, he turned in circles, trying to get a lock on the sense of gluttony, but there was nothing. He couldn't breathe, couldn't focus.

"Bailey!"

Nothing.

Animals screeched. Monkeys whooped. The breeze rustled in the trees.

Someone shoved something at his chest. His hands latched onto the package.

"Find somewhere to put that on," a deep computer-modified voice said. "Just in case someone is watching, or there are cameras about."

Tony looked down. It was a backpack. He looked up. Parker in his Deadly Seven uniform. Pride. Behind him stood Envy, Greed and Wrath. Sloth stood to the side looking at the flexible computer screen pulled out of her sleeve. Liza, still in her civilian clothes, limped to a chair. The creature had gotten her ankles and the poison must be trying to get a hold of her.

"I don't have time," Tony barked. "It's got Bailey. I have to find her."

Parker replied, "Sloth is tracing her as we speak."

"How?"

"Her ring," Sloan replied. "Put a microdot tracker under the diamond."

Relief washed through Tony. He'd never been so happy for his family's invasion of privacy, but... what if the creature was already feeding?

"I can't wait." Tony moved, but Parker yanked him back with a growl.

"Think, man. Can you sense it feeding?"

Tony forced his pulse to calm. Parker was right. No gluttony meant no feeding. Not yet, anyway. He shook his head.

"Then suit up. You will level up your power. We need you." Parker shoved the backpack into him again. "There. Head into the bush."

MOMENTS LATER, Tony jogged through the zoo with his family. Sloan gave them directions, and Tony used his light to help them see the path. They skirted though the labyrinth landscape of man made enclosures and exhibits until finally rounding a corner and coming to a sign. It was almost hidden by palm fronds. Tony shone his light to read.

They were at the orangutan exhibit.

"This it?" he asked Sloan.

She slid the flexible computer screen on her sleeve away and then nodded toward the tall structure. "It's in there."

"Go for the head," Parker said.

"But get Bailey to safety first," Tony reminded them.

Then they moved, combing through the exhibit as one cohesive unit, splitting when they hit the wall separating the enclosure from the public. It went around the exhibit like a castle mote. Just over the wall, the enclosure dipped to a low pit filled with grass and climbing structures, but it was the enormous structure in the middle that held their attention. Climbing at least thirty feet into the sky, it towered above the rest. Made from a mixture of steel and wood, the exotic looking hut came complete with a crows nest and balcony. Ropes attached from the tower to other rocky parts of the enclosure like a web, and ropes dangled down to the ground. The full moon hung low in the sky behind the structure. The last vestiges of the creature's vines

caught Tony's attention as they slid into the main hut. It was definitely in there.

Still no gluttony. He hoped that was a good sign.

"The animals are hiding," Sloan murmured, coming up to him. "I
sense their fear."

"Get them out," Parker ordered quietly, and then pointed at the
rest of his family with military signals. Evan and Griffin to go one
way, Wyatt to go with him.

Sloan moved, but Tony stopped her. "Can you sense Bailey?" Was
she alive?

She nodded, pointed to the hut, and then became a ghost. When
he turned, he saw four shadows drop over the wall and land in the
enclosure. He was next, vaulting the wall in a smooth movement.
When he hit the ground, he tucked and rolled, coming back to his
feet fluidly and breaking into a jog.

This time, the creature wouldn't get away.

One way or another, this would end.

Coming to the foot of the structure, Tony climbed up a rope,
satisfied to see four other shadows rising at different points around
the base. He was the last one up, and almost to the top when a body
flew out of the hut and crash onto one of the spiderweb ropes before
falling. He only spared a glance to make sure whoever it was recovered, then kept climbing, trying not to worry when another body
went flying out of the hut.

Cresting the top, he eased himself onto the wooden platform.
What he saw took his breath away. The creature stood tall and
deformed in the corner, and it used Bailey as a shield. Wyatt and
Griffin were the only two soldiers left, and vines were wrapping
around their bodies like a snake. Indestructible Wyatt tried in vain to
rip the vines from his body, while at the same time protecting Griffin

who was fast being overcome. Bailey pleaded with her eyes. *Help me, please.*

Rooted to the spot, Tony froze as images flashed before his eyes. He felt like he'd been here before. Inconvenient memories bombarded him. His movie. The hostage situation. The final scene. Except, where his gun shot had gone through the hostage to kill the psycho, that would never work here. This was real, unscripted messy life. She could die if he made the wrong choice.

He looked at Bailey again, and the message in her eyes changed. Or he perceived it wrong in the first place. She wasn't saying *help me.* She was looking at him with confidence. With relief. Him. Not the others.

A vine whipped up from the floor and came at him.

He swatted it away with a burning hot hand, then reaching over his shoulder, he released his katana and slashed, cutting more vines in two. More plant-tentacles came, and he kept slashing, never taking his eyes from Bailey. She was unaffected by the poison. The creature must be holding it at bay now that it thought she was his wife.

His wife.

The shocking thought hit him, and then everything spiraled together in his mind. The thing didn't want to hurt Bailey. It thought she was Gabrielle. That meant it had feelings. Daisy had said she'd felt its sorrow.

"Stop!" he shouted. "Everyone stop!"

"What the—" Wyatt growled, mid rip through a limb.

"Not a good idea," Griffin added, one hand out, directing a piece of metal from the hut's skeleton frame to pin one of the plant's limbs.

"Stop. Please. Trust me." Then into his hood mic, "Sloth, get your ass up here."

He didn't have to wait long. Two more shadows came back through the door. Sloan with her bow knocked and sighted, and Evan with his twin katanas out and ready, lightning arcing up his arms. The small hut was crowded, full of hot air and discarded vines. Taking a risk, Tony yanked down his mask and exposed his face so the creature could see him.

"Please, stand down," he said.

"Do as he says." Parker joined them, limping.

Tony's breath caught in his throat at Parker's assent. They were all there. The team stopped fighting the monster. Tony met Bailey's wide eyes, and he nodded. "It's going to be okay, angel."

Her lips flattened. Her jaw tensed, and she nodded back.

"Wayne Bosch," Tony said to the creature's deformed face. "Or whoever you are now, that's not your wife. That's not Gabrielle. That's Bailey, my fiancée."

The creature gnashed his thorny mouth.

"He's sad," Sloan hissed.

Daisy had said it was sad. It didn't like being in the cage it was created. It had wanted freedom, that's why she'd released it. Looking around, Tony saw the metal frame of the hut. He gestured. "Don't keep her in a cage like you were."

The creature paused. It stopped strangling Griffin. It looked around the inside of the hut with its dark eyes. And then it watched Tony.

"We know how you feel," Tony tried again. "We were born in a cage too. We're on the same side. Look—" He put his sword down. "I'm not going to hurt you. I'm not like the people that created you."

His family looked at Tony like he was nuts. Probably because they actually started to believe him. They thought he wouldn't hurt the creature. But he was a good actor.

"Let her go," he said. "She's not your wife."

It swiveled its abnormally twined head, moved its slashes for eyes at Bailey and looked at her again.

"My name is Bailey," she said. "I'm not Gabrielle."

Tony glared at Sloan, and then at the monster, hoping she understood what was happening. She did. She focused on the creature, and soon, elation rippled through Tony as the vines around Bailey loosened. Sloan had the power to influence emotion, and she had cast doubt into the creature's mind. It worked.

Tony swallowed the lump in his throat and gestured for Bailey to come to him. The second their hands touched, he yanked her into his arms, and hugged tight. Only for a second, then he pushed her into Parker's arms and nodded.

Time for anyone who couldn't stand the heat to get out. "Time to go nuclear," he said, and then turned back to the creature. It looked at him. It cocked its head. It looked at Bailey climbing out of the hut with Parker, and it looked at the rest of them, all slowly picking up their weapons.

It knew he'd lied.

Sloan shook her head. "It's not happy."

"*Die*," it hissed.

"This is what you want? You want me to die?" Tony asked, trying to buy time for Bailey to get out. He waved for Sloan, Evan and Griffin to leave too, but they wouldn't. He couldn't let his power out with them there. The suit would only protect so much.

"*Die*," it hissed again, but no attack came. Instead it cowered a little and backed up into a corner.

Sloan released a sob, and her bow dropped. Her head hung low, and she took a deep breath. "It's so sad. I don't think it wants *us* to die. I think *it* wants to die."

"*Yesss. Die. Free.*"

Jesus. An ache spread in Tony's chest and he felt sorry for the thing. If Wayne Bosch somehow lived in there, or even if the creature was its own entity, it was different, unwanted. It didn't know where it fit in this world, and to feed, it had to kill. Tony had never stopped to think if it had feelings. But Daisy had. From the start she had tried to help it.

Even now, when his sister had been trained to kill, a part of her goodness remained. That same part that had tried to sing away his pain when he was little. There was hope yet.

Tony put his sword away. He looked at his family. "You guys go. I got this."

Sniffing, Sloan nodded. She went to leave, but took one last look over her shoulder to the creature. "I'll help you feel better. I'll make it good."

Then she disappeared through the window. Evan hesitated, but left. So did Griffin. Wyatt came up to Tony and lifted his chin. "I'm staying."

Tony gave a curt nod, then he stepped toward the creature. He let the power in his body build. Hot liquid fire burned in his veins. Blue light became white. It blinded them. So close to the being, he could see the eyes weren't slits. They were just deep, deep holes, and within them, he saw the eyes glistening.

"*Yes.*" Viney, bony hands took hold of Tony's wrists and moved his grip to its throat. "*Free.*"

"Yeah, buddy. Free."

And then Tony let his ruin out. He accessed all those parts of himself he'd denied. He accepted everything, because like Bailey had said to him once, ruin could be good. It could be sweet. He freed the creature from the shackles of its life. Sloan must have kept her word because it never cried out in pain.

Smoldering ash burst into the air.

A pungent scent of burning wet things hit him, but he kept going until his fingers closed around nothing but disintegrated wood.

thirty-five
LIZA LAZARUS

THE NIGHT HAD TAKEN a cold turn, and Liza's flimsy and torn dress did little to protect her, but she was determined to stay at the orangutan enclosure until she knew everything. It had been a strange conclusion to an even weirder show. She had to be there to ensure no trace of her family involvement was found; it was the least she could do since she'd been unable to help during the big fight.

The forensics crew had already set up spotlights and cordoned off the crime scene with tape. A few uniformed officers guarded the area and placed evidence markers wherever they found plant matter or weird blobs of ash. The poor orangutans had to be moved to another containment area and tranquilized due to stress, but thanks to Sloan, they were out before Tony's explosion.

Liza glanced up at the metal climbing frame where it had all gone down. Once a hut, now a charred skeleton, scorch marks blended with the dented and warped metal sculpture. There was no way to explain it. She had to pretend she was as marveled as the rest of the cops. At least Bailey was safe. Liza couldn't imagine what it would feel like to lose someone you loved so close to finally connecting with them.

She couldn't imagine it because it was never something she had to worry about. She felt physically sick every time she fucked, so the act was not exactly high on her to do list, despite the lies she'd told her family. Shifting dirt with her bare foot, she winced at the throb in her ankle. The damned venom still worked its way out of her system. She bent down low and rubbed the welt, trying to help the process along. She could be making it worse, but whatevs. It felt better when she rubbed.

A sensation uncurled in her stomach, blossoming like a sick flower. Without having to look, she knew the forensics officer behind her was staring, thinking lustful thoughts, probably ogling her ass as she'd bent down. *Stupid dress.* Sure enough, when she straightened and turned, a man in a bio-hazard mask shifted his eyes from her rear to her face. She scowled, and those eyes quickly skated away, suddenly becoming very interested in the bio-matter he'd discovered from the creature.

"Nice dress." A deep male voice behind had her twirling.

Someone she'd never expected to see in this city again stood before her, dressed in FBI tactical attire. Joey Luciano was her closest, nay, *only* male friend since she left high school when she was fifteen to study the Art of War. She hadn't seen him for the seven years she'd "studied abroad" but they had reconnected in the Police Academy where they became closer friends.

The six-foot-three man had an amused look in his eyes and a slight curve to his lips as he took in her outfit.

The Joey Liza had known was meticulous about keeping himself trimmed. This man was behind. A little scruffy. The five o'clock shadow covering his steel cut jaw was thick and dark. His tactical attire also looked disheveled, and he wore an FBI baseball cap over his head, even though it was night. He only wore a cap when his thick unruly Italian hair needed a cut.

So he'd been busy.

His intense gaze didn't let up.

"Yeah, I'd bet your boyfriend would love it," she quipped.

Joey's jaw flexed, and his eyes turned hard. "Why do you always joke about me having a boyfriend?"

"Because you're gay." She'd thought he'd have admitted it by now. "It's okay. There's nothing wrong with it."

"I'm not. I have a girlfriend."

"You do?"

"For two years."

Oh. She always thought he was gay. Why else would he not feel lust around her? Unless Joey thought of her as a sister. Maybe that was it.

Except she'd never felt his lust, ever. Even as a teenager when boys were meant to have raging hormones. Even when they used to swim together, and she'd caught him ogling her tiny bikini. He certainly wasn't her mate. They'd touched plenty of times during high school. Nothing. He'd never dated. Neither men nor women. Maybe he was asexual.

But she hadn't seen him face-to-face in years. His job had taken him across the country. What did she know anymore?

His scowl drilled into her, and she squirmed. "Good to see you, Joey. What are the feds doing here?"

"Nobody calls me Joey anymore. It's Joe." He shifted his gaze to the mess. "We've been tracking this... *thing* across state lines for weeks."

Shit. Fucking shit. She looked away to hide the alarm in her eyes. There went any chance she had of covering it up with some ridiculous story. How the hell was she going to explain her way out of this? She swallowed hard.

"And what exactly do you think this thing is?"

Those penetrating eyes landed on her again. "You tell me."

This was *not* the Joey she knew. He never used to be so blunt with her. It threw her off.

"Aren't you in the anti-terrorism unit, Agent *Joe* Luciano?"

"It's Special Agent. And I'm in violent crimes now."

"Violent crimes. That's heavy."

"No more than homicide."

"Touché." She'd recently moved from vice, where they'd worked together, to homicide. "So what's it like?"

"Don't change the subject," he snapped.

A breezed wafted in, and she rubbed her arms briskly. The air wasn't the only thing dropping the temperature. She shouldn't have called him gay. Now he was pissed. God, she was always putting her foot in her mouth. She needed to learn to keep her nose in her own business. Friends were hard to come by for her, especially men, and she kinda missed the loser.

"Why would I know what it is?"

"You were here, weren't you?"

Right. Yes, she was.

"I was at the film. Not exactly here, so I didn't see much."

He blinked. Stared hard at her face, then dropped his gaze to her ankles. "Oh really?"

Motherf—

"I know all your tells, Liza," he warned. "I've known you for years. The first time I brought you a coffee order, you pretended to like it, but you stared at me, unblinking. I later saw you tipping it down the sink. And then there was the time you played poker with the boys. You did the stare thing when you had a good hand but pretended you didn't. You can't lie to me."

Oh how she wanted to laugh in his face because she'd been lying to him her entire life. But instead, she sighed and rubbed her eyes. "I'm tired and I'm cold. I want to go home. Can we do this tomorrow?"

He popped some gum into his mouth, scrutinizing her as he chewed.

"Fine," he said. "But don't think you can hide from this."

"Wasn't dreaming of it."

"Good. I'm watching you."

"Don't stare too long, you'll go blind."

He snorted, and his lip twitched up. She smiled inwardly. It was good to see him crack a smile, even if it was small. Working violent crimes wasn't an easy job. It took a toll.

"Hey," she said softly. "Why don't we grab a beer later this week and you can tell me all about the promotion."

Joey stopped chewing. "You ignore my calls for months. Then when I do hear from you, you ask me for information. I ask you for a beer then, you shut me down, and now you just want to go and grab a drink like old times?"

She shrugged and smirked. "I know, right? Isn't it good having a friend you can just catch up with like no time has passed? Plus, I said, maybe some other time. I didn't shut you down."

"Right. Yeah, of course. Except, friends don't avoid friends," he sighed. Someone shouted behind him, and he turned, momentarily distracted. He held up a hand to signal to whoever it was to wait and then came back to Liza. "We'll talk later."

When he walked away, Liza felt a cool sensation settle in her stomach. He was right. She'd avoided him. At the precinct, people had talked. They'd joked about how close the two had been.

When's the wedding?

Taken her to bone-town yet, Joey?

He'd never discouraged them, but she knew he'd not liked her that way. Even if he somehow did, she couldn't ever go there with him. Every relationship she'd had ended the moment she'd crossed the sexual line. She ended anticipating that sick feeling before they got intimate. The psychology of her relationships messed with her mind. Joey didn't like her that way, she never sensed his lust. Even if his lack of lust was an anomaly, or he suddenly changed his mind and decided she was hot, it would all inevitably turn to shit.

Friends don't avoid friends.

As it so happened, she didn't need sex to ruin a good thing with him. She'd fucked things up well enough on her own.

thirty-six

TONY LAZARUS

ON A FRIDAY NIGHT, three weeks after Tony's failed premiere, he sat with Bailey on a porch bench at the sobriety house. He wasn't dark about the premiere, quite the opposite in fact. He thought it was funny. Just another sign that his decision to take a step back from the entertainment industry was a good one.

Down the steps, the streetlights turned on. Night had fallen earlier, and winter's cool touch had landed on Cardinal City. The smell of Indian spices floated in the air.

With his hands entwined with Bailey's, they snuggled into each other to keep the cold at bay and listened to the kids inside, playing music and testing out the new studio. It was good to hear them have fun, and even better to know they were thinking about things other than their problems.

This was the world Tony was fighting for. One where people could come back from their mistakes, instead of being persecuted for them. He'd get back to acting one day, but for now, this was perfect.

"Not to be rude, but how long do we have to wait for your surprise?" Bailey asked.

"You cold?" He inspected her outfit. Maybe her thin cardigan wasn't warm enough. He probably should have told her to bring a coat when they'd left his place. "You want my jacket?"

He was about to shrug out of his, but she stopped him. "No. I'm okay. I just hate surprises."

He lifted his brow. "But it's okay for you to give them?"

She grinned, straightened and gestured excitedly with her hands. "You're going to love it. But I can't show it to you until your surprise is done."

"So, we are at an impasse." He whistled a Wild West stand-off tune.

She rolled her eyes. "We are not. Obviously, you need to get your dramatic urges out more, because that was all wrong."

"Objection." He patted his chest. "I am not dramatic."

"Good Lord, save me now. Right. Anyway, how long do we have to wait?" She squirmed and snuggled back into him.

"Just a few more minutes." He checked his watch and then glanced at the darkening sky. "Almost time."

A sound on the porch roof made Bailey jolt, but Tony put a steadying hand on her arm. "It's okay. It's the surprise."

Two-seconds later, someone cursed above the roof. Something thudded. And then a shadow dropped from the porch roof to the steps below, landing quietly. Then a second shadow lowered, and a third. Three in Deadly Seven uniforms.

It was Evan, Griffin and Sloan, all with their hoods up, and scarfs over their faces.

Bailey jumped up. "I don't understand. Is everything okay?"

A smile tickled Tony's lips. "It's fine. They're here to give the kids a self-defense demo. As the Deadly Seven."

Bailey's eyes bugged out of her head. She darted a glance back to Tony. "Really?"

He nodded. "Every time I've been here, someone has mentioned them, so I thought why not have them come down. And after the attack, I've been thinking about keeping this place protected. Even if the demo fails, word will get around that we're—ahem—*they're* keeping a special eye on the place."

"It's a wonderful idea. I'll go in and make sure they're all ready." She stopped just before she opened the door to the house. "Do you want to… you know, dress up too?"

"Dress up?" he quipped with a grin, standing up too.

"You know what I mean." She waved at his family.

"No," he replied with absolute certainty. "I like being on this side of the show for once."

Bailey's gaze softened. She kissed him on the cheek and then she darted indoors.

He stood there watching the door for a minute, smiling dumbly, so in love with her, and then he turned to his family and jogged down the steps. "Thanks for coming."

"It's a great idea," Griffin answered, his voice low and modified.

Evan took in the house, eyes dancing over the structure. "Nice place. Kind of old school cool."

Sloan's eyes crinkled around the edges, and Tony could tell she wanted to say something snarky, but gloriously kept it to herself. She focused on Tony. "You joining us after? We're going deep into the south-side and then back to base to plan the infiltration of you-know-where to get you-know-who back."

Daisy. His heart swelled. He'd been itching to get her back after having to leave her in the sewer. "Hell yeah, I'll be in for that." He put his hands in his pockets and took a deep breath. It felt good to be asked. "But probably much later. Apparently Bailey has a surprise for me. So"—he waved his communicator watch—"I'll find out where you are and come join later."

"Ooh. Tony and Bailey, kissing in a tree," she sang and then gestured toward the house.

"Don't think it's that kind of surprise." He gave a deprecating laugh. "Come on, I'll introduce you to the kids."

TWO HOURS LATER, Tony waved off the Deadly Seven crew from the front porch. It was getting late and a strict curfew kept the Hudson House in order. Bailey and a handful of the group were with him, chattering loudly. Once his siblings were gone, Bailey tried to usher them all back inside, but they were still pumped from the recent activities.

"Come on," she said. "We're about to break curfew. Agnes will kill me if I don't get you in."

A chorus of groans passed around. Elena and another girl were the loudest, but when Tyson and Simon lended their voices, it got rowdy. They were full of too much energy.

Bailey pulled out a DVD case from behind her back and waggled it before them. "I have a surprise movie for everyone to watch, but we have to go inside."

"What is it?" Elena asked.

Tony narrowed his eyes at Bailey. She lifted her gaze to his.

"Is that what I think it is?" he asked, pointing.

"If you think it's an early screener copy of your film, then yes it is."

"No way!" Elena gasped and snatched it from Bailey and ran into the house. "The one that got smashed up by the monster?"

"Can't believe you just said monster," Tyson teased.

"Shut up. It was real," she replied.

"And Sasquatches and Yetis are too," Simon smirked, but then he lifted his chin at Tony. "Still. It would be pretty cool to watch this before it's out in the cinema."

"Well, it's out tomorrow, so we need to go in now and watch it." Bailey used her forceful stare at them, and they all ducked their heads.

"This is so weird," Tyson mumbled to Simon with a glance thrown at Tony.

Simon took the DVD from Elena. "Weird but cool."

"Just go easy on me, guys," Tony laughed.

They responded with the usual taunts about his acting style and he shooed them inside until it was only Bailey and him left on the porch.

He gathered her into his arms and smiled down at her fondly. "Thank you."

"Thank you too. They loved the demonstration. I think it will help keep trouble away from the house."

She threaded her fingers through his hair and leaned in to kiss him. The warm touch of her lips melted Tony's insides. He sank into her kiss, adding his tongue, growing the pace until she squeaked at his demands.

"Wow," she breathed, pulling away, eyes dazed. "More of that later, but we need to get inside. Not sure how long we have before Agnes kicks us out."

A frown crinkled his forehead when he thought about a certain someone who hadn't been interested in the demo.

"You okay?" Bailey asked.

"Yeah, just noticed someone wasn't participating."

"Don't worry about Akeef." She patted his arm. "He's into the studio and you chat with him when you stop by. Doesn't matter if he's not into the self-defense. At least there's something he's focusing on. All you can do is keep showing up. Eventually, he'll realize it's not just for show and grow to trust you."

Keep showing up.

Tony didn't move. Instead, he looked out into the night where his siblings had gone, and stood with a small smile frozen on his face. They'd all come so far. It wasn't that long ago Sloan had been lazying about, unable to get out of bed. Evan had been fighting in underground cage fights. Griffin had been thieving to keep his internal sin in balance.

Mary had been right. As long as they kept trying, things would get better. He wasn't psychic like Evan, and couldn't say what the future held, but he knew they wouldn't forget Daisy. She was family. Eventually, she'd come to trust them.

epilogue

IN THE DARK office of a building in the Quadrant, Julius Allcott sat, watching recorded televised footage of a movie premiere at his desk computer. Despair stood at his right shoulder, as usual, but this time Levi Van Jansen was there, watching from his left.

"I don't understand," Julius said. Again. He didn't have time for this. "What exactly am I looking for?"

"Wait," Van Jansen said. "It is almost time."

Julius locked his jaw and turned back to the computer screen on his desk. "We've been through this already. They have nothing to link the plant back to us. Why haven't we put this to rest to focus on the replicates?"

"Wait. Wait. There."

Julius squinted, still not understanding. It was a collection of people arriving on the red carpet. Then he noticed familiar faces. The Lazarus family. A blond woman with curly hair walked next to Wrath. He had her held tightly to his side as his eyes scanned the cordoned off area full of cameras and people, always vigilant. But it was when they turned at an angle that Julius sat up. He tapped the screen, zooming in.

"That one. The blond woman," he said.

"Ja. Precisely." Van Jansen smiled. "She is pregnant."

"With a powered Lazarus's child." Julius's heart leapt into his throat and he swiveled in his chair to meet eyes with the geneticist. "You're a genius."

"All his DNA will be unlocked," Van Jansen replied. "Meaning all her stem cells will have similar activated genes. Short of taking one of the Lazarus siblings themselves, and making them pregnant, this was our next bet. Frankly, it's like winning the lotto."

Despair stiffened. Julius tilted his head to catch sight of her in his periphery. Wearing casual clothes, he noted she hadn't been in her white leather enforcer outfit in weeks. It hadn't escaped his notice that she'd been distant lately. Distant and ineffectual. There had been too many blackouts to count. She'd failed at collecting a sample of Gluttony's unlocked DNA. She'd failed at eliminating the plant-creature. It pained him to say that her time with him was coming to an end. She'd been an effective tool. His original plan had been to use her reproductive organs, create his own stem cells, but this was better. They didn't have to wait. Wrath's woman had been heavily pregnant.

A plan formed in his head. He tapped his lip, turning to study Despair with open curiosity.

"What?" she snapped.

He pretended to change his mind and turned back to the screen. "It's nothing. Perhaps I have ruined my chance."

While he stared at the footage, he contained his smile, but when she spoke, he couldn't hold it.

"It's not nothing," she said. "Tell me."

He forced a contrite look on his face. His hand went to the locket around his neck, and he faced her. "My darling, you were right.

Earlier, you accused me of not treating you like family. You are my family, all that is left, and I should hold a piece of you inside this locket. Just in case anything were to happen to you."

Her breath hitched. "Really?"

"Of course. It's terrible that I've been so thoughtless." Opening the drawer on his desk, he took out a small pair of scissors. "Here. Let's sort this out now. Will you give me a lock of your hair?"

For DNA replication, he required the follicle at the root, but she didn't know that.

She hesitated and looked at the screen. Anger swirled in him like a tempest. How dare she second-guess his motives. But then she took a strand of her hair and tugged it from the root, follicle and all.

Julius's heart skipped a beat. Fear trickled into his body.

"That's a good girl." He smiled and took it from her. He frowned as he opened his locket with trembling fingers. "I can't imagine a life without you in it. After all we've been through together. But..." he paused, before he put her hair in the locket.

"But what?" she asked.

Julius met eyes with Van Jansen and then sighed before turning back to Despair. "It's just, without those stem cells, these strands of hair are worthless. If we can't bring you back permanently, then what is the point? If you die, then it will be final, and you won't be able to share in this new wonderful world we are creating."

Her brows puckered in the middle and her eyes turned fierce. "Then I'll get it for you."

He slumped and put his fist on the desk, her hair still contained inside. "It's a fortress there. It's impossible to get close to the pregnant woman."

"Then I'll make them believe I'm coming back to them. I'll start working on a plan right now."

Julius stood up. He kissed her on the cheek and made sure the tears shone in his eyes. "I wouldn't know what to do without you."

She smiled tentatively at him, bowed and then left.

When she was gone, Julius looked down at the open locket in one hand, and Despair's silver strand of hair in the other. Then he snapped the locket shut and threw the hair on the floor.

"You are not keeping it?" Van Jansen asked.

"No," he replied. "There is no coming back from what she is, and there is no room for someone like her in the new world."

characters &
glossary

THE DEADLY SEVEN

(Appearance in order of age from youngest to eldest)

ENVY: Evan Lazarus
SLOTH: Sloan Lazarus
GLUTTONY: Tony Lazarus
GREED: Griffin Lazarus
LUST: Liza Lazarus
WRATH: Wyatt Lazarus
PRIDE: Parker Lazarus
DESPAIR: Daisy Lazarus

Mary Lazarus: Adoptive Mother of the Deadly Seven and ex assassin for the Hildegard Sisterhood
Flint Lazarus: Adoptive Father of the Deadly Seven

OTHER CHARACTERS:

Dr. Grace Go: Surgeon at Cardinal City General Hospital. Mate to Evan Lazarus.

Lilo Likeke: Investigative reporter at the Cardinal Copy. Mate to Griffin Lazarus.

Misha Minski: Yoga instructor, exotic dancer and Mate to Wyatt Lazarus.

Maximillian Johnson: Sloan's mate and owner of the Nightingale Securities firm.

Bailey Haze: Tony's mate and ex CIA operative.

THE SYNDICATE

The Syndicate is a secret organization who believe the only way to save the world from its own harmful self is to eradicate all sinners, even if that means destroying half the world.

THE BOSS: Julius Allcott

SARA MADDEN: Ex-girlfriend of Wyatt Lazarus

FALCON/DESPAIR/DAISY: Enforcer for the Syndicate and lost eldest sister to the Deadly Seven.

BARRY PINKERTON: Old friend of Flint's and ex employee of the Syndicate. He's now in hiding with his daughter.

LEVI VAN JANSEN: Evil Syndicate geneticist.

THE HILDEGARD SISTERHOOD

The Hildegard Sisterhood are nuns with a history reaching back to medieval times when the original Sister Hildegard struggled against a male dominated clergy. Now the world know her as the founder of scientific history in Germany, but back then, her opinions were disregarded until she claimed to have visions from God himself. Belittling herself as a woman in order to be heard was only the beginning of the humiliation the woman faced.

So she started her own abbey filled with women. That same abbey exists today and is a place where women are celebrated and their education encouraged—minus the male influence. Records at the Sisterhood archives reveal they had a hand in the rise of many women over history from *Joan of Arc* to *Indira Gandhi*. From *Catherine the Great* to *Margaret Thatcher*.

Under the surface of the auspicious abbey lays the secret mission that no woman will ever suffer the same struggle as Hildegard and they condition a select few "Sinners" to enforce this mission. These Sinners are trained as assassins for the cause: Sinners like Mary Lazarus. A necessary evil.

In the prequel novella, *Sinner*, Mary Lazarus escaped the Sisterhood who wanted to use the children for their own gain, much like the Syndicate who created them. To this day, she is still on the run.

join lana's vips

Subscribe to Lana's newsletter and receive a free box set, first dibs on giveaways, special printable freebies and more. You won't want to miss out.

subscribe.lanapecherczyk.com

On Facebook? Join Lana's Angels Reader Group https://www. facebook.com/groups/lanasangels

OMG! How do you say my name?

Lana (straight forward enough - Lah-nah) **Pecherczyk** (this is where it gets tricky - Pe-her-chick).

I've been called Lana Price-Check, Lana Pera-Chickywack, Lana Pressed-Chicken, Lana Pech...*that girl!* You name it, they said it. So if it's so hard to spell, why on earth would I use this name instead of an easy pen name?

To put it simply, it belonged to my mother. And she was my dream champion. For most of my life, I've been good at one thing – art. The world around me saw my work, and said I should do more of it, so I did. But, when at the age of eight, I said I wanted to write stories, and even though we were poor, my mother came home with a blank notebook and a pencil saying I should follow my dreams, no matter where they take me for they will make me happy. I wasn't very good at it, but it didn't matter because I had her support and I liked it.

She died when I was thirteen, and left her four daughters orphaned. Suddenly, I had lost my dream champion, I was split from my youngest two sisters and had no one to talk to about the challenge of life.

So, I wrote in secret. I poured my heart out daily to a diary and sometimes imagined that she would listen. At the end of the day, even if she couldn't hear, writing kept that dream alive.

Eventually, after having my own children (two firecrackers in the guise of little boys) and ignoring my inner voice for too long, I decided to lead by example. How could I teach my children to follow their dreams if I wasn't? I became my own dream champion and the rest is history, here I am.

When I'm not writing the next great action-packed romantic novel, or wrangling the rug rats, or rescuing GI Joe from the jaws of my Kelpie, I fight evil by moonlight, win love by daylight and never run from a real fight. I live in Australia, but I'm up for a chat anytime online. Come and find me.

Subscribe & Follow
subscribe.lanapecherczyk.com
lp@lanapecherczyk.com

facebook.com/lanapecherczykauthor

instagram.com/lana_p_author

amazon.com/-/e/B00V2TP0HG

bookbub.com/profile/lana-pecherczyk

tiktok.com/@lanapauthor

goodreads.com/lana_p_author